ECHOES IN THE ABYSS:

THE MEN WHO MADE THE MONSTER

Dr. Amjad Khan

Note from the Author

For as long as I can remember, I have been captivated by history, drawn not just to names and dates but to the stories behind them, to the human forces and philosophical currents that shape the rise and fall of civilizations. Among the countless chapters of the human experience, none has gripped me more deeply than the era of World War II and the shadow cast by the Third Reich.

My fascination began in grade school. While other children read comic books or played outside, I found myself paging through thick history books borrowed from the local library, pouring over black-and-white photographs of bombed cities and broken lives. I was far too young to fully understand the scale of what I was looking at, but even then, I knew I was encountering something profound, something that demanded to be remembered. Hitler and the Nazis, with their strange symbols and terrible ambitions, stood out to me not simply as villains in the story of the 20th century but as warnings: complex, unsettling, and deeply human. That early curiosity never faded. It followed me into adulthood, into my academic pursuits, and beyond. I earned my Bachelor of Arts in Political Science, seeking to understand the structures of power and governance that allowed figures like Hitler to rise. From there, I pursued two Master's degrees, one in Communication and one in Education, disciplines that deepened my understanding of how ideas are transmitted, received, and institutionalized across generations. Finally, I completed my doctoral studies at the University of Dayton, where my passion for research and inquiry reached its fullest expression.

This manuscript is the culmination of that lifelong journey: part academic exploration, part personal reckoning. It is not simply a retelling of what happened but an attempt to understand why it happened, how it happened, and what it continues to mean in the 21st century. I approach this work not as a detached observer but as someone who has spent decades wrestling with the myth, memory, and meaning of Hitlerism. This is not a book about a man. It is a book about the ideas that possessed him, and that, frighteningly, still echo in our time.

In writing this, I have tried to balance rigorous historical analysis with philosophical reflection. I believe that history, to be truly valuable, must illuminate not only the past but the present. It must make us better thinkers, more alert citizens, and more humane participants in the ongoing experiment of civilization.

I offer this work in that spirit. With humility. With urgency. And with the hope that by understanding the darkest corners of our shared history, we might be better prepared to resist the seductions of hatred, fear, and false salvation, wherever and however they may reappear.

-Amjad Khan

<u>Acknowledgements</u>

To my nephew, Weston O'Connor, you are the most important thing in my life. I love you more than anything in this world, and you have changed my life in such a beautiful, unexpected way. Your laughter and presence have filled my heart with a love that I never knew I needed. I love you, kid. Never forget that, and never stop loving yourself.

With deepest gratitude,

Amjad Khan

CONTENTS

CHAPTER 1

HITLERISM IN THE 21ST CENTURY: A TIMELESS REFLECTION ON HUMAN NATURE

As we live in the 21st century, the memory of the terrible events of the 20th century still remains strong. One of the darkest periods was when Adolf Hitler came to power, spreading the ideas of Nazism, a hateful and destructive ideology that caused millions of deaths and reshaped the world. Most people know about the horrors of Hitler's rule, particularly the Holocaust, where six million Jews and countless others were brutally murdered, and the widespread devastation caused by World War II. Even though these events happened decades ago, it's important to keep discussing Hitler and his beliefs today.

Today, with rapid advancements in technology and constantly changing political landscapes, it might seem easier to focus only on the future and leave the past behind. However, the same emotions and ideas that enabled Hitler's rise (such as fear, hatred, division, and manipulation) haven't disappeared. They still influence people and events today.

Across the globe, we witness the rise of extremist groups, populist politicians who exploit people's fears, and authoritarian governments that silence opposition and restrict freedoms. These examples remind us that the dangers of Hitler's ideology still exist. To create a safer, fairer future, we must remember and understand these past horrors, not only to honor those who suffered but also to prevent history from repeating itself.

Understanding Hitlerism and Its Historical Context:

Hitler's rise was possible because Germany faced severe political, economic, and social crises after World War I. Losing the war was devastating, but the harsh terms of the Treaty of Versailles made it even worse. Germany had to pay enormous debts, reduce its military dramatically, and accept blame for starting the war, deeply humiliating the German people. The situation became even worse when the global economic collapse, known as the Great Depression, hit in the early 1930s. Millions lost their jobs, savings disappeared, and desperation spread quickly. People became disillusioned with their government and desperately searched for someone who promised a way out of their misery.

Adolf Hitler, who had personally experienced the humiliation and hardship of World War I, emerged as a charismatic leader who seemed to understand the struggles of ordinary Germans. He promised to restore Germany's pride, rebuild the economy, and create stability. Hitler cleverly directed people's anger and frustration towards Jews, falsely accusing them of controlling world finance, politics and secretly sabotaging Germany from within. His racist beliefs, particularly the idea that Germans belonged to a superior "Aryan" race, appealed to people looking for someone to blame for their suffering.

Central to Hitler's ideology was the concept of Lebensraum, or "living space." Hitler believed that Germany needed more territory, particularly in Eastern Europe, to grow stronger and create an empire of what he falsely claimed were "racially pure" Aryan people. This belief justified military aggression, expansion, and violence against other nations. Hitler and the Nazi Party sought total control, crushing any opposition, silencing critics, and promoting a culture of fear and obedience. Hitler didn't just want power; he aimed to reshape society completely according to his racist, militaristic, and authoritarian vision.

These beliefs led directly to the outbreak of World War II and the horrors of the Holocaust. Hitler's obsessive pursuit of his racist empire resulted in the deaths of tens of millions of people around the world. Despite Nazism being defeated when the war ended in 1945, its harmful ideas did not vanish completely. They have continued to influence various extremist groups and movements, demonstrating that understanding and remembering this dark past is vital to protecting our present and future.

History's Unsettling Habit of Repeating Itself:

One of the most troubling things about human history is how often certain patterns seem to repeat themselves. You'd think we'd learn from our past mistakes, but history rarely moves in a straight line. Instead, it tends to loop back around, and the same ideas and forces that caused disasters in the past can resurface when conditions become ripe again.

Historians like Oswald Spengler and Arnold Toynbee talked about history working in cycles. They believed civilizations rise, reach a peak, decline, and eventually collapse. Although people debate how true this theory is, the basic idea is pretty solid: when things get chaotic or tough, authoritarianism and extremism often find room to grow. Hitlerism is a prime example of this cycle.

After World War II ended, the world tried hard to make sure nothing like Nazi Germany could ever happen again. Liberal democracies spread, and countries set up international organizations to promote peace. The United Nations, the Universal Declaration of Human Rights, and NATO were all part of this big push to create stability and safety globally. But even with these safeguards, extremist ideas never completely vanished. Throughout the Cold War, we saw a struggle between two extreme ideologies: Soviet communism and Western democracy. And even after the Cold War ended, authoritarian ideas kept bubbling up in different parts of the world.

Today, the 21st century has again seen an unsettling comeback of far-right extremism. Nationalist movements, which many thought were just ghosts of the past, have started gaining popularity again across Europe and the Americas. The economic crash of 2008 hit people hard, leaving many, especially young people, feeling lost and left behind by globalization. Far-right populist leaders, who echo some of Hitler's rhetoric, took advantage of this frustration. In countries like Hungary and Poland, nationalist governments have started to limit democratic freedoms and target minorities. In the United States, the election of Donald Trump in 2016 and again in 2024 was viewed by many as proof that something deeper was happening. Trump's policies and speeches often resonated with old fascist themes like racial purity, extreme nationalism, and authoritarian control.

The revival of these dangerous ideologies shows clearly how history repeats itself. When societies experience social, political, or economic upheaval, people often become attracted to extreme solutions, just like they did in the 1930s. This isn't a one-time event; it's a pattern we see again and again during crises. If we don't pay close attention to history, especially how Hitler and his dangerous ideas gained popularity, we risk allowing those same patterns to happen all over again, with devastating consequences.

But to really understand why history repeats itself and why movements like Hitlerism can come back to life, we need to look deeper than just politics or economics. The scariest truths aren't found in treaties or political speeches. They're inside us, deep within human nature itself.

The Latent Potential for Violence and Atrocities in Human Nature:

Beyond the idea that history tends to repeat itself, it's really important to look at the deeper reasons why destructive ideologies like Hitlerism emerge. The truth is humans aren't naturally peaceful creatures. We're driven by all kinds of complicated and often conflicting feelings. Evolutionary psychology, which studies how our minds evolved to help our ancestors survive, tells us that we have certain instincts deeply built into our nature. One of the strongest of these instincts is our desire to belong to a group. This need to connect with others often creates a strong sense of "us versus them."

Think about it like this: it's natural for people to feel closer and more loyal to their own group. But this loyalty has a dark side. Sometimes, it makes us see people outside our group as inferior or even dangerous. This mentality of dividing people into insiders and outsiders has been behind many of history's darkest chapters, including the horrors committed by Hitler and the Nazis.

Hitler used this instinct to devastating effect. His propaganda pushed the idea that Germans, whom he called the "Aryan race," were superior to Jews, Roma, Slavs, and other marginalized groups. By convincing ordinary people to see others as fundamentally different and inferior, he justified unimaginable cruelty and genocide. Even today, leaders who spread racist, xenophobic, or nationalist ideas still exploit this basic human instinct to gather support and gain power.

Another disturbing factor is how people react to authority. Psychological experiments, like Stanley Milgram's famous shock experiments, show us something unsettling: ordinary people can become surprisingly cruel when they're just following orders. In Milgram's studies, participants willingly delivered painful shocks to strangers simply because an authority figure told them to. This explains a lot about Nazi Germany, where regular people (soldiers, doctors, neighbors) became part of the machinery that committed horrific acts. Philosopher Hannah Arendt called this the "banality of evil," emphasizing how ordinary, everyday people can do monstrous things under certain pressures.

So, human nature has a built-in potential for violence and cruelty, and that potential has been exploited by authoritarian leaders like Hitler. Understanding this is essential to stopping future tragedies because it reminds us to be alert and resist ideologies that appeal to our darkest instincts.

But there's still another piece to this puzzle. Understanding why people follow cruel orders helps, but it doesn't fully explain why they're attracted to authoritarianism in the first place. For that, we need to explore the emotional appeal these leaders offer.

The Dangerous Allure of Totalitarianism and Extremism:

There's something dangerously appealing about totalitarianism and extremism. Leaders like Hitler, or even more recent figures, offer straightforward solutions to complex problems. They promise order, security, and national pride, especially during chaotic times. When things feel uncertain, the idea of strong, decisive leadership can be very tempting.

Hitler's rise makes sense when we consider the chaos Germany faced between the two World Wars. The Treaty of Versailles left Germans feeling humiliated, and the Great Depression created terrible poverty and hopelessness. Hitler tapped into these feelings, promising to restore pride, stability, and strength. His message resonated deeply with people who felt forgotten or betrayed by their government and society. By blaming Jews and other minorities for Germany's problems, he provided a simple, clear scapegoat for their suffering.

Sadly, the pull of totalitarianism isn't just history. It's alive today. Modern populist leaders like Donald Trump, Viktor Orbán, and Jair Bolsonaro use similar tactics. They promise to bring back national pride and unity by pointing the finger at immigrants, minorities, and "elites" as enemies. Their message is simple and powerful: "We are the true people, and they are the threat." This narrative becomes especially attractive during times of economic trouble or social unrest when people desperately want someone to blame and something to believe in.

The Necessity of Remembering and Discussing Hitlerism:

If we want to keep dangerous ideologies like Hitlerism from coming back, we have to keep talking openly about what happened during Nazi Germany. You might think that it is just history, something that has nothing to do with today, so why bother understanding any of it? But it is more than just the past; it is something that shaped who we are today. And to see it this way, we have to educate ourselves about it. Schools and universities need to make sure young people understand exactly how Hitler rose to power and what happened when hate was allowed to spread without checks.

Teaching about the Holocaust is a big part of this. It's not just about remembering the victims, though that's incredibly important. It's also about showing clearly where unchecked hatred and extremism can lead. When students learn these things, they become more aware of how easily societies can slip into darkness if we're not careful.

But education alone won't solve everything. We, as a society, need to always stay alert. We need to question leaders who use divisive language and who try to exploit fear to gain power. Populist leaders often rely on turning people against each other, creating division rather than unity. Being vigilant means speaking up, asking tough questions, and not letting hateful or misleading messages go unchallenged.

The media, artists, writers, and community groups all have roles to play, too. Movies, books, art exhibitions, public discussions: all these things help keep memories alive. They help new generations understand the past and remind everyone why it matters so much today.

When we look at everything together, the cycles of history, our psychological vulnerabilities, and the seductive promises of authoritarian leaders, we realize just how delicate our modern world truly is. Remembering and talking about Hitlerism isn't just about knowing history. It's about protecting our future and making sure we never fall into the same traps again.

Conclusion: A Call to Reflection and Vigilance:

Talking about Hitler and the horrors of his regime is more than just a history class; it's about our responsibility today. The forces that made his rise possible haven't disappeared. They're still around us. Understanding what happened in Nazi Germany from historical, psychological, and biological viewpoints helps us spot the signs of trouble today.

We have a moral duty to keep these discussions alive, educate ourselves and our communities, and stay vigilant. Only through constant reflection, awareness, and courage can we ensure that the darkest chapters of history never happen again.

Meet Adolf Hitler: The Person Behind the Infamous Legacy

Adolf Hitler was born in 1889 in Braunau am Inn, a small town in Austria. Today, he remains one of history's most notorious figures because of the central role he played in the rise of Nazi Germany and the catastrophic events of World War II. Even after his death in 1945, Hitler's actions continued to shape global politics and impact the world's consciousness for decades. But to fully grasp how he changed the course of history, it's important not just to look at the horrors his regime committed but also to understand the man himself: the personality, the ideas, and the beliefs that drove him into power.

Early Life: Shaping the Mind of a Future Dictator

Hitler's early years were tough and filled with personal challenges. His father was strict and harsh, whereas his mother was caring but overly protective, leaving him caught between two extremes. At school, Hitler was never remarkable; he struggled academically and frequently clashed with his teachers. Life got even harder when his mother died in 1907. Her death left him lonely, grieving, and lost. Searching for purpose, Hitler moved to Vienna to follow his dream of becoming an artist. Unfortunately, his hopes were shattered when the Vienna Academy of Fine Arts rejected him, not once, but twice. These rejections deeply wounded him, intensifying his feelings of inadequacy and resentment.

Vienna, at that time, was a city full of tension, conflict, and radical ideas, especially about race and nationalism. It was here that Hitler first encountered strong anti-Semitic and nationalist beliefs. He quickly became drawn to groups that preached Aryan superiority and blamed Jews for Europe's social and economic troubles. Hitler adopted these ideas wholeheartedly, convinced that eliminating Jews was essential to the survival and prosperity of the so-called Aryan race. This wasn't a unique viewpoint; racial purity was a widespread idea in Europe known as eugenics, but Hitler became its most notorious advocate.

His painful experiences in Vienna laid the emotional and psychological groundwork for his later ambitions. Personal failures, deep loneliness, and strong exposure to extremist ideas combined into a volatile mix fueling his obsession with power, dominance, and racial purity.

From Soldier to Revolutionary: World War I and Nazi Ideology

World War I dramatically shaped Hitler's worldview. When war broke out in 1914, he eagerly joined the German Army, hoping to prove his loyalty and bravery. Fighting on the brutal Western Front, Hitler experienced firsthand the horror and misery of trench warfare. Millions died around him, and these traumatic experiences left him bitter and angry. Twice wounded (once resulting in temporary blindness) he returned home traumatized and deeply resentful.

The war ended disastrously for Germany, which faced humiliation with the signing of the Treaty of Versailles in 1919. Many Germans, including Hitler, felt betrayed by the treaty's harsh terms, which imposed severe financial penalties and territorial losses. This humiliation created widespread anger, hopelessness, and chaos: perfect conditions for extremist groups to thrive. Hitler found his purpose in this turbulent environment, channeling his anger into politics.

In the early 1920s, Hitler joined the German Workers' Party (DAP), a small nationalist group known for its anti-Semitic, anti-communist beliefs. Quickly, he rose to prominence as the party's most compelling speaker. By 1921, he had taken over the leadership, renaming it the National Socialist German Workers' Party, the Nazi Party. Hitler was a charismatic speaker who tapped into ordinary Germans' frustrations and fears, offering simple solutions: blame the Jews, reclaim German pride, and expand German territory. Using powerful propaganda, mass rallies, and symbols like the swastika, Hitler cultivated a powerful personality cult, making himself synonymous with the Nazi movement.

Hitler's Struggle for Power: Failure, Prison, and Rebirth

Hitler's road to power wasn't straightforward. In 1923, he led an attempted takeover of the German government known as the Beer Hall Putsch. The plan failed, and Hitler was arrested and jailed. However, prison gave him the opportunity to reflect and articulate his dangerous ideology. During this time, he wrote "Mein Kampf" ("My Struggle"), which outlined his beliefs clearly: Aryan supremacy, anti-Semitism, and aggressive territorial expansion. This book became the foundation for the Nazi movement, solidifying Hitler's role as its undisputed leader.

Despite the failure of his initial attempt to seize power, Hitler learned from the experience and changed his approach. After prison, he committed to using legal political channels to gain control. The Great Depression of the late 1920s provided a massive opportunity. As the German economy collapsed, millions faced unemployment and hardship. The government was unable to help, and Hitler capitalized on this despair by promising a return to German strength, stability, and pride.

By 1932, Hitler and the Nazis were among the most powerful political forces in Germany, winning significant support in elections. Although they lacked a clear majority, backroom political negotiations eventually resulted in Hitler becoming Chancellor of Germany in January 1933. Once in office, Hitler wasted no time dismantling Germany's democratic institutions to build a dictatorship.

Consolidating Absolute Power

A crucial turning point came in February 1933 when the Reichstag (German Parliament) caught fire. Hitler blamed the communists for the blaze, using the event as justification to pass the Reichstag Fire Decree, stripping Germans of many civil liberties and allowing the arrest of political rivals. Shortly after, in March 1933, Hitler pushed through the Enabling Act, giving himself total authority to create laws without parliamentary consent. With these moves, Hitler had effectively become a dictator.

Over the following years, Hitler systematically eliminated political opponents and rival parties, establishing the feared Gestapo secret police to enforce his brutal policies. By 1934, after the death of Germany's President, Paul von Hindenburg, Hitler combined the roles of Chancellor and President, taking the title of Führer (leader). With absolute power in his grasp, Hitler set the stage for some of history's darkest chapters.

The Expansion of Nazi Ideology: From Nationalism to Global Conquest:

Once Adolf Hitler took control of Germany, he wanted to restore the country's pride and also to reshape the world. His vision wasn't limited to fixing Germany's economy or politics. He believed that Germans, especially those he called "Aryans," deserved more land, more power, and more influence. This belief turned into an aggressive plan called *Lebensraum*, or "living space," where Hitler aimed to expand eastward into parts of Europe like Poland and the Soviet Union.

But it wasn't just about land. His plan involved pushing out, or wiping out entirely, the people who already lived there. Whole communities were labeled as obstacles to the grand future he imagined for Germany. To him, non-Germans, especially Jews, Slavs, and Roma, didn't belong. He painted them as threats to the so-called purity and strength of the German race.

This obsession with race fueled what would become one of history's most horrifying crimes: the Holocaust. At first, the Nazis tried to isolate Jewish people by taking away their rights, stealing their businesses, and forcing them into overcrowded ghettos. But it didn't stop there. By 1942, at a high-level Nazi meeting known as the Wannsee Conference, they made it official: the "Final Solution" was to murder every Jew in Europe. What followed was industrialized genocide; mass killings were carried out in death camps like Auschwitz, Treblinka, and Sobibor.

But the horror didn't stop with the Jewish community. Hitler's regime also targeted others he considered "undesirable." Roma people, disabled individuals, LGBTQ+ people, political dissidents, and anyone who didn't fit into his racial fantasy were hunted, imprisoned, and often murdered. His dream of a racially "pure" nation came at the cost of millions of lives and the destruction of countless families and communities.

Why We Still Talk About Hitler Today

Adolf Hitler's rise to power is more than just an event in a dusty history book. It's a warning. His story reminds us how dangerous it can be when a charismatic leader taps into fear and division. He didn't come to power through brute force alone. He convinced people that he could fix their problems. He told them who to blame. And in a time when Germany was hurting economically, politically, and socially, his message felt like hope to many.

But that hope quickly turned into something terrifying.

Fast forward to today. As nationalism and far-right movements begin to rise again in different parts of the world, the lessons from Hitler's time feel more relevant than ever. His power grab didn't happen in a vacuum. It was made possible by a society in crisis. When people feel insecure, disconnected, and uncertain about the future, they're more likely to follow someone who claims to have all the answers.

And that's exactly what Hitler did. He offered certainty. He promised glory. He blamed outsiders. And people listened.

That's why understanding Hitler's legacy matters now more than ever. His story shows how democracy can crumble when people stop trusting each other, when fear replaces hope, and when hatred is allowed to grow unchecked.

But this legacy goes even deeper.

When we think of Hitler, we often imagine the obvious symbols: swastikas, parades, speeches, and concentration camps. But what's just as important is understanding the *why* behind all of it.

Hitler didn't just try to control Germany with fear. He seduced people with an entire worldview. The Nazi rallies, the architecture, the uniforms: they weren't just for show. They made people feel like they were part of something big, something meaningful. The Nazi movement was crafted to feel like a kind of religion with rituals, sacred symbols, chants, and even a kind of "salvation" through conquest.

To many Germans, especially after the humiliation of World War I and the chaos that followed, Hitler's vision was emotionally powerful. It told them they were special. That they were destined for greatness. That their suffering had purpose.

This was the genius of Hitler's manipulation. He understood that people don't just want food on the table or a steady job. They want identity. They want to matter. And he gave them a story that made them feel like heroes, no matter how twisted or violent that story became.

So, studying Hitler isn't just about understanding his politics. It's about recognizing how easily human beings, anywhere, at any time, can be pulled into a dangerous fantasy if it promises belonging and purpose.

What Would You Have Done?

There's a question that always creeps in when we learn about Hitler and the Nazis: "What would I have done if I'd lived back then?"

It's not a comfortable question. Most of us would like to think we'd stand up, speak out, and do the right thing. But the truth is, history shows something else. Most people didn't resist. Most weren't villains either. They were bystanders. Silent, uncertain, hoping things would just work themselves out.

That silence is what allowed evil to grow.

And it forces us to look at ourselves today. In our world, full of disinformation, division, and rising authoritarianism, it's easy to think, "That could never happen here." But that's exactly the kind of thinking that makes it possible. Because the truth is, it *can* happen anywhere.

Not because people are bad, but because they're human. And humans are vulnerable to fear, groupthink, and to the comforting idea that someone else has the answers.

One of the most chilling things about Hitler's rise is that it happened in a country many people considered "civilized." Germany had universities, scientists, poets, doctors, philosophers. It was a center of art and culture. And yet, all those institutions, schools, churches, courts, and media were either taken over or fell silent.

This shatters the idea that education or intelligence alone can protect a society from tyranny. Knowledge without ethics isn't a shield. In the wrong hands, it can become a weapon.

So what does that mean for us now?

We live in a world where technology connects us but also divides us. Where facts and fiction blur. Where conspiracy theories flourish, in this environment, it's not hard to imagine how someone could once again tell a story about who we are, who the enemy is, and what must be done that pulls people in the same way Hitler's story did.

The symbols might change. The slogans might sound different. But the underlying forces, like nationalism, fear, and the need to belong, are still here.

Hitler's story isn't just about the past. It's about something deeply human: the longing for safety, identity, and meaning and the danger of seeking those things in hatred and exclusion.

If we want to protect our future, we have to remember not just *what* happened, but *how* it happened. The slow buildup. The excuses. The silences. The moments when people looked away.

And we must pay attention to what's happening around us now: the rise of leaders who divide the world into "us" vs. "them," who turn disagreement into betrayal, who tell stories that sound appealing but are built on lies and fear.

CHAPTER 2

FORGED IN SILENCE:

HITLER'S PARENTS AND THE ARCHITECTURE OF HIS SOUL

From the earliest moments of Adolf Hitler's life, the duality of his household shaped the man he would become: violent, fanatical, emotionally brittle, and deeply wounded. Born on April 20, 1889, in Braunau, Austria-Hungary, Adolf came into a home marked by contradiction. On one side stood Alois Hitler, his father, a stern, brutal, and emotionally inaccessible man. On the other side was Klara, his mother, a gentle, submissive woman whose love, though tender and sincere, could not shield her son from the wrath of his domineering father. These opposing forces, one monstrous and the other saintly, would wage war within their son's psyche for the remainder of his life. In a rare moment of reflection, Hitler once confided that the four years between his father's death in 1903 and his mother's death in 1907 were the happiest years of his life. It was a fleeting reprieve between the two losses, and was the only period when he felt free of his father's shadow and sheltered by his mother's undivided love.

Alois Hitler was a man whose name Adolf would rarely mention in later years. A mid-level customs official in the Austro-Hungarian civil service, Alois was born out of wedlock to a servant woman named Maria Anna Schicklgruber. His own early life was marked by social stigma, and in an effort to legitimize himself, he later assumed the surname "Hitler" from his stepfather, Johann Georg Hiedler. This murky lineage, which possibly included Jewish ancestry (though never proven), haunted Adolf's ideological posturing as a champion of racial purity. More directly, however, it was Alois' treatment of his son that scarred the future dictator. Alois was a heavy drinker, disciplinarian, and utterly devoid of warmth. He treated his children like subordinates in a barracks, demanding obedience, excellence, and deference without question. For young Adolf, who exhibited a dreamy temperament, a passion for drawing, and a distaste for rigid authority, his father's expectations were suffocating.

The abuse was not just verbal. According to neighbors and relatives, Alois frequently beat Adolf with a whip or a cane. These episodes of physical violence were coupled with constant belittlement. Alois viewed Adolf's artistic aspirations as foolish and shameful, insisting instead that the boy prepare for a career in civil service. When Adolf protested, his father doubled down on the abuse. The home became a battleground where a young, sensitive boy waged a silent war for autonomy against a tyrant who saw in his son nothing but disappointment and disobedience. In Hitler's later years, as he ascended to power and projected a cold, commanding persona, the ghost of Alois remained embedded deep in his consciousness. Alois had ruled the home with an iron will, and Adolf, in many ways, modeled his own rule on that template. He would ensure the world, unlike his boyhood self, would bow in submission.

But Hitler's feelings toward his father were not merely those of a wounded son. They were tangled in a strange mix of hatred, fear, and unacknowledged longing. Alois never saw greatness in his child, never glimpsed the charisma, the obsession, the pathological ambition festering beneath the surface. And because of this, Adolf would spend the rest of his life searching for substitute fathers in books, in myth, and in imagined genealogies of strength and purity. The absence of paternal affirmation created a void so large that no earthly man could fill it. Instead, Hitler gravitated toward ideological patriarchs: the philosophers, generals, and racial theorists who echoed the authority his father had wielded without kindness. He did not want their love, only their discipline, their structure, and their ruthless clarity. He devoured the works of German nationalists, military theorists, racial purists, and occasionally non-Germans whom he insisted were Aryan in spirit: Napoleon, Andrew Jackson, Julius Caesar. These figures became his adopted ancestors, a lineage of power forged in ink and blood.

It is not surprising, then, that Hitler never married until the final hours of his life, and more tellingly, never had children. The idea of fatherhood, in his mind, was forever linked to trauma. To be a father meant to be a tyrant or a failure, nothing in between. He lacked the capacity for tenderness, for the self-sacrifice required of a parent. His own childhood had convinced him that children were burdens, not blessings. They were objects upon which a man's inadequacies were projected and punished. Some have argued that Hitler's lack of heirs was tactical, that he feared the vulnerability of a bloodline, the potential weakness it might expose. But the truth is simpler and sadder. He could not fathom bringing a child into a world where they might feel as he had: unwanted, unloved, cursed from the very beginning. He once confided to Eva Braun that it was not worth having a child who could never live up to the expectations of his father.

And cursed he had been, according to his father. There were whispers in the Hitler household that Adolf was a punishment from God. Alois, having married his own niece Klara (his third wife), harbored deep guilt and superstition about their union. He feared divine retribution for the incestuous nature of their relationship, and when Adolf was born, sickly and melancholic, Alois interpreted the boy's frailty as a sign of God's wrath. He viewed the child not as a miracle, but as a curse. These sentiments, spoken aloud in drunken tirades or muttered under breath, seeped into Adolf's bones. To be unwanted by one's father is tragic enough. To be seen as evil by him, to be considered a symbol of shame, branded as the fruit of sin, is a wound from which the soul may never fully recover.

Klara Hitler was the antidote to this horror, though an imperfect one. She loved her son with a devotion that bordered on the sacred. In Adolf, she saw not the curse that Alois proclaimed, but the precious remnant of her hopes and longings. She had suffered multiple miscarriages and the deaths of several young children. Adolf was the only one who survived into adolescence. This fact deepened the bond between mother and son. Klara nurtured him, comforted him, and believed in his talents. She protected him where she could, though she rarely defied Alois openly. Her submission to her husband, while perhaps culturally conditioned, planted in Adolf the seeds of quiet resentment.

He loved her dearly, but he would later recall feeling helpless that she had never saved him. Why hadn't she stopped the beatings? Why hadn't she taken him away?

After Alois died suddenly in 1903, Klara and Adolf moved into a modest apartment. They were poor but freer than they had ever been. These were the years Hitler remembered fondly, the only time in his youth when he felt that life had a rhythm of peace. He wandered the hills, painted scenes of the countryside, and dreamed of attending the Academy of Fine Arts in Vienna. He began to imagine a future where he would be known not as Alois' son, but as Adolf the artist. Klara supported his dreams, even as poverty pressed in on them from all sides. But this brief interlude would come to a crushing end when Klara fell ill in 1906. What began as persistent chest pain turned out to be breast cancer, an incurable disease at the time.

Dr. Eduard Bloch, a Jewish physician who treated the family, would later recall Adolf's heartbreak with vivid clarity. The young man was devoted to his mother's care, pacing the halls, asking endless questions, and watching with silent agony as the woman who had been his sanctuary withered before his eyes. Dr. Bloch administered morphine to ease her pain, but nothing could stave off the inevitable.

As Klara's condition deteriorated, Adolf's grief became unbearable. He slept in short, restless bursts and often spent entire nights beside her bed. In those final weeks, all the rage, all the grandiosity that would later define his adult life, gave way to helplessness. He was a boy again: scared, alone, and losing the only person he had ever truly loved.

Klara died on December 21, 1907, and Adolf was inconsolable. Dr. Bloch described the moment as one of the most heart-wrenching he had ever witnessed. Hitler collapsed into tears, kissed her face repeatedly, and seemed paralyzed by grief. For days afterward, he wandered aimlessly, refusing to eat or speak. He was, in his own words, "shattered." But beneath the mourning was a deeper psychological rupture. Her death marked not just the end of his childhood, but the collapse of his inner world. The only stabilizing force in his life was gone, and what remained was a cauldron of unprocessed anger, despair, and narcissistic fantasy.

The resentment he had buried now began to surface in distorted ways. He blamed fate, modern medicine, and sometimes even the doctor, despite Bloch's kindness and professionalism. He later gave Bloch special protection during the Nazi regime, one of the rare and baffling exceptions to his genocidal policies. Some speculate that this was not compassion, but an attempt to preserve a pristine image of his mother's deathbed. Dr. Bloch had been a witness to Hitler's vulnerability, and sparing him may have been an effort to keep that moment untouched by the larger narrative of blood and conquest that would follow.

Adolf Hitler emerged from his mother's death a changed man. He would go on to fail the entrance exam to the Vienna Academy of Fine Arts twice. He would descend into poverty, sleeping in flophouses and soup kitchens, developing a hatred for the multicultural cosmopolitanism of Vienna. But beneath the antisemitism, the nationalism, and the radicalization that defined those years was a profound loneliness. His father had broken him. His mother had failed to save him. And in their absence, he sought to recreate the world in his image, not a world of love and safety, but one of absolute control, racial purity, and mythic destiny.

In Hitler's Third Reich, there was no room for children, at least not in the traditional sense. The Hitler Youth were not sons and daughters; they were instruments of ideology, extensions of the Führer's will. He demanded loyalty not to parents or families, but to the state, to himself. In this way, Hitler became the father he never had: harsh, unyielding, and feared. But unlike Alois, he commanded millions, not just one small boy. And unlike Klara, he offered no comfort, only the promise of glory through obedience.

The tragedy of Hitler's childhood is not merely that he was abused and abandoned, but that he internalized that pain and projected it onto the world. The boy who had once clung to his mother's bedside became a man who oversaw the mechanized death of millions. The failure of a father to love and a mother to protect produced a psyche that sought redemption not in healing, but in domination. He filled the void left by his parents not with peace, but with fire.

The psychological aftermath of Adolf Hitler's parental relationships continued to shape his adult life in profound and complex ways. The absence of healthy parental modeling, particularly from his father, left Hitler with a fractured understanding of authority, intimacy, and identity. He did not merely mourn his parents; he mythologized them. His father became a symbol of everything he needed to surpass, while his mother became a relic of purity and sacrifice, someone whose love he could never quite repay and whose loss left a gaping emotional wound. This dual inheritance of cruelty and idealized love came to define how Hitler saw the world: split between enemies to be crushed and ideals to be sanctified. There was no middle ground in his thinking, just as there had been no middle ground in his household.

One of the most revealing aspects of Hitler's emotional landscape was his decision to never revisit his childhood home after he rose to power. Unlike other powerful men who sought to reconnect with their roots as a gesture of triumph, Hitler avoided the physical sites of his earliest memories. Braunau was not preserved as a monument to the birth of a leader but was largely forgotten in Nazi mythology. There was no grand parade through the streets of his boyhood. The silence spoke volumes. In his avoidance, we see the guilt, shame, and psychic rupture he carried with him. The past was not a place of inspiration but a pit of memories too dark to confront. He had built a new identity, a messianic figure for a broken Germany, and that identity could not survive the confrontation with the vulnerable, abused child who once trembled under his father's whip.

The death of his mother had left him emotionally unmoored. In the years that followed, he exhibited traits of melancholic narcissism: a deep yearning for unconditional love fused with an inability to form genuine, reciprocal attachments. His relationships with women were distant, fetishized, or controlling. He feared intimacy because it threatened his illusion of invulnerability. Geli Raubal, his half-niece with whom he had an infamously intense and possibly incestuous relationship, died by suicide in 1931 under mysterious circumstances. Though historians continue to debate the nature of their relationship, what remains clear is that Hitler was possessive and manipulative toward her. Some speculated that Geli resembled his mother, not necessarily in appearance but in the intensity of the emotional connection he demanded from her. And when she died, likely by her own hand, Hitler once again collapsed emotionally, locking himself away for days in grief.

These cycles of obsession and loss echoed the patterns of his childhood. His capacity for love was twisted into domination, and his grief was transmuted into rage. His broader worldview mirrored this emotional binary. In Hitler's ideology, there were only two categories: the cherished and the despised, the racially pure and the parasitic, the savior and the traitor. This black-and-white thinking had roots in his personal history, where his father was all cruelty and his mother all sacrifice. He was incapable of accepting ambiguity, of tolerating contradiction, because his earliest experiences had taught him that ambiguity meant danger. The safe parent had been too weak to intervene; the strong one had been too cruel to love. And so, he chose to become one who was never weak, never tender.

Dr. Eduard Bloch, who had witnessed Adolf's most human moment, the death of his mother, was, ironically, a man Hitler never harmed. A Jewish physician in a world that would soon be hunted by Hitler's state, Bloch was granted special protection. Hitler referred to him as a "noble Jew" and allowed him to emigrate with his family. The contradiction is stark: the very man who would sign off on the mass murder of millions of Jews once made an exception for the doctor who had attended to his dying mother. But this exception was not born of mercy; it was born of memory. Bloch was part of a sacred tableau, his mother's final days, the last time Hitler had felt pure, unfiltered love. To destroy Bloch would have been to destroy the last witness to that private sanctum. In sparing him, Hitler preserved a small corner of his shattered innocence.

Still, even this act of "kindness" was laced with self-interest. Hitler's political life was devoid of true sentiment. His capacity to form bonds was almost entirely rooted in his need for control, admiration, or utility. Men like Heinrich Himmler, Joseph Goebbels, and Hermann Göring were not friends; they were instruments. They echoed back to him the version of himself he needed to believe in: the man of destiny, the father of the German volk. And this surrogate fatherhood of a nation allowed Hitler to rewrite the narrative of his own childhood. No longer the unloved child of a failed customs officer and a sickly woman, he would now be the patriarch of a resurrected empire, the embodiment of a people's will. But beneath this grandiosity was still the little boy crying at his mother's bedside.

Even in his aesthetic sensibilities, one sees the residue of childhood grief and longing. Hitler's love of classical architecture, grand pageantry, and idealized representations of the human form were all attempts to impose order on a chaotic world. His obsession with cleanliness, symmetry, and racial purity reflected a deep psychological need for perfection and control, perhaps an unconscious reaction to the unpredictable violence of his father and the helpless decline of his mother. Beauty, in Hitler's universe, was not a matter of taste but of power. It was a fortress against decay and death, a denial of the vulnerability he had witnessed in Klara's final hours.

The absence of children in Hitler's life also speaks volumes about the way his early wounds shaped his values. He once told a confidant that he did not want children because he could not guarantee they would be "worthy of the cause." But the truth is more likely rooted in fear. To become a father would have been to risk repeating the cycle, to watch another life suffer as he had. It would have required empathy, humility, and presence, qualities he had trained himself to suppress. Hitler was a man who preferred masses to individuals, symbols to people, ideals to realities. A child would have required him to live in the present moment, to confront the softness in himself that he had buried long ago.

Moreover, fatherhood might have made him human in the eyes of others, and Hitler desperately clung to a messianic self-image. The carefully curated myth of the Führer, celibate, childless, devoted entirely to the Reich, was incompatible with the compromises of domestic life. While other dictators paraded their families to project an image of stability or relatability, Hitler cloaked himself in solitude and sacrifice. His private life was not merely hidden; it was mythologized into nonexistence. To the public, he was married only to Germany. In reality, he was married to an idea, a twisted vision of strength, purity, and vengeance born from the wreckage of his early life.

As the war wore on and the Reich began to crumble, Hitler's inner world seemed to collapse inward. He withdrew from social life, distrusted even his closest associates, and became obsessed with betrayal, purity, and divine justice. The psychological distance between the young boy in Linz grieving over his mother's death and the man in the Berlin bunker giving orders to destroy his own country was not as wide as it seemed. Both were expressions of the same internal logic: If love ends in loss, then love must be replaced with power. If the world inflicts pain, then the world must be dominated. His entire adult life was an exorcism of childhood pain, a relentless campaign to build a world where he would never again feel powerless.

And yet, even in his final hours, the past refused to loosen its grip. As the Red Army closed in on Berlin, Hitler married Eva Braun in a bizarre and almost desperate ceremony. It was as though he needed, in death, to reclaim a private part of himself that he had long denied. But it was too late. The myth of the invincible Führer had unraveled. The ghosts of Alois and Klara hovered near. In some perverse way, his suicide was not just the end of a regime but the final act of a lifelong drama that began in a small Austrian home, under the shadow of a tyrannical father and a dying mother. The bunker was not just a military headquarters; it was a mausoleum for a man who had never known how to live.

The legacy of Hitler's parental trauma did not end with him. It metastasized into the lives of millions. His inability to resolve the emotional wounds of his childhood became a source of ideological violence and genocidal policy. He weaponized his pain, channeling it into hatred, paranoia, and systemic cruelty. And in this, there is a terrible irony: the boy who once wept at his mother's deathbed became the man who built death camps, the child who feared his father's rage became the adult who inspired terror. The cycle did not break; it expanded.

The psychological profile of Adolf Hitler is not merely a study in pathology but a cautionary tale about the impact of unhealed trauma. The child is indeed father to the man, and in Hitler's case, that child was neglected, abused, and never allowed to grieve safely. He carried that child with him into every speech, every order, every invasion. And though he tried to bury that part of himself beneath layers of ideology and brutality, it remained, the secret architect of his madness.

In the end, the man who could not be a son, who could not be a husband, who could not be a father, turned his nation into a surrogate family. He demanded their loyalty, promised them protection, and punished them for disobedience. But like his own father, he offered no real love. And like his mother, Germany too was left to die, ravaged by disease, hunger, and fire, while the man who claimed to love her took his life in a final act of cowardice and despair.

Hitler's relationship with his parents was not just a personal story; it was a blueprint for his entire life. From the pain of a broken home, he built a broken world. And while history has rightly judged him for his crimes, understanding the roots of his monstrosity remains essential, not to excuse, but to illuminate. For in the shadows of that childhood home, we see not just the making of a tyrant, but the failure of a family to nurture the fragile life entrusted to them. And from that failure came catastrophe.

To fully grasp the magnitude of how Hitler's childhood trauma shaped his worldview, one must explore how the emotional void created by his parents informed not only his political ideology, but also his spiritual and aesthetic sensibilities. Hitler's inner world, which might have developed in the direction of art or quiet reflection under different circumstances, instead hardened into a fortress of absolutist thinking. The intensity with which he clung to ideologies of racial superiority and cultural purification can be traced back to his desperate need for clarity and structure, needs that were systematically violated during his formative years by the unpredictable volatility of his father and the tragic frailty of his mother.

As a young boy, Hitler's perception of family was forged in a crucible of contradiction. The word "home" never conjured images of warmth or safety. Instead, it evoked terror, surveillance, and pain. This inversion of familial affection laid the groundwork for how Hitler would later invert all moral categories in his political philosophy. Compassion was weakness. Mercy was betrayal. Love, in its purest form, was naïve and temporary. These conclusions were not drawn in adulthood through philosophical contemplation; they were etched into his psyche through lived experience. They were conclusions he reached not with the intellect, but with the bruised body of a boy being beaten by a father who never wanted him.

This sense of betrayal extended beyond his father to the broader world, and eventually to his mother. While Hitler revered Klara, elevating her to an almost saintly status after her death, there was a subtle undercurrent of resentment that ran through his memories. She had, after all, failed to protect him. In moments of honesty, Hitler would have to confront the fact that the woman who loved him most did not have the strength to intervene. That dissonance haunted him. It introduced into his mind the dangerous notion that love, no matter how deep, is powerless without force. This belief would crystallize in his politics, where brute strength was the only virtue that mattered. One can trace a direct line from Klara's helplessness to the architecture of Hitler's totalitarian state: a regime that rejected sentiment in favor of terror, that punished weakness and celebrated ruthless domination.

Even Hitler's early failures, his repeated rejection from the Vienna Academy of Fine Arts, his poverty, his homelessness, did not spark empathy or humility. Instead, they confirmed a narrative that had been building since childhood: the world was unjust, rigged, and malicious. It was not merely that he was down on his luck; it was that the universe itself had conspired against him. This sense of cosmic grievance, rooted in the primal injustice of his birth and upbringing, would fester into the genocidal paranoia that defined his later years. The Jews, the Slavs, the Bolsheviks were not merely political enemies but stand-ins for a world that had denied him the love and safety he believed he deserved as a child.

In a sense, Hitler never emotionally matured beyond those early traumas. Though he grew in cunning, ambition, and cruelty, he remained in many ways an emotional adolescent, forever seeking the father's respect he never received, and the mother's protection he ultimately lost. This explains the theatricality of his speeches, the over-compensatory posturing, the compulsive need to be the center of adoration. He was performing not just for the German people but for the ghosts of his parents. Every thunderous rally, every pledge of national rebirth, was a desperate cry into the void: "Am I enough now?"

His aesthetic sensibilities were similarly shaped by this longing. The grand architecture he commissioned, massive neoclassical structures designed by Albert Speer, were not simply monuments to the Reich; they were efforts to build, on a national scale, the kind of unshakable, imposing order he had never experienced at home. These buildings were cold, eternal, and rigid, unlike his father's wrath, which had been chaotic and drunk, or his mother's warmth, which had been fleeting and doomed. The buildings he imagined for Berlin and Nuremberg were meant to endure, to testify forever to his power and vision, so unlike the fragile human relationships he had known.

Even his perception of death, so central to Nazi ideology, was warped by the early loss of Klara. Her death, which he experienced as a profound injustice and a personal abandonment, turned him against the natural order of life. In the years that followed, he would flirt with the occult, with pseudoscientific racial theories, and with apocalyptic visions of purification and rebirth. In each of these, we find the trace of a man trying to reverse the irreversibility of loss, to punish death itself for taking the only person who had loved him. He could not bring Klara back, but he could create a world in which her kind of vulnerability would be eradicated, where only the strong would survive, and the weak would be culled before they could suffer.

This war on vulnerability became the animating force of his political life. In his speeches, Hitler railed against softness, against "degeneracy," against anything that hinted at ambiguity or fragility. He spoke in absolutes because absolutes were safer. They did not weep or falter. They did not, like Klara, deteriorate in front of your eyes no matter how much you loved them. In his mind, the German people had to be hardened, not just militarily, but emotionally and spiritually. They had to be cured of their sentimentality, just as he had been cured, through pain, of his own.

The regime he built reflected this ethos perfectly. The SS, the Gestapo, and the concentration camps were not just instruments of repression; they were expressions of a worldview shaped by childhood trauma. A worldview in which love had failed, protection had failed, and only domination remained. Hitler's inner child, frightened, unloved, and alone, had grown into a man who made the world feel what he had once felt. In doing so, he reversed the roles: he became the inflictor of pain, not its recipient. He became his father, not his mother.

But even as he stepped into this role, he never truly escaped the torment it created. In private, he remained isolated and emotionally stunted. His interactions with others were often awkward, riddled with insecurity masked by aggression. He was notoriously bad at interpersonal intimacy, frequently misreading social cues or retreating into monologues. Those close to him noted his need for constant validation and his inability to accept criticism without flying into rage or despondency. These are the behaviors of a man not at peace with himself, but at war with the wounds he refused to acknowledge.

Perhaps most tragically, Hitler never broke the generational cycle of trauma. Had he become a father, perhaps the opportunity to nurture a child might have softened him or forced him to confront the pain he carried. But he avoided that possibility with the same intensity he had once avoided his father's gaze. And so, the pattern repeated itself on a global scale. The pain he inherited, he transmitted. Not through a bloodline, but through ideology, through policy, through war.

In the end, Hitler's greatest crime was not simply what he did to the world, but what he failed to heal in himself. His story is a chilling reminder that unresolved trauma, when paired with charisma and power, can metastasize into something truly monstrous. The boy who lost his mother and feared his father became the man who made mothers weep and fathers vanish. He turned his personal suffering into collective agony and his private grief into a national catastrophe.

The world would eventually recover from the physical ruins of Hitler's war. Cities would be rebuilt, borders redrawn, governments reconstituted. But the psychological impact, the inheritance of terror, the generational trauma inflicted upon the victims of his regime, would linger for decades. In this way, Hitler's personal history did not end with his suicide in the bunker. It lived on in the survivors' nightmares, in the fractured identities of orphaned children, in the silence of communities erased. His unresolved childhood became humanity's unresolved wound.

And perhaps that is the final, most sobering lesson of his life. The axis upon which all of his crimes turned was not merely geopolitical or economic; it was emotional. It was the small, domestic tragedy of a household devoid of safety, where love was conditional and protection was absent. The road to Auschwitz began not in the halls of power, but in the bruises of a boy and the tears of a dying mother. And in remembering that, we are called not only to condemn, but to understand, so that we may recognize, in time, the quiet wounds from which history's greatest horrors are born.

CHAPTER 3

THE TWO PILLARS OF POWER

If you look at history, you'll notice that people have always looked for strong leaders, especially during tough times. Over and over again, two main types of leaders show up: the *Strongman* and the *Shaman*.

These aren't just people with power. They represent what people *need*. When there's chaos and fear, people want someone strong who can take control and bring order. But when people feel lost or unsure about life, they look for someone who can give them meaning and direction.

The Strongman: Power Through Force:

The Strongman is the type of leader who takes power by force. He doesn't ask for permission or try to win people over with words. He *takes* control and makes people listen. His power comes from being tough, smart in battle, and confident enough that no one dares to challenge him.

You've probably heard of leaders like Julius Caesar, Napoleon, or Stalin. They didn't rise to power by being nice. They fought their way to the top and ruled with a tight grip.

Mussolini, another Strongman, loved to show off his power with big parades and speeches. He made sure everyone knew he was in charge by acting loud, bold, and unstoppable.

To a Strongman, the reason he should lead is simple: "I'm the strongest, so I get to be in charge." His rule is based on fear, strength, and the idea that no one can take him down.

But here's the problem: this kind of power doesn't last forever. Strongmen always have to *look* strong, even when they're not. If they lose a war or show weakness, their whole image can fall apart. That's what happened to Caesar. He was betrayed. Napoleon was kicked out of power. Mussolini was captured and killed. Their power worked. Until it didn't.

The Shaman: Power Through Vision:

Now let's talk about a very different kind of leader: the Shaman. Instead of using fear, the Shaman uses ideas, emotions, and belief to lead people. He might not be the strongest person in the room, but he *knows* how to speak to people's hearts and make them believe in something bigger.

Take Adolf Hitler. He didn't act like the toughest man in Germany. He didn't need to. His power came from making people believe in his vision. He painted a picture of the future that felt powerful and exciting to his followers. To many people, he wasn't just a leader. He was like a prophet, someone with a special purpose.

Hitler even acted like he was different from regular people. He avoided relationships, didn't party or drink, and kept himself very clean and disciplined. This made him seem almost holy, like someone chosen to lead Germany to its destiny.

This idea of the Shaman isn't just about Hitler. All through history, there have been leaders like this. Ancient Egyptian pharaohs said they were gods. Modern-day cult leaders make people follow them without question. What they all have in common is this: they create a story or belief that people trust more than their own eyes.

While the Strongman *forces* people to follow, the Shaman makes them *want* to follow. His followers don't fear him. They *believe* in him. That's what makes this kind of power even more dangerous. Even when the Shaman dies, the ideas he spread can live on for years, even generations.

The Convergence of Archetypes:

Every once in a while, a leader comes along who is both a Strongman and a Shaman. And when that happens, their power is almost unstoppable.

Take Genghis Khan. He was a warrior and was also seen as a spiritual leader. He led huge armies but also brought his people together with shared beliefs and a vision for the future. Even Stalin, who ruled with fear, also made up stories about himself being the "father" of his people. He knew how powerful stories could be.

Hitler, on the other hand, focused more on being the Shaman. He let others, like Himmler and Goebbels, handle the rougher side of power. He focused on spreading the beliefs behind the Nazi movement. He wasn't just in charge. He was building a whole new way for people to think.

When a leader can use *both* force and belief, they can control what people do *and* what they think. That kind of power is rare, but when it happens, it changes the world. Sometimes for good, often for bad. These leaders don't just disappear quietly. They either go down in flames, or leave behind ideas that shape the world long after they're gone.

Even though the world looks totally different from what it was centuries ago (faster, louder, more digital) the roles people play in leadership haven't really changed all that much. Deep down, we still respond to the same types of leaders we always have. In fact, two big personality types, what we might call *archetypes*, keep showing up again and again, especially when it comes to power: the Strongman and the Shaman.

Let's break that down.

The Strongman is the kind of leader who rules with sheer force. Picture someone who takes control, lays down the law, and doesn't hesitate to crush anyone who gets in the way. He wins by being tough, confident, and commanding. You can find this kind of figure in boardrooms too. Imagine a CEO who dominates the market, aggressively pushes out competition, and runs his company like a battlefield.

Now flip the coin, and you get the Shaman. This is the visionary, the one who doesn't just tell people what to do, but makes them *believe* in something bigger. Think of a startup founder who talks about changing the world, someone who doesn't just sell a product, but sells a *story*. The Shaman leads with purpose, with big dreams, and with a sense of meaning that makes people feel like they're part of a movement.

And if you look around, at politics, at tech, at pop culture, you'll see these two types everywhere. Some leaders build their image around strength and order. They talk tough. They promise security. They want to be seen as protectors. Others show up with charisma and bold visions. They speak like prophets. They offer transformation, hope, a new future.

The truth is, both of these archetypes are powerful, and understanding them is incredibly important, whether you want to *be* a leader, or you're just trying to understand the ones already in charge.

Because here's the thing: strength without vision is just bullying. And vision without strength? That's just dreaming. The best leaders, the ones who change the world for the better, know how to walk the line between the two. They use both power and purpose. They know when to be firm, and when to inspire. That balance? That's where real influence lives.

But knowing about these archetypes isn't just for leaders. It's just as important for the rest of us. For people who want to *resist* bad leadership. A Strongman without limits can be dangerous. If no one checks his power, it can turn into something ugly: oppression, fear, even violence. And the Shaman, for all his charm, can be dangerous too. A great story can blind people. When someone starts promising to "save" the world or "redeem" the nation, it's easy to forget to ask *how*. That's how people get swept up in dangerous ideas that sound beautiful on the surface.

No matter how far humanity advances, we'll never stop needing two things: strength and meaning. That's why these archetypes, Strongman and Shaman, always come back. They're part of who we are. One protects our bodies. The other feeds our souls. And in some way, our societies depend on both.

But that also means we face a constant question: which path do we follow? Do we lean into strength? Or do we chase vision? And most importantly: can we tell the difference between a leader who wants to serve us, and one who just wants control?

That's a big question. It's not easy. But it matters. It might even shape the future, not just of one country, but of the whole world.

Because behind all the fireworks of politics, behind the speeches, the uniforms, the rallies, there's something much older going on. Something deep. What we're really watching is a kind of ancient play. A drama about power, and how it moves through people.

These archetypes, the Strongman and the Shaman, they're not just roles someone picks like a costume. They're deeply wired into our psychology. Carl Jung, a famous psychologist, talked a lot about this. He said that deep inside all of us lives a kind of shared memory, a "collective unconscious," that includes these figures: the Warrior, the King, the Magician, the Prophet. They're like old blueprints of human behavior. And when the world starts to fall apart, when people feel scared or lost, these archetypes come alive again. They rise up, sometimes in one person, who becomes the symbol of everything the people need.

That's why extreme leaders often pop up during moments of chaos, when people lose faith in religion, in institutions, or in their sense of purpose. That vacuum, that emptiness? The Shaman archetype rushes in to fill it. Not just with plans, but with meaning. He says, "I will explain the mess. I will lead you to something higher." He doesn't just sound like a politician. He sounds like a prophet.

And sometimes, one person blends both roles, and that's when things get dangerous.

Take Adolf Hitler, for example. What made him so chilling was that he *combined* both archetypes. He didn't choose between the Strongman and the Shaman, he became *both*. He thundered with anger, like a warrior calling for battle. But at the same time, he painted himself as a kind of chosen one, someone sent by fate to change the world. His speeches weren't just political, they were *spiritual performances*. People didn't just follow him. They believed in him. That mix of fear and faith? That's what gave him so much power.

This is why it's so important to understand these patterns. Not just in history, but today. Because every time a crisis shows up, every time people feel unsure, afraid, or hopeless, there's a chance these archetypes will rise again. And someone will step forward claiming they've got the strength to protect us… or the vision to save us.

The Strongman doesn't bother with big spiritual ideas or poetic speeches. His power is simple. You can see it. You can feel it. He doesn't ask, he *commands*, and things get done. The room goes silent when he walks in. People move when he says so. That's the kind of authority that doesn't need to be explained. It just *is*.

But here's the twist: *even* the Strongman needs a little bit of the Shaman's magic if he wants to last.

Take Stalin, for example. He was all about logic and materialism. He dismissed religion. But strangely enough, he built a kind of religion around *himself*. His face was everywhere, in homes, schools, offices, like a saint on a candle. People treated his quotes like sacred text. His backstory was retold like a heroic legend, with the rough edges smoothed out and the drama turned up. He wasn't just being feared. He was being *worshipped.*

Modern dictators do the same. They rewrite their life stories to seem more "relatable" or "divine." They pretend to have come from humble beginnings, painting themselves as underdogs or chosen ones. They create a sense of mystery around who they are. And they use media, rituals, and public events like tools to shape how people see them. Because they know that power isn't just something you hold; it's something you *perform.*

But here's where it gets even trickier.

Sometimes, it's hard to tell the difference between *real* charisma and carefully crafted myth. And to be honest, sometimes it doesn't even matter. What counts is *how people perceive it.*

The sociologist Max Weber once said that charisma isn't something a person just *has*. It's something followers *believe* a person has. It's like an agreement: "You're special because we've decided you are." And once that belief takes hold, once people start seeing a leader as the living symbol of their hopes, fears, and frustrations, it's nearly impossible to question them. That leader becomes more than human. They become a *myth*.

This is where the Shaman archetype becomes even more dangerous than the Strongman.

See, the Strongman can be stopped. If enough people push back hard enough, they can remove him from power. But the Shaman? He's trickier. His legacy lives on even after he's gone. People remember his words. They frame his picture. They tell stories about him, pass down his beliefs, maybe even *kill* in his name. That kind of power goes deep.

Think about Hitler again. The Nazi regime didn't just want people to follow orders. They wanted people to *believe.* They built a kind of religion around him. Kids sang songs praising him. Couples got married in his name. They even adjusted the calendar to center around his life. It was more than just politics. It was spiritual manipulation. They weren't just building loyalty. They were creating *faith.*

And like any faith, it came with rituals.

Authoritarian regimes don't just want control. They want devotion. That's why they change national holidays, invent new symbols, and design massive buildings that make people feel small and awestruck. Hitler's architect, Albert Speer, didn't just make structures, he made shrines. The swastika, an ancient symbol, was twisted into something new, a badge of this dark mythology. Nazi rallies weren't just events. They were massive, choreographed *ceremonies.* It all felt normal at the time. But it was anything *but.*

And that's the most chilling part: it can feel ordinary while it's happening.

Big displays and public participation have a strange effect. They make it easier to believe. When you're in a crowd, singing the same song, waving the same flag, it feels right. It feels like belonging. Doubt starts to fade. Questioning becomes uncomfortable. Soon, people don't just live under a system, they live inside its story. They start thinking in its language. They begin to see the world through its lens. That's how deep the Shaman's influence goes.

And when this mythic influence joins forces with the Strongman's machinery, his police, his army, his spies, you get a kind of power that doesn't just rule people's lives, but also their minds.

Now, let's pause for a second. It's easy to see all of this and think these archetypes are evil. But they're not. They're just human tools, powerful ones, that people reach for when the world feels shaky.

After war or crisis, people crave someone who brings stability. A unifier. When everything feels meaningless, they long for a dreamer, someone who promises purpose. That's when the Strongman and the Shaman step in. And the real danger comes when these leaders start believing their own myth. When they stop seeing themselves as temporary guides and start thinking they *are* destiny itself. That's when things spiral. That's when power goes from being a responsibility… to being a cult.

That's why democracies need more than just rules and institutions. Laws can be changed. Courts can be stacked. Constitutions can be ignored if enough people stop caring. The real fight is over stories. Over who gets to define what's true, what's sacred, and what the future should look like.

This is why authoritarian leaders often go after artists, writers, teachers, and journalists first. Because those people are storytellers too. And if you're trying to build a myth, you *can't* have someone else telling a different story. In a myth-driven regime, facts aren't the threat. Perspectives are.

So here's the takeaway: understanding these archetypes is necessary. It helps us see what's happening beneath the surface. It helps us recognize manipulation, question illusions, and push back when needed.

Because here's the truth: power doesn't just fall on us from above. We agree to it. We participate in it. And we can also take that power back.

But it's not easy.

Saying no to the Strongman means facing chaos. Saying no to the Shaman means letting go of beautiful dreams. It means choosing uncertainty over the comfort of having someone else tell you what to believe. And uncertainty? That's scary for most people.

And maybe that's the hardest truth of all: sometimes, the very leaders we fear… are the ones we helped create.

We long for safety. We crave meaning. And in that longing, we sometimes hand our future to people who promise everything. So the question isn't just, *"How do we stop them?"* It's also, *"Why do we keep calling them back?"*

CHAPTER 4

HITLER THE POSSESSED

Throughout history, some leaders have governed through rational calculation, while others have exercised a different kind of power - one that is based on myth, symbol, and the collective unconscious of a people. Adolf Hitler was not merely a man of political ambition; he was, in many ways, a vessel for something far more sinister. Historians have struggled to categorize him and often describe him as something less than a god but definitely more than just a man. There was something really mysterious about the way he influenced the German people and led them down a path of destruction. Some have suggested that he was probably possessed - if not by a demon, then by an archetype that used him to carry out his global ambitions.

The Cult of Wotan:

Hitler didn't just run a political movement - he stirred up something much older, something almost mythic. It was as if he reached back into the ancient stories that were buried in the German imagination and, pulled them out and dressed them as modern fascism robes of old legends. One of the most powerful symbols he leaned on, whether consciously or not, was Wotan, better known as Odin. In Norse mythology, Wotan is the god of war and wisdom, but he's also a wanderer and a shapeshifter god who walks the world in disguise. He watches, manipulates, and sets events into motion to see who survives and who falls. It wasn't just politics. It felt like fate. And that's what made it so dangerously seductive.

There's an old myth about Wotan, Odin, that says he doesn't start wars to win land or power but to find the strongest warriors. The ones who survive are taken to Valhalla, where they prepare for the final battle of the world, *Ragnarök.* Wotan isn't just a god of war; he's more like a collector of human struggle, choosing the best to join him in something greater.

Hitler's beliefs are a reflection of this myth in many ways that are questionable. He constantly spoke about struggle, *Kampf,* as something necessary and noble. He believed that war could purify a nation and burn away the weak while leaving only the strong. He didn't see himself as just a man but as someone chosen by fate. And to him, Germany wasn't just a country - it was a living thing that had to be solidified by conflict, even if that meant sacrificing the weak.

The Loss of Self:

One of the most disturbing things about Hitler's rise was how he seemed to become one with the will of the German people. He wasn't just a dictator forcing his ideas on them. He also reflected on their hopes, fears, and beliefs.

As he gained power, Hitler seemed to lose his sense of self. The line between him and the nation faded until he was no longer just an individual. He became the voice of a symbol of how Germany saw itself during that time.

This might be the key to understanding how Hitler was able to influence an entire nation. He didn't speak like an outsider giving orders; he spoke as if he *was* the people for them and by them. His speeches didn't sound like commands; they felt like truths being revealed to everyone listening to him. He gave power to the hidden fears, frustrations, and hopes of a generation and made them believe that his fate and theirs were the same - all manipulative tactics.

But there was a darker and stranger side to this loss of self. People who knew Hitler close enough often said that he seemed to be taken over by something beyond him. He talked about visions and moments of insight that felt like they came from another place. Some of his close friends saw him talk about something that made him feel uneasy. It was as if his eyes were glowing from within his head. His childhood friend, August Kubizek, once wrote that Hitler spoke of a great destiny in a voice that didn't sound like his own.

If Hitler was "possessed," it wasn't in a supernatural sense. It was more like he was taken over by an idea.

The Transformation in the Trenches:

Before he was the Fuhrer or before he even entered politics, Hitler was a failed artist. He was a man whose life seemed to be headed toward nothing but a series of miseries. He was prone to fits of depression and even attempted suicide. By all accounts, he was a nobody.

Then came the First World War:

Hitler joined the German army and was sent to fight in France, where he witnessed firsthand the brutal reality of modern war. But instead of breaking him, the experience seemed to transform him. While he was there in the trenches, he read the work of philosopher Arthur Schopenhauer, who believed that life is driven by a blind, irrational force and that suffering is at the heart of existence. To Schopenhauer, only those who accepted this harsh truth could rise above it.

Hitler took these ideas very seriously. The war became a turning point for him. It became a place where he let go of his old self and accepted the idea of struggle as a way of life. He didn't come out of the war defeated; he came out hardened and with a single purpose: to fulfill what he believed was Germany's destiny.

The Death He Desired:

By the end of World War II, when Germany collapsed and lost the war, there was a tone in Hitler's speech. He no longer talked about winning - he spoke about destruction and war. He began to blame the German people, saying they had failed him and didn't deserve the future he had promised.

In a way, his death was the final chapter of his story. Like Wotan in the myth of Ragnarök, Hitler never expected to survive the war. He saw it as a test of Germany's strength, and in his eyes, Germany had failed. His death felt like part of the nation's death and like a final act in a war which he had always seen as apocalyptic.

What's most disturbing is that he didn't fear the outcome of all the chaos he spread. He just embraced it almost as if he was expecting it. Just as he lost his identity in the rise of the Reich, he was ready to give up his life in its fall. In that sense, he wasn't just a leader; he became the living symbol of a destructive story that was playing out through him.

Possession by History:

Whether you believe Hitler was literally possessed or just swept up by the forces of history, one thing is clear: he was more than just a man. He became an idea in human form, shaped by myth, war, and the darkest parts of the human mind.

That's what makes people like Hitler so hard to understand. We want to see them as insane or as exceptions, but they're something scarier. These people are reflections of the societies that produce them, with collective hopes, fears, and hidden desires.

To truly understand Hitler, we have to look beyond the man himself. We have to study the myths, philosophies, and psychological forces that made his rise possible. And in doing so, we face a hard truth: figures like him don't come from nowhere. They are brewed.

And if it's happened before, it can definitely happen again. That's why studying Hitler isn't just about a sad history lesson - it's a warning. As long as the forces he represented still exist, the world remains vulnerable to another leader just like him. All it takes are the right conditions, and history may once again bring such a person to the surface.

Calling Hitler "possessed" isn't about superstition or demons - it's about recognizing how deeply he was motivated by something that was much larger than himself. His rise didn't feel like ambition alone. It felt like his destiny. He believed it was his destiny to rise to power and change the history of Germany.

What set Hitler apart from most dictators was how completely he blended himself with his ideology. Other leaders can bend or drop their beliefs when needed, but Hitler *was* his belief. There was no personal life that softened or contradicted his public image. This total fusion made him more dangerous and actually harder to understand. His speeches didn't feel or sound like politics. They felt like rituals that he practiced religiously. His followers didn't respond with thought but with emotion, even ecstasy.

Spiritually, you might say he was taken over. Either way, the result is the same: the person disappears, and a symbol takes their place. Hitler stopped being Adolf, the failed artist who was rejected admission to the university for studying arts; he became the Führer, the voice of vengeance and a hope of rebirth of Germans.

Carl Jung and other thinkers have pointed out that there are these deep, almost ancient patterns in our minds that get passed down through generations. Sometimes, these can take over a person, and when that happens, they stop acting based on their own will and start acting on something much bigger, something from the collective unconscious.

The real danger is when that medium that takes control isn't something positive, like a wise leader or a healer, but it's sinister, like the force of anger, destruction, or cruelty. And it seems that's exactly what happened with Hitler.

What's even more chilling is that the German people, in their pain and hopelessness, seemed to reflect that same dark force. He wasn't just a leader; he was an event and a rupture in history. Some postwar psychologists described him not just as a narcissist or a sociopath but as someone who carried psychic contamination in his head.

If Hitler was a medium, then his rise was not just the result of propaganda, militarism, or economic collapse; it was a psychic phenomenon. He gave form to formless fear, voice to rage, and direction to humiliated desires. In this sense, he functioned like a prophet, though a false one, whose revelation led not to salvation but to ruin.

There's something here that connects to ancient cultures. In shamanic traditions, being possessed by a spirit, whether divine or malevolent, was seen as both a gift and a curse. The possessed person was treated with awe but also with caution. They could speak truths that others couldn't hear, but there was always a *price* to pay: loneliness, madness, or an early death. With Hitler, that price wasn't just paid by him but was paid by millions.

Another comparison worth considering is the idea of the *puer aeternus*, the "eternal boy." In many ways, Hitler never truly grew up. He held on to a black-and-white view of the world that left no room for compromise or complexity. He had rigid, obsessive, and ascetic habits, like a child, that reflected this mindset. But this wasn't just any child; it was a child who was possessed by the spirit of war, a kind of Peter Pan with apocalyptic dreams.

As Hitler became more "possessed" by his vision, he also became more isolated. His inner circle, which had once been filled with advisors and rivals, shrank to just yes-men and worshippers who followed him. He couldn't tolerate anyone disagreeing with him anymore. He shut out outside opinions and retreated into his own dreams, sometimes quite literally.

By the last years of the war, his decisions weren't based on military strategy; they were shaped by how he perceived certain places and ideas. He refused to let the German army retreat from cities he thought had some great significance, even when it meant great defeat. His belief in destiny had become so firm that even as everything was collapsing around him, he couldn't shake it.

And collapse came.

In the final days of the Reich, when he was trapped in the crumbling Berlin bunker, Hitler played out the last scene of his own story. It was like the "twilight of the gods, "Götterdämmerung. He was angry with betrayal, blamed the people for being so weak, and accepted his own destruction.

His suicide wasn't just a way to escape; it was the last act in a drama he'd been writing for years. He didn't die quietly - he went out with the delusion of grandeur still firmly in his head. What makes this story really terrifying is not its uniqueness but its familiarity.

History is full of figures who seem "possessed" by destiny, and there are so many leaders who arise in times of chaos and speak with absolute conviction while influencing everyone. The danger is not only that they exist but that we invite them into our lives. We do that when we get tired of democracy's compromises, when we want clarity over complexity, and when our beliefs no longer help us. In those moments, we turn not to reason but to revelation.

To call Hitler possessed is, in the end, to ask what we ourselves are capable of being possessed by. Ideology? Identity? Anger? How easily do we surrender when someone offers to carry our burden, help us in our suffering, and punish our enemies?

In this way, Hitler's possession was not solitary. It was shared. He drew his power not just from within but from the willing projection of a people desperate for meaning.

This isn't something that's unique to Germany or just the 20th century. It's a pattern that can repeat throughout history at any time or place. When the conditions are right: economic hardship, cultural shame, and political disarray, then we know that the stage is set for another figure like Hitler to rise. The names and symbols may change, but the underlying dynamic stays the same.

So, what can we do about it?

The first step is recognizing the danger. We need to learn to see not just the signs of external tyranny but also the internal conditions that make us vulnerable to it. We need to develop a kind of psychological awareness alongside historical knowledge. It's not enough to ask, "What happened?" We also have to ask, "Why did we fall for it?" Most importantly, we can't give in to the temptation to reduce Hitler to some kind of monster. As comforting as that view may be, it lets us off the hook.

He wasn't a demon. He was a man who had terrifying beliefs that became his voice and unleashed massive destruction. Understanding him is not about excusing him for the horrific things he did - it's a way of understanding ourselves.

CHAPTER 5

THE NAZI MASTER PLAN FOR POST-WAR DOMINATION

The Third Reich's ambitions extended far beyond the battlefield victories of World War II. Nazi leadership, particularly Adolf Hitler and his inner circle, had a vision for a post-war world shaped by German control. This so-called "Master Plan" was not just about theory, but it was a blueprint for a radically transformed global order under the dominion of the Aryan race. After Germany's defeat, there were documents and plans discovered that provided a chilling glimpse into what could have happened if Hitler and his allies had won the war.

The Vision of a Thousand-Year Reich:

Nazi ideology was based on the concept of a vast Germanic empire, the "Thousand-Year Reich," which meant that the world would be remade through territorial takeover, racial purification, and economic control. Hitler and his associates imagined an empire stretching from the Atlantic to the Ural Mountains, where the local population would have no choice but to serve the interests of an elite Aryan ruling class.

Hitler believed that Germany's destiny was to be on top of everyone as the preeminent world power, which would be far more influential than the British Empire and the United States. The Nazis believed in expanding their power and believed war was a justified way to do it. They imagined a world where Germans were at the top and all other people were treated as lower and controlled.

Generalplan Ost: The Blueprint for Eastern Europe:

One of the Nazis' biggest post-war plans was called "General plan Ost" or "General Plan for the East." It was meant to turn Eastern Europe into a German colony by killing, enslaving, or removing Slavic people, Jews, and others they saw as unwanted. Key Components of General plan Ost:

1. Population Reduction and Forced Deportation

   - It called for the extermination or expulsion of up to 50 million Slavic people from Eastern Europe.

   - Ethnic Germans (Volksdeutsche) would be resettled in newly occupied territories.

   - Entire cities such as Leningrad and Moscow were to be depopulated and destroyed.

2. Germanization of Eastern Europe

- Slavs deemed "racially valuable" might be forcibly assimilated into German culture.

- New German cities and settlements were to be established, particularly in Poland, Ukraine, and western Russia.

- Infrastructure such as roads, railways, and fortifications would be built using forced labor to integrate the new territories into the Reich.

3. Exploitation of Resources

- The occupied lands would serve as a breadbasket for the Reich.

- Slavic populations would be used as a labor force under conditions close to slavery.

- Industrial centers in occupied territories would be pulled to pieces and relocated to Germany.

4. The Role of the SS and Special Forces

- The SS played an important role in planning and implementing Generalplan Ost, managing mass deportations and executions.

- Einsatzgruppen (mobile killing squads) would continue their campaign of terror, eliminating resistance and unwanted populations.

- Concentration camps would be expanded to accommodate the large-scale imprisonment of millions of people.

The Fate of Western Europe:

Unlike Eastern Europe, which the Nazis wanted to take over completely, Western European countries like France, the Netherlands, and Scandinavia were meant to become controlled partners or "vassal states." They would keep some local power, but Germany would be in charge, making sure their economies and armies helped the Nazi cause.

France

- France would become a weaker state that served German needs.
- The people would be closely watched to stop any uprisings.
- Paris would still be a cultural city but controlled by German officials.

Britain

- At first, Hitler hoped Britain might join Germany as an ally.

- Later, he planned to take control of Britain and replace its royal family and government if Germany won the war.

- The British monarchy and government would be replaced with a fascist puppet regime led by pro-Nazi sympathizers.

- The British people would have strict political and ideological reeducation.

- German bases would be established throughout the British Isles to prevent any uprisings in the future.

The Role of the United States:

Hitler saw the U.S. as a future enemy but only planned to deal with it after Germany had full control over Europe. His long-term plan included:

- Creating conflict within the U.S. by stirring up racial and political tensions.

- Supporting fascist groups in America to weaken its democracy.

- Building advanced weapons like long-range bombers and missiles to attack U.S. cities.

Nazi Economic Plans: The Global Economic Order

The Nazis wanted to create a big economic zone called the "Greater Economic Space" controlled by Germany.

This system would:

- End free trade and instead let Germany set the rules for other countries under its control.
- Take raw materials from conquered lands and use them for German factories.
- Stop other countries, like Britain and the U.S., from competing with Germany economically.

The Nazis also wanted Germany to be self-sufficient, using large farms and factories, especially in Eastern Europe, where local Slavic people would be forced to work under German control.

The Future of Science and Technology:

The Nazis gave a lot of importance to scientific progress, especially in areas like rocket science, aircraft design, and nuclear research. If they had won the war, the following technological advances would likely have shaped the world after World War II.

1. Nuclear Weapons - Germany was engaged in atomic research, and a victorious Reich might have developed nuclear capabilities to impose its dominance.

2. Space Exploration - Wernher von Braun and other Nazi scientists planned a future where Germany expanded its influence beyond Earth, possibly leveraging rocket technology for military and exploratory purposes.

3. Eugenics and Human Experimentation - Because the Nazis believed in racial superiority, they would have expanded their programs involving human experiments and genetic engineering to try to create what they called a "master race."

4. Advanced Warfare - The Nazis also planned to keep developing new military technology, such as faster jets, guided missiles, and biological weapons, to stay stronger than other countries.

Apart from expanding their territory, Nazi beliefs aimed to build a new world order based on the idea that Aryans were the most superior race. This system would have been kept in place through the following methods:

- **State-Controlled Propaganda** - The Nazis would have set up a worldwide system to spread their messages, making sure that everyone followed their way of thinking and didn't question it.

- **Education Reforms** - Schools would have been changed so that children were taught Nazi beliefs and values from a very young age, shaping their minds to fully accept Nazi ideas.

- **Eradication of Religious and Cultural Opposition** - Religions like Christianity, and other cultural beliefs that didn't match Nazi thinking, would have been either destroyed or taken over and changed to support Nazi views.

- **The Cult of Hitler** - Hitler would have been turned into a god-like figure. His image would be everywhere through statues, monuments, and official ceremonies, and people would be forced to honor and praise him all across the Nazi empire.

Conclusion:

Even though the Nazi Master Plan was never carried out, the fact that it was so carefully planned shows just how big Hitler's goals were and how terrible things could have been if Germany had won the war. The world would have looked very different, with extreme levels of cruelty, control, and mass killings. Discovering these plans is a powerful warning about how dangerous totalitarian beliefs can be and why it's so important to stay alert and protect democratic rights and freedoms.

To truly understand how big Hitler's ambitions were, we shouldn't start by looking at maps or military actions but at deeper beliefs. The Nazi way of thinking wasn't just about taking over land. It aimed to completely reshape the universe. Hitler's idea of a Thousand-Year Reich wasn't just a political goal; it was like a myth or a legend meant to restart human civilization based on a racially "pure" ideal. In this way, the Nazi "master plan" was not just a military or political plan; it was treated like something sacred, written in the language of fate and destiny, not in terms of regular politics or diplomacy.

At the center of it all was the belief that the Aryan race had a sacred right to rule the world. This belief mixed false science, old myths, and harsh political thinking. It wasn't about building an empire in the usual way. It was about taking over through violence and land ownership, controlled by a racial belief system that divided people into biological groups and judged their value based on a made-up ranking taken from myths.

What the Nazis wanted wasn't just a global dictatorship like the ones we know, but a whole new worldview, a reimagined Earth divided into racial territories, each controlled by rulers chosen by biology.

This new world wouldn't just manage borders; it would control who could be educated, who could have children, who could speak, and who could live. The concept of individual rights, as we know them in liberal democracies, was to be completely destroyed, not just changed or ignored, but completely eliminated.

The ideal world Hitler imagined stretched far into the future in very specific and frightening ways. Entire generations were to be raised according to Nazi beliefs. Children in the Reich would be trained from an early age, first through groups like the Hitler Youth, then through military or family roles. Even thinking differently would be seen as a genetic flaw. The ultimate goal was not just control but change: to remake humanity in the image of the Aryan ideal.

While Generalplan Ost explained how the Nazis would carry out mass killings and forced removals in Eastern Europe, it was just one piece of their bigger empire plan. They intended to build whole new cities in the East, ideal Aryan centers designed from the ground up. These cities would feature German-style buildings, museums celebrating their conquests, and grand monuments to racial victory.

In these plans, the Nazis didn't view Slavs, Jews, Roma, and others as usual enemies. They saw them as blocks to their goal of racial purity. Allowing these groups to live, they believed, would spoil the "natural order" they aimed to restore. Extermination was treated like a public health measure, removing supposed "racial germs" to keep their society healthy.

The officials who set up the trains to the death camps focused on making the system run smoothly, driven not by personal hatred, but by ideological obedience. In Nazi thinking, evil wasn't about individual malice. It was a matter of cold, efficient procedure.

One of the most frightening parts of the Nazi plan was how logical it seemed to its own supporters. Every horrific act was given a reason. Every killing was framed as a step toward a better future. That's what made the plan so dangerous: it wasn't wild insanity but a cold, careful application of their beliefs. Its strength came from its internal consistency and ruthless precision. It didn't promise chaos.

It promised a strict and terrifying order.

Even beyond Europe, the Nazis had huge plans. Their partnership with Japan was more about practical gain than shared beliefs, but they imagined dividing the world's eastern half into two racial empires. Germany would rule Europe, much of Africa, and the Middle East, while Japan would control East and Southeast Asia. They expected a kind of racial Cold War between these two superstates, but even then, Germany's ultimate aim of dominating the entire globe would remain supreme.

The Nazis also planned to control the Atlantic. They imagined building a navy after the war that could rival British and American fleets. Hitler respected the British Empire but was also jealous of it. In their vision, Britain would either become a smaller country under Germany's control or be fully absorbed into the German Reich. Its noble class would be replaced by people who fit Nazi racial rules, and its overseas colonies would be handed out in ways that served Germany's strategic goals.

The Nazis saw the Americas as a different kind of challenge, not one of military attack, but of spreading their ideas. Hitler never seriously planned to invade the United States, but he imagined a future where America would fall apart due to internal problems like racial conflict, economic failure, and ideological division. Nazi propagandists created materials to help make this happen, trying to stir up racist feelings, anti-Semitic ideas, and fear of communism.

While the war in Europe was fought with tanks and bullets, the fight in the West would be through stories, ideas, and creating divisions.

Even space wasn't left out of Nazi dreams. People in the Reich, including Wernher von Braun, talked about developing long-range rockets not just for war but for space travel in the future. To them, this wasn't just an idea from science fiction - it was their destiny. If humans were to reach the stars, it had to be done by the "master race." They believed that Hitler's Germany wasn't the final stage of history but the true beginning of it. The stars, just like the Earth, were meant to be controlled by Aryans.

The foundation of this plan was a total rejection of the idea that all people share a common human bond. Enlightenment thinkers believed in equal rights for everyone, but Hitler saw a strict ranking of races. Where democracies valued equality, he thought it weakened the strong. He saw his fight not just as a struggle between nations but as a battle against the belief that everyone is equally worthy. In his view, power was not just the final word; it was the only right imposed by divine and racial laws.

After Germany lost the war, traces of these ideas continued to hide in the shadows. Even though the Nazi government collapsed, its vision lived on in the minds of escaped leaders, in new fascist groups, and in hidden writings and conspiracy myths. Some former Nazis escaped to South America with stolen money and secret plans. Others held on to dreams of a Fourth Reich, waiting quietly for their chance.

This survival of Nazi thinking teaches us that ideas do not surrender like armies do. They pull back, change form, and come back in new ways. When people forget or underestimate them, they reappear, not in uniforms, but in speeches, laws, and cultural trends.

The master plan may have died in Hitler's bunker, but its core ideas; the drive for domination, racial destiny, and approved violence is, still present in our world's systems.

When we look at the Nazi master plan, we are not just studying history. We are seeing what could still happen if ideology wins over conscience if myths replace facts, and if violence is dressed up as a necessity. Hitler's dream was huge, terrifying, and eventually fragile. Yet it was not madness; it was a real possibility.

And that is why we cannot forget it.

CHAPTER 6

THE RELATIONSHIP BETWEEN GOD AND HITLER

The relationship between Adolf Hitler and religion is complicated. At first glance, it might seem like he believed in God. He talked about God in public, mentioned faith in his speeches, and used religious words to connect with everyday people. But when you look closer, you see a different picture. His real goal was to replace it with something else entirely: his own twisted version of truth, built around Nazi beliefs.

Let's go back to the beginning to understand how this unfolded.

Adolf Hitler was born in Austria in 1889. He was raised Roman Catholic, baptized as a baby, and confirmed in the church. Like many kids at the time, he went to church, learned Bible stories, and followed the rituals. Religion was a big part of daily life. Some say he believed in God when he was young. Others think he was never very religious, just going through the motions. (We should mention that he wanted to be an altar boy).

As he got older, something shifted. His views started changing, especially as he got more involved in nationalist politics and started blaming Jews for Germany's problems. The teachings of love and humility in Christianity started to clash with the harsh ideas he was forming about race, power, and destiny.

Using Religion to Win People Over

Even though his beliefs were changing, Hitler knew how powerful religion was, especially in a country where many people still went to church and believed in God. So, he used it to his advantage.

When he spoke to crowds, he often talked about "God's will" and painted himself as someone chosen to save Germany. After World War I, the country was humiliated, broke, and desperate. Hitler stepped in and said, "I'm the one who will lead us back. This is my divine mission."

He used religious ideas like sacrifice and redemption. Words people already understood. Many Christians, both Protestants and Catholics, wanted to believe him. To them, he seemed like a defender of old-fashioned values, standing up against communism and godlessness. (We should mention Hitlers alliance with the Roman Catholic Church in the Concordat between the Holy See and the German Reich.)

But even while Hitler was quoting God in public, behind closed doors he had a very different opinion. He didn't respect Christianity. He saw it as weak, too focused on forgiveness and compassion. Not what he wanted for his brutal, power-driven movement.

The Nazis pushed their own version of religion, something they called "Positive Christianity." It looked Christian on the outside, but they stripped it of anything connected to Judaism or traditional teachings. Basically, they rewrote it to fit Nazi ideas.

They also went after church leaders who didn't play along. Some pastors spoke out, especially from the Confessing Church, a group that tried to keep real Christianity alive. Many of them were threatened, arrested, or killed.

Creating a New Kind of Religion

Hitler didn't just want to twist religion. He wanted to replace it. His dream was to build a belief system where the Nazi party became like a religion itself.

He tried to swap Christian symbols for Nazi ones: the cross for the swastika, the Bible for *Mein Kampf*. Instead of churches teaching love and humility, he wanted the state to teach loyalty, strength, and obedience to him.

Groups like the Hitler Youth were a big part of this. Kids were trained in Nazi beliefs. They were taught to admire Hitler like he was some kind of prophet. The system felt religious: rituals, songs, symbols, all focused on worshiping the Nazi cause.

So… Did Hitler Believe in God?

This is a question historians still argue about.

He definitely talked about God in speeches. But in private, it sounds like he saw God more as a symbol of power than a loving creator. He didn't pray or show real faith. Instead, he admired religions that promoted strength and discipline, like certain interpretations of Islam or ancient pagan traditions.

To him, God wasn't someone to worship with humility. It was more like a force of fate, something that justified his actions and made him feel unstoppable.

The Contradiction of Nazi Theology

On the surface, Hitler talked about God and Christianity. But behind the scenes, it was a different story.

Christianity is about love, kindness, humility, and forgiveness. Hitler's beliefs were the opposite. He believed in hate, violence, and control. He wanted to change Christian teachings to fit his cruel agenda.

Some experts say Hitler's religion wasn't faith at all. It was just a tool to make people trust and follow him more easily.

Christian Resistance and Complicity

Not all churches responded the same way. Some religious leaders stood up against him, even when it cost their lives. One example is Dietrich Bonhoeffer, a pastor who spoke out and was eventually killed.

But many others stayed silent, or supported the Nazis. Some clergy chose to go along instead of standing up for what was right. Maybe they were afraid. Maybe they thought they were protecting their churches. Either way, their silence let wrong go unchallenged.

This raises a question: What should religious people do when something clearly wrong is happening? Should they speak up, even if it's dangerous? Or stay quiet to protect themselves?

Religion, Power, and Manipulation

Hitler wasn't religious in a true sense. He used religion like a mask. He used words like "God" and "faith" to make people feel like he was one of them. That made it easier to get their support. But he was twisting faith into something dark.

His use of religious belief for political gain shows how faith can be manipulated to justify immoral actions. It shows how dangerous it can be when someone powerful uses religion to get what they want. When people stop thinking and start blindly following a leader who says, "God is on my side," terrible things can happen.

So, another question: Should religion stay out of politics? Or should it get involved to stop bad things from happening? There's no easy answer, but history shows how messy it can get.

The Morality of Hitler's Actions

From a moral view, Hitler's use of religion was a deep failure. His actions went against basic ethical principles, like the value of human life and dignity.

Moral philosophers say what he did wasn't just wrong politically. It was morally rotten. He didn't just want people to obey. He wanted them to worship the government. He wanted to be at the center, like a false god.

Lessons for the Modern World

This whole story teaches us something important. It's a warning about what can happen when people stop questioning and let leaders speak for God without thinking critically.

It reminds us to stay alert. To ask questions. To never let hate hide behind holy words.

And for religious communities, it's a reminder to stand up for what's right, even when it's hard. Because staying silent in times of injustice can end up doing just as much harm.

Conclusion:

Hitler's connection with religion is a strange and twisted story. On the surface, he talked about God and Christianity to win people over. But behind the scenes, he had a very different plan. He wasn't interested in supporting religion. His goal was to replace it with something centered around himself and Nazi ideology. It was a dangerous mix of faith and manipulation that raises tough questions: How can religion be twisted for power? What happens when people of faith stay silent during dark times? And how do we tell the difference between real belief and something that just looks holy on the outside?

Trying to understand how Hitler saw God is like walking into a maze. Religion, politics, and psychology are all tangled together. Unlike rulers in the past who claimed God's blessing, Hitler didn't attack God directly or claim to be divine. Instead, he acted like fate had chosen him to lead. He made it seem like his leadership was part of some bigger plan, blurring the line between spiritual belief and political obsession. Religious-sounding ideas became a cover for personal ambition.

Hitler and the Nazis didn't try to wipe out Christianity completely. They tried something more chilling. They rewrote it. They kept familiar words like "sacrifice" and "redemption" but changed their meaning. Instead of love and forgiveness, their version focused on race and power. When Hitler spoke of "Divine Providence," he didn't mean a loving God. He meant a force that rewarded the strong and eliminated the weak. In his mind, life was struggle, not grace.

To Hitler, this "god" wasn't someone to love. It was a tool to justify his actions. Winning a war became a holy ritual. Gaining power became a kind of prayer. The Jewish people weren't just political targets. They were framed as threats to German purity. Getting rid of them became, in his twisted logic, a kind of "cleansing," like a spiritual duty.

This raises a disturbing question: if someone uses religious words for evil purposes, do we still recognize it as evil? Hitler used words like mission, sacrifice, destiny. It confused people. Was he just a madman, or a terrifying product of his time? Did he kill faith, or create a fake version of it?

The Nazi regime borrowed from religion's structure. It had its own rules, symbols, holidays. It had martyrs and rituals.

Nazi rallies resembled religious ceremonies. The swastika replaced the cross. In some churches, Hitler's picture even hung where Jesus once did. Children weren't raised to follow Christ. They were raised to worship Hitler. It was all designed to fill the gap left by a struggling church and a desperate nation. People were looking for hope. Hitler offered something that looked like salvation, but wasn't.

The Nazis flipped Christian ideas. Where Jesus taught love and mercy, Hitler preached hate and strength. Christianity says all people are equal before God. Hitler claimed some races were superior. The Gospel speaks of forgiveness. Hitler promoted revenge and purity.

Some religious thinkers call Hitler's movement an "anti-Christology," not just spiritually, but structurally. Germans were treated like the chosen people. Hitler was the prophet. World War I was the fall. War became sacrifice. The "Thousand-Year Reich" was the promised kingdom. Even Hitler's last days in the bunker echoed religious sacrifice in a twisted form.

What's painful is how many Christians, Catholic and Protestant, went along with it. Some thought Hitler was saving Europe from communism. Others were caught up in national pride. A few brave people, like those in the Confessing Church, resisted, but they were rare. Most either believed the lie or stayed quiet.

That silence raises questions. Should faith be private, or does it come with responsibility? When does being quiet become complicity? How do religious groups end up supporting tyranny, not through violence, but through slow praise and flattery?

It's easy to call Hitler evil and move on. But the truth is more uncomfortable. He knew how to use people's deepest beliefs about God, identity, and purpose and twist them. He turned religion into a show. He made morality sound like myth. That shows us something terrifying. When faith is separated from conscience, it can be used as a weapon.

At his core, Hitler believed in survival of the fittest more than anything spiritual. He didn't see the world as a peaceful garden made by God, but a brutal battlefield where only the strongest survived. He admired animals not for their beauty, but for their harsh order. Kindness and forgiveness were weakness. His idea of "god" was not a loving father, but a harsh judge.

There are echoes of Nietzsche's "will to power" in all this. But Nietzsche warned against worshiping power. Hitler ignored that. He fused power with racism and called it divine.

And that may be the worst offense of all. Hitler didn't just reject God. He tried to create a new one in his image. A god of blood and steel. A god who didn't forgive or heal, only judged. A god who asked not for love, but for loyalty. That's what made Nazism spiritually dangerous. It didn't erase faith. It hijacked it.

After the Holocaust, religious communities asked: Is it even possible to believe in God after this? Where was God when children were taken? When priests stood by? When churches stayed silent?

Some gave up on God. Others rethought faith, seeing God not as ruler, but as one who suffers with us. Some believed God was always there, but people turned away.

Whatever someone believes, the challenge remains. How do we tell the difference between real faith and something fake? Between the God who lifts up, and the one used to push others down? Between conscience and control?

Hitler's story forces every faith to look in the mirror. It's a warning. Religion can be used for horror if we don't protect its heart. In the end, Hitler wasn't a man of faith. He was an exploiter of it. He co-opted the sacred, drained it of meaning, and used it to justify hate. And he didn't act alone. He was welcomed and, in fact, applauded,, even by people who should've known better.

Faith, however, is never just an abstract question. It is also a personal one. If religion can be twisted to serve evil, then understanding the beliefs of the man who orchestrated that evil becomes unavoidable. To confront the moral collapse of an era, we must also confront its spiritual distortions. What did God mean to Hitler, if anything at all? Was he a true believer, a manipulator, or something in between? Answering that question not only exposes the emptiness behind his ideology but also reveals how faith, when stripped of its moral core, can become a weapon.

God & Hitler

From the earliest years of Adolf Hitler's ideological formation, the question of God loomed large, not in the form of traditional piety, but as a complex, ever-evolving abstraction shaped by myth, militarism, and mystical longing. Hitler's relationship with the divine was not linear nor devout in the classical Christian sense. Instead, it became a syncretic fusion of pantheistic awe, Germanic myth, racialized Christianity, and political utility. For Hitler, God was not a father in heaven who demanded meekness or forgiveness. God was will, power, and destiny. And in this image, Hitler reshaped the moral and spiritual landscape of Nazi Germany.

As a child raised in a predominantly Catholic region, Hitler was exposed early to Christian dogma. He even served briefly as an altar boy and attended a Benedictine monastery school. But the faith that might have offered solace in the face of paternal brutality and maternal loss never penetrated him in a traditional sense. Instead, it became a vessel into which he would later pour radically different content. Christianity, for Hitler, would be reinterpreted not as a religion of love and sacrifice, but as a corrupted faith, a once noble Aryan tradition poisoned by Jewish influence. In his adult years, especially in the secrecy of private conversation, Hitler derided the Church and its teachings, ridiculing its calls for humility, peace, and mercy. He believed that such values weakened the racial and spiritual fortitude of the German people. The Jesus he revered was not the turn-the-other-cheek Nazarene, but a defiant Aryan warrior who stood against the "Jewish world order."

This racialized Christ became a key element in the ideological campaigns of Nazi propagandists. Figures like Alfred Rosenberg and Heinrich Himmler developed the idea of the "Aryan Jesus," a figure purged of Semitic origins and cast instead as a proto-Germanic revolutionary. This Jesus was imagined as a fighter, not a savior, a man of action who challenged authority and cleansed the world of impurity. The goal was to strip Christianity of its Jewish roots and realign it with the supposed martial virtues of the Germanic race. In this narrative, Christ was no longer the son of the Jewish God of Abraham, but rather the divine embodiment of racial destiny, a spiritual prototype of the Führer himself.

Yet even this Aryanized Christianity could not fully satisfy Hitler's spiritual hunger. His vision of the divine often veered into pantheism, a belief in the sacredness of nature, the cosmos, and fate. In his private writings and table talk, Hitler frequently referenced "Providence" rather than God in the traditional sense. This Providence was not a loving, paternal figure but a force of selection, trial, and testing. It rewarded the strong and annihilated the weak. For Hitler, nature itself was divine, and nature was merciless. The survival of the fittest was not merely a biological reality; it was a spiritual law. As such, his God was inseparable from struggle, victory, and blood. In his speeches, he often invoked Providence as the guiding hand behind his rise to power and Germany's racial purification, couching his political will in a mystic mandate.

This pantheistic streak found reinforcement in the mythos of Norse and Germanic gods, particularly Wotan, also known as Odin, the one-eyed deity of wisdom, war, and sacrifice. Wotan was not merely a relic of ancient tales; for Hitler and many of the Nazi ideologues, he was a living archetype, a cultural symbol that resonated with the racial memory of the German people. Wotan represented the ancestral spirit of conquest and transcendence. In Carl Jung's famous 1936 essay, "Wotan," he observed the reawakening of this archetype in the soul of the German nation, linking Hitler's rise to a psychological resurgence of Wotan-like energy. For Hitler, Wotan's characteristics (ferocity, cunning, ruthlessness, vision) mirrored the qualities he believed were necessary for Germany's rebirth. The Norse pantheon offered an alternative to Christian meekness, grounding Nazi myth-making in blood, soil, and steel.

While Hitler never publicly declared allegiance to Norse paganism, the imagery and ritualism of the Nazi Party were soaked in its influence. Swastikas, runes, and torchlit processions were not just political theater; they were invocations of a spiritual heritage Hitler believed predated and superseded Christianity. Himmler's SS, in particular, adopted Wotanist symbols and practices with religious zeal. Their rites at Wewelsburg Castle were attempts to resurrect a new priesthood, one rooted in Germanic myth and racial purity. Hitler tolerated, if not encouraged, these developments, seeing them as means of establishing a new spiritual order aligned with his vision.

And yet, Hitler's religious imagination extended even further. In the figure of the Prophet Muhammad, he found another historical model of how religion could be wielded for political consolidation and cultural unification. Hitler admired Islam not for its theology, but for its sociopolitical structure, its call to disciplined action, and its history of expansionism. He believed that Islam's emphasis on strength, loyalty, and submission to divine will mirrored many of the qualities he wished to instill in the German Volk. In private conversations, he lamented that Christianity had taken root in Europe rather than Islam, believing that the latter would have been a better fit for the Aryan temperament. Islam, in his view, was a religion that forged empires; Christianity, a religion that softened them.

The comparison with Muhammad went beyond admiration. Hitler saw in the Prophet a template for the sacred leader, one who unified a fractured people under a banner of divine destiny, instituted a legal and spiritual code, and led armies in defense of that revelation. Muhammad's synthesis of the spiritual and the temporal provided a precedent for Hitler's own ambition to fuse church and state under the Nazi banner. The concept of the Führerprinzip, the absolute authority of the leader, echoed the prophetic model of combining religious legitimacy with political dominance. But where Muhammad's message was one of monotheism, community, and ethical law, Hitler's interpretation was stripped of mercy and justice, repurposed for the aims of racial conquest.

The result of this ideological alchemy: Christian symbolism, pantheistic reverence for nature, Norse myth, and Islamic statecraft, was a theological chimera: a God that reflected Hitler's own image and ambitions. It was a God of blood and iron, of sacred violence and racial hierarchy. In Nazi Germany, this vision of the divine seeped into all aspects of life. School curricula were revised to include "Positive Christianity," which denied Christ's Jewish heritage.

Churches were pressured to align with the Reich's spiritual objectives or risk dissolution. Prayer and scripture were replaced in many schools with oaths of loyalty to Hitler. Even baptismal ceremonies were substituted with state-sponsored rituals celebrating Aryan birth and racial belonging. God had not disappeared from public life. He had been conscripted.

This spiritual transformation reached its most grotesque expression in the cult of Hitler himself. As Nazi power grew, Hitler ceased to be merely a political figure; he became a messianic icon. Posters, statues, and paintings often depicted him with outstretched arms, surrounded by radiant light, a modern imitation of Christ or Wotan incarnate. Children were taught to revere him as the redeemer of Germany, the chosen one sent by Providence to lead the people through their national Passion and Resurrection. "Hitler is Germany, and Germany is Hitler," proclaimed one popular slogan. Churches that refused to align with this doctrine were persecuted, pastors imprisoned or executed, and theological dissent stamped out with military precision.

Despite his deep contempt for institutional Christianity, Hitler understood its symbolic power. He co-opted its vocabulary and repurposed its rituals, turning religious holidays into national celebrations of Nazi ideology. Christmas became less about the birth of Christ and more about the birth of the German nation. Easter was celebrated not as a resurrection of divine love, but of German strength. Crosses were replaced with swastikas, hymns with nationalist anthems. The Reich was not just a political entity. It was a new religious order, and Hitler its high priest.

This spiritual narrative was crucial to maintaining control over the masses. It offered meaning in a time of uncertainty, transcendence in the midst of suffering, and justification for violence. By fusing religious sentiment with racial ideology, Hitler was able to elevate politics to the level of salvation. The extermination of the Jews, the conquest of Lebensraum, the sacrifices of war: these were no longer merely strategic goals; they were sacred duties. Dying for the Reich became a holy act. And in this framework, God was not the judge of nations, but the force that animated their rise and fall, the divine Will coursing through the veins of the Aryan race.

But even as Hitler invoked God and destiny, there was a curious emptiness at the heart of his theology. It was not about communion, redemption, or love. It was about domination, purification, and hierarchy. God was no longer Other; He was immanent in the blood and destiny of the chosen people. This deification of race, coupled with the sacralization of political authority, created a closed system of belief where dissent was not just treason. It was heresy.

By the end of the war, as Germany lay in ruins and the dream of the Thousand-Year Reich collapsed into rubble, Hitler's theology of power revealed its spiritual bankruptcy. In his final days in the Berlin bunker, there were no prayers for forgiveness, no appeals to mercy. There was only rage, paranoia, and a chilling detachment. The man who had once invoked Providence as the author of his destiny now railed against the German people for failing him, accusing them of unworthiness and betrayal. His god had been himself all along, a god who demanded absolute faith but offered no grace.

And so, Hitler died as he lived: not as a man in dialogue with the divine, but as a self-anointed prophet of a false religion, one built not on love or truth, but on death and delusion. The role that God played in Hitler's mind was ultimately that of a mirror, reflecting back his own hunger for power, his obsession with order, and his hatred of weakness. He summoned deities not to humble himself before them, but to cloak his will in their names. And in doing so, he forged one of the most terrifying theologies in human history, one that turned the sacred into the profane and justified the unthinkable in the name of Providence.

The spiritual world Hitler constructed for himself, and eventually imposed upon the German people, was one devoid of repentance. It had no place for inner transformation, no room for the brokenhearted, no sacred refuge for the meek. In the traditional Judeo-Christian understanding, the concept of sin implies a need for humility before a moral order that transcends the self. But Hitler could not abide the idea of subordination, especially not to a God of compassion. He despised what he saw as Christianity's obsession with forgiveness, especially forgiveness for those deemed weak, impure, or inferior. In his theological reinterpretation, there was no sin in extermination, no moral burden in conquest. There was only the duty to fulfill the sacred law of strength and purity. In this way, Hitler's vision of God became indistinguishable from the image of the Aryan man triumphant over all forces of decay.

This transformation of theology into anthropology, of divinity into blood, was not simply philosophical; it was operational. The Nazi regime developed what could only be described as a sacrificial theology, in which millions were deemed necessary offerings to the new world order Hitler sought to birth. The death camps were not merely instruments of political repression; they were temples of racial purification, presided over by high priests in SS uniforms. The meticulous record-keeping, the ritualistic procedures, the cold, mechanical efficiency: these were not just bureaucratic practices, but part of a perverse liturgy. Just as ancient priests would prepare offerings to appease their gods, the Nazis prepared their victims as offerings to the idol of Aryan supremacy.

This ritualization of death reached a point where even nature itself, once seen through Hitler's pantheistic lens as sacred and ordered, became a stage for divine testing. He believed that the Eastern Front, the vast and brutal theater of war against the Soviet Union, was not merely a strategic imperative but a sacred proving ground. There, in the snow-covered forests and bombed-out cities, the fate of civilizations would be decided. It was Armageddon, not in the biblical sense of a final reckoning between good and evil, but in the Nordic sense of Ragnarök: the twilight of the gods, where fire and blood would purify the world and usher in a new, racially redeemed age.

And just as the gods of old were fated to die and be reborn in myth, Hitler saw in himself the dual role of destroyer and creator. He had to tear down the existing world order, decadent, multicultural, democratic, in order to raise in its place a Reich built on myth, race, and steel. In his mind, this destruction was not just justified; it was sanctified. The burning of synagogues, the annihilation of villages, the mass deportations: these were not crimes but rituals, bloody steps toward a new dawn. The absence of empathy, the cold detachment in orchestrating genocide, makes sense only within this religious framework where morality had been entirely re-engineered.

Nazi Germany, then, did not simply function as a state; it operated as a cult. Its symbols, songs, salutes, uniforms, and ceremonies were part of a totalizing religion of the Reich. The swastika was not just a political emblem; it was a solar symbol drawn from ancient Indo-European iconography, representing the eternal cycle of rebirth and conquest. The Nuremberg rallies were not merely political gatherings; they were spiritual revivals where the individual was absorbed into the collective will of the Volk, baptized by fire, sound, and spectacle. Hitler, standing at the center of these rituals, played the role of prophet and messiah, absorbing adulation with the serene detachment of a demigod.

In this constructed cosmology, martyrdom took on a new meaning. To die for Germany was no longer an act of patriotic sacrifice alone; it was an initiation into eternal glory. The fallen soldier was envisioned as joining a spiritual army of the dead, a spectral force that would watch over the Reich as guardian spirits, much like the Einherjar of Norse mythology, those warriors who died in battle and ascended to Valhalla to await the final war. Nazi propaganda films and literature emphasized this transcendental dimension, creating a mythology in which sacrifice for the nation was indistinguishable from communion with the divine. A theology of blood had replaced the theology of grace.

In contrast to the biblical image of Jesus as a suffering servant, Hitler's preferred Christ-figure was a militant redeemer, a racial messiah who bore not the sins of the world, but the sword of its purification. In this theology, Jesus was no longer the lamb led to slaughter, but a lion, a proto-Führer who defied corrupt religious elites and drove out money-changers with a whip. And whereas the crucifixion in Christian doctrine represented the ultimate sacrifice of God's love for humanity, the Nazi version replaced that message with one of racial betrayal and vengeance. Christ was no longer crucified by the sins of mankind, but by an alien enemy, the Jew, whom the Aryan world must now expel in retribution. This inversion of sacred narrative enabled the Nazis to twist Christianity into a tool of hate while retaining its emotional power and cultural reach.

Even the concept of the afterlife was subtly reconfigured in this worldview. Traditional Christian doctrine promises heaven as a place of rest, reward, and reunion. But in Hitler's theology, the afterlife was imagined more in line with Wotanist and warrior ideologies: not a peaceful kingdom but an eternal battlefield. The ideal German man, if he died in war or service to the Reich, would become part of an unending cosmic struggle. The dead were not released from duty; they were consecrated into it. This belief helped fuel the fanatical bravery of many German soldiers who fought to the bitter end, refusing surrender even when defeat was certain. They were not merely defending a nation; they were enacting a mythic role, affirming their place in an eternal cycle of struggle and transcendence.

The Prophet Muhammad's legacy also echoed through Hitler's strategic imagination. While Hitler was fundamentally a European nationalist with no deep theological connection to Islam, his admiration for the Prophet's life had a distinct purpose. Muhammad had unified tribes under a divine mission, established religious law as state law, and built an empire through both preaching and some level of warfare. Hitler envisioned himself performing a similar function for the German people. His speeches mimicked the cadence of revelation, his edicts carried the weight of scripture, and his military conquests were cast as sacred campaigns of renewal. Where Muhammad received the Qur'an, Hitler claimed to channel the voice of Providence through *Mein Kampf*. It was, for him, not merely a manifesto but a scripture, a text that would guide generations, filled with revelations born of struggle and divine insight.

And just as the early Islamic community faced external enemies who sought to destroy them, Hitler positioned the Nazi movement as a persecuted yet chosen group. The Jews, the Communists, the liberal democracies of the West, these were painted not just as political adversaries, but as satanic forces bent on thwarting a holy mission. Every military victory was a sign of divine favor; every setback a test of faith. The Führer-state was meant to be a total system of worship, in which every German, knowingly or not, became a supplicant to a divine calling cloaked in iron and fire.

What emerges from all this is a portrait of Hitler's God not as a singular deity, but as an amalgam: a dark synthesis of pagan force, racial essentialism, apocalyptic prophecy, and political absolutism. His God had no commandments beyond victory, no grace beyond loyalty, and no paradise beyond the borders of a purified homeland. He had taken fragments from disparate spiritual traditions and twisted them into a theology of will, a cosmology where the only sin was weakness and the only virtue was domination.

By 1945, as Berlin fell into ruin and Hitler's dream lay in ashes, his silence on God was perhaps the loudest theological statement of his life. In his final political testament, there were no invocations of divine justice or appeals for eternal peace. There were only denunciations of betrayal, blinding rage against imagined enemies, and a final call for vengeance against a world that had rejected his vision. The man who once claimed to walk with Providence exited the stage of history without a single prayer. He left no word of hope, no spiritual legacy, only a hollow ideology built on death and illusion.

In this sense, the role of God in Hitler's mind, and in Nazi Germany more broadly, was less about communion and more about construction. God was not someone to be worshipped, but a symbol to be repurposed. Not a being to love, but a force to imitate. And once that force no longer served him, Hitler discarded it, just as he had discarded every human bond that once tied him to the world. What remained was only power: brutal, empty, and final.

Thus ended the most heretical religion of the modern age. It masqueraded in symbols of holiness but bore no soul. It spoke of destiny but delivered annihilation. It summoned gods but offered no salvation. And its prophet, Adolf Hitler, died not as a martyr, but as the architect of a spiritual void so deep that the world is still struggling to climb out of it.

The theological void Hitler created, one where God was replaced by will, nature was sanctified as merciless, and human life was valued only through a racial lens, left a chilling imprint on the German conscience. Even after the Reich collapsed, the residue of that ideology persisted like an open wound. Survivors, soldiers, ordinary citizens, many were forced to confront the aftermath of a regime that had draped itself in sacred language while perpetrating some of the worst atrocities in human history. The dissonance between divine justification and demonic reality demanded reckoning. But Hitler, until his final breath, refused any such reckoning. To the end, he insisted that his mission was righteous, his enemies evil, and that Providence itself had been betrayed, not by him, but by a world that lacked the strength to follow through on its destiny.

In the postwar years, theologians, historians, and psychologists struggled to explain how a supposedly Christian nation had embraced such a system. Many pointed to the way Hitler had systematically dismantled the ethical framework of traditional religion and replaced it with a religion of blood. But the deeper truth is more disturbing: Hitler understood the spiritual hunger of his time. He knew that Germans, like many across Europe after the trauma of the First World War, felt abandoned by the old gods, disillusioned by institutions, broken by poverty, humiliated by defeat. Into this vacuum, he offered a new revelation: a messianic myth that promised rebirth through struggle, unity through purity, and eternity through sacrifice.

The transformation was not instantaneous, nor universal. Many Germans resisted, privately or publicly, the creeping encroachment of Nazi spirituality. The Confessing Church, led by figures like Dietrich Bonhoeffer, stood against the Nazi appropriation of Christianity, emphasizing the incompatibility between the teachings of Jesus and the ideology of the Reich. Yet these voices were few, and often silenced. The majority either conformed out of fear or were seduced by the emotional appeal of a leader who offered not only political salvation but metaphysical purpose. Hitler did not merely seek to lead a nation; he sought to redeem it, not from sin, but from weakness. And to those who accepted his gospel, obedience became a sacrament, and dissent a betrayal not just of country, but of fate.

What makes Hitler's theology so dangerous, and so difficult to fully dismantle, is how it weaponized some of humanity's most noble impulses. The desire for meaning, for unity, for transcendence, these were the very yearnings he twisted into tools of manipulation. He did not reject the spiritual impulse in mankind; he exploited it. He offered his people rituals, symbols, sacred songs, and shared myths. He gave them a new heaven, cleansed of foreign influence, and a new earth, conquered and reordered according to racial law. In doing so, he mirrored the structure of traditional religion while inverting its core values. Where true faith calls for humility, he demanded arrogance. Where it calls for love, he offered hate. Where it calls for repentance, he imposed vengeance.

There is perhaps no greater irony in modern history than the fact that Hitler, a man who so bitterly resented his own religious upbringing, became one of the most effective theologians of the twentieth century, not by preaching God, but by replacing Him. He constructed a belief system more totalitarian than any theocracy, more demanding than any church. In his world, there was no room for mystery, for grace, or for the sacredness of the individual soul. Every person was a vessel, either of Aryan destiny or of racial poison. Every moment of history was interpreted through the lens of his divine mission. This rigidity, this absolutism, created a system impervious to reform and incapable of reflection.

In the broader arc of history, Hitler's manipulation of religious ideas fits into a longstanding pattern: tyrants who claim divine mandate, regimes that wrap themselves in spiritual legitimacy to justify conquest and repression. But what made the Nazi system unique was the way it blended ancient myth with modern propaganda, tribal theology with industrial murder. The Holocaust was not only a genocide; it was the culmination of a doctrine that had turned God into a racial principle and sacredness into biological destiny. The smoke rising from Auschwitz was not just the evidence of political failure; it was the burnt offering of a theology gone mad.

The story of Hitler and God, then, is not merely one of rejection or heresy; it is a story of profound inversion. He did not erase the idea of God; he absorbed it into himself. In the ancient world, the gravest sin was hubris, the mortal who dared place himself on the level of the divine. Hitler committed this sin on a civilizational scale. He demanded worship, he determined fate, he judged the worth of nations and peoples, and in the end, he authored his own apocalypse. His conception of God was less about the divine other and more about divine reflection. His God looked like him, thought like him, and ruled like him.

As the war ended and the world began to count the cost, many Germans and global observers attempted to rediscover their relationship to real divinity, not the distorted idol Hitler had offered, but the transcendent truth beyond ideology. Churches were rebuilt. Hymns returned to their original lyrics. The swastika was cast into the ash heap of history, and the name of Hitler became synonymous with evil. And yet, the question remained: how could such a man, so twisted and so destructive, have commanded such devotion?

The answer lies not only in fear, nor in nationalism, nor in the machinery of propaganda, but in the spiritual deformation of an entire people. Hitler's genius, his terrible genius, was his understanding that the human soul does not crave facts, but meaning. That people will endure hardship, war, and even moral compromise if they believe they are participating in something greater than themselves. By masquerading as a prophet, by cloaking his brutality in spiritual grandeur, Hitler gave millions a false sense of transcendence. They were not just citizens; they were chosen. Not just soldiers; they were crusaders. Not just voters; they were disciples.

The danger of such a spiritual counterfeit remains with us. In every generation, there are those who seek to transform politics into religion, who promise redemption through identity, who paint their enemies not merely as opponents but as cosmic threats. The legacy of Hitler's theology is a warning not only about the past, but about the future. It reminds us that God, when severed from mercy and truth, becomes a weapon. That faith, when stripped of humility, becomes fanaticism. And that man, when he places himself at the center of the universe, becomes a monster.

In the ruins of Berlin, amid the shattered cathedrals and the broken idols, the world began to rebuild, not just its cities, but its soul. And in that process, one truth became painfully clear: the God of Hitler was never God at all. He was an invention, a reflection of rage and fear, a specter born of trauma and inflated into apocalypse. The real God, whether seen through the eyes of Christ, the voice of the Prophet, the whisper of the forest, or the quiet conscience of the human heart, was absent from Hitler's theology, not because God had abandoned man, but because man had abandoned God.

In the end, Hitler's theology was a mirror, and in that mirror he saw only himself. And what he built from that reflection was not heaven on earth, but a hell that the world would spend generations trying to escape.

In the haunting and visceral 1889 painting *The Wild Chase* by Franz von Stuck, we see a spectral rider galloping across a shadowed sky, cloaked in wrath and otherworldly fervor. The painting depicts the Germanic god Wotan, or Odin in Norse tradition, leading the ghostly horde of the dead through storm-filled skies in an apocalyptic vision drawn from ancient myth. Wotan's face is twisted in feral intensity, one eye gleaming while the other gapes as an abyss, echoing his sacrifice of sight in exchange for wisdom. Beneath him gallop the spirits of the restless dead, a chaotic stampede of fury and fate. This terrifying image of death, destiny, and divine wrath would not remain an obscure mythological fantasy. For Adolf Hitler, born in the same year the painting was completed, *The Wild Chase* would become a symbol so potent that it seemed to haunt his psyche and worldview until his final breath. The parallels between Wotan's ghostly ride and Hitler's rise, reign, and fall are not merely poetic; they offer deep insight into the mythic and psychological underpinnings of Hitler's self-image and the spiritual narrative of the Third Reich.

Hitler's life was permeated by myth, not just in the ideological sense but in the way he understood his own journey. From an early age, he regarded his existence as part of a larger, preordained destiny. The notion of fate, of being chosen, of standing at the helm of a national or cosmic mission, saturated his thinking. Wotan's ride in *The Wild Chase* embodied the very archetype of the furious god sweeping through time with divine mandate: ruthless, transcendent, and apocalyptic. It was not simply a painting to be admired; it was an icon of leadership as terror, of destiny as war. The Wild Hunt legend that inspired the painting had long been part of Germanic folklore, a ghostly procession through the night skies, often an omen of catastrophe or the signal of impending transformation. In Hitler's understanding, catastrophe and transformation were inextricable. One did not usher in the future without blood, without horror, without sacrifice.

The painting, with its dark palette and dynamic brushwork, resonated with the Wagnerian mythos that so deeply influenced Hitler's imagination. Richard Wagner, whom Hitler revered almost religiously, had explored similar themes of godlike vengeance and redemption through fire in his operatic works. Von Stuck's portrayal of Wotan captured that same emotional intensity: the collision of beauty and terror, glory and annihilation. For Hitler, who considered art not merely as an aesthetic pursuit but as a revelation of national spirit, *The Wild Chase* represented a divine mandate for fury. Art, in his view, was prophecy. And in this painting, the prophecy was unmistakable: a chosen figure would rise, unyielding, possessed by ancient will, and lead the souls of the dead into a final reckoning.

Though Hitler never publicly commented on *The Wild Chase*, the alignment of its imagery with his persona and ideological project is striking. From the stormy skies to the skeletal faces of the damned, the painting offered a portrait of a leader who is not merely mortal, but possessed, consumed by a calling that demands obliteration before rebirth. Hitler's own speeches, particularly those given in the early 1930s, often evoked this sense of spectral leadership. He spoke of the blood of the martyrs, the ancestors who cried out for vengeance, the spirits of German soldiers who had died in the Great War and demanded justice. He described himself not as a man grasping for power, but as a vessel through which history, nature, and fate would speak. In this way, he became Wotan, not in name, but in spirit.

Moreover, *The Wild Chase* represents a specific fusion of masculine energy, death-worship, and transcendence that Hitler and his propagandists elevated to the level of state religion. Wotan, after all, is not merely a warrior; he is a wanderer, a seeker of wisdom, a god of both war and poetry. In the image of the one-eyed deity galloping through the storm, there is both chaos and clarity, destruction and vision. Hitler fashioned himself after this mold. He too cultivated the image of the ascetic visionary, a man who had sacrificed everything (family, comfort, even love) in pursuit of a higher goal. Like Wotan, who wandered the earth in disguise, Hitler spent years in Vienna and Munich in relative obscurity before rising in a blaze of revolutionary violence. He painted himself as misunderstood, maligned, but ultimately awakened to divine insight. The idea that suffering refines the soul, that trial is the gateway to truth, was central to his narrative, and central to the mythology that *The Wild Chase* evokes.

This painting also reflects the spiritual despair and nihilism that undergirded Nazism at its core. Wotan in the painting is not a benevolent god; he is fierce, detached, almost demonic. He commands the souls of the restless dead, not to lead them to salvation but to wage eternal war. This reflects the core of Hitler's project: not salvation, but purification through annihilation. Nazism was not concerned with building a better future through humane progress; it sought to burn the present and past in order to construct a mythic empire of the strong. Hitler did not aim to save humanity; he sought to purify it by fire. In *The Wild Chase*, we see the same dynamic: a leader emerging not with olive branches, but with thunder, riding ahead of death, consuming the world in his wake.

Furthermore, the year of the painting's completion, 1889, was the very year of Hitler's birth. While coincidence should not be mistaken for causality, the symbolic resonance is difficult to ignore. In a nation increasingly obsessed with signs and myth, such a detail would have carried immense weight. Hitler himself was acutely aware of signs, symbols, dates, and archetypes. He believed in destiny as an unfolding script, one written in blood and prophecy. The idea that he was born in the same year Wotan's ride was immortalized in paint would not have struck him as trivial. It would have confirmed, in his own mythology, the belief that he had been summoned to restore something ancient, to avenge a cosmic imbalance, to revive the Volkisch soul of the Germanic race.

The Wild Hunt legend that inspired *The Wild Chase* had always been tied to death and the liminal space between the living and the dead. In older Germanic folklore, the leader of the Hunt, whether Wotan, a ghostly knight, or another cursed soul, was both feared and venerated. The hunt often heralded plague, war, or winter: a time of reckoning. This symbolism resonated deeply in Nazi ideology. Hitler's speeches repeatedly invoked the need to cleanse the body politic, to purge weakness, to enter a new era of strength. Like the Wild Hunt, Nazism emerged as a spectral force out of the chaos of the Weimar Republic, offering not reasoned solutions but violent rupture. It promised not peace, but transformation through conflict. The storm would come, and in its wake, only the strong would remain.

In this context, *The Wild Chase* can be seen as more than a painting; it is a visual prophecy of the Nazi era's spiritual aesthetics. It articulates the allure of apocalyptic leadership, of the messianic destroyer who promises salvation through annihilation. The stormy skies, the howling beasts, the skeletal army, all mirror the reality that unfolded between

1933 and 1945. Under Hitler's command, Germany did indeed become a kind of Wild Hunt, charging across Europe, trailing the ghosts of war behind it. Cities burned, populations were uprooted or exterminated, and the skies, like those in von Stuck's vision, were filled with smoke and thunder. Hitler was not merely leading a nation; he was leading a crusade of the dead.

And just as Wotan in *The Wild Chase* is fated to ride eternally, haunted by his choices and bound to a destiny of wrath, so too was Hitler consumed by the fire he unleashed. By 1945, as his empire collapsed, he resembled not the triumphant savior but the doomed god, trapped in the very storm he summoned, betrayed by his illusions, and condemned by history. The painting, therefore, serves not only as a depiction of fury and grandeur, but also as a cautionary tale. It shows the price of hubris, the cost of divine pretensions. Wotan's ride does not end in glory; it ends in madness.

Franz von Stuck's *The Wild Chase* would go on to influence not just Hitler's imagination but that of many artists, philosophers, and cultural critics in the early twentieth century. Carl Jung, in his analysis of German national psychology, pointed to Wotan as the archetype reawakened in the soul of the German people. He argued that the old god had returned, not literally, but psychologically, and that Hitler was the manifestation of that return. Hitler, like Wotan, was not simply a leader; he was a storm, a psychic event, a rupture in the fabric of reason. In that framework, *The Wild Chase* becomes the artistic expression of a collective unconscious hurtling toward catastrophe.

The deeper tragedy of this connection is how art, something that might have elevated the human spirit, was used to justify its destruction. Hitler, who once aspired to be an artist, who saw himself as a man of aesthetic sensibilities, ultimately twisted the meaning of art into a mirror of death. He admired paintings like *The Wild Chase* not for their beauty, but for their violence. He did not draw inspiration from pastoral scenes or sacred serenity, but from images of conquest, apocalypse, and wrath. His was not the eye of a creator, but of a destroyer disguised as an artist. In that sense, *The Wild Chase* reflects not only his ideals but his failures: the failure to see art as redemptive, the failure to understand power as responsibility.

And yet, the painting endures: haunting, enigmatic, sublime. It stands as a relic of the nineteenth-century Romantic imagination and a premonition of the twentieth century's horrors. Through its brushstrokes, we glimpse the raw power of myth, the danger of archetype unmoored from conscience. In its ghostly gallop, we see the tragic figure of Adolf Hitler, riding not toward glory, but into the abyss, trailing the souls of millions behind him, his eyes fixed on a heaven that never was, and a destiny he never deserved.

The symbolic power of *The Wild Chase* extends beyond its aesthetic into the metaphysical, particularly when considered through the lens of Hitler's obsession with death and destiny. The restless dead who gallop behind Wotan in von Stuck's vision mirror the ideological role of the fallen in Hitler's Germany. In Hitler's rhetoric, the dead of World War I were never truly gone; they were invoked constantly as sacred witnesses to the betrayal of the Versailles Treaty, as fuel for nationalist vengeance, and as spiritual guarantors of Germany's right to rise again. Hitler cast himself as the medium through which their cries for justice would be answered. The dead, like those storm-bound souls in *The Wild Chase*, were not to be mourned or released; they were to be weaponized, mobilized in the ghostly armies of racial rebirth. This conception of death not as an end but as a call to arms reflects one of the most chilling parallels between Hitler's worldview and the ethos captured in von Stuck's canvas.

That Hitler saw himself as part of a metaphysical narrative, one spanning from mythic past to apocalyptic future, is a notion corroborated by his speeches, his symbolic use of time and memory, and his belief in cyclical catastrophe. He frequently framed German history as a sacred tragedy that required not mere correction, but total redemption. The idea that Germany had to "ride out" a storm of enemies, to gallop through history like Wotan through the tempest, had powerful appeal in a country humiliated by defeat and economic despair. Hitler offered himself as the stormbringer, the man who would not only avenge the dead, but join them in spirit to destroy the world that had dishonored their sacrifice. Thus, like Wotan, Hitler placed himself at the intersection of life and death, the material and the mythic, the now and the eternal.

The figure of Wotan, as rendered in *The Wild Chase*, also allowed for a uniquely masculine mythos that suited the hyper-masculine aesthetic of Nazi Germany. There is no softness in Wotan's ride, no sentiment, no negotiation. He is motion and fury, with a gaze fixed forward, beyond morality, beyond reason. In many ways, Hitler's politics were a reenactment of this vision. The cult of manliness propagated by the Third Reich, the glorification of the soldier's body, the elevation of stoicism, the suppression of emotional vulnerability, can all be seen as extensions of this archetypal framework. Wotan does not weep. He rides. He commands. He kills. And so too, in the Nazi imagination, must the ideal German man. The emotional economy of Nazi masculinity was one of suppression and sacrifice. Mercy was betrayal. Pity was decadence. The only emotion permitted was rage against the impure and pride in the bloodline.

This emotional ethos extended to the German youth indoctrinated under Hitler's regime. In Hitler Youth camps and education systems, boys were taught to see themselves as heirs to a cosmic struggle, to imagine their lives as part of an eternal chase through history in defense of the Volk. The myth of Wotan, with its wild, transcendent momentum, became not just a cultural relic but a living blueprint for how to act, fight, and die. *The Wild Chase* visualized the emotional texture of what Hitler demanded: a people possessed by a mission so great that even death was no escape. The wild-eyed god, bearing down on an unseen enemy, reflected the inner world of a generation raised to believe that their highest calling was to destroy and be destroyed.

One of the most terrifying implications of *The Wild Chase* in relation to Hitler's vision is the absence of destination.

Wotan rides forward, but toward what? There is no haven in the sky, no holy land on the horizon. Only darkness, wind, and chaos. This mirrors the nihilism at the heart of Hitler's worldview, masked though it was in the language of idealism and rebirth. For all his talk of a Thousand-Year Reich, Hitler built nothing truly enduring. He left behind no institutions of peace, no enduring philosophical legacy, no constructive vision of human flourishing. His was a politics of pure motion: perpetual war, endless purges, infinite expansion. Like Wotan's wild chase, it was forward always, never homeward. The Reich was not a nation; it was a storm system.

This storm-thinking had practical consequences. The invasion of the Soviet Union, the insistence on fighting to the last man at Stalingrad, the declaration of total war, these were not rational strategies but theological performances. Hitler could not retreat because Wotan does not turn back. He could not negotiate peace because the god in *The Wild Chase* does not speak; he thunders. Even in the final weeks of the war, as cities crumbled and civilians starved, Hitler refused to alter course. Like the god he had internalized, he would ride into the abyss rather than dismount and surrender. His refusal to abandon Berlin, his decision to take his own life beneath the ruins of his empire, all bear the unmistakable echo of *The Wild Chase*: a fate embraced rather than avoided, a ruin mistaken for transcendence.

The influence of this mythic imagery also explains why Hitler was obsessed with creating his own visual culture. The Nazi aesthetic project, from Leni Riefenstahl's films to Albert Speer's architectural megalomania, was an attempt to translate this same mythic momentum into concrete form. Cities were to be built not for function, but for eternity. Parades were choreographed not merely for celebration, but for spiritual submission. The Nazi regime was less a political structure than an art installation of control, a Wagnerian opera in which the people were extras in an eternal act. *The Wild Chase* did not hang in Hitler's office, but it hung in his mind, and he remade the world in its image.

Hitler's peculiar relationship to art, then, was not one of appreciation, but of possession. Art was sacred only if it served myth. Degenerate art was condemned not because it was aesthetically offensive, but because it disrupted the narrative of divine order. In the wild-eyed chaos of *The Wild Chase*, Hitler saw a cosmos that needed no questioning, only obedience. His preference for heroic sculpture, mythic paintings, and monumental architecture reveals his desire to evoke awe and submission. His aesthetic tastes were not shallow; they were theological. Everything had to reinforce the myth of the chase: the leader in front, the spirits of the past behind, and the storm forever rising.

That *The Wild Chase* was painted the year Hitler was born adds a poetic final note to its role in the Hitlerian mythos. Though no documents place the painting explicitly in Hitler's collection or private reflections, the synchronicity of their birthdates, and the thematic alignment of its vision with his political life, suggest a deeper metaphysical connection. In his mind, Hitler was not simply a man of his time; he was outside time, a rider summoned by history itself to settle ancient scores. Just as Wotan was a god of both vision and destruction, Hitler saw himself as both the prophet and the sword. And like Wotan, his legacy was not peace, but haunting.

In the decades since Hitler's death, *The Wild Chase* has continued to invite speculation, reverence, and dread. Art historians and cultural critics have debated its place in German symbolism and its contribution to the aesthetic of doom that characterized late Romanticism. But when viewed through the lens of Hitler's life and ideology, it takes on a uniquely sinister role. It is not merely a painting about a god; it is a prophecy about a man who thought himself one. And in the storm-churned skies of von Stuck's masterpiece, we see not just myth, but memory; not just legend, but history. We see the terrifying power of beauty corrupted by belief, of myth wielded as a weapon, of art summoned not to heal, but to hurl the world into darkness.

Hitler died in the bowels of Berlin, isolated and betrayed, a spectral figure in his own right. But the echoes of the wild chase he had initiated did not stop with him. The chaos, the fury, the spiritual disorder he unleashed continues to haunt the modern world, not because we revere him, but because the myths he manipulated remain embedded in the human psyche. The image of the god who destroys to purify, who rides ahead of the dead, who sacrifices his eye for wisdom and his heart for rage, this image did not die in 1945. It sleeps, it whispers, and in times of fear, it tempts.

In this way, *The Wild Chase* remains a warning, not just of what Hitler became, but of what any man may become who confuses myth with morality, power with providence, fury with faith. Franz von Stuck could not have known, when he painted that furious rider in 1889, that a child had just been born who would one day enact that vision upon the world. But history, like art, is full of dark harmonies. And in those harmonies, we hear the gallop of ghosts, not just the past calling back, but the future, asking if we will chase blindly into storm again, or finally learn to rein in the fury that rides within us.

CHAPTER 7

SETTING THE STAGE FOR BARBAROSSA

Adolf Hitler's plans for the Soviet Union were deeply influenced by his extreme ideological beliefs. To him, the Soviet state wasn't just an enemy on the battlefield. It also represented everything he opposed: Bolshevism and what he falsely saw as Jewish domination. Hitler viewed the Soviet Union as a critical target in his broader plan for reshaping Europe. At the heart of this vision was something he called *Lebensraum,* meaning "living space." He believed Germany needed to expand eastward to grow strong and powerful, occupying territories across Eastern Europe.

In Hitler's worldview, the Slavic people who lived in Eastern Europe were inferior. Nazis considered them lesser humans who should be either controlled or eliminated. Sadly, this racist thinking wasn't just talk but became official Nazi policy.

If we look at Hitler's earlier writings, especially his book *Mein Kampf,* it's clear he had long dreamed of conquering the East to remove what he perceived as a Soviet threat. Even when Germany signed the Molotov-Ribbentrop Pact with the Soviet Union in 1939, a temporary agreement not to attack each other, Hitler never really trusted the Soviets. To him, this was just a short pause to buy time and deal with Western Europe first.

Hitler knew all along that one day, Germany would invade the Soviet Union.

Pre-Barbarossa Planning

Long before the June 1941 launch of Operation Barbarossa, Hitler saw conquest of the East long before Operation Barbarossa officially began in June 1941. In other words, Hitler and his generals were already planning out how to dominate the Soviet territories. They didn't just aim to defeat the Soviet military. They planned something far bigger: total control over the land and its people. Nazi planners, influenced by Hitler's beliefs, started creating strategies focused not only on military victory but also on harsh racial domination, economic exploitation, and colonization.

By 1940, with Western Europe largely under his control, Hitler's attention turned fully to the Soviet Union. He was convinced that a lasting peace was impossible, especially since the Molotov-Ribbentrop Pact had never really erased his suspicions. Preparations began to accelerate, and the plans for Operation Barbarossa took final shape, guided heavily by his extreme beliefs about race and territory.

The Launch of Operation Barbarossa

When Germany launched Operation Barbarossa on June 22, 1941, it became the largest military operation ever attempted up to that point. Over three million German soldiers poured into Soviet territory, aiming to capture important cities quickly, including Leningrad, Moscow, and key oil fields in the south. But Hitler wasn't just after military victory. The deeper goal behind this massive invasion was ideological: he wanted to completely wipe out what he saw as a corrupted and inferior system.

At first, things looked promising for the Germans. They made rapid progress, seizing large areas of Soviet land. But soon enough, serious problems began emerging. The Soviet Union was vast. Far larger than Hitler had anticipated. Supply lines became overstretched, meaning soldiers lacked basic supplies like food, ammunition, and proper winter clothing. Hitler had also seriously underestimated the strength and determination of the Soviet people, as well as the brutal Russian winter, which soon began to take a toll on his troops.

The Campaign: Early Successes and Strategic Mistakes

Early successes during Barbarossa masked some significant strategic mistakes. By September 1941, German troops were close to major cities like Moscow and Leningrad. But instead of focusing entirely on defeating Soviet military forces, Hitler often became obsessed with capturing cities because of their symbolic meaning. His fixation on cities like Stalingrad later diverted resources and attention away from more critical military objectives, weakening his overall campaign.

Logistics quickly became a nightmare. German soldiers were ill-prepared for the harsh Soviet winter, lacking adequate winter uniforms and supplies. Roads turned to mud, freezing temperatures hit, and vehicles often broke down. On top of that, Nazi soldiers committed horrific atrocities, like the killings carried out by special units called Einsatzgruppen. These brutal acts only fueled fierce local resistance, causing even those who initially welcomed the Germans as liberators from Stalin's oppressive regime to turn against them.

Hitler's Changing Plans for the Soviet Union During the Invasion

As the invasion went on, Hitler's vision shifted from purely military goals to aggressive plans for colonization and ethnic cleansing. A detailed blueprint, known as Generalplan Ost, outlined how Nazis intended to eliminate or enslave millions of Slavic people and replace them with German settlers. This was meant to secure Hitler's radical idea of racial purity and territorial dominance.

However, reality soon set in. Occupying and controlling the massive Soviet territories turned out to be far harder than Hitler had imagined. The local population fiercely resisted the Nazi invaders, forming partisan groups and launching continuous attacks behind German lines. At the same time, the Red Army rallied, fighting back with increasing effectiveness.

By winter of 1941–1942, the Germans found themselves stuck. The harsh Russian winter halted their advance, and during the Battle of Moscow, Soviet forces launched a massive counterattack, turning the tide of the invasion. The Soviets had cleverly relocated many of their factories and workers far beyond German reach, enabling them to rebuild their strength quickly and fight back fiercely.

At this critical turning point, Hitler could have adjusted his strategy to better match the reality on the ground. Instead, he stubbornly clung to his ideological goals. He became obsessed with capturing cities like Stalingrad, seeing them not just as strategic targets but as symbols of victory. This refusal to adapt to changing circumstances only deepened Germany's military struggles.

Ultimately, Hitler's rigid beliefs about race and conquest, combined with severe miscalculations, logistical failures, and fierce Soviet resistance, led to disastrous outcomes for Germany. His refusal to change course when things went wrong accelerated the decline of German military power on the Eastern Front, marking a crucial turning point in World War II.

Aftermath: The Collapse of Nazi Plans for the Soviet Union

After the defeat at Stalingrad in early 1943, Hitler's grand dreams for the Soviet Union started falling apart. Instead of conquering more territory, the Nazis were suddenly forced onto the defensive. The Soviet armies pushed back with powerful counterattacks, regaining land and driving German soldiers into a chaotic, exhausting retreat. The once ambitious vision of a vast German-controlled Eastern empire quickly faded into a desperate fight just to survive.

As the war dragged on, the Eastern Front became one of the most brutal, deadly conflicts the world had ever seen. Operation Barbarossa's failure drained Germany's resources and morale, weakening their forces severely. Instead of victory, the Nazis found themselves stuck in a costly, losing battle that slowly chipped away at their strength.

Conclusion: What Could Have Been and the Legacy of Barbarossa:

Looking back, it's startling to consider what might have happened if Operation Barbarossa had actually succeeded. Hitler would have had access to the immense natural resources of the Soviet Union: things like oil, coal, food, and manpower. With these resources at hand, Nazi Germany could have grown stronger, possibly extending its brutal rule and reshaping Europe in frightening ways. But the operation failed because of Hitler's extreme ideology, rigid thinking, and crucial strategic mistakes.

One of Hitler's biggest miscalculations was underestimating the strength, resilience, and determination of the Soviet people. With support from their allies, particularly the United States and Britain, the Soviets managed not only to hold their ground but eventually push back hard, completely stopping the Nazis from expanding further.

But Operation Barbarossa was always about more than just military conquest. At its core, it was driven by Hitler's extreme racial ideology. He saw the Soviet Union as a place that needed to be destroyed. A land both hated and desired. For him, conquering the East was not just a military necessity; it was also a moral duty, a mission to purify and remake Europe according to his racist ideals.

This kind of thinking wasn't entirely new. Hitler's ideas drew from centuries-old German desires to expand eastward, something known as *Drang nach Osten*, meaning "Drive to the East." But Hitler's version of this idea was far more brutal and extreme. He didn't just want new territories for Germans to settle; he aimed to eliminate millions of people already living there. Plans like the "Hunger Plan," designed to starve millions to death, and the *Einsatzgruppen* massacres, systematic mass killings carried out by special

Nazi units, showed clearly just how horrific and intentional these genocidal policies were.

Hitler genuinely believed that by destroying entire Soviet cities and deliberately starving millions of innocent people, he could somehow cleanse the land, making room for German settlers. But he severely underestimated the resilience and fighting spirit of the Soviet people, as well as their ability to endure immense suffering. His beliefs blinded him from recognizing the strength and complexity of his opponent. What he initially believed would be a quick, decisive victory turned into a long, grinding, and exhausting war.

Interestingly, Operation Barbarossa was named after Frederick Barbarossa, the Emperor of the Holy Roman Empire.

The Soviet Union's ability to survive and push back the Nazi invasion wasn't just about military numbers or industrial production. It was also about the mindset and desperation that both Hitler and Stalin forced upon their people. From the start, the Nazis made it clear they weren't fighting a normal war. They were fighting a war of extermination. Soviet soldiers and civilians understood that surrender didn't mean being taken prisoner; it meant being killed. Entire villages were wiped out. Orders from German commanders even told soldiers not to take prisoners during the early stages of the invasion.

This fear created what ancient strategist Sun Tzu called "death ground," a situation where the only choice is to fight with everything you have because surrender means certain death.

On the Soviet side, Stalin added to this pressure by making retreat nearly impossible. His famous Order No. 227, known for the line "Not a step back!", meant that anyone who tried to flee could be executed by their own side. Penal battalions were formed for those accused of cowardice, and special troops were placed behind Soviet lines to shoot deserters. It was brutal, but it worked. Soviet soldiers were trapped between two deadly forces: the Nazi army ahead and their own commanders behind. So fighting was the only option for survival.

Civilians knew this too. Under Nazi occupation, people faced starvation, executions, and deportation. So they resisted however they could: by joining the fight, supporting the Red Army, or sabotaging the invaders. The idea that surrender could mean the death of entire communities created a powerful sense of unity and determination.

Ironically, the Nazis thought that terror would break Soviet morale. But it did the opposite. It made people angrier, tougher, and more determined to fight. Stories of atrocities spread quickly, and they fueled a deep hatred for the enemy. Every act of brutality made Soviet resistance stronger.

Even as defeat became increasingly clear, Hitler stubbornly clung to his vision, treating each setback as a test of his fanatical beliefs. His refusal to adapt to reality ultimately made things even worse for the German forces. Operation Barbarossa became the point at which Hitler's dreams collided violently with reality. Its disastrous failure opened a massive second front in World War II, stretching Nazi resources thin and exposing their vulnerabilities. It also forced the world to confront the true horror of Hitler's genocidal ideology head-on.

The damage caused by Operation Barbarossa in Eastern Europe was unimaginable, with tens of millions losing their lives. Entire regions were devastated, cities reduced to ruins, and countless innocent people displaced or killed.

In the end, Barbarossa was more than just another military failure. It was a catastrophic attempt to put Hitler's hateful vision into practice. It became a brutal lesson in how dangerous unchecked ideology can be. And more than anything, it showed what happens when people are pushed to the edge. When the only path left is to stand and fight or be destroyed. Studying Operation Barbarossa helps us understand how distorted beliefs and fanaticism, combined with ignorance of reality, can lead entire nations into disaster.

<h1 style="text-align:center">CHAPTER 8</h1>

THE NAZIS AND THE OCCULT: A QUEST FOR POWER THROUGH MYSTICISM AND ANCIENT RELICS

When we think about the rise of Adolf Hitler and the Nazi regime, the first things that come to mind are often the horrors of World War II, the brutal enforcement of Aryan supremacy, and the Holocaust, the systematic extermination of millions of innocent lives. It was a time defined by violence, hatred, and power-hungry politics. But underneath all that, there was another strange and unsettling layer that many people don't hear about: the Nazis were obsessed with the occult.

They weren't just focused on conquering territories or reshaping governments. Some of Hitler's top leaders genuinely believed in ancient myths, mystical energies, and the existence of sacred objects that could grant supernatural power. They thought that relics like the Holy Grail, the Spear of Destiny, and even the Ark of the Covenant were more than just religious symbols or historical artifacts. They were tools that could control the future, decide the fate of nations, and maybe even make them invincible.

To outsiders, this might sound like fiction or fantasy but these beliefs were not separate from their politics. They were deeply woven into their ideological framework. The Nazi leadership didn't view these relics as mere trophies of history; they saw them as evidence of divine favor, proof that they were meant to lead a new world order. In their minds, possessing such objects could validate their claim to power, not just politically, but spiritually.

The Nazi Fascination with the Occult: Origins and Influences

To understand how this all started, we need to look at what was happening in Germany and Europe after World War I. That was a time of chaos and confusion. Germany had just lost the war and was facing economic disaster, political unrest, and national humiliation, especially because of the harsh terms of the Treaty of Versailles.

In the middle of all this instability, people began searching for something: a deeper meaning, a sense of identity, or even a spiritual answer to the mess they were in. That's when all sorts of unusual ideas started to gain popularity. Nationalist, mystical, and occult philosophies became surprisingly common. People were drawn to stories of ancient civilizations, lost powers, and racial purity. Many believed that Germany had once been great and could be great again, if only they could reconnect with their ancient roots.

One of the most influential groups during this time was something called the Thule Society. It was formed in Munich in 1918, and while it may sound like just another secret club, its beliefs had a huge impact on what would eventually become Nazi ideology.

Members of the Thule Society believed that there had once been a powerful, pre-Christian Aryan civilization, full of spiritual wisdom and strength. They were obsessed with ideas of racial superiority, especially the idea that "Aryans" were not just better physically or mentally, but spiritually superior, too. The society mixed these beliefs with anti-Semitism, pagan rituals, and symbols that dated back to ancient times.

To them, Aryans were like a chosen race, guardians of lost mystical powers. The goal wasn't just to rule the world politically, but to restore a kind of ancient spiritual order, one that had supposedly existed before history was "corrupted" by modern religions and cultures.

Now, Hitler himself wasn't someone you'd call religious in the usual sense. He didn't go to church or talk much about God in a personal way. But he was deeply influenced by a movement called "völkisch," which mixed extreme nationalism with folklore, pagan myths, and spiritual ideas from Germany's past.

This movement believed that the true soul of Germany could be found by looking backward into the myths, symbols, and values of ancient Germanic tribes. Hitler liked this idea. He believed that by reviving those ancient traditions, Germany could rise again. That's part of why the Nazis chose the swastika as their symbol. While many people now see it as a hateful emblem, back then it was taken from ancient Indo-European cultures, where it represented good fortune and power.

To Hitler, symbols were tools for shaping minds. He believed that if people saw and believed in these old signs of power, they'd start to feel the same spirit awaken inside them.

Of all the top Nazis, no one was more obsessed with the occult than Heinrich Himmler, the head of the SS (the Nazi paramilitary elite force). Himmler didn't just see the SS as soldiers but saw them as modern-day knights, guardians of an ancient and sacred mission. Under Himmler's leadership, the SS became something like a cult. He gave them rituals, symbols, and a strict code of behavior, all inspired by old Germanic traditions, myths, and mystical beliefs. He even redesigned old castles to serve as SS training centers, complete with rune carvings and ceremonial chambers.

Himmler believed that the SS were the living embodiment of the "master race," chosen to guide Germany, and the world, into a new age. To him, winning the war was about spiritual destiny, a cosmic struggle between the forces of purity and corruption.

When we look at all of this (the search for magical relics, the belief in mystical Aryan roots, the use of ancient symbols and rituals) it paints a chilling picture. The Nazi regime didn't just try to control the world through force. They tried to reshape reality itself, using myth, mysticism, and propaganda to create a new world order based on an imagined past.

It's a reminder of how dangerous ideas can become when they're mixed with power and fanaticism. What started as strange beliefs in hidden wisdom and lost civilizations became part of a violent machine that destroyed millions of lives.

Even today, the strange relationship between the Nazis and the occult remains a haunting example of how ideology can be twisted into something dark and destructive, especially when people are looking for meaning in the middle of chaos.

The Ahnenerbe: A Center of Nazi Occultism

Back in 1935, Heinrich Himmler started an organization called the **Ahnenerbe**, which means "Ancestral Heritage." On the surface, it looked like a serious scientific group focused on studying German history and culture. But as time went on, it became clear that this wasn't just about history. The Ahnenerbe had a much stranger and darker mission: it was obsessed with mystical knowledge, ancient secrets, and powerful relics.

Himmler truly believed that if the Nazis could uncover forgotten ancient wisdom and powerful artifacts, it would not only prove that the Aryan race was superior but also give their regime a kind of magical or spiritual authority. To him, the past was a source of power that could shape the future.

To chase this dream, the Ahnenerbe funded several expeditions across the world, especially to places that were believed to hold clues about the ancient Aryan race. One of the most famous of these missions was to Tibet. Some Nazi thinkers believed that the Aryans, the so-called "master race" in Nazi ideology, had originally come from somewhere in Central Asia, and Tibet seemed like a promising place to find proof. Nazi officers went there not just to study the land or people, but to look for any kind of evidence (bones, symbols, ruins) that might support this theory.

One key figure in this strange world of Nazi mysticism was Karl Maria Wiligut. Before joining the SS, Wiligut was an occultist, someone deeply involved in spiritualism, magic, and ancient beliefs. When Himmler met him, he was fascinated by Wiligut's ideas, especially his connection to old Germanic paganism and rituals. Himmler made him a spiritual advisor and gave him a role in shaping what the SS believed in at a deeper, almost religious level. Wiligut helped create a strange belief system for the SS that mixed pagan traditions, mysticism, and Nazi ideology.

The Ahnenerbe's most famous and legendary efforts were focused on finding two powerful objects: the Holy Grail and the Spear of Destiny. The Holy Grail, in legend, is the cup used by Jesus at the Last Supper and is said to have magical powers. The Spear of Destiny, also known as the Lance of Longinus, is the spear that was believed to have pierced Jesus' side during the crucifixion, and many believed it could give great power to whoever possessed it. The Nazis were convinced that these relics were real and could actually help them win the war or at least give them control over their enemies.

So, what started as a group pretending to protect history quickly turned into something far more dangerous: a team of true believers, chasing mystical powers, ancient secrets, and magical artifacts, all in the hope of making the Nazi regime seem unstoppable and almost god-like.

The Holy Grail: A Divine Symbol of Power

The Holy Grail is one of the most legendary and mysterious objects in history. Most people know it as the cup that Jesus drank from during the Last Supper. In Christian tradition, it's believed to have special, even miraculous, powers. Some say it can heal, others say it brings eternal life.

But for the Nazis, the Grail meant something very different. They believed it was a divine object that could give its owner the right to rule the world. So, for them, finding the Grail wasn't just about history or religion, but about power, destiny, and control.

One of the most obsessed Nazi leaders with the Grail was Heinrich Himmler. He believed that whoever possessed it could help secure the Nazi dream of creating a massive empire, the so-called "Thousand-Year Reich." To Himmler, the Grail was like a key that could unlock their rightful place as rulers of the world.

So, he sent people on real-life treasure hunts. Nazi expeditions traveled to places like Montserrat in Spain, where legends claimed the Grail might be hidden. They were also fascinated by the stories linking the Grail to the Knights Templar, mysterious group of warrior monks from the Middle Ages who were said to guard powerful secrets. The Nazis even funded archaeological digs in areas tied to these legends, hoping to find something that would prove their beliefs true.

But despite all the efforts, the Grail was never found. It stayed hidden, if it even existed at all. But the hunt for it became more than just a search for a physical object. It turned into a powerful symbol of Nazi thinking. It showed how far they were willing to go to connect their rule to something higher, something divine.

The Spear of Destiny: The Weapon of Power

The Spear of Destiny is another object that's surrounded by myth and mystery. According to Christian legend, it was the spear used by a Roman soldier named Longinus to pierce Jesus's side during the crucifixion. That moment, as the story goes, gave the spear incredible power. Many believed that whoever held the Spear could control the future, or even rule the world.

Throughout history, the Spear was said to have been in the hands of powerful rulers like Charlemagne and Napoleon. Some thought its presence helped them rise to power. So when the Nazis took over Austria in 1938, they made sure to grab the Spear, which was being kept in Vienna at the time. They moved it to Nuremberg, one of their most symbolic cities, and put it on display as a show of their strength and connection to something greater.

Hitler, in particular, was fascinated by the Spear. He believed it could give him the power to conquer his enemies and make his vision of world domination a reality. He took its presence seriously and made sure it was carefully preserved, almost like it was a piece of sacred treasure.

To the Nazis, the Spear was a sign that their rule was blessed by fate. Just like with the Holy Grail, their obsession with the Spear showed how deeply they believed in mixing myth, magic, and power.

Other Mystical Artifacts: The Ark of the Covenant and the Ring of the Nibelung

The Holy Grail and the Spear of Destiny weren't the only legendary objects the Nazis were after. They were also obsessed with finding other mystical relics, especially the Ark of the Covenant and the Ring of the Nibelung. To them, these were powerful tools. Symbols that could supposedly help them win wars, rule the world, and claim a kind of "divine right" to power.

Let's start with the Ark of the Covenant. According to the Bible, the Ark was a sacred chest that held the stone tablets of the Ten Commandments: laws that God gave to Moses on Mount Sinai. The Ark was believed to carry an overwhelming spiritual force. In ancient times, it was said to bring victory in battle and even cause destruction to those who dared to touch it without permission. For believers, it was the ultimate symbol of God's presence on Earth.

The Nazis were drawn to the Ark because they believed it could grant them divine favor, or in simpler terms, they thought it could prove that they were chosen to lead. Himmler and his inner circle treated religious relics like these not just as holy objects but as ancient technologies or tools with real, usable power. If they could find the Ark, they believed it would help them defeat their enemies and strengthen their claim to a new world order.

Then there was the Ring of the Nibelung, which came from old Germanic myths: stories full of dragons, dwarves, and enchanted gold. The most famous version of the tale was brought to life by composer Richard Wagner, whose powerful operas inspired many of the Nazis' ideas about ancient Germanic glory and Aryan heritage. In the myth, the ring is forged from cursed gold and gives its owner the power to rule the world, but at a terrible cost. Anyone who owns the ring is doomed by its curse.

For Himmler, this legendary ring was a real thing. He saw it as a symbol of the supposed superiority of the Aryan race. Wagner's music and mythology had a huge influence on Nazi ideology, and the Ring became wrapped up in their vision of power, destiny, and mythic German roots. They believed that these old legends were part of a hidden truth about their race and their mission.

Of course, neither the Ark nor the Ring was ever found. But that didn't stop the Nazis from pouring money and manpower into searching for them. These quests, for them, were part of a larger effort to rewrite history, blend myth with politics, and make their brutal empire seem like it was backed by fate, magic, or even divine will.

Conclusion: Occultism, Power, and the Legacy of the Nazis

What we learn from all this is that the Nazis were deeply fascinated by the occult, largely because they believed it could give them power and control. This might sound strange, but for them, magic, ancient symbols, and mystical ideas weren't just fantasy, but part of a bigger belief system that tied into their dangerous ideology. They truly believed they had a divine right to rule, and that certain ancient relics or supernatural forces could help them hold on to that power.

This wasn't just a side interest for a few people in the regime. Their search for mystical objects, things like the Holy Grail or ancient runes, was linked to their belief that these items held real, cosmic power. They thought finding them could somehow unlock secret knowledge or strength that would help them dominate the world. These beliefs helped them justify some of the most horrific things they did, including the Holocaust.

In the end, the Nazis never found the powerful relics they were searching for. But their efforts, and the strange, shadowy beliefs behind them, are still a chilling part of history. Their obsession with the occult showed just how dangerous it can be when politics and mystical thinking are mixed together.

The Nazi regime wasn't just about rules, weapons, and soldiers. It also operated through powerful symbols, dramatic rituals, and made-up myths. Their use of mysticism shaped everything from the way they built their buildings to the way they spread propaganda. They used grand, theatrical ceremonies and symbols to stir up emotion and make their movement feel larger than life, almost like a religion.

One of the key figures behind all this was Heinrich Himmler, the head of the SS. He was deeply involved in turning the SS into something like a secret brotherhood, similar to the knights of old legends. He wanted it to feel noble, sacred, and powerful. To do this, he built up a whole world of made-up myths, rituals, and beliefs for the SS to follow.

Wewelsburg Castle became the center of these strange ideas. Himmler saw it as the heart of a new mystical empire, a kind of spiritual headquarters for the Nazi elite. The castle was filled with symbols and designs meant to create a sense of mystery and sacred purpose. One of these symbols was the Black Sun, a dark and complex design that has since become associated with Nazi mysticism and is still used today by some extremist groups.

At the core of this strange belief system was a rejection of science, logic, and modern thinking. Instead, they looked to ancient ideas, myths, and supposed spiritual truths. They believed that race wasn't just a biological fact, but a spiritual force too. To them, ancestry had almost magical meaning. Your bloodline could make you more powerful or pure in a cosmic sense.

To prove and promote these ideas, the Nazis created Ahnenerbe. This organization carried out fake "scientific" research, hoping to uncover hidden Aryan knowledge. They sent teams to far-off places like Tibet, Scandinavia, and the Middle East, looking for signs of a lost "pure" civilization they believed had once ruled the world. Basically, they were trying to rewrite history to fit their beliefs, mixing archaeology with fantasy.

They also revived old symbols and runes, treating them like magical tools. The SS symbol, the double lightning bolt rune, and the swastika weren't chosen just because they looked striking. These symbols had ancient roots and were believed to carry deep mystical energy. To the Nazis, they were talismans of power.

Some of these ideas came from a secretive group called the Thule Society, which helped shape early Nazi thinking. The Thule Society believed in a lost Aryan civilization and held strong anti-Semitic views. They saw the Jews as enemies not just politically, but spiritually. Within this twisted myth, mass murder was framed as part of some cosmic struggle. It's terrifying, but they made genocide seem like a kind of sacred duty.

People still argue about whether Hitler himself truly believed in all this. He didn't take part in rituals or lead secret ceremonies, but he understood the emotional power of these ideas. His speeches were full of religious energy. He often spoke like a prophet or a chosen one. He seemed to believe he had a special role in history, like he was carrying out some larger destiny.

What makes Nazi occultism so disturbing is how it combined ancient myths with modern technology. Rockets and ruins. Eugenics and runes. Science was twisted to serve superstition. War was treated as a kind of cleansing. And genocide? That was seen as a necessary step toward some imagined spiritual rebirth.

That's what should really scare us. When people stop relying on reason and start believing in myths to guide their actions, terrible things can happen. Evil doesn't always show up in the form of obvious monsters. Sometimes it wears robes, lights candles, and talks about healing and destiny, while planning horrors behind the scenes.

Even today, some extremist groups still hold on to these Nazi occult ideas. They use the same symbols. They read the same texts. It's proof that these ideas haven't completely disappeared, and that we need to keep paying attention.

Looking back at this dark chapter forces us to face a painful truth: when dangerous ideas are wrapped in mystical language, they can feel powerful and sacred. But in reality, they can lead to devastating consequences. That's why it's so important to question myths that justify harm, and to recognize how easily belief can be twisted into something deadly.

CHAPTER 9

THE ROLES OF HERMAN GÖRING, HEINRICH HIMMLER, AND JOSEPH GOEBBELS IN HITLER'S RULE OVER GERMANY

When people talk about Adolf Hitler's rise to power and how he managed to lead Nazi Germany from 1933 to 1945, they often focus just on him. But the truth is, Hitler didn't do it all alone. There were a few key people who stood right beside him every step of the way, people who not only believed in his ideas but also helped make them a terrifying reality. Without them, Hitler's vision might never have turned into the brutal regime we now know as the Third Reich.

This chapter takes a closer look at three of the most important figures in Hitler's inner circle: Hermann Göring, Heinrich Himmler, and Joseph Goebbels. These weren't just followers; they were leaders in their own right. They helped Hitler build his power in party politics, control the German population, and carry out some of the darkest actions in modern history.

Let's start with the first of them: Hermann Göring.

HERMAN GÖRING: The Architect of Nazi Germany's Economic and Military Expansion

Hermann Göring wasn't just another Nazi official but was one of Hitler's closest allies and most powerful supporters. His influence stretched across the military, the economy, and the government. Long before the Nazis took control of Germany, Göring had already made a name for himself. He was a decorated World War I pilot, known for his bravery and sharp instincts. When he joined the Nazi Party in the early 1920s, he quickly became one of its rising stars. His charm and military background helped him earn Hitler's trust early on.

The Role in the Economy: Plundering Resources for the War Effort

When Hitler became Chancellor in 1933, he gave Göring a big role right away. At first, Göring was made "Minister without Portfolio," a vague title, but one that gave him a seat at the table for all the big decisions. But it was in 1936 that Göring took on an even bigger job: running the Four-Year Plan.

So, what was the Four-Year Plan? Simply put, it was a strategy to get Germany ready for war, fast. Göring's task was to prepare the country's economy so it could support a full-scale military campaign within four years. That meant focusing on things like making synthetic oil and rubber, boosting weapons production, and making Germany less dependent on foreign imports. This idea of economic self-sufficiency was known as "autarky."

Göring worked closely with major German companies, especially those that supported Nazi goals, and gave them massive government contracts. These companies, in return, helped build up the German military by producing weapons, tanks, planes, and ammunition. It was a tight partnership between industry and state, and Göring was the one pulling the strings.

But his role wasn't just limited to building factories. As the Nazis invaded and occupied more territory during the war, Göring played a key role in stealing resources from those lands. He approved the plundering of raw materials, food, and goods from countries like Poland and the Soviet Union. He also helped set up systems of forced labor, where people, mostly from Eastern Europe, were taken from their homes and forced to work in brutal conditions to support the Nazi war effort.

So, Göring was planning the war and also fed it by whatever means necessary, no matter the cost in human suffering.

The Role in the Military: Luftwaffe and the Pursuit of Air Supremacy

Göring's influence didn't stop at the economy. He also headed the Luftwaffe, the German Air Force. Hitler gave him the job of creating a powerful air force that could help Germany dominate Europe. And at first, Göring delivered. He helped build a modern air force from the ground up, one that played a major role in early Nazi victories, like the invasions of Poland and France, and even during the Battle of Britain.

But things started to fall apart as the war dragged on. Göring became overconfident and made several poor strategic choices. He underestimated the strength and tactics of the British Royal Air Force, and his promise to destroy it before a German invasion of Britain failed badly. Later in the war, he struggled to keep the Luftwaffe supplied and properly equipped, partly because of the growing Allied bombings and Germany's shrinking resources.

His inability to adapt to the changing conditions of war made a real difference. By the time the tide of war turned against Germany, the Luftwaffe had lost much of its strength, and Göring's influence began to fade. Even so, he remained loyal to Hitler until the very end, staying close even as the Nazi regime crumbled around them. But that eventually changed.

The relationship between Hermann Göring and Adolf Hitler, once marked by loyalty and mutual admiration, ended in betrayal and bitterness. As the Third Reich crumbled in April 1945, Göring, viewing himself as Hitler's legal successor, sent a telegram proposing to assume leadership. Hitler, isolated in his Berlin bunker and increasingly paranoid, saw this as an act of treason. Furious, he stripped Göring of all titles and ordered his arrest. Their bond, forged in the early Nazi movement and solidified through years of shared ambition, disintegrated in Hitler's final days, leaving Göring disgraced and alienated as the regime collapsed around them.

HEINRICH HIMMLER: The Protector of Nazi Ideology and Architect of the Holocaust

Heinrich Himmler was one of the most terrifying and powerful people in Nazi Germany. He did more than just follow orders. He helped *shape* some of the cruelest ideas the Nazis believed in. As the head of the SS, a special Nazi force, Himmler played a leading role in carrying out Hitler's harshest and most violent plans. He pushed the idea that Germany had to be "racially pure," and he helped set up the system that would lead to the murder of millions, especially Jews, during what became known as the Holocaust.

The SS: Enforcing Terror and Loyalty

The SS (short for *Schutzstaffel*, or "Protection Squad") didn't start as the huge force it became. When it began in 1925, it was just a small group of guards protecting Hitler. But when Himmler took control, he turned it into a powerful and dangerous organization that did much more than bodyguard work.

Himmler expanded the SS into an elite group of soldiers and police who were completely loyal to Hitler. Their job wasn't just to protect but to crush anyone who didn't agree with the Nazis. They arrested people who spoke out, broke up protests, and made sure everyone was loyal to the Nazi cause. Fear was their weapon, and they used it everywhere.

Under Himmler, the SS became deeply involved in running concentration camps. These camps were places of horror, where people were starved, tortured, and killed simply because of their religion, political beliefs, or background. Jews, Romani people, political enemies, people with disabilities, and others the Nazis called "undesirable" were rounded up and taken away, often never to return. One of the SS's darkest creations was the *Einsatzgruppen*, roving death squads that followed the German army into Eastern Europe, shooting entire communities, often in cold blood.

The Final Solution: The Holocaust

The most horrifying part of Himmler's legacy was his role in what the Nazis called "The Final Solution." This was their plan to completely wipe out the Jewish people in Europe. Himmler helped design and run the whole thing.

He supervised the creation of death camps like Auschwitz, Treblinka, and Sobibor, places built with one purpose: to kill as many people as possible. These weren't like regular prisons. People were packed into trains, sent to the camps, and either forced into backbreaking labor or killed right away in gas chambers. Many starved to death or died from disease and abuse. It was genocide on an industrial scale, and Himmler was at the center of it.

What made Himmler especially chilling was the way he carried out these crimes. He believed completely in the Nazi idea that some races were "inferior" and didn't belong in society. To him, this mass murder wasn't personal. It was part of a "clean-up" job. He talked about these horrifying acts as if they were just another task on his to-do list.

Himmler made Hitler's deadly plans possible. He built the system, trained the killers, and kept everything running. Without Himmler, the Holocaust wouldn't have happened the way it did. He wasn't just enforcing Nazi policies; he *was* one of the key minds behind them.

JOSEPH GOEBBELS: The Master of Propaganda and Public Manipulation

Joseph Goebbels wasn't a soldier or a general, but he played one of the most powerful roles in Nazi Germany. He controlled what millions of people thought, felt, and believed. As Hitler's Minister of Propaganda, Goebbels made sure the Nazi message was everywhere. He used newspapers, radio, films, posters, anything that reached people, to shape how they saw the world. His job was to make Hitler look like a savior, to make Nazi policies seem fair and necessary, and to turn enemies, real or imagined, into monsters.

He didn't just spread ideas. He shaped reality. Goebbels was so skilled that many Germans truly believed what they were being told, even as their cities were bombed and their neighbors disappeared. He created a world where questioning the Nazi message felt wrong, even dangerous. His words and images helped Hitler gain power, and keep it, even as the country began falling apart during the war.

Propaganda may sound like just exaggeration or political messaging, but under Goebbels, it became a powerful weapon. It was used to control, to deceive, and to crush dissent. And Goebbels knew exactly how to use it.

Early Life and Political Rise:

Goebbels' path to power was shaped by a life full of disappointments. Born in 1897 in a small German town to a modest Catholic family, Joseph was a bright student who loved reading and writing. He earned a doctorate in literature and philosophy, which gave him a sharp mind, but not a clear future. He dreamed of being a novelist or playwright, but publishers rejected his work again and again. He also struggled with feelings of inferiority due to his physical disability, a clubfoot that made walking difficult and sometimes painful. In a society that valued strength and perfection, Goebbels often felt like he didn't measure up.

But it was these struggles, this mix of ambition, bitterness, and a desire to prove himself, that drove him toward politics. After reading about the failed Beer Hall Putsch, Goebbels joined the Nazi Party while Hitler was incarcerated at Lanzburg prison. Goebbels, being a skilled orator himself, quickly gained attention within the party and was considered the new leader of the National Socialist movement. In fact, while Hitler was in prison, Goebbels encouraged the party to completely divorce itself from him. When he first met Adolf Hitler, something clicked. Goebbels was drawn in by Hitler's energy and vision, and he quickly became one of his most passionate supporters. He wasn't just a follower. He saw himself as someone who could help bring that vision to life.

By the time Hitler was released from prison after the failed Beer Hall Putsch in 1923, Goebbels had already joined the party. He rose fast. He had a gift for writing fiery speeches and connecting with people. His emotional style of speaking, filled with drama and symbolism, grabbed attention and stirred up crowds. He didn't just repeat Hitler's ideas; he amplified them.

By the early 1930s, Goebbels was running the Nazi Party's entire media strategy. When Hitler became Chancellor in 1933, Goebbels was appointed Minister of Propaganda, a position that gave him full control over what Germans could see, hear, and read.

The Cult of Hitler's Personality: Creating a Charismatic Leader

One of Goebbels' biggest missions was building a god-like image of Hitler. He wanted people to see Hitler not just as a politician, but as Germany's savior, someone chosen by fate to rescue the nation from humiliation and poverty. And Goebbels made sure that image was everywhere.

The Nazis staged massive rallies with dramatic lighting, marching bands, and thousands of swastika flags. These events were designed to feel powerful and emotional. Films like *Triumph of the Will*, directed by Leni Riefenstahl with Goebbels' support, made Hitler look like a divine figure: strong, calm, and destined to lead. Photos showed him surrounded by adoring crowds. Posters showed him as the father of the nation.

Goebbels carefully controlled how Hitler appeared in public. Hitler was rarely photographed in awkward poses or casual moments. Everything was staged to support the myth. His walk, his speeches, even his silence. He became, in the eyes of many, almost superhuman.

This "Führer cult" helped hold the country together, especially when things got tough. People clung to the idea that Hitler had a plan, even when food was running out or bombs were falling. Goebbels' strategy was simple: If people believed in the man, they would follow the mission, no matter how extreme it became.

Anti-Semitic Propaganda: Fueling Hatred and Persecution

Goebbels promoted the Nazi vision and helped destroy anyone who stood in its way. And at the heart of Nazi hatred was anti-Semitism. Goebbels played a key role in spreading lies and fear about Jewish people, turning neighbors against neighbors.

He used every form of media to make Jews seem like a threat. Articles called them greedy or dishonest. Cartoons portrayed them with exaggerated features. Children's books taught that Jews were dangerous. Goebbels wanted Jewish people to seem like the cause of Germany's problems, and it worked. Over time, many Germans came to believe that Jews were not just different, but evil.

The film *The Eternal Jew* (1940) was one of Goebbels' most horrifying projects. It portrayed Jews as filthy, sneaky, and animal-like. It was designed to stir up disgust and fear. And it helped lay the emotional groundwork for what came next: the Holocaust.

Goebbels' propaganda made it easier for the public to accept Nazi actions like the Nuremberg Laws, which stripped Jews of their citizenship, and Kristallnacht (Night of Broken Glass) in 1938, when Jewish homes, shops, and synagogues were attacked in one terrifying night. Later, when Jews were deported to ghettos and camps, many Germans stayed silent, some because they were afraid, but others because they had been taught to believe it was justified.

The War Effort: Maintaining Morale During the Holocaust

When World War II began in 1939, Goebbels' role became even more important. He needed to keep the public on board, even as the cost of war became unbearable. At first, his job was easy. German victories in Poland, France, and elsewhere gave people hope. Goebbels celebrated every success with bold headlines and speeches about German strength.

But as the war dragged on and losses mounted, especially after the failed invasion of the Soviet Union, Goebbels had to work harder to keep morale up. He gave speeches about sacrifice and survival. He said Germany was fighting not just for land, but for its soul. He painted the Allies as monsters who wanted to destroy German culture and families.

Goebbels also turned Hitler into a symbol of endurance. Even when people questioned the war, many still believed in their leader, because Goebbels had built that belief into something sacred.

Behind the scenes, he censored bad news, spun defeats into "strategic withdrawals," and broadcast stories of heroism and loyalty. But by 1944, the truth could no longer be hidden. Germany was falling apart, and even Goebbels couldn't cover it up anymore.

As the Allies closed in on Berlin, Hitler refused to surrender, and so did Goebbels. He moved into the underground Führerbunker with Hitler and a few other top officials. There, as bombs exploded overhead, Goebbels kept writing speeches and calling for resistance, even as most Germans were simply trying to survive.

In one of the darkest acts of the Nazi leadership, Goebbels and his wife, Magda, made a horrifying choice. Believing that life without Hitler and National Socialism wasn't worth living, they poisoned their six young children before taking their own lives on May 1, 1945. Hitler had committed suicide the day before.

Their deaths marked the end of the Nazi regime's inner circle, but the damage Goebbels had done through his propaganda would last far beyond the war.

Joseph Goebbels may be gone, but the way he used media to shape reality remains a powerful warning. He proved that lies, when repeated enough times, can seem like truth. He showed how fear, anger, and identity can be manipulated to control entire populations. And he taught future dictators and spin doctors just how dangerous propaganda can be when mixed with ambition and hate.

Conclusion: The Unholy Trio of Nazi Power

Herman Göring, Heinrich Himmler, and Joseph Goebbels were three of the most important people who helped Hitler stay in power in Germany. Each had a different job: Göring handled the economy and the military, Himmler ran the terrifying SS that enforced Nazi beliefs, and Goebbels controlled the propaganda that shaped what people saw, heard, and believed. Together, they created a powerful system that kept the Nazi regime going for over ten years. They were in charge of different parts: money, force, and ideas, but worked toward the same goal. And because of their actions and their loyalty to Hitler, they played major roles in causing the horrors of World War II and the Holocaust. Their names are now forever tied to one of the darkest times in history.

At first glance, the Nazi government looked strict, organized, and efficient, like a well-oiled machine. But inside, it worked more like a maze than a clock. It was chaotic and full of competing powers. And that wasn't an accident. It was planned that way. The confusion made Hitler even more powerful. He didn't run things by controlling every little detail. Instead, he became the center of everything, the one figure everyone revolved around.

To really understand how the Nazi system worked, you have to forget how regular governments are supposed to work. There wasn't a clear chain of command. Ministries and departments often stepped on each other's toes. Officials had tons of power with almost no rules to follow. Jobs and duties would shift suddenly, with no explanation. Yet somehow, the system still worked. Terribly and violently, but it worked. That's because it didn't act like a government. It acted more like a cult.

And at the heart of that cult was Hitler himself. As Führer, he didn't need to give direct orders all the time. Just his general wishes were enough. What really mattered was guessing what he wanted. His top men started doing something people later called "working toward the Führer." That meant they'd listen to his speeches, read between the lines, and then come up with more extreme ideas on their own to impress him.

This created a strange mix of strict control and wild improvisation. All power technically came from Hitler, but he stayed hands-off. He let his closest men fight among themselves because that made him even stronger at the top. Men like Göring, Himmler, Goebbels, and Bormann all fought for Hitler's favor. They each built their own little kingdoms inside the regime. Their power was huge, but always shaky, depending on how much Hitler liked or trusted them at any given moment.

The Nazi government ended up as a tangled web of departments and power centers. There was no regular cabinet. Rules could be skipped with a simple decree. It was often unclear who was in charge of what. This mess led to constant turf wars, but that actually helped the system stay aggressive and fast-moving. People made quick, brutal decisions without waiting for approvals.

One of the clearest signs of this system was how the Nazi Party operated alongside the regular state. The normal government (courts, civil service, the army) was still there, but the Nazis slowly took it over. Party leaders often had their own roles that overlapped or even overruled official state positions. A single town might be run by a state governor, a Nazi official (called a Gauleiter), and an SS commander, all supposedly reporting to Berlin but actually doing their own thing.

This gave the Nazis a lot of flexibility, and a lot of room to be cruel. Local officials could act on their own, and the most extreme ones often rose the fastest. Promotions didn't come from hard work or talent. They came from being loyal and willing to go further than anyone else. The more radical your idea, the more likely you were to get noticed. That's how terrible policies became reality. Hitler didn't always give orders. Many times, his people were trying to outdo each other to win his praise.

The SS is a perfect example of this. It started out as Hitler's bodyguard but grew under Himmler into a massive organization. It became part police, part military, and part Nazi brainwashing machine. The SS had its own spy network, ran the Gestapo (the secret police), controlled concentration camps, and even operated businesses using forced labor. It was like its own mini-state, with its own rules and beliefs.

But the SS wasn't just about force. It was a vision for the future. Himmler imagined it as the purest part of the Nazi race. SS members had to pass strict racial tests and go through intense training. The soldiers were true believers. Their black uniforms and skull symbols weren't just scary. They were worn with pride, symbols of a "new breed" shaped by Nazi ideology and stripped of anything seen as weak.

At the same time, the regular German army, the Wehrmacht, was slowly being taken over too. Many officers thought they could stay neutral or stick to old traditions. But they learned fast that loyalty to Hitler was the only thing that mattered. Those who questioned him were removed. Over time, Hitler took more control of the military. And as that happened, things started to fall apart on the battlefield.

Propaganda was another huge part of how the Nazis kept control. Goebbels, as head of propaganda, didn't just spread messages. He created an entire reality. His ministry changed how people saw the world through newspapers, radio, movies, and even school lessons. Everything was shaped to fit the story of a strong Germany fighting for survival and rebirth. People weren't just told what to think. They were shown a whole new way to see the world.

Even words were twisted. The Nazis used cold, official-sounding language to hide their crimes. "Resettlement" meant forcing people out. "Special treatment" meant killing. "Evacuation" often meant death. These words helped people look the other way. Bureaucrats and soldiers could tell themselves they were just doing paperwork, not taking part in mass murder.

Economically, the Nazis mixed big business with robbery. They didn't take over companies directly, but they worked closely with them. The government gave them contracts, rewards, and tied their success to Nazi goals. Many large firms, especially in steel, chemicals, and cars, made huge profits from war production and forced labor. The line between business and government disappeared, and so did the line between making money and helping commit crimes.

Inside Germany, things looked legal on the surface. Courts still ran, elections were held (but only one party was allowed), and laws were passed. But under that surface, the Gestapo kept everyone in line. Informants were everywhere. People lived in fear. You didn't need mass protests to scare people. You just needed a few brutal examples to keep the rest quiet.

One reason the Nazi system lasted so long was because people learned to separate their feelings. Many Germans managed to live what felt like normal lives while also being part of a terrifying regime. This wasn't an accident. It was built that way. People were told they were part of something historic and heroic. The trains to Auschwitz didn't need guards at every turn. They just needed drivers, schedulers, and office workers doing "their job."

This spread-out system of guilt meant everyone was involved, but no one felt fully responsible. That was part of the system's dark genius. It didn't need to watch every citizen. Once people bought into the Nazi story, the system kept going on its own.

And yet, behind all the speeches and uniforms, the Nazi regime was full of contradictions. Its leaders fought with each other. Its policies changed all the time. Its ideas didn't always make sense. But none of that mattered as long as people believed the illusion. As long as they thought Hitler had a plan, that the Reich would last forever, and that all the chaos was leading to something great.

But once the war started going badly for Germany, that illusion broke down. The system's flaws became obvious.

Bureaucracy collapsed. Power struggles got worse. Leaders turned on each other. And in its final moments, the truth came out: the Nazi system was never really about order. It was about power. Personal, total, and based on myth, not reality.

CHAPTER 10

THE FÜHRER AND THE MAESTRO: HITLER'S RELATIONSHIP WITH WAGNER

Adolf Hitler's connection with the music and ideas of the composer Richard Wagner went deeper than just enjoying beautiful music. It was personal, emotional, and tied closely to Hitler's political beliefs and vision for Germany. Wagner's operas, filled with myth, heroism, and strong nationalist messages, spoke directly to Hitler's heart and mind. They helped shape not just his taste in music, but also his view of the world and what he wanted the future of Germany to look like.

To really understand how much Wagner meant to Hitler, we have to look at three things:

- how Wagner's music impacted Hitler when he was young,
- what ideas Wagner believed in,
- and how the Nazi regime used Wagner's legacy to promote their own agenda.

The Influence of Wagner's Music on Hitler's Early Years:

Hitler first heard Richard Wagner's music when he was a teenager, long before he had any real political power. It was during this time, in his early years living in Vienna, that he attended a performance of Wagner's opera *Rienzi* at the Vienna State Opera. He later wrote about the experience in *Mein Kampf*, his autobiography mixed with political beliefs. That moment made a huge impact on him. He was entertained, yes, but was emotionally overwhelmed too.

In *Rienzi*, the main character, Cola di Rienzi, is a revolutionary who rises up from being a regular person to becoming a powerful leader who fights for the people. For young Hitler, this story felt personal. He saw himself in Rienzi, a man who wanted to rise from obscurity, lead a nation, and bring about a grand transformation. This opera became more than just a night out; it became a symbol of what Hitler wanted his own life to become.

Wagner's music itself also spoke to Hitler in a very emotional and dramatic way. His operas are full of large, powerful themes: heroes battling against odds, epic journeys, deep love, sacrifice, and destiny. The music is loud, bold, and emotional, with dramatic orchestration that makes the stories feel huge and important. For Hitler, this was a vision of greatness. Operas like *The Ring of the Nibelung*, *Parsifal*, and *Tristan and Isolde* became almost sacred to him. They seemed to tell stories about heroic struggle and triumph that mirrored his own beliefs about what Germany needed to go through.

And Wagner's stories weren't set in everyday life. They were based in German myths and legends, full of gods, warriors, and magical lands. These mythological elements made everything feel even more grand, and they gave Hitler the sense that Germany had a deep, noble past that needed to be restored. Wagner's work made it easy for Hitler to imagine himself as a character in a myth, a man chosen by fate to bring back Germany's lost greatness.

But it wasn't just the stories or the music that mattered to Hitler. He also connected with the deeper messages and ideas hidden within Wagner's operas. Wagner was more than a composer. He was a thinker. His works often carried philosophical meanings about race, culture, sacrifice, purity, and national identity. Hitler picked up on those messages. To him, Wagner's music seemed to express the same intensity and purpose he wanted to instill in the German people. It stirred something in him emotionally and reinforced the idea that Germany's destiny was something almost spiritual. Wagner's art, other than being a part of the cultural, became a tool of belief.

Ideological Convergence: Wagner's Nationalism and Anti-Semitism

Even though Richard Wagner is still considered one of the greatest composers in history, his legacy is deeply stained by his anti-Semitic views. He didn't just quietly dislike Jews, but was vocal and unapologetic about it. In his essay *Das Judenthum in der Musik* (which means "Jewishness in Music"), Wagner blamed Jewish musicians and intellectuals for what he believed was the decline of pure German art and culture. He said that Jews, because of their background and supposed lack of "true feeling," could never really understand or create genuine German music. These ideas were racist and meant to exclude Jewish people from having any role in cultural life.

For Hitler, reading Wagner's ideas was like finding someone who shared his views, and he put them into intellectual terms. Wagner gave Hitler a kind of "cultural reasoning" behind his own racism. It helped make his hateful ideas feel justified or supported by someone respected in the art world.

Now, it's important to say that Hitler didn't become anti-Semitic *because* of Wagner. He already had these beliefs. But Wagner's writing made it easier for Hitler to feel right about them. Wagner gave him something that sounded intelligent and respectable to back up his prejudice. In speeches and writings, Hitler often praised Wagner as a genius who had captured the soul of the German Volk (a word that meant not just people, but the true ethnic and spiritual identity of the nation).

Wagner's strong belief in German purity and in building a culture that was free from outside, especially Jewish influences, fit perfectly with the Nazi worldview. Hitler wanted to create a "pure" Germany, not just in terms of race, but in art, music, and society as a whole. And Wagner had already written about these ideas decades earlier. To Hitler, it was as if Wagner had predicted and supported the goals of the Nazi movement long before it existed.

Wagner also used mythology to tell stories about German identity, drawing from old legends and folklore. These stories were a way of creating a shared past, something that felt ancient, heroic, and deeply rooted in the German spirit. This matched Hitler's own goals exactly. He wanted to rule a country and also wanted to create a myth of rebirth, where the Nazis were seen as continuing the legacy of a great, ancient people. Wagner's operas helped provide that myth. His characters and stories were used to make the Nazis seem like part of something eternal and noble.

Bayreuth: The Cultural Heart of Nazi Ideology

One of the most important parts of Hitler's connection to Richard Wagner was also about the people around Wagner, especially the Wagner family. In particular, Winifred Wagner, who was married to Wagner's son Siegfried, played a big role. She became the head of the Bayreuth Festival, an annual event that celebrated Wagner's operas in the very town where he had lived and worked.

Winifred was more than just a festival organizer. She was a devoted supporter of Hitler. She admired him deeply, even before he came to full power, and she helped create a close bond between him and the Wagner family. Through her, Hitler gained access to Bayreuth's inner circle, and it became a place where he felt welcomed not only as a political leader but as someone who shared in Wagner's cultural vision.

Winifred gave Hitler gifts, personal stationery, and her unwavering support. She treated him as someone special, almost like a chosen one to carry on Wagner's legacy.

For Hitler, Bayreuth became much more than just a music festival. He treated it almost like a sacred site, a place where art, politics, and myth came together. He visited regularly and used the festival as a kind of stage to promote the Nazi cultural agenda. Only high-ranking Nazis and trusted guests were invited, turning Bayreuth into an elite event, where Wagner's work was seen as the ultimate symbol of Aryan pride and cultural superiority.

Hitler believed that Wagner's music and the values in his operas were the perfect expression of the Nazi spirit: strong, heroic, deeply rooted in Germanic myth and racial identity. With Winifred Wagner's help, he made sure that Wagner's legacy became tied directly to the image of the Nazi regime. In Nazi Germany, Wagner wasn't just a composer anymore. His work had become part of the official identity of the state.

Wagner in Nazi Propaganda and the War Effort:

Once Hitler was in power, Wagner's music became a major tool for propaganda. The Nazis used it everywhere: at public rallies, in films, during speeches, and in grand parades. The music helped stir up emotions, create a sense of unity, and make the Nazi movement feel powerful and historic. It was part of the messaging. Wagner's operas gave the Nazis a dramatic, heroic soundtrack for their story.

One opera in particular, *Die Meistersinger von Nürnberg*, was heavily promoted. Its themes of German cultural pride and the celebration of "true" German art made it a favorite. The Nazis used it as a kind of cultural anthem, proof that Germany had a rich artistic tradition that needed to be preserved and purified. Another opera, *Götterdämmerung* (the last part of *The Ring Cycle*), became a symbol of the Nazi dream of rebirth, and, later, of its downfall. It reflected the idea of a great nation falling in flames, yet somehow, remaining noble and meaningful during its destruction.

Wagner's music was even used during World War II in ways that are now seen as deeply disturbing. The Nazis played it during military campaigns, and even in concentration camps, where prisoners were forced to hear it. The goal was to control emotions. To intimidate, confuse, or manipulate. The beauty and intensity of the music were twisted into tools of fear and oppression. This chilling use of art shows how far the regime went to link Wagner's music with its violent and totalitarian rule.

But Wagner's music was also something very personal for Hitler. He often turned to Wagner's operas during hard times. When things started going badly in the war, Hitler retreated more and more into music, especially Wagner's. He would listen for hours, sometimes alone, trying to find comfort in the powerful emotions and the idealistic, mythical world the operas portrayed. It was his escape from a reality where his vision of domination was falling apart.

In those final years, as Germany collapsed around him, Wagner's music became like a personal refuge, a way for Hitler to shut out the defeat and pretend, for a little while, that the dream was still alive.

Hitler had a deep obsession with the music of Richard Wagner. He admired Wagner so much that he saw him not just as a brilliant composer, but almost like a guiding light for his own vision of the world. But here's where things get strange: Wagner's music and ideas weren't meant to support hate or violence. In fact, the way Hitler used Wagner's legacy is full of contradictions.

Wagner was a groundbreaking artist who changed the way people thought about opera. His works were full of powerful music, big emotions, and rich stories. But they were never meant to be used as a political weapon, let alone tied to something as horrific as genocide. Still, Hitler clung to Wagner's name and reputation, using it to give his own beliefs a sense of cultural and historical weight.

To make things even more complicated, the Wagner family later became openly supportive of the Nazi regime. They welcomed Hitler into their circle, and that connection has left a lasting stain on Wagner's legacy. It raises tough questions: Can we truly separate an artist's work from the ideologies it gets tied to? Especially when the artist himself wasn't alive to defend or explain it?

And here's something that people often overlook: not all of Wagner's operas actually align with Nazi values. Take *Parsifal*, for instance. It's a story that centers on kindness, forgiveness, and spiritual healing. These ideas are completely at odds with the violence, cruelty, and hatred that the Nazis stood for. Another example is *Tristan und Isolde*, which is all about love, longing, and the emotional struggles of being human. Not power, conquest, or racial purity.

So, how did Hitler justify his obsession? The truth is, he cherry-picked what he wanted from Wagner's work. He ignored the parts that didn't fit his vision and focused only on what he could manipulate to serve his message. He wasn't appreciating Wagner as an artist in full, but was using bits and pieces of his music and stories to make Nazism seem more noble or culturally rooted.

In the end, Hitler's use of Wagner tells us a lot about how he operated. He didn't just try to take over land or people. He tried to take over culture, too. And in doing so, he turned something beautiful and complex into a tool for something ugly and destructive.

Conclusion: Wagner's Enduring Legacy Beyond Hitler

Wagner was a brilliant composer whose operas changed the world of music forever. His works are still celebrated for their beauty and depth. But because Hitler loved Wagner so much, and used his music to support the Nazi vision, there's now a dark cloud hanging over Wagner's name.

After World War II ended and the Nazi regime was crushed, Wagner's music became controversial, especially in places like Germany and Israel. In Israel, performances of his work were never officially banned, but they were strongly discouraged because of how deeply his music had become linked to the horrors of the Holocaust.

Still, it's important to understand something: Wagner was long gone before Hitler came to power. His music had nothing to do with the Nazis when it was written. The real tragedy is how Hitler took something beautiful, Wagner's art, and used it to serve his hateful ideology. This story is a powerful example of how art can be misused when it falls into the wrong hands.

When we look at why Hitler was so drawn to Wagner, we start to see just how dangerous myths and music can become when they're turned into propaganda. Hitler believed Wagner's operas expressed the kind of heroic, almost godlike vision he had for Germany. He saw himself as the central figure in a similar myth, a savior of his people. But Wagner's music, full of emotion and drama, was never meant to justify violence or genocide.

Even today, Wagner's legacy is complicated. His music continues to inspire composers and opera lovers all over the world. But at the same time, we can't ignore how it was once used to support one of the darkest chapters in human history. That's why we need to look at this history closely, not just to understand the past, but to learn how easily culture can be turned into a weapon when used by those chasing power.

As the Nazi empire collapsed, the huge myth that had held it together began to fall apart too. For over a decade, Hitler and his followers had wrapped Germany in a powerful story: one about greatness, strength, destiny, and rebirth. They promised a "thousand-year empire," a nation reborn. But by 1945, that dream had turned into a nightmare.

By the spring of that year, what was once a vast empire was reduced to broken pieces. The mighty Third Reich was now just scattered troops, a crumbling Berlin, and a damp underground bunker beneath the Reich Chancellery. That bunker, claustrophobic, dimly lit, and full of fear, wasn't just where Hitler hid from the world. It became the tomb of everything he had promised.

Inside the Führerbunker, things were surreal. Outside, Soviet artillery thundered as the Red Army closed in. Inside,

Hitler's closest allies tried to act like everything was still under control, clinging to their myth of victory. But behind closed doors, that control was slipping fast. People argued, trust broke down, some planned escape, and others quietly prepared for death.

Hitler himself seemed to lose touch with reality. Once known for powerful speeches that stirred crowds, he now ranted to the walls, angry, paranoid, and convinced that betrayal, not defeat, had ruined his plans. He lashed out at everyone: his generals, the German people, even fate. He reportedly said, "The German people are not worthy of me," showing just how deeply he believed in his own myth. He didn't see the people as citizens but as tools for his vision. And when they failed him, they no longer mattered.

This final stage wasn't just the end of a government. It was the collapse of a fantasy that had controlled millions. The grand speeches and the promises of glory gave way to fear, confusion, and despair.

Above ground, Berlin had turned into something almost out of a nightmare. People were starving, buildings were rubble, and young boys were sent to fight tanks with nothing but grenades. Hospitals overflowed. Communication systems failed. The government fell apart. Men who once wore proud SS uniforms ran away dressed like civilians. They burned documents and abandoned plans. The so-called "empire of order" had become a kingdom of chaos.

And yet, even in the middle of this complete collapse, the Nazis kept acting out the rituals of power. They handed out medals, promoted officers, and even held a wedding. Eva Braun, who had been by Hitler's side for years, finally married him, just hours before they both took their lives. It was like a twisted play, a final scene in the theater of lies that had defined the Nazi regime.

There was something strangely theatrical about it all. Almost like a Wagner opera. Grand, tragic, and doomed. In fact, Hitler had always been inspired by Wagner's stories of heroic downfall and destruction. And in his final days, life imitated that myth. Rather than surrender, negotiate, or face justice, Hitler chose to burn with his dream, like a fallen god consumed by the fire of his own prophecy.

On April 30, 1945, Hitler and Eva Braun ended their lives. But their suicide wasn't a peaceful exit. It was an attempt to control the ending, to avoid capture, and to remain larger-than-life even in death. Their bodies were burned with gasoline. It was meant to erase them from judgment and history.

But history doesn't forget that easily.

Just days later, Allied forces began to uncover the truth about what the Nazi regime had really done. They opened the gates to concentration camps. Survivors gave testimony. Photos were taken. Documents were found. The full horror of the Holocaust came into the light. It wasn't exaggeration. It was real. The myth of noble German destiny crumbled beneath the weight of mass graves and the machinery of death.

The suicide in the bunker marked the death of Hitler and also of a lie so big, so deeply believed, that its fall shook the entire world. Millions had followed this dream. They had fought, killed, and died for it. And now it was clear: it had all been based on hate, delusion, and cruelty.

But even as the Reich disappeared, its shadow didn't. Some Nazis escaped, helped by sympathizers or by the chaos of the Cold War. Others quietly blended into new lives in other countries or even postwar governments. The myth didn't die completely. It lingered in secret conversations, hidden symbols, and new movements that carried the same poison.

And that's the frightening part.

Because it shows us that when a regime ends, its ideas don't necessarily die with it. Ideas can hide, change shape, and wait. The story of Nazi Germany isn't just a history lesson. It's a warning. A warning that totalitarianism doesn't always collapse overnight. It unravels slowly. It turns into ritual, theater, myth, and then vanishes into something harder to fight: memory and nostalgia.

That's why understanding these final days is so important. We can't just study them; we have to learn from them. What began with hope and promises ended in ashes and despair. What claimed to uplift a nation ended up destroying it. And what was sold as salvation turned out to be a lie so massive that it still echoes today.

CHAPTER 11

HITLER'S INTELLECTUAL AND HISTORICAL INSPIRATIONS: NIETZSCHE, GRANT, FREDERICK THE GREAT, AND NAPOLEON

Adolf Hitler's vision for Nazi Germany, the so-called "Third Reich," didn't come out of nowhere. It was shaped by a mix of philosophy, racial theories, and military history. But instead of understanding these ideas clearly or honestly, Hitler picked out certain parts that matched what he already believed and ignored the rest. He changed the meanings of the words and ideas of people like Friedrich Nietzsche, Madison Grant, Frederick the Great, and Napoleon Bonaparte to fit into his own worldview. Even when his understanding was shallow or completely wrong, he used these figures to make his plans for war and mass killing seem more credible.

Friedrich Nietzsche: The Philosopher of Power

Friedrich Nietzsche (1844–1900) was one of the most complex and misunderstood philosophers of modern times, and Hitler's take on him is one of the most extreme examples of that confusion. Nietzsche's books, such as *Thus Spoke Zarathustra, Beyond Good and Evil,* and *The Will to Power,* were filled with bold ideas, poetic language, and deep challenges to how society thought about good and evil. They were never easy to interpret, even for scholars. But Hitler, and later the Nazi state, took pieces of Nietzsche's writings out of context and changed them to fit their own nationalism and authoritarian beliefs.

One of the ideas Hitler grabbed onto was Nietzsche's concept of the Übermensch, or "Overman" (sometimes translated as "Superman"). In Nietzsche's original writing, the Übermensch wasn't about a race of people being better than others. It was a symbol of an individual who rises above traditional moral rules and lives by his own values. Someone who dares to question society, religion, and herd thinking. Nietzsche imagined this figure as someone who created new meaning in a world where old beliefs were falling apart.

But Hitler didn't see it that way. He turned the idea of the Übermensch into something racial. To him, it meant the dominance of a so-called "master race," the Aryans. He used Nietzsche's idea as a way to justify treating other races as inferior, which completely ignored what Nietzsche actually stood for. Nietzsche was not a nationalist, and he strongly criticized anti-Semitism. In fact, he once broke off a friendship because his friend had become anti-Semitic. Hitler chose to ignore this.

Part of the problem was that Hitler read versions of Nietzsche's work that had already been altered. After Nietzsche's death, his sister Elisabeth Förster-Nietzsche, who supported anti-Semitic and nationalist views, took over his estate and edited his writings to make them seem more in line with her own politics. She even promoted Nietzsche as a kind of early supporter of fascist ideas, which he absolutely wasn't. These distorted versions of Nietzsche's work were the ones Hitler had access to.

Even so, Hitler and the Nazis went out of their way to present Nietzsche as a kind of "intellectual father" of their movement. They made sure his books were taught in schools and quoted in speeches. They staged events like public visits to the Nietzsche Archive in Weimar to show the world that Nazi ideology was backed by "deep" German philosophy. It was all part of an effort to make Nazism look smart and serious, to give it intellectual weight.

But if Nietzsche had been alive during Hitler's time, there's every reason to believe he would have rejected the Nazi system entirely. He hated nationalism. He considered anti-Semitism a sign of weakness and cowardice. And he believed people should rise above tribal thinking, not become more tied to it. The fact that Hitler claimed Nietzsche as a source of inspiration shows how dangerous it can be when powerful people misuse big ideas. It also shows how easily deep philosophy can be manipulated into tools of hate when taken out of context.

Madison Grant: The Architect of Scientific Racism

While Nietzsche's ideas were philosophical and often abstract, the ideas of Madison Grant (1865–1937) were very concrete, and deeply racist. Grant was an American lawyer, writer, and conservationist who became one of the most influential voices in the early 20th-century eugenics movement. His most well-known book, *The Passing of the Great Race* (1916), argued that the "Nordic race," which he believed included people from Northern Europe, was superior to all others and was in danger of disappearing due to immigration and racial mixing.

Hitler was deeply influenced by this book. In fact, he reportedly called it his "bible." While Grant's theories were already seen by many scientists of the time as flawed or outright wrong, Hitler embraced them completely. He believed that keeping the Aryan race "pure" was essential for the survival of Germany, and Grant's book gave him what seemed like scientific backing for those beliefs. It helped him justify extreme policies like forced sterilization, racial segregation, and eventually, mass murder.

Many of the ideas in *The Passing of the Great Race* were reflected in Nazi laws. For example, in the United States, Grant had supported laws that banned interracial marriage and allowed the sterilization of people with disabilities. Hitler admired these policies and copied them in Germany. The Nazis created programs to sterilize people they saw as unfit to reproduce: those with physical or mental disabilities, as well as Roma (Gypsies), Jews, and others. These actions were presented as ways to "improve" the German population, even though they were cruel, inhumane, and based on false science.

Grant also promoted the idea of Lebensraum, or "living space," although he didn't use that exact word. He believed that superior races needed more land to thrive and that they had a right to take it from "lesser" peoples. Hitler adopted this idea and made it central to his foreign policy. He believed that Germany had to expand eastward into countries like Poland and Russia to make room for the growing Aryan population. To him, it was about racial destiny.

Even though Grant focused mostly on America and the threats he saw there, Hitler took his theories even further. He turned them into a justification for world war and genocide. Where Grant had warned about racial decline, Hitler acted on it with violence. He used these ideas to explain why Germany needed to dominate Europe and why certain groups needed to be removed from society altogether.

This connection between Grant's eugenic theories and Hitler's real-world policies can be seen most clearly in the Nazi T4 Program. This was a secret campaign where the Nazis murdered tens of thousands of people with disabilities, calling it "mercy killing" or "euthanasia." But there was nothing merciful about it. It was part of a larger goal to "cleanse" the population and build a stronger race, just as Grant had recommended in his writing. The terrifying difference is that Hitler had the power, and the will, to carry those ideas out on a massive scale.

The story of how Hitler used Grant's work shows how dangerous it is when bad science meets hateful ideology. What starts as a book full of racist theories can become a blueprint for real-world horror when put in the hands of a dictator.

Frederick the Great: The Prussian Model of Leadership

One of the people Hitler looked up to the most wasn't a modern leader or politician. It was Frederick the Great, the 18th-century King of Prussia. To Hitler, Frederick was the perfect example of strong leadership. He saw him as a brilliant military commander, a strict ruler who kept things in order, and someone who brought power and pride back to Germany at a time when it was surrounded by enemies.

Hitler didn't just admire Frederick from a distance. He made his admiration public. He visited Frederick's tomb in Potsdam many times, almost as if he were visiting the grave of a national hero or even a spiritual guide. He called Frederick a kind of guiding light for Nazi Germany and used his story to inspire his own followers. During the early years of World War II, when things were still going well for Germany, Hitler often compared himself to Frederick. He reminded people how Frederick had managed to turn the small kingdom of Prussia into a major European power during the Seven Years' War, even though he had to fight against bigger, stronger countries. It was Hitler's way of saying, "Look, we've done this before, and we can do it again."

But, like with so many of the historical figures he admired, Hitler only saw what he wanted to see. Frederick wasn't just a war leader. He was also a man of ideas. He believed in Enlightenment values: things like reason, open thinking, religious tolerance, and reform. He allowed people of different faiths to live peacefully in his kingdom. He supported freedom of thought, improved education, and worked to modernize his government. These were things that went completely against Hitler's Nazi beliefs. Hitler didn't care about tolerance or freedom. He controlled ideas, banned books, and punished anyone who disagreed with him.

Even the way they handled war was different. Frederick was known for being smart and flexible on the battlefield. He was able to change his plans when needed and knew when to retreat to save his troops. Hitler, by contrast, became more and more stubborn as the war went on. He made decisions based on pride and ideology instead of strategy. A good example of this was the Battle of Stalingrad. The German army was surrounded and running out of supplies, and his generals begged him to let them pull back. But Hitler refused. He thought retreat was a sign of weakness. That decision led to one of the worst defeats of the war and cost thousands of German lives.

Still, even when things were falling apart, Hitler clung to the idea that he was following in Frederick's footsteps. In 1945, just before the fall of Berlin, he had a portrait of Frederick brought into his underground bunker. It was a symbolic gesture and his way of showing that he still believed he could turn things around, just like Frederick had. But unlike Frederick, Hitler wasn't facing reality. He wasn't planning clever comebacks. He was losing control.

So while Hitler liked to present himself as the "new Frederick the Great," the truth was very different. He had misunderstood Frederick's legacy, ignored the parts that didn't fit his agenda, and used him more as a propaganda tool than as a real role model. In the end, where Frederick had used reason and adaptation to survive and succeed, Hitler used blind ambition and fantasy, and it led to total destruction.

Napoleon Bonaparte: The Ambition of Empire

Another major figure in history that fascinated Hitler was Napoleon Bonaparte, the famous French general and emperor. Like Frederick, Napoleon wasn't just a military genius. He was someone who reshaped Europe. And like Hitler, he rose from humble beginnings and climbed his way to absolute power. Hitler saw himself in Napoleon. He thought they were both men of destiny.

Hitler especially admired how Napoleon had built a massive empire across Europe through quick and decisive military action. He was amazed by how Napoleon turned post-revolutionary France into a powerful and organized force that could take on the older, more traditional European powers. Hitler tried to do the same with Germany: take a broken country and turn it into a dominating empire. He admired how Napoleon brought law and order to France and unified a divided country under his leadership.

But Hitler also studied Napoleon's mistakes, and yet he still repeated them. The biggest of these was invading Russia. In 1812, Napoleon led a huge army into Russia, thinking he could conquer it quickly. Instead, he ran into bitter cold, long supply lines, and fierce resistance. His army was eventually forced to retreat, and most of his soldiers died. Hitler read about this and understood the risk. But in 1941, he did the exact same thing. He launched Operation Barbarossa, sending millions of German soldiers into the Soviet Union, convinced they would win before winter. He underestimated the Russian resistance and the weather, and just like Napoleon, it turned into a disaster that crippled his army and helped seal his fate.

There were other big differences too. Napoleon, for all his ambition, also left behind real reforms. He created the Napoleonic Code, a set of laws that helped shape legal systems across Europe. He improved administration, education, and infrastructure. He wanted to modernize and organize the countries he controlled. Hitler, on the other hand, wasn't interested in building lasting institutions. His focus was on racial ideology, war, and wiping out entire groups of people. He didn't leave behind reforms but destruction.

In truth, Hitler didn't deeply understand these historical figures. He didn't try to learn from them in a meaningful way. He just picked the parts of their stories that made him feel powerful or important and ignored everything else. He wasn't really following in their footsteps. He was just using their images to make himself look grand.

The Myth of Hitlerism: How a Man Became More Than a Man

What gave Hitler so much power wasn't just politics or laws. It was myth. The Nazi movement was more than merely passing rules or running a country. It was about telling a story. A story that made people believe they were part of something huge and meaningful. In this story, Hitler wasn't just a leader. He was painted as a savior, someone chosen by fate to bring Germany back from the edge.

And like all powerful myths, this one wasn't based on facts. It was built on emotion, symbols, and belief. It connected with people on a deep, almost spiritual level. Germany had gone through hard times after World War I: losing the war, facing the harsh terms of the Treaty of Versailles, and struggling through poverty and shame. The Nazi myth took all of that real pain and turned it into a story about betrayal and redemption. It said: "Germany didn't just lose. It was stabbed in the back. But now, we will rise again."

And in this story, Hitler was the one who would lead that rise. His life was retold like a hero's journey. He had been poor, he had served as a soldier, gone to prison, written a book (Mein Kampf), and returned stronger than ever. Every step in his life was reimagined as something important and meaningful, like he was destined for greatness. People said that when he spoke, it felt like he understood their pain, their fears, and their dreams. His speeches were dramatic and emotional, less like political talks and more like performances that stirred the soul.

Nazi rallies, especially the huge ones in Nuremberg, weren't just political gatherings. They were like religious ceremonies. Imagine thousands of people standing in perfect rows, holding banners and torches, with music playing and speeches timed like theater. These weren't just shows of strength, yes, but more than that, it was designed to make people feel part of something sacred, something bigger than themselves. Hitler was offering a kind of belonging.

And symbols played a huge part in this myth. The swastika, for example, was originally an ancient symbol used in Indian and Indo-European cultures. But the Nazis gave it a new meaning. To them, it became the sign of the "Aryan soul," a symbol of power, rebirth, and destiny. They used it everywhere, in flags, uniforms, posters, until it felt timeless and all-powerful.

Even the land of Germany, its forests, rivers, and old buildings, was given spiritual meaning. It was no longer just geography; it was turned into holy ground, proof of an ancient, noble past. And when German soldiers died, their blood was mourned and *glorified.* They were treated as martyrs, heroes whose deaths had made the nation stronger.

But maybe the most frightening part of this myth was how it made hatred seem noble. In Nazi ideology, Jews weren't seen as people with different beliefs or backgrounds. They were turned into a threat to everything sacred. Blamed for Germany's pain, corruption, and weakness. This wasn't just racism. It was made to feel like a spiritual war. And because of that, the murder of Jews wasn't presented as evil. It was called necessary; seen as cleansing, not genocide.

And Hitler himself? He became the center of the entire myth. His face was everywhere: in schools, homes, government buildings. People treated his voice, his words, even his posture like they were sacred.

This is what made Hitlerism so dangerous. It didn't try to win people over with logic. It didn't rely on facts. It worked through feelings. It told a story that felt right, even if it wasn't true. And it was powerful. Hitler once said that people are more likely to believe a big lie than a small one. And he was right. The bigger the story, the more it could explain. Myths work that way. They don't need to be true. They just need to make sense emotionally.

Even after Nazi Germany fell, the myth didn't completely die. It changed shape. Neo-Nazis, white supremacists, and other fringe groups still use the symbols, the slogans, and the fantasies of Hitlerism: not because they truly believe the original history, but because they still feel the emotional power of the story. In the darker corners of the internet, people still talk about "Aryan blood" and "spiritual war." Some even worship Hitler as a kind of god or warrior-king.

And even in mainstream culture, the way Hitler is shown, as either a genius or a monster, can make him feel larger than life. But that, too, feeds the myth. It makes him seem not fully human. And that's dangerous.

So what can we do? We need to break the myth. Not just say "Nazism is wrong," but look at the story behind it and take it apart. We need to stop treating its symbols like they have magic. We need to challenge the emotions that fuel it.

And most importantly, we need to remember: Hitler was not a god, not a savior, not a symbol. *HE WAS A MAN.* A deeply broken and dangerous man. And when we forget that, the myth wins.

Because Hitlerism isn't just about one man or one moment in history. It's a pattern. A pattern where pain becomes anger, anger becomes identity, and identity turns into violence. Myths can help people find meaning, but some myths are built on hate, and when they demand blood, they must be destroyed.

CHAPTER 12

THE EARLY YEARS: CAUTIOUS OBSERVATIONS (1920–1933)

The relationship between Adolf Hitler and Joseph Stalin didn't begin with open conflict or direct communication. It started quietly through distant awareness. Both men were rising to power in their own countries, and each knew the other existed, but they didn't engage with one another right away. Instead, they were like two storm clouds forming on opposite sides of the continent, watching the skies but focused on their own paths.

In the early 1920s, Hitler was beginning to make a name for himself in Germany as the head of the National Socialist German Workers' Party, more commonly known as the Nazi Party. Even in these early years, he stood out because of how openly and aggressively he spread his beliefs. He was deeply anti-Semitic, blaming Jewish people for many of Germany's problems. He was a passionate nationalist, obsessed with the idea of reviving German pride and power after the humiliating loss of World War I. And, perhaps most importantly, in terms of Stalin, Hitler was ferociously anti-communist. He saw communism not just as a political opponent but as a dangerous, even poisonous, ideology that had to be destroyed. He often linked communism with Jews in his speeches and writings, painting both as enemies of Germany's future.

Meanwhile, in the Soviet Union, Stalin was working his way into the highest position of power following the death of Vladimir Lenin. By the mid-1920s, he had succeeded in becoming the undisputed leader of the Communist Party. But Stalin's rise was not just about stepping into Lenin's shoes. It involved a long and ruthless struggle within the party. He systematically eliminated rivals, secured loyalty from key figures, and built a political machine that revolved entirely around him. His focus during these years was not international politics but power: consolidating it, expanding it, and making sure no one could take it from him.

Stalin's view of Hitler in these early days was cautious but not panicked. He watched Germany from a distance, keeping track of what was going on, but he didn't see Hitler as an urgent concern. Germany itself was in deep trouble. After losing World War I, it was weighed down by the harsh terms of the Treaty of Versailles: crippling reparations, economic instability, and a shaky democratic government known as the Weimar Republic. From Stalin's point of view, Germany was in no shape to pose a threat, and Hitler seemed like just one more loud, angry figure trying to take advantage of the chaos. Fascism was spreading across parts of Europe, but it hadn't yet become a force that demanded immediate attention.

In Stalin's mind, what mattered most at this stage wasn't external threats: it was the transformation happening inside the Soviet Union. He was leading the country through massive changes: the forced collectivization of agriculture, where millions of peasants were pushed into state-run farms, and the implementation of the first Five-Year Plan, which aimed to rapidly industrialize the nation. These changes were supposedly to modernize the USSR and make it a global superpower, but they came at a brutal cost. Widespread famine, mass arrests, and violent suppression of dissent became part of daily life. Stalin believed that for communism to survive and succeed, he had to crush all internal resistance first. Foreign threats, including Hitler, were a lower priority for now.

So when Hitler tried to stage a coup in Munich in 1923, a failed attempt known as the Beer Hall Putsch, Stalin didn't see it as particularly alarming. Hitler's coup ended in disaster, and he was arrested and sentenced to prison. From

Stalin's point of view, this showed just how weak and fringe Hitler's movement really was. It likely confirmed Stalin's belief that Hitler was more of a symbol of unrest than a serious political force. At this stage, there was no reason to see Hitler's Nazi ideology as anything more than background noise in the larger European landscape.

The Gathering Storm: Antagonism and Tactical Engagement (1933–1939)

Things changed dramatically in 1933. That year, Hitler was appointed Chancellor of Germany. Suddenly, the man who had once been viewed as a fringe radical was now in charge of one of Europe's most powerful countries. For Stalin, this was a turning point. Hitler was no longer just a voice shouting from the sidelines. He was now in a position to act on his ideas. And those ideas directly threatened everything the Soviet Union stood for.

Stalin couldn't afford to ignore the danger anymore. Even if he had once kept his distance from Hitler's rise, the Nazis open hostility toward communism made it impossible to stay indifferent. Hitler's hatred of communism was the core of his entire political vision. In his book *Mein Kampf*, written while he was in prison after the failed coup, Hitler laid out his belief in "Lebensraum," or "living space." He argued that Germany needed to expand eastward to grow, and he saw the Soviet Union as the place to do it. This wasn't just about geography; it was about destroying Soviet communism and claiming the land and resources of the East for the German people.

In other words, if Hitler got his way, a war with Stalin's USSR was not just possible: it was inevitable. And yet, Stalin didn't jump into a fight. His reaction was more measured, even reserved. That's partly because the Soviet Union, at that time, was still struggling with deep internal problems. The economy was unstable, political fear was everywhere, and the military was being torn apart by Stalin's own hand. In the late 1930s, Stalin carried out massive purges: arresting, exiling, or executing anyone he saw as a threat, including many top officers in the Red Army. These purges weakened the Soviet military just as the Nazi threat was becoming real. So Stalin knew that the USSR wasn't ready for a full-scale conflict.

Instead of confrontation, Stalin adopted a strategy of patience. He continued to monitor Hitler's moves carefully but avoided provoking him. At the same time, Stalin's government began reaching out to Nazi Germany in more practical ways. Not because they shared any values but because there were things both sides could gain.

Throughout the 1930s, the Soviet Union and Nazi Germany started cooperating quietly, especially in areas like trade and military development. These agreements were based on cold, strategic calculations. For example, Germany was secretly allowed to test weapons and military tactics on Soviet soil. It was something it couldn't do openly because of restrictions from the Treaty of Versailles. In return, the Soviets gained access to modern German military technology and knowledge.

This behind-the-scenes cooperation wasn't based on trust. Stalin despised Hitler's ideology, and Hitler considered the USSR his enemy. But both were willing to look past their hatred temporarily if it meant strengthening their own positions. Stalin, always the pragmatist, saw these deals as a way to buy time, learn from Germany's strengths, and keep the USSR secure while he continued rebuilding and controlling his empire.

So even as tensions in Europe grew and Hitler made his intentions increasingly clear, Stalin's approach was one of strategic engagement: watching, waiting, and preparing for the storm that everyone knew was coming.

The Devil's Bargain: The Nazi-Soviet Pact (1939–1941)

By the time the late 1930s rolled around, Stalin's opinion of Hitler had changed quite a bit. At first, he had underestimated just how extreme and dangerous Hitler's ambitions really were. Stalin was willing to keep things practical. He thought that maybe, even if they didn't like each other, they could still find ways to benefit from each other. But as Nazi Germany started swallowing up more and more land in Europe, Stalin grew uneasy. Hitler was now taking action, and his moves were getting bolder.

Then, in 1939, Hitler invaded Czechoslovakia. This was a turning point. Stalin could no longer pretend that Hitler was just another ambitious leader. He saw clearly now that Hitler was unpredictable, ruthless, and determined to expand German power no matter what. Still, instead of preparing for war, Stalin made a surprising and deeply controversial choice. In a move that shocked the world, he agreed to work with Hitler. That agreement came to be known as the **Molotov-Ribbentrop Pact**, a deal that would be remembered as one of the most cynical, cold-blooded diplomatic moves in modern history.

Signed on August 23, 1939, the Molotov-Ribbentrop Pact was presented publicly as a simple non-aggression agreement. It meant that Nazi Germany and the Soviet Union promised not to attack each other. But behind closed doors, it was much more than that. The pact included a secret protocol, an agreement that divided Eastern Europe between the two powers. Poland, for example, was split into two parts, with one half going to Germany and the other to the Soviet Union. Other parts of the region, like the Baltic States (Estonia, Latvia, and Lithuania), were also carved up and assigned to Stalin.

To outsiders, especially those who believed in Stalin's anti-fascist promises, the pact felt like a betrayal. Stalin had spent years condemning fascism and claiming to stand for the global fight against it. But here he was, shaking hands with the very symbol of fascism: Adolf Hitler.

Why would he do that?

Stalin's reasons were complicated. For one, he knew the Soviet Union wasn't ready for a war against Germany. The

Red Army was still recovering from the purges, and the country needed more time to prepare. So, the pact was a way to buy time. It was a temporary safety net. Second, Stalin saw a chance to expand Soviet territory without having to go to war. The deal gave him control over parts of Eastern Europe, which he had long wanted. Third, and perhaps most importantly, Stalin believed he could outsmart Hitler. He thought that by cooperating for now, he could protect the USSR and, eventually, turn the situation to his advantage.

But the pact came at a heavy cost. It shattered any hope of building a united international front against fascism. Britain and France, who had been trying to contain Hitler, were stunned. Many people around the world couldn't believe what Stalin had done. Two of the most powerful men in Europe, sworn enemies in ideology, were now political partners, using each other for their own gain. Stalin and Hitler weren't friends. But for a brief time, they were collaborators, each trying to outplay the other while pretending to cooperate.

Betrayal and Survival: Operation Barbarossa (1941–1942)

That fragile alliance didn't last long.

On June 22, 1941, Hitler launched Operation Barbarossa, a massive surprise invasion of the Soviet Union. For Stalin, it was a devastating betrayal. He had believed that the Molotov-Ribbentrop Pact would protect the USSR, at least for a while. But Hitler had never truly meant to keep the peace. His goal had always been to destroy communism and conquer the East, and now he was making his move.

When the German tanks rolled across the Soviet border, Stalin was completely caught off guard. Despite warnings from spies and foreign governments, he refused to believe that Hitler would attack. When it happened, the shock was so deep that Stalin disappeared from public view for several days. He reportedly locked himself away, too stunned to speak or lead. This hesitation, this moment of paralysis, was one of Stalin's greatest missteps. In a country where leadership meant everything, his silence created confusion and fear, and it gave the Nazis time to advance quickly.

Hitler's army made terrifying progress at first. They captured huge stretches of land and killed or captured hundreds of thousands of Soviet troops. But Hitler had made a grave mistake. He underestimated the size of the Soviet Union, the fierceness of its people, and the punishing power of the Russian winter. As his forces pushed deeper, the war became harder and bloodier than he had imagined. The further they went, the more resistance they met.

For Stalin, everything changed. Any trace of hope or strategy that involved working with Hitler was gone. He now saw Hitler for what he truly was: a political enemy, yes, but more than that, a dangerous fanatic bent on destroying the entire Soviet system. This wasn't just a fight for land anymore but a fight for survival.

Stalin's leadership during this stage of the war was a mix of harsh control and national rallying. He ruled with an iron fist, but he also knew how to stir the hearts of the people when it mattered most. One of his most famous orders came during the darkest days of the war: "Not one step back!" It may sound like a mere slogan, but it was a command to stand and fight no matter what. This became a powerful cry for unity and resistance, pushing soldiers and civilians alike to hold their ground.

From that point on, Stalin's hatred for Hitler became personal and absolute. There was no more calculation, no more diplomacy. It was now a war of total resistance. Stalin was fully committed to crushing Hitler, no matter the cost.

The Relentless Counteroffensive: The Turning Tide (1943–1945)

As World War II went on, Stalin began to see Hitler differently. At first, Hitler had seemed like a strong and unstoppable enemy. But by the middle of the war, Stalin saw him as someone stuck in a battle that was slowly draining him. This kind of war, called a war of attrition, wears both sides down. But Stalin believed that Hitler and his army couldn't last forever.

Then came a huge turning point: the Battle of Stalingrad in 1942. Hitler was determined to capture the city: not just because it was important strategically, but because it was named after Stalin. Taking it would've been a big blow to Soviet pride. But things didn't go as Hitler planned. The Soviets fought fiercely. The German army was pushed into a terrible situation. Winter came in full force, temperatures dropped below freezing, and supplies ran out. Surrounded by Soviet troops, the Germans were forced to surrender.

For Stalin, this was a moment he had been waiting for. The victory at Stalingrad was a symbol that the Nazis could be stopped. It gave the Soviet people hope and gave Stalin the confidence to go on the offensive.

By 1943, the Soviet Union had taken back much of its territory. Stalin was in a stronger position, and he became even more focused on one goal: defeating Nazi Germany completely. For him, this wasn't just about reclaiming land. It was about justice, revenge, and protecting the future of the Soviet Union. After all the suffering caused by the Nazis, he wanted to make sure they were completely destroyed.

So, the Red Army began its massive counterattack. And it wasn't just a small push: it was a full-force campaign to drive the Germans out of Eastern Europe. Bit by bit, town by town, the Soviet forces moved forward. The fighting was intense and brutal, but they didn't let up. Their mission was clear: reach Berlin and finish what the Germans had started.

Stalin also closely watched how Hitler handled things. He noticed that Hitler refused to face the reality of the situation. Instead of pulling back when it made sense, Hitler insisted on holding every inch of land the Germans had taken. Even when it meant huge losses, he refused to retreat. Stalin saw this as a major weakness.

While Stalin could be harsh and ruthless, he was also practical. He was willing to lose battles if it meant winning the war. He didn't cling to pride or empty victories. He wanted results. However, Hitler's decisions were guided by ideology and stubbornness. He believed giving up land was a sign of weakness, even if it cost thousands of lives. In a way, Stalin used that to his advantage. Every time Hitler refused to adjust, it gave the Red Army another opening.

Stalin's Final Judgment: The Fall of Hitler (1945)

By 1945, the war was coming to an end, and things looked very different. Soviet troops were closing in on Berlin from the east, and the Allied forces were pushing in from the west. Hitler was losing ground fast, and he looked nothing like the confident leader he had once been. Stalin now saw him as desperate, isolated, and broken.

At this stage, Stalin had one big goal left: he wanted to capture Hitler alive. He believed it would be the ultimate symbol of victory. After all the destruction Hitler had caused, Stalin wanted him to be brought to justice. He imagined Hitler in a courtroom, facing the world and being held accountable for everything: the war, the deaths, the devastation. Stalin wanted to show that no dictator could escape responsibility.

But that moment never came. On April 30, 1945, as Soviet troops were surrounding Berlin, news came in: Hitler had taken his own life in his bunker. At first, Stalin didn't believe it. It was hard to imagine that someone who had caused so much destruction could just end it all in private. No trial. No justice. Just an escape through death.

Stalin's final thoughts on Hitler were filled with anger and disgust. In his eyes, Hitler wasn't just a military failure but a coward who had ruined his own country. Hitler had promised a powerful German empire, but in the end, he left behind only ruins and loss. Instead of standing up and facing the consequences, he chose to disappear.

For Stalin, this wasn't just the end of the war. It was personal. He had watched his people suffer, watched his cities burn, and now, the man who started it all was gone. Stalin felt like he had defeated the man who had caused some of the worst pain his country had ever known. That made the victory feel even more complete.

Conclusion: A Relationship Defined by Deception and Contempt

The relationship between Hitler and Stalin was anything but warm or straightforward. It was a complicated game of strategy, manipulation, and cold pragmatism, with each man using the other only as long as it suited their own goals. They weren't friends nor true allies. They were two ruthless leaders, each convinced of their own greatness, willing to play along until they no longer needed each other.

At first, Stalin kept a close eye on Hitler, watching him from a distance, unsure of his intentions. Stalin didn't trust easily, and he had every reason to be wary. Hitler, for his part, saw Stalin as a potential tool, someone to keep off his back while he focused on conquering the rest of Europe. Their early agreements, like the Nazi-Soviet Pact of 1939, weren't based on shared values. They were tactical, temporary arrangements designed to buy time and avoid direct conflict. But this fragile cooperation was doomed from the start. Deep down, they despised each other.

Eventually, that quiet tension turned into open hostility. Hitler broke the pact by launching Operation Barbarossa in 1941, invading the Soviet Union without warning. Stalin, caught off guard, was furious. From that moment on, their relationship became intensely personal. Stalin didn't just see Hitler as an enemy but as a reckless, arrogant man who had made a catastrophic mistake and was now speeding toward self-destruction.

When Hitler died in 1945, it marked the end of his horrific experiment: his attempt to reshape Europe through violence, fear, and genocide. Stalin, on the other hand, emerged from the war as a victor. The Soviet Union had paid a staggering price in blood and destruction, but it came out of the conflict as one of the two dominant superpowers alongside the United States. Stalin's triumph was political and symbolic. He had outlasted Hitler. But that victory also came with consequences. The world didn't find peace after World War II; instead, it entered a new kind of conflict: the Cold War: an ideological standoff between East and West that lasted for decades.

In the big picture, both Hitler and Stalin were men who used fear and force to shape the world as they saw fit. They ruled and tried to redesign entire societies around their beliefs. But the damage they caused was enormous. Their rivalry and the wars they waged left behind a legacy of destruction, suffering, and instability that echoed throughout the 20th century and beyond. Their story is a stark reminder of what can happen when power goes unchecked.

***

You would think that after all the horror Hitler caused, his name and image would quietly fade into history. But strangely, that hasn't happened. Hitler died but left behind a shadow that still hangs over the modern world. Unlike many other dictators who are remembered only in history books or museums, Hitler remains unsettlingly visible. He pops up in documentaries, movies, political debates, video games, protest signs, and even memes. His mustache alone is enough to conjure thoughts of dictatorship. His name still sparks outrage, fear, and sometimes even dangerous fascination.

This constant presence is a mixed bag. On the one hand, it helps keep people aware. It's like a flashing red warning light reminding us how bad things can get when hatred and authoritarianism take hold. But on the other side, seeing Hitler everywhere, especially in jokes or casual references, can start to wear down that sense of horror. When he becomes just a meme or a Halloween costume, the seriousness of his crimes, like the Holocaust, can begin to feel less real. And that's a big risk.

What makes Hitler so enduring in culture is that he has become the ultimate symbol of evil. He represents a kind of moral extreme that's easy to understand: the clear villain. In a world where so many things feel complicated or unclear, Hitler is a figure people can point to and say, "That was pure evil." In movies, books, and even casual conversation, he becomes the gold standard of wrongdoing: the person against whom all others are compared.

But that kind of simplification can be dangerous. It turns Hitler into a kind of myth, something larger than life, less like a real human being and more like a monster from legend. And when that happens, people forget that he wasn't supernatural. He wasn't a one-of-a-kind demon. He was a man who was elected, followed, supported, and empowered by millions of ordinary people. If we see him only as a freak exception, we miss the warning signs that could show up again.

And here's where things get especially disturbing: for some people today, Hitler's evil isn't a reason to avoid him. It's the reason they're drawn to him. In certain dark corners of the internet, he's not remembered as a historical villain but instead as a kind of rebellious figure. Among some extremist groups, especially neo-Nazis and radical accelerationists, Hitler becomes a symbol of total defiance. To them, his destruction and cruelty aren't failures. They're part of the appeal.

These people aren't studying history. They're fantasizing about destruction. They see Hitler as a kind of mythic figure who dared to go all the way. For people who feel isolated, angry, or hopeless, this image of Hitler offers something twisted: a fantasy of revenge, of cleansing the world, of burning everything down to start over.

And the internet has made this worse. In the digital world, especially on anonymous forums and fringe platforms, it's easy to find spaces where extremist ideas spread freely. People who start by posting "edgy" jokes or memes about Hitler can slowly find themselves slipping deeper into communities that take those ideas seriously. Irony fades. The jokes become beliefs. And eventually, the line between mocking Hitler and admiring him disappears.

Even on mainstream platforms like YouTube, TikTok, and Twitter, Hitler-related content gets shared all the time.

Sometimes, it's educational or critical, but other times, it's thinly disguised praise. The way this content is presented often makes it hard to tell what the message really is, and the more people see it, the more normal it starts to feel. This is how historical memory fades, not with some big dramatic event, but slowly, through repetition and half-laughs.

Outside the internet, Hitler's ideas still echo in the real world, especially in politics. While most modern authoritarian leaders don't mention Hitler directly, many use the same tactics he once did: blaming minorities, stirring up national pride through shame or fear, building their power through media control, and slowly weakening democratic systems.

Some political figures even flirt with the same language Hitler once used: talking about "purity," warning about cultural "decay," or pushing ideas about invasion and decline. These are not coincidences. They speak to the same emotions Hitler once manipulated: fear of change, a desire to return to some imagined glory, and the belief that violence or conflict might be the only way to restore order.

Ironically, many of these leaders will say, "Don't compare me to Hitler," as if that alone proves they're not dangerous.

But meanwhile, they hold massive rallies, attack the press, and scapegoat vulnerable groups. The idea is: "As long as I'm not as bad as Hitler, it's okay." That's a dangerous mindset. It lowers the bar for what we're willing to accept and allows cruelty to grow slowly under our noses.

This is why studying Hitler today matters. Not just to condemn him but to truly understand what made him possible and why his image still pulls people in. We need to ask hard questions: What makes people fascinated by him? What makes them sympathize with such hatred? And how can we make sure our societies don't fall into the same traps?

Education is key here, but it can't just be about memorizing dates or visiting museums. Young people need to be taught how to spot the early warning signs: rising hate speech, scapegoating, the breakdown of democratic norms, and the psychology behind mobs. We have to teach not just what Nazism was but what led to it and what kind of social and emotional conditions allowed it to grow.

We also need to think about how Hitler is shown in movies, books, and art. It's not about banning his image, but we do need to ask: how is he being portrayed? Is he shown as human or as superhuman? Are we meant to understand the damage he caused or just be dazzled by his rise and fall? These choices matter. They shape how future generations will see him.

Maybe the hardest part of all this is accepting that Hitler wasn't some supernatural monster. He was a human being: flawed, hateful, but human. That's uncomfortable to admit. Because if he was just a freak of nature, then we don't have to worry. It could never happen again. But if he was a product of real human choices, real systems, and real emotions, then we have to face the possibility that something like it could happen again under different circumstances.

That's why the challenge isn't to forget Hitler or hide his story. It's to understand it, live with it, and learn from it. We need to keep reminding ourselves what he did and why people followed him. And most importantly, we need to recognize that we, too, are capable of being swept up in dangerous ideas if we're not careful.

Hitler's image isn't going away. He's become part of the mental landscape of our time, a symbol of evil, trauma, and the dark pull of power. The question now is: how will we remember him? And what will we do with that memory?

Because the biggest danger is not just forgetting what he did.

It's thinking we could never do it ourselves.

250

CHAPTER 13

THE AMERICAN BLUEPRINT: HITLER'S ADMIRATION FOR ANDREW JACKSON AND THE RACIAL EMPIRE OF THE WEST

When Adolf Hitler was imagining what his perfect empire should look like, one built on racial "purity," he didn't just turn to European history for ideas. Strangely, he also looked across the ocean to the United States. One part of American history especially caught his attention: the country's westward expansion during the 1800s. And among the American leaders of that time, one man stood out to him: Andrew Jackson.

Jackson, who became the seventh president of the United States, was known for being both admired and hated. He was admired by some for being a strong leader, but also deeply criticized for the way he treated Native Americans. He pushed hard for their removal from their lands, believing white settlers had the right to take over. Jackson didn't try to hide it and openly supported the idea that white people should dominate the land. And to Hitler, this made him a role model. He saw in Jackson the kind of tough, unapologetic leadership needed to build an empire by force; an empire that removed anyone considered "undesirable" in the name of racial superiority.

But Hitler's interest in the American example was also about strategy. He believed the way Americans had expanded westward, pushing Native people off their land and claiming it for themselves, offered a kind of blueprint for what Germany could do in Eastern Europe. In his book *Mein Kampf*, Hitler even praised how the U.S. had, as he put it, "gunned down the millions of Red Indians to a few hundred thousand." He didn't see this as a tragedy. To him, it was proof that a country could justify mass violence if it claimed to be acting for a higher purpose, like the survival or growth of a so-called "superior" race.

Andrew Jackson, in particular, symbolized that idea. As both a general and president, he pushed for what was called *Manifest Destiny*, the belief that the U.S. had a divine right to expand westward. In 1830, Jackson signed the Indian Removal Act, which forced thousands of Native Americans off their land. This led to what became known as the *Trail of Tears*, where many died from hunger, disease, and exhaustion during forced relocations. Jackson's actions weren't seen by many Americans at the time as extreme or wrong; they were seen as fulfilling the country's destiny. His mix of strongman politics, racial views, and national pride set an example of how a leader could use democratic language to push deeply violent and authoritarian policies.

Hitler took all this in. He started to see Eastern Europe: places like Poland, Ukraine, and Russia: as Germany's own version of the American frontier. Just like Americans had believed the West was empty land meant for white civilization, Hitler believed Eastern Europe was the future "living space," or Lebensraum, for the German people. He used the same kind of logic American settlers had: for "us" to live and grow, "they" need to go. In both cases, it wasn't just about land: it was about the belief that one group had more right to exist and expand than another.

Even the methods were similar. In the U.S., the government had made treaties with Native tribes only to break them later. They used military force, starvation, forced marches, and relocation to destroy Indigenous nations. Hitler studied this. He planned to use a similar mix of lies, laws, and brutal violence to remove Slavic peoples and Jewish communities from the lands he wanted. His regime even created a plan called *Generalplan Ost*, a horrifying vision of clearing out huge areas of Eastern Europe through hunger, displacement, and mass killing. In some ways, it echoed what Jackson's policies had done in the U.S. a century earlier.

Hitler even went so far as to refer to Russia as Germany's future "Indian territory." To him, it was where the German empire would grow, once the people already living there were removed. Just like the U.S. had pushed Native Americans onto reservations or wiped them out, Hitler wanted to do the same in Eastern Europe, only on an even larger scale.

What really caught Hitler's attention about Andrew Jackson wasn't just that he took land through war or forced people out; it was the way Jackson saw the world. Jackson believed deeply in white dominance. He didn't shy away from it. He dismissed anyone who disagreed, glorified the idea of a tough, manly pioneer spirit, and claimed that even God supported his mission. To Hitler, this was familiar and personal. He saw himself the same way: as a man chosen by fate to lead his people to greatness, no matter the cost.

In Jackson, Hitler saw a powerful example of what he wanted to be: a leader who didn't ask for permission, who broke the rules when they got in the way, and who believed in using violence to build something "greater" for his people.

Jackson pushed forward even when the courts or political elites tried to stop him. To Hitler, that kind of defiance was strength. He believed that true leadership meant doing what needed to be done, even if it went against the law or public opinion. In his mind, that was the real "will of the people": strong, pure, and unafraid to crush weakness.

But this admiration for Jackson wasn't just a personal thing for Hitler. It became part of the bigger Nazi way of thinking. He encouraged his top officers, generals, and political thinkers to learn from what the U.S. had done during its westward expansion. He pointed to the American frontier as a model for how to conquer and settle new territory. In the U.S., settlers had been backed by the government, supported by militias, and allowed to take over Native land, even if that meant breaking laws or ignoring rights. And the government often found ways to make it all seem legal.

The Nazis copied this playbook. In the lands they invaded, especially in Eastern Europe, they planned to bring in German settlers to replace local communities they saw as racially "inferior." Just like in America, this was done with a mix of military power, propaganda, and law-bending. The Nazis used the SS to enforce their vision, while pretending it was all part of a noble mission to create order and spread civilization. In Hitler's eyes, what Jackson had done to Native Americans was exactly the kind of empire-building Germany needed to do in the East.

What makes all of this even more unsettling is what it reveals about the connection between American democracy and European fascism. We're often taught to see them as total opposites: America standing for freedom and rights, while Nazi Germany represented hate and dictatorship. But Hitler's admiration for Jackson blurs that line. Jackson wasn't a dictator. He was a democratically elected U.S. president. His face is still on the $20 bill. He's studied in American schools and is praised by some modern politicians for his populist style. And yet, Hitler saw him as a hero. That tells us something uncomfortable: when democracy is used to promote racism and conquest, it can start to look a lot like fascism.

Both Hitler and Jackson knew the power of storytelling. They built myths around themselves to connect with people emotionally. Jackson portrayed himself as a rugged war hero, a man of the people who fought against the elites and defended everyday Americans. Hitler did something very similar. He told the story of a poor soldier who rose from the trenches of World War I to lead his country out of humiliation. He wasn't just a politician; he claimed to be a kind of savior. These myths helped them bring people together, not through hope or inclusion, but through fear, anger, and the promise of greatness built on someone else's suffering. For Jackson, that unity came through whiteness. For Hitler, it came through the idea of a pure Aryan race.

One big thing that impressed Hitler about America was how it turned land grabs into a story about freedom. The U.S. had taken land from Native tribes and presented it as a victory for liberty and opportunity. Settlers weren't seen as invaders but pioneers, heroes. The Native people were painted as uncivilized obstacles standing in the way of progress. This idea really stuck with Hitler. He wanted to do the same thing in Eastern Europe. In his version, German settlers wouldn't be conquerors. They'd be brave pioneers bringing farming, order, and "civilization" to wild, disorganized lands. That's why Nazi propaganda portrayed Slavic people as primitive and Jewish people as harmful parasites. The goal was to make violence look like justice.

Hitler's admiration didn't stop at Jackson. He respected the entire American system of settler colonialism. Everything from forced marches to starvation, from taking land to building systems that kept races apart: it all showed him that these brutal strategies could actually work. What fascinated him most was how the U.S. had used legal tools: treaties, courts, and policies: to cover up the violence. Even when the U.S. broke its promises to Native tribes, it still managed to keep a public image of being lawful and just.

Hitler understood this trick well. He believed laws didn't have to stop power. They could be used to protect it. And in this, he once again followed Jackson's lead. Jackson had ignored court rulings that tried to protect Native American land. He believed the president's will was more important than any judge's opinion. Hitler agreed completely. In his view, laws existed not to protect people, but to help strong leaders get what they wanted while looking like they were playing by the rules.

One of the most unsettling parts of the connection between Hitler and Andrew Jackson shows up in how both dealt with the idea of genocide: even if they approached it differently. Jackson never used the word "genocide," but his actions led to the deaths and forced removal of tens of thousands of Native Americans. Hitler, on the other hand, made his genocidal plans very clear. But he took a disturbing lesson from American history: that a nation could commit mass violence and still present it as a necessary part of national growth. To him, the removal of entire peoples wasn't just possible. It could even be justified if it was seen as progress.

The term *Lebensraum*, or "living space," didn't come out of nowhere. Hitler used it to describe his dream of expanding eastward into places like Poland and Ukraine. But this idea had roots in global history: powerful countries had long been taking land from weaker people and calling it destiny. The U.S. did it in the 1800s, pushing westward and taking Native land in the name of freedom and development. Andrew Jackson was one of the boldest leaders behind that push, and to Hitler, that gave his own vision a kind of historical approval. If America could do it and become stronger, why couldn't Germany?

Hitler's admiration for America: and Jackson: also showed in what he read. He was a big fan of Karl May, a German writer who told dramatic cowboy-and-Indian stories set in the American West. These tales painted white settlers as brave heroes and Native Americans as wild enemies that had to be conquered. Hitler loved the way these stories celebrated violence and expansion as part of some great, heroic journey. He believed they captured the spirit of what Germany needed to do in Eastern Europe. He even recommended these books to his officers, saying they could learn from how America saw itself and use those lessons in building a new German empire.

Modern historians like Timothy Snyder, Carroll Kakel, and James Q. Whitman have looked closely at how much American ideas influenced Nazi thinking. In *Hitler's American Model*, Whitman shows how the Nazis actually studied U.S. laws on immigration and segregation while writing their own racist Nuremberg Laws. Kakel and Snyder explain that Hitler didn't just admire the American West as a place: he saw it as a plan. It was a guide on how to build an empire, how to remove people, and how to reshape an entire region to fit a racial vision. And at the heart of that plan was Jackson: not just a president, but a kind of warlord who used democracy to lead a brutal campaign of conquest.

The Trail of Tears: the forced march of Native Americans after Jackson signed the Indian Removal Act: left thousands dead. Most Americans today see it as a dark and tragic chapter. But to Hitler, it wasn't a tragedy at all. It was an example of success. A whole population had been removed to make room for white settlers, and the country didn't fall apart. In fact, it grew stronger. American democracy didn't just survive it: it supported it. That gave Hitler confidence. He believed Germany could do something similar: remove

Jews and Slavs, and the nation wouldn't just survive. It would thrive. If America could come out of such violence stronger, why not Germany?

Hitler was also fascinated by how Americans remembered: or forgot: this history. Jackson wasn't remembered as a villain. His actions weren't labeled as genocide in most history books. Instead, he was remembered as a strong leader, someone who helped grow the nation. The suffering of Native Americans was often left out or brushed aside. To Hitler, this showed the power of storytelling. If you controlled the story, you could control how people remembered the past. That's why he put so much trust in Joseph Goebbels and the Nazi propaganda machine. He wanted to shape memory just like America had: with monuments, stories, and national pride that covered up the horrors.

Hitler's obsession with Jackson also tells us something deeper about how certain leaders rise in troubled times. Jackson became popular during a time of change and uncertainty in early America, when the country was expanding and people were feeling left behind. He used that unrest to push bold, often brutal policies, especially against Native Americans. He also fought against anyone who supported ending slavery. In doing so, he brought many white Americans, especially in the South and West, together with a shared belief in white supremacy.

Hitler did something very similar. After Germany lost World War I and fell into political chaos during the Weimar Republic, people were angry, poor, and confused. Hitler used those feelings to blame Jews, Slavs, and others for the country's problems. He offered a simple answer: racial purity and national pride. Like Jackson, he turned pain into unity, at the cost of innocent lives.

Both men built their image around being strong leaders who could break the rules for a bigger cause. Jackson ignored court rulings that tried to protect Native Americans, believing that as president, he had the final say. Hitler took this even further. He created the *Führerprinzip*, or "leader principle," which meant that the leader's word was law. There were no more checks and balances; just one man with total control, justified by the idea of destiny and racial mission. In both cases, the idea of law gave way to the power of the story: the myth that their leadership was necessary to save the nation.

But perhaps the most chilling part of all this is how Hitler thought he could repeat Jackson's trick: rewriting history. The Trail of Tears wasn't often taught as genocide. It was seen by many as a sad but necessary step for American progress. Native people were reduced to background characters in a bigger tale of national success. Hitler believed the Holocaust could be treated the same way. That it wouldn't be remembered as a crime, but as part of Germany's rebirth. Like Jackson, he believed that if you won, you could decide what was right. That history wouldn't judge you by your actions, but by your victory.

There's something chilling about how both Andrew Jackson and Adolf Hitler used the idea of "civilization" to excuse violence. Jackson talked about bringing peace and order to the American frontier. Hitler, in a similar way, claimed he was bringing culture and stability to Eastern Europe. But behind these lofty words, the reality was much darker. What actually happened in both cases was the destruction of entire cultures, the deaths of countless people, and the building of societies where some races were seen as superior to others.

They used powerful words, like progress, destiny, and civilization, to cover up the cruelty of their actions. Instead of talking about rights or fairness, they spoke about duty, greatness, and the future. And in doing so, they made it seem like wiping out whole communities was not only necessary, but noble.

Today, when we look back at these connections, it challenges the stories we often tell ourselves, especially in the U.S. If someone like Hitler found inspiration in Andrew Jackson, what does that say about how American identity was shaped? This isn't about saying the two men were exactly the same. It's about noticing the deeper links between settler colonialism, like what happened in the U.S., and fascism, what Hitler built in Germany. Both were driven by similar beliefs: that it was acceptable to take over land and erase people for the sake of national power.

For a long time, Jackson's story in American history books was told as one of strength and leadership. But when you view him through Hitler's eyes, his legacy becomes far more troubling. Suddenly, the picture becomes clearer: a leader who turned democracy into a tool for violent expansion, and whose actions influenced one of the darkest chapters in human history.

This also makes us rethink how empires are remembered. Both the American West and Nazi-occupied Eastern Europe were described at the time as empty, wild lands, just waiting for the "right" people to come and settle them. But that was never true. These lands were home to real nations, with their own cultures, languages, and long histories. Still, those people were treated as if they didn't matter, just obstacles in the way of someone else's dream.

The fact that whole populations were labeled as expendable shows just how brutal these systems were. But it also shows how powerful national myths can be. Hitler believed that if the U.S. could erase its crimes and still be seen as a symbol of freedom and strength, then Germany could do the same. He saw America's example not just as a story of conquest, but as proof that you could reshape the truth if you controlled the narrative.

The example Hitler saw in Jackson was a roadmap for how to forget. It was a blueprint for building a nation's greatness on racial violence, then slowly turning that violence into patriotic pride. If the story was told the right way, and told often enough, then people would stop seeing it as evil and start seeing it as necessary. In Jackson, Hitler didn't just find a military model. He found someone who had shown how to use memory, storytelling, and national pride to cover up cruelty.

So, as Hitler stood looking over maps of Eastern Europe, deciding which communities would be moved, imprisoned, or killed, he wasn't just thinking of German history. He was also thinking of places like Georgia and Mississippi, and of the wide plains of North America. He was thinking about how one republic, America, had expanded violently and still kept its identity as a proud, free nation. And he believed Germany could do the same. That it could remove the people it deemed "undesirable," expand its borders, and still be seen as powerful and civilized.

The connection between Hitler and Jackson isn't just symbolic; it shows how ideas of imperialism and racial conquest have deeply shaped how modern governments operate. When Hitler studied what Jackson had done, he wasn't just admiring a strong leader. He was studying a political system, a democracy that had found a way to make racism, forced removals, and war part of its everyday workings. What fascinated Hitler most was how America had managed to do these things while still appearing fair, legal, and moral to the world.

From Hitler's point of view, that was the genius of Jacksonian America: it made violence look normal. It turned attacks on entire populations into legal policy. It wrapped it all in flags, laws, and speeches about freedom. This blend of brutality and public respectability was something Hitler desperately wanted to copy. t gave him ideas for how to create his own empire, and how to make sure people believed in it.

One thing that stood out to Hitler in particular was how the U.S. used law to expand its empire. It wasn't just about guns and soldiers. The U.S. passed treaties, changed laws, and created property rules that let settlers claim land that had belonged to Native peoples for centuries. Through legal tricks and definitions, like who counts as a citizen or what makes land "civilized," the government made it look like everything was fair and official. But in reality, it was a system built to push Native Americans out and replace them with white settlers.

To Hitler, this was not a contradiction but a lesson. Law didn't have to stop violence. It could be used to organize it. It could make cruelty look neat, proper, and even just. That's exactly what he tried to do later with the Nuremberg Laws. These laws stripped Jewish people of their rights, redefined them as outsiders, and made it "legal" to exclude, persecute, and eventually eliminate them. Just like in America, Hitler used law not as a shield for the weak, but as a weapon for the strong.

Hitler was deeply impressed by how Andrew Jackson used populism (that is, appealing to ordinary people) to win support for policies that were actually quite cruel. Take the removal of Native Americans, for example. Jackson didn't describe it as a brutal act. Instead, he made it sound like something necessary to protect and help everyday white workers. He framed it as if he was looking out for "the little guy."

Hitler picked up on this idea. In his time, he used the same kind of language. He told the German people, specifically the so-called "Aryan" Germans, that they needed more land, more food, and better chances in life. And just like Jackson, he said that achieving this meant removing others, especially Jews and groups he labeled as "undesirables." Both men gave their followers someone to blame and a dream to chase. They painted a picture of an ideal, hardworking citizen who was being held back by someone else, and then promised to fix it by getting rid of that "enemy."

This use of *populism as a weapon* was one of Hitler's most powerful political tools. And it's clear he borrowed it from

American history. Jackson had painted himself as a man of the people, fighting against the rich elites of the East. Hitler copied that strategy too. He railed against the so-called "November criminals" who, he claimed, had ruined Germany after World War I. He also blamed Jews, Marxists, and wealthy bankers, tying them all together as enemies of the people.

Hitler promised to restore the pride of the Volk, the German people, just as Jackson promised to defend the rugged American settler. Both leaders used the same old trick: stir up anger about class and poverty, but instead of fixing the real problems, direct that anger at racial or ethnic groups. It made people feel united, but only by turning them against someone else.

Another chilling thing Hitler admired was how the U.S. government handled Native Americans through the *reservation system*. He saw how America had created a way to move entire communities off their land, put them in isolated areas, and control them, all while pretending it was for their own good. This idea of forced separation and slow destruction gave Hitler ideas for his own plans, like Jewish ghettos and, eventually, extermination camps.

To Hitler, the reservation system showed how a government could erase a people's freedom, identity, and future, not all at once but bit by bit, using laws, poverty, and social isolation. It wasn't loud and obvious violence; it was a kind of slow-motion genocide, hidden under polite words and official policies.

There was also a *psychological element* to Hitler's thinking. He admired the way American culture turned its brutal history into something heroic. The myth of the frontier, where white settlers were seen as brave pioneers and Native people as dangerous enemies, gave Hitler a kind of moral story he could use for himself. In that American story, conquest was seen as brave, resistance as savage, and whiteness as civilized.

So, Hitler took that mindset and applied it to Eastern Europe. In his eyes, it was Germany's version of the American frontier. He believed German settlers should move in, bring their culture, and take over the land, while pushing out or destroying the people already living there. That story, in his mind, wasn't evil; it was destiny. He believed he was building something new, even if it required destruction along the way.

Even when it came to *symbols and imagery*, Hitler copied from American traditions. His use of the swastika was meant to feel both ancient and powerful, like a new beginning built on something sacred. It was a symbol meant to inspire hope and pride in a racially pure future.

In the same way, Jackson used powerful American symbols like the log cabin, the coonskin cap, and the frontier rifle. These weren't just for show. They told a story. A story where strength came from struggle, and greatness came from race and violence. Hitler saw the impact those images had, and he created his own, like the eagle, the torch, and the brown uniform of the Nazi stormtroopers. He understood that symbols could turn ordinary people into believers.

Another thing both leaders shared was the belief in *historical destiny*. Jackson often said that removing Native Americans was sad but unavoidable, like it was just something history required. Hitler said the same about his own racial policies. He called it a biological struggle, where the strong would naturally defeat the weak. Both men believed they had been chosen by history to carry out its harsh demands.

And that belief, that they were just following fate, made what they did even more dangerous. When leaders claim they are acting on behalf of history itself, they stop feeling responsible for their actions. They think they're above morality. Every act of cruelty becomes a necessary step toward some future glory.

Jackson believed that the suffering of Native Americans would lead to a stronger America. Hitler believed that exterminating Jews and Slavs would create a racially pure empire. For both of them, genocide wasn't a failure of the system. It was the system. It was working just as they thought it should.

This brings us to a tough and uncomfortable truth: ideas like racism, land theft, and power through division weren't just created in dictatorships. They also came from places like the United States, countries that call themselves democracies. Hitler didn't invent these ideas. He borrowed them from America's colonial past, from the way it treated Native Americans, and from the way it justified conquest through national pride.

That doesn't mean Hitler wasn't responsible for his crimes. He absolutely was. But it does mean we need to take a closer look at the roots of those crimes. They weren't some strange, foreign evil. They grew out of the modern world. They were part of its darker side.

When Hitler looked at Andrew Jackson, he saw more than a president. He saw proof that you could take land by force, erase entire cultures, and still be remembered as a national hero. He saw that stories could be rewritten, statues could outlast the truth, and history could be edited to suit the powerful.

He understood that winning wasn't just about guns and battles. It was about *narratives*. About who tells the story, who writes the textbooks, and who decides what's right and wrong for the next generation.

That's why this connection between Hitler and Jackson isn't just about the past. It's also a lesson. It shows us that empires don't just need soldiers. They need *storytellers*. It reminds us that genocide can be dressed up as destiny. And it warns us that democracy, if we're not careful, can become a mask for tyranny.

Looking at this connection isn't about being dramatic. It's about being honest. It's about asking hard questions: Have we confused cruelty with greatness? Have we let comforting myths hide uncomfortable truths? Are we still vulnerable to the same dangerous ideas wrapped up in flags, symbols, and stories that make us feel proud?

These are the questions that history asks of us, and we have to be brave enough to answer.

In the end, Hitler's admiration for Andrew Jackson wasn't just a passing thought. It was something much deeper. It was part of the foundation of how he built his own ideas. It shows us that the mindset behind genocide doesn't always come from wild, chaotic minds. Sometimes, it grows from the very systems and institutions of respected democracies. It reminds us that the path to a place like Auschwitz might begin in places like the Trail of Tears; that one kind of tragedy can plant the seeds for another, even worse one.

This is the hard truth history wants us to face. Not so we can hate the past, but so we can understand it. And maybe, if we're honest about it, begin to do better. Because if we don't face it, we leave the door wide open for it to happen again. The same blueprint, the same ideas, the same excuses. And the same kind of leader who once looked at that blueprint and admired it.

What makes this even more unsettling is that Hitler's admiration for Jackson didn't just belong to the past. It reached into the future. Even though Hitler and the Nazis were defeated in World War II, the ideas they drew on, especially the ones borrowed from American history, didn't disappear. The link between Hitler's vision and America's history of expansion and conquest didn't die with him. In fact, the legacy of *settler colonialism*, the idea that certain people can be pushed aside to make way for others, continued to influence how many nations handled things like war, displacement, and national identity.

If Jackson's policies helped inspire Hitler's dream of pushing east and getting rid of whole populations, then we have to ask a tough question: how many times has that same idea shown up again, in different places, with different names, but the same brutal logic?

To answer that, we have to understand how deeply Jackson's way of thinking became part of American identity. The belief that the U.S. had a special, divine mission to spread westward and "civilize" the land was never just a Jackson thing. It turned into something bigger. Something that lived in school textbooks, political speeches, and patriotic songs.

It became known as *Manifest Destiny*, the belief that America was meant to expand, no matter the cost.

But Manifest Destiny wasn't just a slogan. It was a way of seeing the world. It said expansion was good, conquest was noble, and nonwhite people were obstacles to progress. That kind of thinking, wrapped in the language of freedom and democracy, was exactly what Hitler found so appealing. It showed him how power could be taken, and kept, by turning injustice into a proud story.

In this version of the American story, the West wasn't just a place on a map. It became the heart of a national identit. One built around race. To be white didn't just mean having a certain skin color. It meant being "civilized," hardworking, and worthy of land and rights. If you weren't white (whether Native American, Black, or later, an immigrant), you were seen as a problem. You didn't fit the story. You were either pushed aside, ignored, or destroyed.

This *either-or* way of defining who belonged and who didn't became the unspoken rule of empire, and Hitler noticed. He didn't admire American democracy because it was fair or free. He admired how *practical* it was. He saw how the U.S. had managed to unite all kinds of European immigrants

(Irish, Germans, Italians) under one label: *white*. They might have been seen as outsiders at first, but as long as they joined the project of building the empire and turned against people of color, they were accepted.

Hitler took this idea and ran with it. He didn't just want to say Germans were superior. He wanted to *unite* all Germans, across different classes and regions, under one racial mission. He believed that if he gave them a common enemy (the Jews, the Slavs, the Communists), they would rally together. Just like American settlers had done when they were told to fear the "savage."

That's also why Hitler cared so much about *stories*. He saw how the U.S. had turned racial violence into a national legend. Andrew Jackson wasn't remembered as the man behind the Trail of Tears. He was remembered as a hero, a founder of the nation. The suffering and death of thousands of Native Americans was rewritten as a necessary part of a bigger story about freedom and strength.

Hitler wanted the same thing. He didn't worry about being judged in the future. He planned to *control* that future. He wanted to write the version of history people would learn.

He understood that people can accept terrible things if they believe those things are part of a noble cause.

That's why the Nazis focused so much on shaping collective memory. They were fighting for how those battles would be remembered. Statues, flags, parades, schoolbooks would tell a version of the story that felt clean and proud, even if it was built on horror. Just like Jackson had been celebrated in American history, Hitler wanted to be remembered as the man who brought Germany back to greatness.

This was a psychological warfare. Hitler had learned what Jackson had shown: that memory is powerful. It is about identity. It shapes how people see themselves, their country, and their future.

And Hitler didn't only admire what Jackson did to Native Americans. He also studied how the U.S. handled *slavery*. Even though Germany didn't have a history of plantations, Hitler respected how the American system made slavery feel "normal" and even *legal*. He was struck by how U.S. law could strip Black people of rights and humanity, all while still claiming to be a land of freedom and justice.

To Hitler, this wasn't a contradiction. It was clever. It showed that you could create a strict racial hierarchy and still have a functioning legal system. It showed that modern, educated societies didn't have to treat everyone equally. They just had to write the rules in a certain way.

This idea became central to how Nazi Germany operated. In 1935, the Nazis passed the *Nuremberg Laws*, which stripped Jews of citizenship and banned marriages between Jews and Aryans. These laws weren't slapped together last minute. They were carefully crafted, and part of that process involved studying U.S. laws.

Legal experts in Nazi Germany looked closely at how American states defined race. They were especially interested in how some states used the "one-drop rule," where a person with even one Black ancestor was considered Black. They debated whether they should copy that rule or make their own definition of Jewishness.

In the end, they came up with a system that looked a lot like Jim Crow America. It had all the same parts: people divided by race, rights taken away by law, and fear used as a weapon. Segregation was encouraged and enforced by the state. Violence was part of the design.

The similarities didn't stop with laws. Even when it came to shaping people's minds, what we might call *social engineering*, Hitler again looked to the American example for ideas.

In the U.S., Native American children were often taken from their families and placed into boarding schools. These schools weren't just about education. They were designed to erase everything that made those children who they were: their language, their traditions, their beliefs. The goal was to turn them into something else entirely: into "proper" Americans. It wasn't just about controlling land; it was about wiping out identity.

Hitler tried to do something very similar. In parts of Eastern Europe, especially in Poland and what was then Czechoslovakia, he ordered the kidnapping of children who had "Aryan" features: blonde hair, blue eyes, fair skin. These kids were taken from their families and raised as Germans. They were taught to forget their origins. The idea was to steal souls, to replace entire cultures with the Nazi vision of what was "pure" and "proper."

In both cases, this wasn't just about military power. It was about *cultural destruction*. It was a war fought through schools, language, and rituals. It was about breaking people from the inside.

But Hitler's plan went even further. He wasn't just trying to get rid of people physically. He wanted them wiped from *memory*. What he understood, and what Jackson had already shown, is that genocide doesn't really end when people die. It ends when they're *forgotten*. When no one talks about them anymore. When their names aren't in the books. When their stories aren't told. When the monuments go up for the killers and the victims are left in silence. That's when the second death happens.

And that's why Hitler was obsessed with controlling the narrative: the story that people would remember. If no one remembers the crime, it's as if it never happened. If the textbooks don't mention it, if the statues only honor the victors, then the truth fades away. And without truth, there's no justice.

This idea has serious meaning for us today. In recent years, we've seen a rise in right-wing populism across both Europe and the United States. And while today's situations aren't exactly the same as the 1930s, the way some leaders talk can feel eerily familiar. They stir up racial pride. They blame minorities. They talk longingly about a "better past" that never truly existed. They complain about democracy getting in the way.

This is why the link between Jackson and Hitler isn't just a footnote in history. It's a warning. It shows how old tools, like racist myths, biased laws, and violent nationalism, can be reused again and again, as long as they're wrapped in flags and painted as patriotic.

We see it today in fights over monuments, school curriculums, and national memory. Some people say Jackson should be judged by the standards of his own time, not by today's values. But here's the problem with that: *Hitler* judged Jackson by those same "old" standards, and *he* thought they were great.

When we excuse atrocities by calling them "normal for their time," we make room for those same ideas to return. We send a message that those crimes were just part of how things were done. That kind of thinking doesn't stop the past from repeating. It *guarantees* it.

This is why we need to take a hard look at the people we label as heroes. Jackson was a man with personal prejudices and a symbol of an entire system built on conquering others and keeping them out. His actions weren't just personal choices; they were part of a bigger pattern, one that said power belonged to some and not to others.

And *that* was what Hitler admired. Not just the man, but the *system*: the way it worked, the way it told its story, the way it turned cruelty into greatness.

In the end, Hitler's respect for Jackson tells us as much about *America* as it does about *Germany*. It makes us face something we often don't want to admit: that fascist thinking doesn't always come from some faraway place. Sometimes, it grows right at home. Sometimes, it's hiding inside the very stories we tell about our national pride. And sometimes, if we're not careful, it can come back under new names, with new slogans, and new uniforms.

So now we're left with a choice.

We can keep honoring Jackson as a bold leader and ignore the human cost of what he did. Or we can look honestly at the legacy that inspired one of history's worst dictators, and break apart the myths that keep giving dangerous people a path to power.

If we choose honesty, if we choose to remember not just the victors but the victims, then we do more than fix the record. We begin to reclaim something much more important: *Our humanity*.

CHAPTER 14

THE DARWINIAN SHADOW: EVOLUTION, STRUGGLE, AND THE RACIAL IMAGINATION OF ADOLF HITLER

Long before the sound of marching boots filled the streets of Germany and Nazi flags waved over city squares, something much quieter had already taken root: something that didn't begin with armies or angry crowds, but in the world of science. It all started with ideas, wrapped in the language of nature and biology, and they seemed to carry the weight of truth because they came from science. The man behind these ideas was Charles Darwin, an English naturalist whose famous book *On the Origin of Species*, published in 1859, changed the way people thought about life on Earth.

Darwin's theory of evolution explained how living things slowly change over time to adapt to their surroundings. He talked about natural selection; how animals and plants that were better suited to survive in their environments passed on their traits to the next generation. But Darwin also warned people not to over-simplify his ideas. He knew evolution was a complex, slow-moving process. Still, once his theories began to spread across Europe, they started to take on meanings he never intended, especially when twisted to fit political or racist beliefs.

In the late 1800s and early 1900s, many thinkers in Germany and Austria took Darwin's scientific theory and turned it into something else. Something dangerous. They mixed evolution with racist ideas, turning it into what became known as "Social Darwinism." This was no longer about animals adapting to nature; it became a way to judge which human groups were "strong" and which were "weak." According to this distorted view, life was a constant fight for survival, and some people believed that the strong had not only the right but the duty to dominate the weak. For them, this wasn't just science; it became a kind of belief system.

This was the intellectual world a young Adolf Hitler grew up in. He wasn't deeply interested in Darwin as a scientist. But the *idea* of struggle, of a constant, brutal fight where only the strongest survive, deeply influenced him. Hitler didn't need the real Darwin; he followed a made-up version of Darwin's theory that had been reshaped to support ideas about race, war, and power.

Hitler was born in the Austro-Hungarian Empire, a place where people were already divided by language, ethnicity, and social class. From a young age, he was exposed to ideas that ranked some cultures as superior to others. But it was after World War I when Germany was defeated and in political and economic chaos that Hitler's thinking really hardened. The humiliation of losing the war, the collapse of the German Empire, and the struggles of the Weimar Republic made him look for someone, or something, to blame.

That's when his racist ideas truly took shape. He believed that life was all about struggle. He saw it not as a world where people should help one another, but as a kind of battlefield where the strong must rise and the weak must fall. In this harsh view of the world, there was no room for compassion or fairness, but only strength and survival.

In his infamous book *Mein Kampf*, Hitler wrote openly about this belief.

"He who wants to live must fight," he said.

He described life as a constant war, where struggle was the rule and weakness meant defeat. These weren't just dramatic words; they revealed his entire worldview. He believed human beings were like wild animals, ruled by the same brutal laws of nature. For him, kindness, justice, or cooperation were lies….things that weakened society. Only power and racial "purity" mattered.

Now, Darwin had talked about how species evolve and branch out over time. He imagined a tree of life, where different species slowly develop in their own directions. But in Hitler's mind, this became a ladder with some races at the top and others at the bottom. He manipulated Darwin's tree into a hierarchy, with the so-called "Aryan" race at the top. He imagined Aryans as the highest form of human evolution: strong, noble, destined to rule. Meanwhile, he painted Jews as the opposite: weak, corrupt, and dangerous. This wasn't science but an ideology pretending to be science. Evolution, as Hitler used it, became a myth built around blood and race.

To Hitler, the state wasn't just a government. He saw it as a kind of living body. And like any body, he believed it had to be kept "pure" and "healthy." So he saw anyone who didn't fit his idea of racial perfection, the Jews, disabled people, LGBTQ individuals, people with mental illnesses, as infections, as dangers to the health of the nation. These ideas led to horrific policies: forced sterilizations, euthanasia programs, and ultimately genocide. And all of it was justified using the language of biology and evolution, dressed up as if it were medical truth.

But Hitler didn't come up with these ideas by himself. Decades earlier, German scientists and thinkers were already paving the way. One of them was Ernst Haeckel, a famous biologist and a strong supporter of Darwin's work. But Haeckel took Darwin's theory and added his own racist beliefs. He argued that different races had evolved at different speeds, and that some were more advanced than others. He even claimed that some non-European groups were closer to apes than to white Europeans. These kinds of ideas were taught in schools, published in books, and accepted by many scientists at the time. So by the time Hitler entered politics, these beliefs were already part of the cultural mindset.

During this period, the idea of eugenics was also gaining popularity. Eugenics was a movement that claimed society could improve the human race by controlling who had children and who didn't. It started in Britain, with Francis Galton, who happened to be Darwin's cousin, and quickly spread across Europe and the U.S. Eugenics sounded scientific, but it was used to support harmful and discriminatory practices. People believed they could "speed up" evolution by choosing who was fit to reproduce.

Hitler accepted these ideas and took them to the extreme. Under his leadership, Nazi Germany launched the most aggressive and deadly eugenics program in modern history. Hundreds of thousands of people were forcibly sterilized. Hundreds of thousands were killed through the T4 Euthanasia Program, a secret plan that targeted people with disabilities. All of this was carried out in the name of science, but it had nothing to do with real science. It was ideology, hatred, and power disguised in lab coats.

The Nazi obsession with things like bloodlines, breeding, and who was "fit" to live wasn't just some extreme side belief; it was right at the heart of their thinking. These ideas affected everything: who could get married, what kids learned in school, and even how buildings and cities were designed. The goal wasn't just to win a war or rebuild a country. Hitler and his followers wanted to create what they saw as a new kind of human: A "perfect" German race, cleansed of anything they believed was weak or impure. In their minds, the war indeed included borders or politics, but more than that, it was about cleaning out what they saw as bad genes. It was, horrifyingly, an attempt to reset human evolution through violence.

And that's how they saw the Holocaust too….not just as hate or revenge, but as a kind of racial "clean-up," a way to protect the supposed health of the German bloodline. Of course, this was all built on centuries of antisemitism, but now it was being framed as if it were a scientific necessity.

But here's the thing: Darwin never intended any of this. He wasn't telling people how to act or what kind of society to build. He was simply trying to explain how animals and plants changed over time. He didn't say that struggle should be celebrated or that some people were better than others. In fact, in his later book *The Descent of Man*, Darwin talked about how kindness, sympathy, and cooperation were important parts of what made us human. He believed those traits actually helped humans survive and grow as a species.

But once ideas are out in the world, they don't always stay in the hands of the people who created them. Others pick them up and twist them into something new. And that's what happened here. Darwin's name and theories were pulled into something much darker, something he never would have supported. His scientific work became fuel for an ideology that used biology as an excuse to kill.

Now, it's tempting to draw a straight line from Darwin to Hitler, like Darwin's ideas directly caused the Holocaust. But that wouldn't be fair or accurate. The real connection is more complicated. What connects the two is not a cause-and-effect chain, but a series of misinterpretations. Darwin's ideas were taken by others, changed, distorted, and used to justify racist beliefs. It wasn't Darwin the scientist who inspired Hitler; it was Darwin as a myth. A symbol of "survival of the fittest" turned into a sick moral code, one that said the strong should dominate the weak, no matter the cost.

To understand why these ideas took hold, we also have to look at what was happening in the world at the time. By the late 1800s, many people were feeling lost. Traditional beliefs, especially religious ones, were being questioned. Science was showing that life wasn't guided by a higher power, but by random chance and natural forces. Evolution said there was no divine plan. Just change, struggle, and adaptation. For some, this was freeing. For others, it was terrifying.

Hitler was one of those people who hated the idea of weakness or uncertainty. He wanted clear, hard answers. In Darwinian struggle, he thought he'd found a new kind of truth: a brutal, cold logic where only the strong deserved to survive. He believed that Germany's problems came from being "soft" or "contaminated" by weaker races and groups. So he promised to purify and strengthen the nation through force.

And talked about these ideas and actually acted on them. His speeches and policies were full of talk about blood, land, and the need for constant struggle. He told the German people that they were victims, polluted by foreign races and betrayed by history. His plan was to restore them through war and cleansing. When Germany invaded the Soviet Union, Hitler didn't see it as just another battle. To him, it was a racial war. A fight between "pure" Aryans and what he called the "mongrel" mix of Jews, Slavs, and Communists. The mass killings that followed, the Holocaust, the starvation of millions, the mass shootings, weren't seen as crimes in his eyes. They were part of a cold, twisted logic. They were, to him, acts of "biological necessity."

What's even more disturbing is how many doctors, scientists, and university professors went along with it. These weren't uneducated thugs. They were highly trained professionals; people who had studied biology, medicine, and philosophy. And yet they used their knowledge to help carry out mass murder. They performed medical experiments on prisoners, ran sterilization programs, and helped design systems for euthanasia. They believed they were improving the future by "weeding out" the weak. It's a chilling reminder of what happens when science is used without ethics, when facts are stripped of humanity.

After the war, many people tried to separate Darwin's name from the horrors of Nazism, and rightly so. Darwin's work was one of the greatest contributions to human knowledge. But we can't pretend that his ideas weren't misused. The path from *The Origin of Species* to Auschwitz wasn't straight, but it was real. It shows us how even the most brilliant discoveries can be manipulated when people want to turn truth into a tool for control and cruelty.

For Hitler, Darwin became something more than a scientist.; a kind of prophet, not of peace or progress, but of struggle and blood. Hitler built a new religion around these ideas, a harsh religion without forgiveness, where only the strong mattered. He saw himself as both the preacher and the judge, leading Germany into a brutal new era. The swastika, once an ancient symbol, became the flag of this cruel vision. And in the smoke rising from the crematoriums, Hitler believed he had fulfilled the destiny of evolution.

But the misuse of Darwin's ideas didn't start, or end, in Germany. Even before Hitler, parts of the world were already using science to justify racism and control. In Britain, Darwin's cousin, Francis Galton, had taken evolution and turned it into something called eugenics. This was the belief that humans could be "improved" by controlling who was allowed to have children. Galton believed that traits like intelligence or morality were inherited, like eye color, and that if you stopped the "wrong" people from reproducing, society would get better over time.

Unlike Darwin, Galton wasn't shy about telling people what to do. He believed governments should actively guide human evolution by encouraging the "fit" to have more kids and preventing the "unfit" from doing so. His ideas caught on quickly, especially in Britain and the United States.

In America, eugenics became part of government policy. By the 1930s, more than 30 U.S. states had laws allowing forced sterilization of people labeled as mentally ill, disabled, or simply "unfit." These weren't small programs. Thousands of people were sterilized, often without their full knowledge or consent. And the U.S. Supreme Court supported it. In a famous case called *Buck v. Bell*, Justice Oliver Wendell Holmes defended sterilization by saying, "Three generations of imbeciles are enough." It was a cruel and cold-hearted ruling, and it showed just how far these ideas had spread.

Hitler's ideas didn't just come out of nowhere. They were shaped by a mix of older European beliefs and some newer, especially American, ways of thinking about race and society. He didn't see himself as someone inventing something new; he thought he was fixing what had been broken. In his mind, nature had a certain "biological order," and modern ideas like freedom, equality, and democracy had messed it up.

In *Mein Kampf*, Hitler wrote about the state not as something that should protect people's individual rights or freedoms, but as something that should serve the goals of a specific race. He looked to America for inspiration, particularly the way the U.S. had strict immigration laws and divided people by race. He was especially impressed by the 1924 Immigration Act, which limited immigration from southern and eastern Europe while favoring people from northern Europe. To Nazi thinkers, this was a great example of "racial hygiene," a term they used to talk about keeping a race "pure."

Hitler closely followed these developments in other countries because they made him feel like he wasn't alone. He believed that the whole world was waking up to the idea that biology, meaning race and heredity, should shape politics and society.

But in Germany, the way these ideas were twisted took on a much darker and almost religious tone. After World War I, Germany was broken. Its economy had crashed, its politics were a mess, and many people felt lost and ashamed. This created the perfect environment for extreme ideas to take root. Hitler and his followers wanted to change politics *and* remake humanity itself.

They believed that the German people had once been strong and pure, but had become weak because of racial mixing, city life, and moral decay. To "fix" this, they thought the nation had to go through a kind of rebirth, one that involved cleansing and hardening the population.

That's why Nazi propaganda was full of comparisons between Jews and diseases. Jews weren't just seen as outsiders or enemies; they were described as infections or parasites. This was cruel language, treated like a medical truth. Nazi films, textbooks, and posters painted Jews as dangerous to the health of the nation.

And in this logic, Hitler saw himself not as a destroyer, but as a kind of doctor. He believed he was performing surgery and getting rid of the "infection" to save the body. Killing millions became, in his mind, a necessary act to protect the future of the Aryan race. Genocide, horrifyingly, was seen as a kind of medicine.

These ideas were backed by what was called "scientific racism." At the time, many scientists claimed they could prove that some races were better than others using things like skull measurements, eye shapes, and IQ tests. They said criminal behavior, mental illness, or even laziness could be inherited, passed down through "bad" genes.

This wasn't some fringe idea. These theories were taught in respected universities, printed in scholarly journals, and used to shape laws. In Germany, places like the Kaiser Wilhelm Institute were deeply involved. Scientists there worked directly with the Nazis, running cruel experiments on twins, studying forced sterilizations, and helping to decide who was racially fit or unfit. Science, instead of seeking truth, became a tool for promoting Nazi ideology.

But it wasn't just about science. Hitler's beliefs were also wrapped up in myth and emotion. He didn't just think the Aryan race was biologically better. He thought it was sacred, almost holy. The Nazi mission became something like a religious war, where "saving" the race was the ultimate goal.

He mixed the language of Darwin, about survival and evolution, with romantic ideas from German mythology, heroic struggle, and love for the land. "Blood and soil," "sacrifice," and "struggle" became part of a new kind of faith, where being born Aryan was like being chosen by destiny. In this view, history was a battle where only the strongest, purest race deserved to survive and rule.

One of the most disturbing parts of this thinking was the Lebensborn program. The Nazis wanted to increase the number of Aryan children, so they created special homes where women considered racially "pure" were encouraged to have babies, often with SS officers, even if they weren't married. These babies were treated like future warriors for the Nazi state.

At the same time, babies from non-Aryan families, especially in conquered countries, were often taken away. If they looked "Aryan enough," they were adopted and raised as Germans. If not, they were killed. Life and death became decisions made by the state. It wasn't about morals anymore, but racial goals. The government decided who should live, who should have children, and who should disappear.

This same mindset was behind Operation Barbarossa, the massive Nazi invasion of the Soviet Union. To Hitler, this wasn't just a war over land. It was a racial war, a battle for survival. He believed the vast eastern lands, like Ukraine and Russia, should become "Lebensraum," living space for the German people.

The Slavs, who lived there, were not seen as equals or even as people worth protecting. Hitler saw them as an inferior race, fit only for slavery or extermination. One of the Nazi plans, called the Hunger Plan, was to starve tens of millions of Soviet citizens to make room for German settlers.

This war strategy had become more about a belief that nature demanded strong races to rise and dominate. If Germany didn't take over the East, someone else would. In Hitler's mind, there was no place for mercy. The forests, farms, and fields of Eastern Europe became testing grounds for these beliefs, where racial theory was put into bloody action.

To truly understand Hitler's view of the world, we have to face one of the darkest chapters in human history: the Holocaust. While hatred toward Jews had existed in Europe for centuries, Hitler brought something new to it; he turned that hatred into a matter of biology. For him, Jews weren't just people with a different religion or culture. He saw them as a completely different and dangerous species, like a genetic mistake that needed to be wiped out.

This idea led to the "Final Solution," Hitler's plan to completely get rid of the Jewish people. In his mind, this was science. He saw the Holocaust as a way to protect the "racial health" of the German people. The death camps weren't the result of chaos or insanity. They were carefully planned and organized, as if part of a huge, cold, industrial process. Like how farmers might get rid of animals with genetic defects, Hitler believed certain humans had to be "removed" for the sake of the future. It was evolution without compassion, biology without a soul.

But even inside the Nazi regime, not everyone agreed on how to understand race and evolution. Some Nazi leaders, especially those in the SS like Heinrich Himmler, leaned more toward myths and spiritual beliefs. They didn't just focus on genes and science; they believed in ancient symbols, magical history, and mystical destiny. Himmler, for example, was fascinated by Nordic legends, runes, and even thought the Aryan race came from a lost civilization near the North Pole. For him, it wasn't just about survival of the fittest, but being spiritually "pure" and living out some kind of sacred past.

Still, whether people followed the scientific version or the mystical one, the message was the same: not all humans were equal. Some were seen as naturally superior, while others were labeled weak, dirty, or dangerous. And it wasn't just Nazi leaders who believed this. Many regular Germans did too.

The ideas of racial struggle, cleanliness, and purity were everywhere. They were in children's stories, in school textbooks, in doctor's offices, and even in church sermons.

Kids were raised in the Hitler Youth to believe in loyalty to their race, strength, and obedience. Schools taught them that some people were born better than others. Even marriage wasn't just about love; it had to be approved by the state to make sure both people were "racially pure."

Over time, it became hard to tell where science ended and propaganda began. The same ideas that were once taught in biology class were now being used to decide who deserved rights, who could have children, and who should live or die.

After the fall of the Nazi regime, the world had to come to terms with what had happened. During the Nuremberg Trials, the role of doctors and scientists in the Holocaust came into full view. Many of them defended themselves by saying they were just following "scientific facts." But the world now saw the truth: when science loses its moral compass, it can become a tool for evil.

This led to the birth of something new: bioethics, the study of how science and medicine should always be guided by human values. People began to understand that science doesn't exist in a bubble. It's always connected to the society, politics, and people who use it.

Even today, Darwin's theory of evolution is considered one of the most important ideas in all of science. It explains how species change and adapt over time, and it's backed by tons of evidence. But like many powerful ideas, it can be misunderstood, or worse, misused.

Darwin never said that evolution should be used to decide who deserves to live or die. He never said that strong people should rule over weak ones. But when people like Hitler took Darwin's ideas and changed them into ideology, they used them to justify some of the worst crimes in history. When the theory of evolution was mixed with extreme nationalism and racism, it became something deadly.

Hitler didn't create his beliefs in a vacuum. He was influenced by a wider world that was already steeped in ideas of racial superiority, colonial conquest, and "survival of the fittest." By the late 1800s and early 1900s, many scientists, writers, and politicians had already started using evolution to support their own agendas. They weren't using it to understand life, but to justify who should have power, and who shouldn't.

Hitler's beliefs were shaped by this atmosphere. He took Darwin's scientific theory, stripped it of its careful, thoughtful meaning, and turned it into a brutal rulebook for society. In his world, life was a battle, and only the "strongest race" had the right to survive and expand.

This belief became a kind of religion. It had its own gospel, its own commandments, and it demanded sacrifice. And millions paid the price.

Looking back, it forces us to ask hard questions about ourselves. How easily can the things we create for good, like science and knowledge, be turned into tools for hate? How quickly can reason be twisted into cruelty when it's used without empathy?

To study Hitler isn't just to learn about a dictator; it's to look in the mirror. He shows us how deeply human beings long for order, purpose, and meaning, especially in times of chaos. But when we use powerful ideas like evolution to create rigid hierarchies or justify violence, we betray those ideas, and our own humanity.

Darwin gave the world a theory of change. Hitler turned it into a belief in eternal, unchanging racial destiny. That shift from science to ideology is not just a historical tragedy. It's a warning for all of us.

This way of twisting Darwin's ideas, using them to justify power and control, was especially clear in the British Empire. As the empire spread across the world, the people running it needed a reason to believe their rule was right. For many of them, imperial officials, politicians, and academics, evolution seemed to offer that reason. They used Darwin's theory to claim that British rule wasn't just strong, clever and *natural*. They believed the British were more "evolved," and that gave them the right to rule over others.

In this mindset, British dominance, especially by the Anglo-Saxon people, was seen as proof that they were biologically superior. Winning wars, building colonies, and ruling faraway lands were seen as signs of evolutionary success. Progress meant expansion. And expansion was seen as part of nature's plan. From elite universities like Oxford to colonial offices in India and Africa, people began to see Darwinism not as a neutral science, but as a story that explained why the British deserved to lead the world. It became, in a way, a kind of anthem for empire.

Hitler noticed this. He admired the British for how they ran such a large empire using racial order and hierarchy. What fascinated him most was how a small number of British officials and soldiers were able to control a place as big and complex as India. To him, this could only mean one thing: the British were racially superior. Their ability to rule over hundreds of millions wasn't just about training or organization; it had to be in their blood.

To Hitler, the British weren't just another world power, but living proof that race could shape history. They had taken the idea of evolution and applied it overseas. What Hitler wanted was to do something similar, but inside Germany first, and then across Eastern Europe. Where Britain ruled through colonialism, Hitler planned to rule through what he called Lebensraum, living space.

He also looked to America. The U.S. offered him another model of how to build a racially ordered society. The westward expansion across the American frontier, the violent removal of Native Americans, the history of slavery, Hitler didn't see these as moral failures. In his eyes, they were victories. To him, they showed how one race had pushed forward by overpowering others.

He was especially interested in how America had used laws to support this racial structure. He studied U.S. policies that enforced racial segregation, sterilized people deemed unfit to reproduce, and controlled immigration based on race. All of these things, he believed, showed that America had taken Darwin's ideas and turned them into a working system. Hitler deeply admired the American belief in "Manifest Destiny," the idea that the U.S. had the right to expand westward and claim land. He saw this as a perfect example of evolutionary thinking in action.

That belief in a people's right to expand and dominate helped shape Hitler's own plan for Germany. Just as Americans had taken the West, Hitler wanted Germany to take the East. He dreamed of German families settling the lands of Poland, Ukraine, and Russia, pushing out the existing populations, claiming the land, and reshaping it to fit his racial vision. In his mind, Eastern Europe would become Germany's version of the American frontier.

Understanding this global backdrop is key. Hitler didn't create these ideas on his own. Around the world, Darwin's theory had already been reshaped into something much bigger, and much more dangerous, than what Darwin himself intended. People were desperate for certainty in a time when old beliefs were falling apart. Religion was losing its power, industrial life was changing everything, and the old systems of kings and aristocrats were crumbling. Science seemed to offer answers, but instead of humility, many people chose arrogance.

The same energy that created new inventions and technology was also used to build systems that ranked people by race. These systems weren't truly scientific and often based on biased thinking, politics, and fear. But because they used the language of science, they seemed believable. They were taught, published, and enforced.

Philosophers and social thinkers added to this dangerous mix. Friedrich Nietzsche was one of the most famous. Even though the Nazis often misunderstood his work, they borrowed some of his language, especially his talk about strength, power, and the idea of the *Übermensch*, or "superman," who rises above the ordinary crowd.

Nietzsche was deeply critical of compassion and democracy. He believed that many moral values were made by weak people to hold strong people back. He didn't follow Darwin directly, but his idea of life as a constant struggle fit well with the Social Darwinist thinking that Hitler loved. In Nietzsche's world, destruction could be creative, and moral rules could be broken if they stood in the way of greatness. Hitler found these ideas useful. He believed that modern morality, especially ideas like equality and empathy, had to be destroyed so that the strong could rise.

Other thinkers also helped shape the racial theories that Hitler believed in. Arthur de Gobineau was one of the first to claim that different races had unequal value. In his *Essay on the Inequality of the Human Races*, he argued that the white race, especially the Aryan branch, was responsible for creating civilization, and that mixing with other races only led to decline. His theories weren't backed by real science, but they felt convincing to many people at the time.

Later, Houston Stewart Chamberlain, an English writer who became a fierce German nationalist, expanded on these ideas in his book *The Foundations of the Nineteenth Century*. That book had a big influence on Hitler. Chamberlain claimed that the Teutonic race (basically northern Europeans) carried all the best qualities of Western civilization. But, he warned, those qualities were in danger. He blamed Jews for weakening the cultural and racial strength of Europe.

To Hitler, Chamberlain was almost like a prophet. His words confirmed everything Hitler already believed: that history was shaped by race, that purity was power, and that Germany had to act before it was too late.

By the early 1900s, ideas about race and biology had become so common that people didn't even question them anymore. They were just part of everyday thinking. Schools taught that humanity could be divided into fixed racial categories, almost like scientific facts. Museums displayed human skulls arranged in what they claimed were "racial hierarchies," suggesting some races were smarter or more advanced than others. Public health campaigns talked about things like "genetic cleanliness," as if people could be judged or treated based on their genes alone.

Worse still, governments in many places, including the U.S., started seeing it as their duty to "protect" the gene pool. This meant forcing people who were disabled or mentally ill to be sterilized, so they couldn't have children. That wasn't seen as cruel at the time. It was considered responsible. That was the kind of world Hitler was born into; one where science wasn't just about facts, but about shaping society's morals. Evolutionary theory had been twisted into a set of cold, unbending rules about who should live, who should lead, and who didn't belong.

What made Hitler so dangerous wasn't that he invented these ideas, but that he pulled them all together into one big, powerful story. He mixed the belief in racial superiority, the idea of constant struggle from Darwin's theory, old imperial myths, and German nationalism. And he turned it into something that felt like a natural truth, something people couldn't argue with. He didn't need to convince the German people that his policies were good or kind. He just needed them to believe they were *necessary*. He told them this was how nature worked: the strong survive, the weak perish. Nature doesn't care about feelings, and neither should we.

This idea became the foundation of the Nazi state. Hitler didn't talk about compassion or fairness in his speeches. He talked about blood, struggle, fate, and racial purity. He used phrases like "the law of life," "the iron logic of nature," and "the racial soul of the people." In his view, to question his ideas was to fight against nature itself. And if nature didn't have room for the weak, neither should Germany.

This way of thinking had terrifying consequences. If struggle is the highest truth, then war becomes something holy. If only the strong deserve to live, then anyone defeated, whether in battle or in life, deserves to disappear. If showing kindness to the weak makes the nation weaker, then kindness itself becomes a problem. These weren't just ideas in books. They became real policies. You could see them in the ghettos of Warsaw, in the mass graves in the East, and in the death camps like Dachau. They showed up in dull bureaucratic forms: train schedules, sterilization records, medical reports. But behind the paperwork was a belief system that had taken root deep in people's minds. It wasn't just biology being twisted; it was people's souls, their understanding of right and wrong.

And maybe that's the darkest truth of all: that when an ideology hides behind the mask of science, it doesn't just become convincing; it becomes *total*. It doesn't just offer people a goal for the future. It gives them permission for what they're doing right now. It helps them sleep at night. It wraps evil in the calm voice of logic. It makes murder seem like healing. Racism becomes medicine. Genocide becomes "purification." Hitler embraced modern science and used it to justify every horror, and he did it with confidence, purpose, and frightening clarity.

This isn't just history. These kinds of beliefs can resurface, even today. With modern breakthroughs in genetics, neuroscience, and artificial intelligence, we now have powerful tools to study human differences. But if we're not careful, those tools can be used to rank people again, to judge their value by biology or data. The real warning from the Nazi era isn't just about how Darwin was misused. It's about how fragile our ethics can be when we fall in love with certainty. The nightmare isn't just what was done, but how easily it was defended.

And here's something else: Hitler didn't need to twist Darwin's ideas beyond recognition. He didn't invent some strange theory. He simply took the most extreme interpretations of the time, the ones already being spread by respected scholars, scientists, judges, and priests, and pushed them to their limits. These weren't underground opinions. They were mainstream. They were taught in schools, promoted in public, and passed into law. In that kind of world, the distance from theory to genocide was shockingly short.

Charles Darwin himself, especially in his later years, spoke about kindness and the importance of morality in human evolution. He worried about human suffering. But once his ideas were out in the world, he couldn't control how others would use them. His theory, that species change and adapt over time, was meant to explain life. But others turned it into a tool for empire-building, racism, and mass murder. Darwin held up a mirror to nature. Others picked it up and turned it into a weapon.

For Hitler, that weapon was essential. It gave his plans a kind of cold, scientific logic. His dream of a Thousand-Year Reich wasn't just about politics; it was, in his mind, an evolutionary mission. He didn't claim to be shaping Germany; he claimed to be shaping the future of the human species. In the end, it wasn't ideology alone that fueled the death camps and the gas chambers. It was the belief that evolution demanded it. The people who were killed were seen as failed experiments, evolutionary dead-ends.

And maybe the most chilling idea of all is this: that a human mind, while honestly trying to make sense of the world, can build a system so logical, so orderly, so seemingly "right," that it loses all feeling. That reason itself, when stripped of empathy, can lead to cruelty beyond imagination. Hitler didn't throw reason away but followed it, step by step, to its most horrifying conclusion. And he convinced a nation to follow him.

CHAPTER 15

THE RACE POPE: HANS F. K. GÜNTHER AND THE CODIFICATION OF HITLER'S RACIAL VISION

When it comes to the people who built the ideas behind National Socialism, few names are as big or as troubling as Hans Friedrich Karl Günther. Back then, many of his followers actually called him the "Race Pope," and that title says a lot. He wasn't just someone with theories about race; he was the one who gave shape and structure to a whole worldview. Like an architect, but of ideology. He drew the map for how the Nazis saw humanity. Where Hitler spoke with fire and passion, Günther brought a cold, organized logic. Hitler gave voice to the beliefs; Günther gave them a system.

Günther's work gave Hitler's racial ideas a kind of academic cover. It made them look like serious science. It added rules and labels and a sense of authority. In many ways, Günther was the "scientific conscience" behind a regime that believed your biology (specifically, your race) determined your destiny.

A Childhood Surrounded by Nationalism and Education

Hans Günther was born on February 16, 1891, in Freiburg, Germany, at a time when German nationalism and intellectual debates were everywhere. He came from a comfortable middle-class family. His father worked as a civil servant, which meant Günther grew up in a home that valued education and public service.

He studied at some of Germany's top universities: Freiburg, Heidelberg, and Berlin. There, he focused on comparative linguistics, anthropology, and psychology. From early on, he had a strong interest in classification: that is, sorting things into groups, especially people. He wanted to bring order to the wide variety of human appearances and behaviors. While many people saw human diversity as natural and rich, Günther saw it as something that could be sorted and explained. This need to organize and label people became the heart of everything he did later.

Even though Günther started out studying languages, he soon shifted toward race theory. This shift happened as he became influenced by the growing popularity of eugenics and anthropology in the early 20th century. These fields were starting to redefine people not based on character or soul, but by their genes and physical traits.

At that time, science was moving fast. Discoveries in biology, medicine, and genetics were changing the way people thought. But alongside this progress came some very dangerous ideas. People started thinking that science could be used to control or "improve" society by managing which groups were allowed to reproduce.

Thinkers twisted Darwin's theory of evolution into something it was never meant to be: a ranking of races. Mendel's genetic laws were misused to justify sterilizing people or keeping them out of society. In that kind of atmosphere, Günther's way of thinking didn't seem extreme. It was even celebrated by many.

The Book That Defined His Career

Günther's first big work was published in 1922. It was called Rassenkunde des deutschen Volkes, or Racial Science of the German People. This book made him famous and gave him a leading role among Germany's racial theorists. It quickly became a bestseller and an important guide for nationalist movements during the Weimar Republic.

In the book, Günther laid out a system for classifying different European "racial types." He listed five: Nordic, Mediterranean, Dinaric, Alpine, and East Baltic. But he wasn't just describing how people looked. He claimed each type had certain moral, intellectual, and spiritual qualities too. For Günther, race was more than skin deep.

He believed the Nordic race, with its tall height, light eyes, and long skull, was the most superior. He said they were not only better-looking but also smarter, more virtuous, and more capable of leadership. On the other hand, he described other racial types as being emotionally unstable, less intelligent, or spiritually weak.

What made Günther's ideas so powerful, and so dangerous, was how he mixed scientific language with myth-like storytelling. He didn't just present data. He told a story. One where the Nordic man wasn't just a person but a symbol of greatness, a kind of hero from the past.

He turned his theories into something that felt almost sacred, like a belief system. His version of racial science wasn't neutral; it was more like a gospel for those who believed in the superiority of one race. And when Adolf Hitler came along, Günther found a political leader who was ready to turn that gospel into real-life policies.

Although Günther and Hitler didn't work together every day, Hitler read his books and often spoke highly of them. Günther's work was even required reading in Nazi schools. Their connection was more about shared beliefs than regular meetings. They didn't have to plan side by side. They already saw the world in the same way.

In Mein Kampf, Hitler's famous book, you can see Günther's influence clearly. Hitler talked about racial struggle, purity, and hierarchies using the same terms and ideas Günther had written about. Hitler's worship of the Aryan race closely matched Günther's idealization of the Nordic type.

Both men believed that racial mixing would weaken the nation, and both feared what they called degeneration. They thought Germany's future didn't depend on politics or the economy; it depended on racial purity. For Hitler, Günther was the one who gave a scientific voice to what he already felt emotionally. Günther put those instincts into words, diagrams, and lessons.

Once the Nazis gained more power, Günther's career rose quickly. In 1930, he was appointed as a professor of social anthropology at the University of Jena, a move that had Hitler's personal support behind it.

After the Nazi Party took control in 1933, Günther's influence grew even more. He became one of the main voices behind Nazi racial science. He helped write textbooks, shape school lessons, and gave talks attended by top officials from the SS and the Nazi Party.

His books were used in classrooms, and SS officers in training were required to study his work. In 1941, he received one of the highest honors from the Nazi regime: the Goethe Medal for Art and Science. He was admired by powerful Nazi figures like Himmler, Goebbels, and Rosenberg.

One of the most dangerous things about Günther's influence was how it helped make policies of exclusion, sterilization, and even extermination seem acceptable. His racial theories weren't just ideas on paper; they were used to justify real laws, like the Nuremberg Laws, which banned marriage and sexual relationships between so-called Aryans and Jews.

These laws weren't just about rules. They were based on Günther's deep belief that racial purity was the key to a healthy nation. The Nazi idea of "Rassenschande," which means "racial defilement," was basically Günther's thinking turned into law. It made love, family, and even private relationships illegal if they crossed the racial lines Günther had drawn in his books.

More than almost anyone else, Günther gave Nazi Germany a kind of false scientific language that made horrible things seem reasonable. While Hitler spoke emotionally, using metaphors and fiery speeches, Günther used charts, measurements, and anatomical diagrams. He would measure skulls, record eye colors, and try to link things like facial angles with personality traits. He used the language of science, but instead of using it to seek truth, he used it to promote ideological prejudice.

This created a system where mass murder looked like public health policy, and genocide was framed as a biological necessity.

Günther's writings didn't just shape domestic policy. They also had an impact on the Nazi campaigns in Eastern Europe. He portrayed Slavs and other Eastern European groups as racially inferior, giving the Nazis a so-called intellectual excuse for their brutal actions. The plan called Generalplan Ost, which aimed to remove entire populations from Eastern Europe to make room for Nordic settlers, was built on ideas found in Günther's academic work. These ideas didn't come out of nowhere. They were the direct result of the theories Günther had been developing for years.

Still, even with all his influence, Günther wasn't completely free of criticism inside the Nazi leadership. Some top Nazis didn't fully agree with his work. For example, Alfred Rosenberg, who generally shared Günther's views, felt that some of his racial categories were too rigid or too simplistic. And Heinrich Himmler, who was deeply into racial mysticism, sometimes preferred more spiritual or occult racial theories instead of Günther's dry academic style.

But in the end, those disagreements didn't matter much. Most Nazi leaders still believed that Günther's work was essential. Even Hitler, who usually didn't trust intellectuals, respected Günther deeply, calling his racial theories crucial for the survival of the German people.

After the War

When the Third Reich fell, Günther didn't face harsh punishment like many others. While some Nazi thinkers and leaders were executed or imprisoned, Günther mostly escaped serious consequences. After the war, he was briefly held and went through a denazification process, where former Nazis were categorized based on their involvement.

In 1948, Günther was classified as a "fellow traveler," which was a relatively light label. It meant he had supported the regime but wasn't seen as a major criminal. Because of that, he was allowed to go back to normal life.

He returned to writing, but this time his tone had changed. His postwar books were more defensive. He wasn't proudly promoting his ideas anymore. Instead, he tried to distance himself from how the Nazis had used his theories. Still, he kept believing in racial separation, and he warned against what he called the "biological chaos" of modern life. But those days of influence and fame were over. In the postwar world, Günther found himself pushed to the margins, no longer taken seriously by most academics or the public.

He died in Freiburg on September 25, 1968, mostly unrepentant. Even near the end, he still believed in his racial worldview.

In the years that followed, Günther's name became a symbol of how science can be twisted to serve dangerous ideologies. Historians and scholars didn't study his work to learn from it; they studied it to understand how knowledge can be corrupted. Günther became a clear example of how something that looks like science can actually be used to support lies. His legacy shows how rational thinking can be turned into rationalization, how data can be used to spread dogma, and how scientific tools can become weapons when used by people who believe some lives matter more than others.

Günther's story isn't just part of the past. It's a warning for the future. His writings show how dangerous it is when harmful ideas hide behind the mask of science. His charts, diagrams, and racial categories weren't neutral. They were carefully constructed arguments, deadly ones, about who should live, who should die, and who deserved a place in history.

Hitler may have given the orders, but it was Günther who wrote the blueprint. He was the scholar behind the Holocaust, the professor of the Final Solution.

One big question still hangs over Günther's life: How did he come to believe these things, and why did so many others follow him? The answer lies in the mix of fear, national pride, science, and myth that was spreading through Germany at the time. In Günther's world, racial theory seemed to offer answers to the deep problems of the modern era. It promised to bring order during chaos and meaning during despair. It told Germans they were special, chosen, and biologically destined to lead. And because these messages came dressed up as science, they were even more convincing and harder to resist.

Hans F. K. Günther didn't invent racism, but he gave it structure. He took vague feelings of superiority and turned them into textbooks. He transformed whispers of hate into academic theories. His life shows that the most dangerous ideas don't always come from angry mobs or loud speeches. Sometimes they come from classrooms, from books, and from people who think they are simply being "rational."

In the long and painful story of Adolf Hitler and the Nazi regime, Günther was the one who gave the madness a method. He gave a tyrant the tools to make his darkest visions real.

Günther wasn't born a monster. He was born a scholar. But in early 20th-century Germany, a country struggling with the loss of its empire, economic collapse, and deep national fear, his academic work turned into a weapon. His pen became a scalpel. His obsession with classifying people helped build the intellectual foundation of the most murderous regime in modern history.

People once called him the "Rassenpapst," the Race Pope. And it was Günther who gave Hitler something he desperately needed: the illusion that his racial vision was grounded in science.

Where Hitler acted on emotion, Günther provided the structure. His theories were a mix of bad science, romantic nostalgia, and cold, exact measurements of human traits. But those theories gave the Nazi worldview its precise, chilling framework and its lasting cruelty.

Hans Günther was born on February 16, 1891, in Freiburg im Breisgau, which was then part of the German Empire. He entered a world filled with both confidence and instability. Germany had only recently become a unified nation, and the country was buzzing with nationalist pride, romantic ideals, and a strong belief in scientific progress.

Günther grew up in a disciplined home. His father worked as a civil servant, and his early education was shaped by a classical upbringing, one that valued order, hierarchy, and structure. These values would later become central to how Günther saw the world.

As a young man, Günther became interested in classical languages, anthropology, and a new field that was gaining attention at the time: eugenics. Eugenics promised to be a "science of human improvement," claiming that humanity could be made better through controlled breeding and the elimination of so-called undesirable traits. Günther studied at top German universities: Freiburg, Heidelberg, and Berlin, where he focused on linguistics and ethnology (the study of human cultures and races).

Even though his education was highly academic and demanding, Günther's imagination was already moving beyond facts and evidence. He was drawn toward speculative ideas and essentialist thinking: the belief that people could be defined by fixed, unchanging traits.

A World Ripe for Racial Theories

The early 20th century was a time when racial theories were spreading rapidly. Across Europe and the United States, scientists, doctors, and ideologues were trying to use evolution, genetics, and physical measurements to define and rank different human groups.

Charles Darwin's ideas, which originally explained natural selection, were being twisted into new ideologies that claimed some races were meant to dominate others. Social Darwinism, eugenics, and racial hygiene weren't fringe ideas; they were mainstream and widely accepted. This was the world Günther stepped into. He didn't invent these ideas, but he became one of their most powerful voices.

In 1922, Günther published the book that would define his life's work: Rassenkunde des deutschen Volkes (Racial Science of the German People). In this book, he divided Germans into five racial types: Nordic, Mediterranean, Dinaric, Alpine, and East Baltic.

But this wasn't just a list or a neutral classification. It was a ranking, a system of values pretending to be science. According to Günther, the Nordic race was the highest and most advanced. He described them as tall, blond, blue-eyed, long-headed, and said they had the noblest traits: bravery, creativity, intelligence, and a special ability to build and lead societies.

The other racial types, in his view, were lower in value. They were less capable, less stable, and better suited for passive roles or even servitude. What Günther called "science" was actually ideology dressed up with charts and numbers.

Günther's racial theories quickly became popular among nationalists in Weimar Germany. At the time, the country was struggling: the Treaty of Versailles had left many Germans feeling humiliated, the government was unstable, and the economy was in crisis due to hyperinflation.

People were desperate for answers. Günther's ideas gave them one. Germany had lost its way not because of bad leaders or political mistakes, but because its bloodline had been weakened. Foreign influence and racial mixing were blamed for the country's downfall. His theories supported the growing belief that Germany was in decline, not politically, but racially. The solution he hinted at was purification: first cultural, then racial, and eventually, as history showed, genocidal.

Adolf Hitler was very interested in ideas like Günther's. He wasn't a trained scholar, but he read widely, especially anything that matched his own prejudices. Günther's work (especially Rassenkunde) gave Hitler the scientific-sounding language he needed to support his beliefs.

In Mein Kampf, Hitler talked about the Aryan race, but his ideas were vague and filled with myth. Günther gave those ideas structure: a detailed vocabulary, a racial system that could be turned into real policies and laws.

They didn't work closely together, but their connection was clear. Hitler spoke highly of Günther in private and made sure his books were widely distributed in schools, government offices, and Nazi training programs. Günther's work was used in classrooms, read by SS recruits, and relied on by doctors and judges to decide who could marry, who should be sterilized, and who was seen as racially valuable. His writings helped shape the entire Nazi worldview.

Because Günther's ideas lined up so perfectly with Hitler's goals, they didn't need to collaborate directly. Günther wasn't a Nazi propagandist; he was their chief racial theorist.

When the Nazis came to power in 1933, Günther's career soared. That same year, he was appointed Professor of Racial Science at the University of Jena. The appointment came with Hitler's personal approval, showing that it wasn't just about one man. It was about supporting a whole field of study.

Racial science was now an official part of German academia, and Günther was at the center of it. From his new position, he trained future doctors, teachers, and administrators in the Nazi racial ideology. Nazi officials and SS members attended his lectures. His racial tables and diagrams appeared in pamphlets, schoolbooks, and even government forms.

At the heart of Günther's thinking was the belief that races didn't just exist. They were not equal, and never would be. He rejected the Enlightenment belief that all people had equal potential. Instead, he believed in fixed racial hierarchies: unchangeable laws of nature where the Nordic man was always on top.

This belief turned discrimination into something that seemed natural and necessary. It wasn't just policy; it was "how nature worked." In Günther's eyes, Jews weren't just culturally different. They were racially foreign, described as "Oriental," with physical and spiritual traits that made them incompatible with the German soul. He said similar things about Slavs, Roma, and other non-European groups.

His words dehumanized entire populations and made it seem "logical" to separate, sterilize, and eventually exterminate them.

Günther's influence reached into the lives of ordinary people. His students, now trained as racial experts, evaluated people applying for marriage licenses, jobs, and citizenship. They used skull measurements, eye color charts, and family trees to decide who was "Nordic enough."

The effects were real and devastating. Günther's work was used in court rulings, in marriage denials, and even in deportation cases. He made racism look scientific, organized, and inevitable.

Even though he was deeply involved in Nazi policy, Günther wasn't a Nazi in the usual political sense. He didn't join the

SS or SA, and he didn't hold government office. His influence was quieter, but just as dangerous. He was the regime's intellectual conscience, the one who gave Hitler the tools to believe that his hatred was backed by science.

After the war, Günther tried to downplay his role, claiming he had just been a theorist, a scholar whose ideas had been misused. But the truth is much darker. Günther knew exactly how his work was being applied. He took part in racial selection, advised Nazi officials, and kept publishing throughout the war.

He wasn't standing off to the side. He was fully involved: a craftsman of exclusion.

During the height of Nazi power, Hans Günther was celebrated and rewarded. In 1941, he received the Goethe Medal for Art and Science, one of the highest honors of the time, personally awarded by Hitler. Within Nazi Germany, Günther was not just respected; he was praised by academics, featured in Nazi publications, and treated like a guiding light by powerful men like Heinrich Himmler and Alfred Rosenberg.

He didn't work alone. Günther also kept in touch with other racial theorists across Europe, sharing ideas and helping shape racial policies outside of Germany too. His reach wasn't just national. It was international, and the influence he had was, in many ways, terrifying.

Even as World War II turned against Germany, Günther stayed in his university position. He kept writing and teaching his ideas. He didn't take part in the military or attend important Nazi meetings like the Wannsee Conference, where the Holocaust was officially planned. He wasn't at any of the death camps either.

But the truth is, the men who did plan and carry out the Holocaust read his books. They used his ideas as part of their logic. The entire idea behind the Final Solution, the Nazi plan to murder millions, was built on the foundation Günther had helped create. In the minds of the Nazis, killing was not just hatred; it was "cleaning up" the population. They called it hygiene. And Günther was one of the architects of that twisted way of thinking.

When the Third Reich collapsed in 1945, Günther was captured by American forces and briefly held in custody. During the postwar denazification trials, he defended himself by saying he was just an academic, not a political figure. He claimed he was against violence, insisted his work was only theoretical, and argued that he had been misunderstood.

Sadly, these excuses worked. In 1948, Günther was labeled a "Mitläufer," which means a fellow traveler, someone who went along with the regime but didn't actively participate. Because of that classification, he never went to prison.

Instead, he returned to academic life and kept writing until he died in 1968.

Even in his final years, Günther never admitted he was wrong. He continued to defend his racial theories, criticized racial mixing in postwar Germany, and warned about what he called "biological chaos." He had lost his official status and position, but he still had a small, loyal following, especially among neo-Nazis and white supremacists, both in Germany and in other countries.

Some of these groups saw Günther as a kind of martyr: a man who had told the "truth" and been punished for it. They whispered his name as if he were a misunderstood prophet who had only been rejected because he wasn't "politically correct."

After the war, the world tried to move on and leave Günther behind. But his ideas didn't disappear. Racial essentialism, eugenics, and scientific racism kept showing up again and again, changed, disguised, but still present.

In the decades after his death, scholars didn't look back at Günther with admiration. They studied him as a warning. He became a symbol of how science can be twisted, how knowledge can be used as a weapon, and how intellectuals can become dangerous when they lose sight of morality.

Günther's influence on Hitler wasn't like that of a schoolteacher; it was more like a mirror. He didn't teach Hitler new ideas. Instead, he took what Hitler already believed and organized it, validated it, and gave it the appearance of science.

That was the most dangerous part. By wrapping hatred in scientific language, Günther gave the Nazi movement a powerful tool: the feeling that what they were doing was unavoidable. If biology demands separation, then who are we to question it? If nature rewards the strong and discards the weak, then showing mercy feels like betrayal.

Günther's racial science didn't just support Nazi ideology. It removed all doubt. He turned belief into math, and prejudice into policy. With his charts and classifications, murder became a calculation, and genocide became a logical step.

In the end, Hans F. K. Günther's story isn't just about one man. It's about how giving up on truth helped make the Holocaust possible. He was the kind of academic who gave up honesty in favor of status, and a scientist who replaced curiosity with the desire to control. He represents a chilling question: what happens when knowledge becomes obedience?

Even though Günther worked mainly through books and universities, his influence reached deep into the Nazi system, especially into the SS. Many of his racial theories were taken up as official policy. Under Heinrich Himmler, the SS became more than just a paramilitary force. It became a group bound by what they believed was their shared "Nordic" bloodline. Himmler imagined the SS as a sort of racial nobility, the biological elite of Germany, and Günther's ideas played a key role in shaping how SS members were chosen and trained. Every applicant had to go through intense racial checks, including detailed family background searches and physical exams. These were based directly on Günther's racial categories.

The SS Race and Settlement Main Office (RuSHA) was the part of the SS that put Günther's racial theories into action. They kept detailed family records, approved marriages between SS members, and carried out racial evaluations of entire populations in occupied areas. All of this came from Günther's belief that a nation's future depended on keeping its racial bloodline "pure." These weren't just paperwork tasks. They became almost sacred rituals, backed by fake science. Even the SS's everyday language, words like Blutsgemeinschaft (blood community) and Rassenschande (racial defilement), reflected Günther's way of thinking, where physical traits carried moral meaning.

But not everyone in the Nazi regime fully agreed with Günther. Other Nazi thinkers like Alfred Rosenberg and Walter Darré had their own ideas about race, which sometimes clashed with Günther's strict categories. Rosenberg was more mystical. He saw race as something spiritual and historical, not just biological. Darré, who led SS agricultural policy and pushed the "Blood and Soil" idea, focused on tying race to the land, believing in a racially pure group of farmers rooted in German countryside life. While all three believed the "Nordic" race was best, they emphasized different things. Günther focused on body measurements and features, Rosenberg on spirit and culture, and Darré on farming and tradition.

These differences showed that even inside the Nazi system, racial ideology wasn't always consistent. Sometimes, Nazi beliefs outpaced the science meant to support them. The regime often needed everyone to agree, even when the experts' results didn't match the official line. There were awkward moments when top Nazi officials were found to have features that didn't fit the ideal "Nordic" look. In those cases, the results were either ignored or twisted to fit. Günther was sometimes criticized for being too rigid, and his strict categories didn't always work with the regime's shifting goals, especially as the war grew.

Still, Günther kept his status. His books were regularly updated and re-released throughout the 1930s and 1940s, often with praise from high-ranking Nazis. He had access to university publishers, was invited to events across Nazi Germany, and was often mentioned in official writings. Even when the Nazis used his ideas selectively or bent them when needed, the core message, biological ranking and the need for racial purity, was never questioned. His thinking showed up in everything from policies to "Germanize" occupied lands to the Lebensborn program, which encouraged the birth of racially "ideal" children.

In Eastern Europe, especially places like Poland and the Soviet Union, Günther's ideas were used to carry out violent state actions. RuSHA officials trained in his methods screened entire populations for "Nordic" traits. Children who passed were taken from their families and raised as Germans. Those who didn't were forced into labor or killed. These decisions were made coldly, following Günther's way of seeing people as numbers in a racial formula, judged by things like skull shape and eye color.

Günther's classifications also played a role in how German Jews were treated. His writings helped push the idea that Jews weren't just a religious group, but a separate and unchangeable race. That shift turned regular anti-Semitism into official racial policy. Once Jews were labeled as a race, it didn't matter how they acted, believed, or lived. They were marked for exclusion. In Nazi eyes, they became something dangerous to be removed. Günther never openly called for their extermination, but his logic made it seem acceptable, even necessary, to those chasing the dream of a racially pure Germany.

Ironically, Günther's own background may not have met the racial standards he promoted. Some reports said he might not have been fully "Nordic" himself, leading people to question whether he should even be judging others. But this kind of hypocrisy wasn't unusual in the Nazi system. Many of the people creating rules of racial "purity" couldn't live up to them. What really mattered was loyalty to the ideology. Günther made himself valuable by giving the Nazis exactly what they wanted: an intellectual framework that made mass murder seem like routine policy.

After the war, once the truth about Nazi crimes came out, Günther tried to distance himself. In the 1950s and 60s, he claimed he was just a scientist, not someone involved in politics. He said people had misunderstood his work, that he hadn't encouraged violence, and that his racial ideas were about preserving cultures, not destroying them. These explanations didn't hold up, but in postwar Germany, where many people wanted to move on and forget, his excuses were often accepted.

Günther never showed regret for the part he played in supporting the Holocaust. He kept writing about race, sometimes under fake names or in smaller journals that supported nationalist or racist views. In these writings, he warned about Europe's supposed decline, the dangers of mixing races, and the loss of "natural order." His tone became more careful, but his beliefs stayed the same. He still believed that racial purity was the foundation of a strong civilization.

What makes Günther stand out from other Nazi thinkers is how long his ideas lasted. Even after he died, his work was picked up by far-right and white nationalist groups in both Europe and the U.S. Neo-Nazi magazines quoted him. Holocaust deniers used his categories to argue that Jews and Slavs were biologically inferior. Online forums passed around his racial charts as if they were real science. In these dark corners, Günther's ghost still lingers, where race decides your worth and biology seals your fate.

****

In the years after World War II, experts in fields like anthropology, genetics, and social science worked hard to take apart the fake science that Hans F. K. Günther had supported. They showed that race is not a biological fact, but a social idea, something people made up. They also proved that the lines between racial categories are blurry and that all human beings share the vast majority of their DNA. But by then, the damage was already done. Günther's ideas had helped make inequality seem normal, had been used to justify violence, and had played a part in the dehumanization of millions.

Günther's impact didn't come from any real science. It came from the emotional and ideological power of his words. He offered people a sense of order during chaotic times, made them feel superior when they felt defeated, and gave them a reason to hate, wrapped up in what looked like reason.

To Günther, race explained everything: culture, morality, intelligence, creativity, even a person's future. His thinking was total and absolute. It took away all the complexity of life and replaced it with a strict ranking system. In doing so, Günther played two roles. He was both the scientist and the preacher of the Nazi worldview. His charts and racial categories weren't just academic tools; they were treated almost like holy texts, used with the passion of someone who truly believed in them. Reducing all human variety to five racial types wasn't just a mistake. It was a terrible crime.

And the people who suffered because of those beliefs weren't just statistics. They were real human beings, destroyed by a way of thinking that cared more about skull shapes than the value of life.

Even now, long after Nazi Germany collapsed, Günther's legacy is a powerful warning. It shows that being smart doesn't make someone immune to doing evil. In fact, some of the most dangerous ideas come not from ignorance but from clever people using logic to justify fear and hatred. Günther's work didn't happen in a vacuum. It was shaped by the time he lived in, supported by institutions, and accepted by a society that chose order over compassion and control over fairness.

To understand Günther is to understand more than just the man. It means looking closely at a way of thinking: a mindset that divides people, lowers their worth, and destroys in the name of purity. It shows us what happens when science loses its sense of ethics. Behind every chart, every label, every diagram, there were real people whose lives were erased, not by accident, but on purpose.

Günther never led an army or planned battles, but his racial theories had a huge impact, especially on Adolf Hitler, who took those ideas deeply to heart. The most tragic part of Günther's legacy isn't just that it justified mass killing. It also influenced how the most important war in history was fought and lost. To Hitler, Nazism wasn't just politics. It was a sacred belief system. And at its center was the idea that the Aryan race was superior. That belief shaped everything he did: his speeches, his decisions, and the orders he gave.

To really understand Hitler's military failures, you have to understand how much he let ideology override common sense. Günther's racial ideas weren't just part of domestic policy; they twisted Hitler's entire approach to war. In the beginning, Hitler had some major wins. He quickly took over Poland, humiliated France, and swept through the Balkans. It looked like his worldview and military strategy were in sync. But beneath the surface, there was a serious conflict. Hitler saw war not just as a battle between armies, but as a way to cleanse and reshape races. He wasn't after victory for its own sake. He wanted racial reordering, and that obsession kept getting in the way of smart strategy.

This became crystal clear when Hitler decided to invade the Soviet Union. Operation Barbarossa, launched in June 1941, wasn't just about military goals. To Hitler, it was a racial mission. He saw Slavs as subhuman and believed communism was a Jewish plot. So the war in the East was framed as a fight for racial survival. Many of his generals warned him to be cautious or focus on one target, but Hitler ignored them. He split his army and aimed at Moscow, Leningrad, and the Caucasus all at once. Each of those places held symbolic racial meaning for him: Moscow as the heart of Jewish-Bolshevik power, Leningrad as a symbol of Slavic pride, and the oil fields of the Caucasus as key to German colonization.

This spread his forces too thin. The German army was soon stuck, cut off, freezing in the Russian winter, and badly supplied. But even then, Hitler wouldn't allow a retreat. This wasn't just about pride; it was about ideology. Backing down would mean admitting that Slavs were worthy opponents, and he couldn't accept that. He believed Soviet resistance was just a temporary glitch before the Aryan race took over. His speeches during this time were full of racial fire, not military planning, but talk of good versus evil, of pure versus impure.

Hitler's racial obsession also shaped how he viewed the North African front. His generals knew that controlling the Suez Canal and oil-rich regions was strategically important, but Hitler didn't care much about it. He saw the region as unimportant and racially beneath his attention. Even though the Afrika Korps, led by Rommel, showed real skill, Hitler never gave them the full support they needed. Again, racial beliefs got in the way of military success.

Even worse, Hitler took key military resources (like trains, fuel, and manpower) and used them for the Final Solution instead of the battlefield. At the height of the war, as German soldiers were dying by the thousands, he prioritized sending Jews to extermination camps. For Hitler, killing Jews mattered more than winning the war. That choice says everything about his priorities. He had once said that if Germany couldn't remain racially pure, it wasn't worth saving. And he stayed true to that terrifying belief.

As the war turned against Germany, Hitler only dug deeper into his ideology. When the Allies landed in Normandy in June 1944, his generals wanted to adjust plans, regroup, or retreat. Hitler said no. He believed that the Western armies, "weakened" by Jews and racial mixing, could never beat German soldiers. When they did, he blamed betrayal, not his own bad strategy. To him, any loss was a sign of weakness in others, not himself.

This paranoia grew. As Soviet troops got closer to Berlin, Hitler became bitter and angry at the German people. In March 1945, he gave the Nero Decree, ordering the destruction of German infrastructure (bridges, factories, railroads) so nothing would fall into enemy hands. His minister, Albert Speer, quietly ignored the order, but the message was clear: if Germany couldn't fulfill his dream, it didn't deserve to survive. This wasn't about patriotism. It was about devotion to an idea. Hitler didn't serve Germany; he expected Germany to serve his ideology. And if the country fell apart, at least his belief system stayed pure.

Hitler's loyalty wasn't to his people. It was to a myth. Günther's image of the perfect "Nordic" man became Hitler's ultimate goal. Every decision he made came down to one thing: did it serve the racial ideal? He didn't see war as a battle of weapons or resources, but as a test of racial strength. When the army failed, he blamed racial impurity. When civilians suffered, he pointed to Jewish sabotage or communist corruption, not his own actions.

This thinking even shaped how he handled potential allies. He could have worked with colonized people under British and French rule, like Indian freedom fighters, African revolutionaries, or Middle Eastern rebels, but he didn't. He saw them as racially inferior and not worth supporting. Even in Europe, he waited far too long to form non-German SS units that could've helped fight the Soviets. When he finally allowed it, the war was already slipping away. His belief in racial purity blinded him to practical alliances.

Nowhere did this blind faith in ideology hurt more than at Stalingrad. Hitler was obsessed with the city, partly because it was named after his rival Stalin. He saw capturing it as a huge symbolic win. He refused to let his generals pull back, even when the German army was surrounded and running out of supplies. The entire Sixth Army was wiped out. This battle marked a turning point in the war. But for Hitler, it wasn't about smart tactics. It was about racial pride and symbolic victory, even if it meant losing everything.

In his final days, hiding in the bunker under Berlin, Hitler still clung to the same beliefs. Even with the war lost, he kept talking about the rise of the Aryan race, the threat of the Jew, and the importance of struggle. As everything collapsed around him, he dictated a final political statement that repeated all the same racial ideas. He never apologized. He never reconsidered. He died still holding on to his twisted vision. His death wasn't just a way out. It was, in his mind, a sacred ending. If Germany couldn't become his racial dream, then he didn't want it to exist at all.

Hans F. K. Günther wasn't in that bunker, but his ideas echoed in Hitler's last words, last thoughts, and final decisions. The fantasy of Nordic superiority, the myth of racial destiny, and the fake science of "purity" were all still there. The Nazi regime had fallen, but the racial dream lived on in Hitler's mind, untouched.

The great tragedy of Nazism is that it destroyed itself from the inside. Hitler's complete devotion to Günther's racial theory made him blind to reality, unwilling to compromise, and unable to adapt. In the end, it wasn't just the Allies who beat Hitler. It was his own ideology. By putting race above reason, he chose destruction over change, dreams over facts, and death over defeat.

The lesson from all of this isn't just that racism is wrong. It's that racism is self-destructive. It asks people to sacrifice truth for fantasy, to replace real people with stereotypes, and to follow belief instead of facts. That's the real warning in Günther's legacy: when ideas matter more than human life, the result isn't progress. It's devastation.

CHAPTER 16

THE DIALECTIC OF DESTINY – HEGEL'S SHADOW OVER HITLER

Adolf Hitler wasn't a philosopher in the usual sense. He didn't carefully study ideas or write in a logical, thoughtful way like real philosophers do. Instead, he thought in symbols, feelings, and big dramatic stories. But even though he wasn't a deep thinker, the way he saw the world was surprisingly similar to the ideas of one of Germany's most important philosophers: Georg Wilhelm Friedrich Hegel.

Hitler had read Hegel's books and learned from them. He didn't talk about Hegel often, but Hegel's influence was still there, quietly shaping the way Hitler thought about history, power, and the world. Hegel's ideas had already spread throughout German schools, politics, and culture by then. They helped create the way many Germans thought, and Hitler grew up surrounded by these ideas.

One of Hegel's biggest ideas was that history had a purpose. He believed that everything that happened, good or bad, was part of a big plan. For Hegel, the state (the government) wasn't just for laws and rules. He thought it was something almost holy, a way for a higher power to work through the world. This kind of thinking made a deep impression on Hitler. It made him believe that things didn't just happen by chance. Everything was part of fate. Germany, he thought, had a special role in history.

Hegel was born in 1770 in a city called Stuttgart. He lived during the Enlightenment, a time when people were excited about science and reason. But Hegel didn't just believe in clear answers or logic. He believed in contradictions and conflict. His way of thinking followed a pattern: first an idea appears (the thesis), then an opposite idea pushes against it (the antithesis), and finally, the two ideas mix into something new (the synthesis). He saw this as the way history moved forward.

Hegel thought that history wasn't just random events. It was like a story with meaning. He said the world was like a stage where something called the Spirit (or Geist in German) revealed itself over time, through nations, leaders, and big events. In this story, conflict wasn't bad. In fact, it was needed. Without struggle, there was no progress. Without pain, no growth. Hegel believed that freedom was created through time and challenges, like iron being shaped by fire.

These ideas gave hope to 1800s Germany. At that time, Germany wasn't one strong country. It was divided and uncertain. Many Germans felt ashamed after being beaten by foreign powers. But Hegel made them feel proud. He said the German people were at the center of history's journey, and that the Prussian state showed the best form of freedom and order. For him, the state wasn't just politics. It was a deep moral and spiritual power. He once wrote, "The state is the march of God through the world." That's a powerful sentence. It later inspired dangerous ideas, but Hegel meant it as a belief in reason and progress, not in dictatorship.

When Hitler was born in 1889, Hegel's ideas were already everywhere in German life. They influenced schools, legal systems, and government offices. But over time, these ideas had split into two sides. One side, the right-Hegelians, focused on power, order, and the importance of the state. The other side, the left-Hegelians, focused on freedom, change, and questioning the system. Karl Marx came from the left side. He used Hegel's method of thinking to talk about class struggle and revolution. On the other side, nationalists and royalists used Hegel to support strong states and unity.

Even though Hitler wasn't very educated, he grew up surrounded by this mix of ideas. He didn't really understand the deeper philosophy, but he picked up the big messages. In Vienna, as a young man, he didn't go to school much. But he read newspapers, went to operas, and listened to speeches. All of these were full of Hegel-style thinking, even if no one said Hegel's name. People around him believed Germany had a special role in history. That it was chosen for something great.

Writers who supported pan-German ideas, racial theories, and strong nationalism all believed that history had a direction. They thought things were meant to happen. Hitler didn't invent this thinking. It was already popular. But he took it further. He believed Germany had to rise, had to win, and had to stay "pure." Anything else would go against nature.

One big idea that Hitler got from Hegel was that history is a fight between opposites. And through that fight, a new, better thing is created. Hitler even saw his own life this way. He believed that his hard life, being poor, rejected, and struggling, was part of a bigger plan. He thought those difficulties were meant to prepare him to lead. When Germany was falling apart after World War I, with different political groups fighting each other, Hitler didn't see it as the end. He saw it as a beginning.

He believed that National Socialism, his political movement, was the answer that would bring everything together. He saw it as the solution to Germany's problems, mixing race, state, and destiny into one united force. Just like Hegel said the Spirit becomes more aware through history, Hitler believed that the German people were waking up to who they really were through struggle and pain.

But for Hitler, this wasn't just politics. It felt more like a religion. Hegel's idea of the Spirit working through the state showed up in Hitler's speeches too. He didn't talk about Germans as just citizens. He talked about them as part of something holy, something greater. National Socialism wasn't just about rules. It was about truth. Hitler believed he wasn't chasing power for himself. He thought he was just doing what destiny had already decided. He once said, "I go the way that Providence dictates with the assurance of a sleepwalker." He didn't mean it as a humble thought. He meant it like a man who believed history itself was moving through him.

Hegel's influence on Hitler showed up clearly in the way Hitler completely ignored basic ideas of right and wrong. Hegel had taught that personal feelings about morality, what you as an individual think is right or wrong, don't matter as much as what the community believes. For Hegel, ethics meant following the shared values of the state or society, not your personal conscience.

Hitler took that idea and changed it into something truly horrifying. In his Nazi worldview, what a person felt in their heart didn't count. What mattered was the so-called racial community, what the Nazis called the Volksgemeinschaft. According to this belief, something was considered "good" if it helped the race, even if it involved cruelty, violence, or murder.

So, in Hitler's eyes, killing Jews wasn't wrong if it helped the Aryan race. Taking land from Slavic people wasn't bad if it fulfilled what he believed was Germany's historical mission. In this logic, morality didn't matter. Only racial goals did. This is how Hitler justified mass murder: by saying it was part of history's plan. Hegel had once written, "World history is not the ground of happiness. The periods of happiness are empty pages in it." Hitler seemed to agree. He didn't care about peace or comfort. He believed that history had to be harsh to move forward.

One of the most disturbing things about Hitler was how willing he was to sacrifice people's lives in the name of this so-called historical purpose. He didn't just see war as a way to gain power. He saw it as something almost holy. Hegel had said that war keeps nations from becoming weak, that it forces people to grow and change. Hitler took that idea and turned it into a rule to live by. To him, peace was weakness. War was truth.

He believed the Aryan race could only reach its destiny through violence and conquest, not through peace or discussion. He thought destruction was necessary to create a new world. That's why the horrors of the Holocaust, including Auschwitz, weren't seen by him as something awful that went wrong. He saw them as part of the larger plan. In his mind, the Final Solution wasn't a mistake. It was the next step in history.

Even Hitler's idea of leadership came from Hegel. Hegel had talked about something called the "world-historical individual," a person through whom history moves forward. These were people like Napoleon or Caesar, who weren't limited by normal laws or rules. They weren't ordinary. They were tools of something greater, helping to break down the old world and build the new.

Hitler saw himself exactly that way. He didn't believe he had to answer to voters, laws, or even his own political party. He saw himself as above all of them, the chosen one through whom history was working. His power wasn't about winning elections or following rules. It was based on personality and belief. He had total power, and nobody could question him. He even visited Napoleon's tomb with deep respect, seeing himself as part of the same group of history-shaping leaders. But Hitler believed he wasn't chosen by God. He was chosen by history itself.

Hegel's idea that the state is a spiritual force, something more than just a government, reached its darkest form in Hitler's regime. In Nazi Germany, the state wasn't just in charge of laws and policies. It was treated like a living thing, the physical body of the German race. If someone betrayed the state, they were betraying the race. If they obeyed the state, they were following their destiny. It wasn't just politics. It was treated like a religion.

That's why Nazi Germany had all the symbols, rituals, and loyalty to the Führer. The Nazi Party, the state, and the people were all tied together. It was his own version of Hegel's vision: spirit without freedom, unity without mercy.

Even Hitler's approach to law and justice followed this thinking. Hegel had said the state is the final authority: it decides what's right. Hitler fully accepted that. For him, laws weren't there to limit power. They were tools of power. In

Nazi Germany, laws weren't about fairness. They were about protecting the race. For example, the Nuremberg Laws, which stripped Jews of their rights, weren't seen by the Nazis as abuse. They believed they were doing what the state demanded.

The courts weren't there to ensure justice anymore. They were there to enforce Nazi beliefs, punishing people not for crimes, but for being seen as "impure." Step by step, the law changed from being about fairness and freedom to being about control. And in the end, that led to full-blown tyranny.

As Germany started losing the war, Hitler's beliefs didn't soften; they became even more extreme. Every loss, like the failure at Stalingrad or the Allied invasion of Normandy, didn't make him question his plan. He didn't see them as mistakes. He saw them as tests. He believed that before history could be reborn, it had to be destroyed.

The worse things got, the more extreme and hopeless his thinking became. In his last days, trapped in his bunker, he wasn't planning a peaceful end. He talked about cleansing and destruction. He said the German people had failed the great idea. They weren't worthy of it anymore, so they could die.

Hegel had said, "The real is the rational." But in Hitler's final vision, the world had flipped. Now the irrational (violence, death, and madness) had become real. And in that dark final belief, death itself was seen as the only truth left.

Saying that Hitler was a true follower of Hegel would be both wrong and right. On one hand, Hitler didn't have the deep understanding or the discipline to grasp Hegel's complex philosophy. He wasn't a thinker; he didn't have the patience or depth for that. But on the other hand, he acted out a new version of Hegel's ideas about history.

Hitler behaved as if history itself had chosen him. He ruled as if the state was some kind of holy force. He treated war like it was sacred. And in the end, when everything was falling apart, he accepted defeat as if it were part of a final, cleansing fire. He didn't carry Hegel's ideas like a student might. Instead, he took them and turned them into something dark and monstrous.

Hegel's influence didn't come to Hitler directly through reading books. It came through the culture around him. It was passed down through German nationalism, old ideas about race, strict military thinking from Prussia, and the school systems of the 1800s. It came through the schools

Hitler attended, the speeches he listened to, the operas he loved.

These ideas were part of the air in Central Europe at the time, and even though Hitler wasn't very well-educated, he breathed them in deeply. He may not have truly understood Hegel's complex thinking, but he believed that history had a direction, that it was heading somewhere. He ignored Hegel's focus on reason and freedom, but he clung to the belief that history had meaning. And that belief gave him all the justification he needed to do terrible things.

Now, to be clear: Hegel did not cause Nazism. But the sad truth is that his ideas, once separated from ethics and turned into myths, helped make it all feel like it was meant to happen. Hitler took Hegel's idea of a historical process and turned it into a fixed belief system. He made the state into something holy. He turned history into a tool for killing. He flipped Hegel's dream of freedom into a nightmare of control. And by doing that, Hitler showed how even the most thoughtful philosophy, if misused, can become the foundation for something truly evil.

Hitler's view of time and history also carried the fingerprints of Hegel's thinking, even if it was a distorted version. Hegel believed that time wasn't just empty space. It was the path through which the Spirit slowly reveals itself. For Hegel, history wasn't a circle, repeating forever. And it wasn't just a straight line of progress, either. It moved through conflict, tension, and finally, a kind of deeper unity. That's the dialectic: thesis, antithesis, and synthesis.

Hitler had a similar view of history. He didn't think things happened randomly. He believed they followed a sacred story. In his eyes, the fall of Germany after World War I wasn't just a national crisis. It was like a death that had to come before a resurrection. He often spoke of Germany rising again, not just as a country, but as something almost holy, something better and more complete than before.

Because of this belief, Hitler saw compromise as weakness. He hated negotiation. He didn't think he was making political choices; he thought he was unveiling destiny. He saw himself as someone Hegel might've called a world-historical individual, a person who pushes history forward, who doesn't follow old rules but makes new ones. People like that, in Hegel's view, couldn't be judged by regular morality. They were the tools of the Absolute, the next step in the great story.

In this logic, Hitler found a way to excuse any cruelty. His speeches often said that Germany's pain wasn't just necessary. It was spiritual. He told people to embrace suffering because it would lead to something greater. War and sacrifice were painted as the birth pains of a better world. Every defeat was just a test. Every terrible act was part of building a racially pure future. He took out Hegel's belief in reason and replaced it with race, but kept the idea that history had a purpose and would reach a final goal.

Hitler's obsession with the Volksgemeinschaft, the national and racial community, was also a twisted version of Hegel's idea of ethical life (or *Sittlichkeit*). For Hegel, real freedom wasn't about doing whatever you want as an individual. It was about becoming part of something bigger, like family, society, and the state, that worked together to create a free and rational world. The community wasn't just a group of people; it was something more, almost like a spiritual whole.

Hitler took that idea and bent it into something dangerous. To him, the German community wasn't political. It was racial. It was made of blood, ancestry, and shared fate. If someone didn't belong to this group, they were seen as a threat. Disagreement wasn't just a different opinion; it was like a disease that needed to be removed. To oppose the Volksgemeinschaft was to go against the natural path of history.

This kind of thinking led to real-world consequences. It gave the Nazis a reason to remove anyone who didn't fit into their idea of the racial whole. People with mental or physical disabilities, Roma, Slavs, and especially Jews were all seen as outsiders. They weren't just different; they were seen as polluting the unity that Hitler wanted to create.

Hegel's dialectic was about overcoming opposites and finding a new unity. But in Hitler's mind, this meant wiping out anything that didn't fit. Hegel talked about a process called *Aufhebung*, where contradictions are both canceled and preserved to create something new. But in Hitler's version, it was only about canceling. To keep the Aryan race, the Jew had to disappear. There was no space for living side by side. There was only domination, and then purity.

Even the way Hitler gave his speeches followed a kind of dialectical pattern, although it was much more basic. He would start by pointing out a problem or an enemy, like Jews, communists, or foreign bankers. Then he would describe the German people as the heroes: good, noble, and unfairly treated. Then came the answer: National Socialism, with Hitler as the leader who could fix it all.

This simple structure (problem, enemy, and solution) was a rough version of Hegel's thesis-antithesis-synthesis idea. It wasn't deep, but it worked. It gave people a clear story to believe in. Millions of people followed that rhythm, drawn in by the promise that all their problems, economic, social, racial, could be solved by joining the racial state.

Even Hitler's ideas for architecture reflected his belief in history and destiny. He worked with Albert Speer, his chief architect, on plans to redesign Berlin into a new world capital called "Germania." These buildings weren't just meant to look grand; they were meant to send a message. The huge size, perfect symmetry, and classical style were designed to show order, strength, and the feeling that the Nazi state would last forever. This fit with Hegel's idea that the state represents reason and stability. For Hitler, these buildings were more than stone and concrete. They were symbols that history had reached its highest point in Nazi Germany.

But Germania was never finished. And instead of feeling defeated by that, Hitler believed it proved something else: that he was a kind of tragic hero, someone who came close to fulfilling history's plan but was stopped by betrayal.

In his last months, Hitler gave orders to destroy German cities, bridges, railways, and everything. It may seem like madness, but to him, it made perfect sense. He believed that if the German people failed to win, then they had failed history. If they couldn't fulfill their destiny, then they didn't deserve to live. He said, "If the German people are not strong enough to give their blood for their existence, then they shall perish." This wasn't just anger; it was a belief that history would move forward without them, like a judgment from something higher.

Hitler also saw history as a battle between huge forces: nations, races, and ideas, not between individual people. He rejected the idea that history is made through small choices by individuals. Instead, he believed in a kind of cosmic fight. In his eyes, the Aryans and the Jews weren't just two groups of people; they were total opposites. Their fight wasn't just political; it was about the very meaning of existence. This way of thinking, though twisted, was similar to Hegel's belief in big forces shaping history. But instead of the clash of ideas, Hitler replaced it with a clash of races.

This kind of thinking allowed Hitler to talk about genocide as if it were just something natural, like a storm or a disease. He didn't speak about it with guilt. He saw it as something necessary and unavoidable.

Hitler also hated democracy, and this too tied into his distorted version of Hegel's ideas. Hegel had worried that if you only followed public opinion, things might fall into chaos. He believed real freedom came through strong and thoughtful institutions, not just popular votes. Hitler took this idea and manipulated it even further. To him, democracy was weak, messy, and fake. He believed that compromise was betrayal and that equality was a lie.

That's why he followed the idea of the *Führerprinzip*, or "leader principle." In his view, the leader wasn't chosen by the people. He was the people. He didn't rise from them; he embodied them. Once the leader was revealed, no one could question him. The connection between the leader and the people had to be total.

In the end, Hitler didn't take exact ideas from Hegel. He took a way of seeing the world, a mood, a belief that history had meaning, that contradictions must be resolved, that the state was more than a government. It was a spiritual force. He replaced Hegel's Spirit (*Geist*) with Blood (*Blut*), reason with race, universal freedom with tribal loyalty. But the structure remained. The belief that history moves forward with purpose, that struggle is necessary, and that politics is tied to something greater: these were all still there.

The sad truth is that Hegel himself believed in progress, reason, and freedom. His ideas were meant to help people grow and unite. He saw the state not as a tyrant, but as a way to bring liberty and law together. But Hitler took that structure and used it to create something horrifying. He kept the frame, but filled it with violence. Hegel's philosophy, meant to be a path to human growth, was turned into a system for destruction.

That's the danger of powerful ideas when they lose their moral grounding. Hitler didn't read Hegel like a philosopher. He used Hegel's structure to build a world of hate. He turned the dialectic into destruction. He turned Spirit into race. And instead of giving people freedom, he gave them fanaticism.

The path from Hegel to Hitler isn't a straight line. It wasn't guaranteed to happen. But it teaches us something important. It shows how big ideas, once they're out in the world, can be bent and used as weapons. Philosophy can lead to beautiful things like cathedrals, but also terrible things like concentration camps. And it shows how someone like Hitler, who wasn't a real philosopher but who grew up surrounded by those ideas, could take a vision of freedom and turn it into a system of slavery based on race.

Hegel didn't write Mein Kampf, but his influence is still there: between the lines, in the way Hitler thought and wrote, and in his belief that history had a fixed path. Hitler didn't see history as full of choices. He saw it as a map he was meant to follow. That belief gave him the excuse for everything he did. In his own mind, he wasn't just a man; he was the living force of history.

Hitler also believed that the individual didn't matter unless they were part of the greater whole: the Volk, or the racial community. This idea goes back to Hegel, who believed freedom came from being part of a shared ethical life. But Hegel tried to balance that with personal freedom. Hitler didn't. In his world, a person's value only came from serving the race. There was no room for private thoughts or personal choices. Conscience, that inner voice telling us right from wrong, was replaced by blind loyalty to the Führer. And so, people were trained to stop thinking for themselves. Their hearts and souls now belonged to the state.

This was a key reason why ordinary Germans took part in terrible things. A bureaucrat who signed a deportation order, a teacher who taught kids about racial superiority, or a soldier who shot civilians, many didn't see themselves as individuals making choices. They believed they were just parts of a larger machine, doing what history required. Hegel once said that personal morality has to step aside for the greater good of the state. He never meant that to justify mass killings. But in Hitler's world, stripped of ethics and compassion, it became an excuse to follow orders without question.

Hitler also built up a belief around himself that he was necessary: that history needed him. He spoke often about how struggle and harsh decisions were unavoidable. He said, "The world does not belong to the weak," showing his belief that only those who pass history's brutal tests deserve to win. If his plans failed, he didn't blame himself. He blamed the German people. In his final speeches, he said they had let him down, and their defeat proved they were not worthy. It was a dark version of Hegel's idea that history rewards those who push through conflict.

To Hitler, the Aryan wasn't just a race; it was a spiritual force. Aryans were, in his words, creators of culture and order. Jews, in contrast, were blamed for everything that caused disorder and confusion. This wasn't just racism. It was a worldview where people were turned into symbols of good and evil. It echoed Hegel's idea that history is shaped by opposing forces, but Hitler changed it. In his version, there would be no coming together. The "enemy" had to be completely wiped out.

The SS, more than any other group, followed this belief system. They didn't see themselves as just soldiers. They believed they were building a new world. They were taught racial science, filled with Nazi beliefs, and trained to see themselves as a kind of spiritual army. Heinrich Himmler, the SS leader, said they were like priests of a new order: a world without democracy, freedom, or individuality. In this new world, only racial unity and blind belief would remain. This was Hegel's idea of historical movement, but turned into a system of domination.

Hitler and his top leaders also believed deeply in the power of time. They talked about a "Thousand-Year Reich" and a new era for civilization. They believed they were creating not just a new country, but a new world. Hitler often used images of fire, rebirth, and revolution in his speeches. He didn't just want to continue German history; he wanted to transform it completely. That matched Hegel's idea that history is not just repetition: it's revelation, a constant becoming. But Hitler added violence. He didn't just want to move beyond the past; he wanted to destroy it. Churches, books, people, anything that didn't fit the new order had to be erased.

Even when everything was falling apart, bombs dropping, cities burning, Hitler didn't change his mind. In the last days, hiding in his bunker, he still believed he was part of a greater plan. He told his team that this destruction was a cleansing, and that through fire and death, a new world would be born. This wasn't just politics. It was more like religious prophecy. He had stopped being a leader. He had become a prophet of destruction. And in that final vision, we see the darkest twist of Hegel's ideas: the belief that even death and suffering can be justified if they're part of history's next step.

Hitler's Germany was a disaster built on misused philosophy. It turned deep ideas into deadly tools. It took metaphysics, the study of meaning and spirit, and turned it into mass murder. But we have to remember: Hitler didn't invent these ideas. He picked them up, absorbed them, and twisted them. Hegel's ideas about history, spirit, the state, and conflict were passed down through culture. Not through careful study, but through stories, symbols, and myths. Hitler wasn't reading footnotes. He was reading legends. But even legends carry deep ideas. And he believed in the biggest one: that history has a purpose, that struggle reveals truth, and that the individual must disappear into the whole.

What started as a way to understand human freedom became, in Hitler's hands, a plan for domination. So we must study Hegel's influence not just to see what it inspired, but to understand what can happen when powerful ideas lose their moral grounding. In Nazi Germany, the dialectic, meant to guide us to truth, led instead to darkness.

CHAPTER 17

THE REDEEMER RECAST – JESUS OF NAZARETH, HITLER, AND THE STRUGGLE FOR SPIRITUAL SUPREMACY - NAZAREEN

Adolf Hitler was born into a deeply Catholic world. He was baptized in a small Austrian town called Braunau am Inn, which was a very normal thing back then. As a young boy, he went to schools run by Benedictine monks. Everywhere he looked, he saw religious symbols, especially the crucifix, which hung in every classroom. The community followed all the usual church traditions: daily prayers, regular masses, and religious processions. It was simply part of life.

But even though Hitler grew up surrounded by Christian rituals, something deeper and more complicated was going on inside him. He absorbed the look and feel of Christianity, but he never truly followed its teachings. He wasn't drawn to the gentle and loving side of Jesus, the one who taught kindness, forgiveness, and compassion. Instead, the version of Jesus that captured Hitler's imagination was much darker: a Jesus who judged, punished, and came with fire and a sword. This was the image that stuck with him.

As a boy, Hitler gave mixed signals about his religious feelings. For a short time, he sang in a church choir, and some say he even thought about becoming a priest. But when you look closer, it seems like it wasn't a true calling. He wasn't really interested in God or faith. What fascinated him was the drama of it all: the rituals, the robes, the smell of incense, the power that came with it. These weren't just decorations to him; they were symbols of authority. As he grew older and drifted away from religion, he never forgot how powerful these images could be. Later, he would use that same emotional force to control others.

By the time he moved to Vienna in his late teens, Hitler had already started to let go of his Christian beliefs. In the busy, political atmosphere of the Austro-Hungarian Empire, he came across a mix of ideas that would shape his future. These included extreme German nationalism, antisemitism, racial theories, and even some strange mystical and occult beliefs. He turned away from Christian values like love and humility, but he didn't forget the powerful Christian stories and symbols. In his own mind, he started to see himself in a messiah-like role, not as the Son of God, but as the one sent to save Germany.

In this twisted version of history, Germany was like a suffering people: betrayed, beaten down, and humiliated after losing World War I and being punished by the Treaty of Versailles. Hitler saw himself as their rescuer, the one who would pull them out of the pain and give them a new future. He didn't see himself as just another politician. He believed he was a savior leading his people from suffering to rebirth.

This way of presenting himself wasn't random. It was planned. Hitler understood that people, especially in hard times, often search for something to believe in. They want hope. They want purpose. And in a country where many had lost faith in their government, he filled that gap with himself. In speech after speech, he told people he was chosen by fate. He painted himself as someone who had been poor, rejected, and even thrown into prison, but who had risen through it all with a higher mission. The way he told his story sounded a lot like religious tales, but turned upside down.

When Hitler got out of prison after writing *Mein Kampf*, his followers treated him almost like a holy figure. His words were read like sacred text. His pictures were hung up where people used to hang crosses. His life was presented like a martyr's story: misunderstood as a young man, punished unfairly, but finally glorified. To his supporters, it felt like they were following a prophet.

But this imitation of Christ didn't stop at symbols. It went even further. The Nazis actually tried to rewrite parts of Christianity itself. One of their main goals was to change the image of Jesus. For Hitler and his followers, the idea that Jesus was Jewish didn't fit with their racist beliefs. They couldn't accept that the central figure of Christianity came from the very group they hated.

So they tried to "Aryanize" Jesus. Nazi writers and some friendly theologians started painting Jesus as a strong, blue-eyed, blond hero, someone more like a German warrior than a Jewish teacher. In their twisted version, Jesus wasn't a peaceful rabbi, but a fighter who opposed corrupt Jews and the Roman Empire. They turned him into a kind of early Nazi, a symbol of racial purity and betrayal.

And this wasn't just something said by a few fringe thinkers. It became a full movement. A group called the "German Christians" (Deutsche Christen) worked to change Christianity from the inside. They tried to remove the Old Testament, replacing it with Germanic myths and stories. They edited parts of the New Testament too, downplaying anything that made Jesus seem Jewish. They even reinterpreted his fights with religious leaders like the Pharisees as racial battles instead of theological ones. In Hitler's Germany, the Christian cross didn't disappear. It was taken over and slowly replaced by the swastika.

This transformation was done step by step. Nazi celebrations took the place of Christian holidays. For example, the Christmas season was turned into a winter solstice festival that celebrated nature and race instead of the birth of Christ. Hymns were rewritten to reflect Nazi values. Marriage ceremonies were redesigned to fit the Nazi ideal. The idea of a "Reich Church" was introduced, a national church with no real theology, just devotion to race and homeland.

Anyone who stood against this shift paid a heavy price. Pastors and priests who refused to go along were pushed aside, arrested, or even killed. One of the most famous examples was Dietrich Bonhoeffer, a brave Christian who stood up against the Nazis and lost his life because of it. In Hitler's regime, there was no room for a Jesus who forgave enemies or loved the weak.

At the center of this whole transformation was something dark. Hitler was replacing Jesus with himself. He erased

Jesus as a Jewish figure and placed himself in the role of redeemer. In this new belief system, Hitler was the one who connected the German people to their destiny. His speeches sounded like sermons. His rallies looked like church revivals. The torches, the flags, and the chants weren't just politics. They were acts of worship.

Hitler didn't just want control over laws and land. He wanted people's hearts and souls. And he knew that in a country where Christianity had shaped minds for centuries, he couldn't just get rid of religion. He had to offer something new. So he built a new version of faith, centered around race, power, and himself.

Still, no matter how hard he tried, he couldn't completely erase Jesus. The real teachings of Christ stood in direct opposition to Nazism. "Blessed are the peacemakers," said Jesus, but Hitler preached war. "Love your neighbor as yourself" clashed with Nazi hatred. "What you do for the least of these" condemned the persecution of the weak. Deep down, Hitler hated these teachings. He saw Christianity as soft, feminine, and weak.

He even admired Islam, not for its beliefs, but because he thought it was stronger. He liked that it combined religion with politics and demanded loyalty and discipline. To him, Jesus was not someone to follow. He was someone to replace.

Even so, Hitler often used Christian words when it suited him. He talked about "Providence" and "divine will" as if he were guided by God. But this wasn't real faith. It was a way to make himself sound more important and trustworthy. By talking about God, he wrapped himself in a sacred image. He wasn't trying to destroy religion completely. He wanted to complete it, with himself as the final figure. Just like Christians believe the New Testament fulfills the Old, Hitler's new faith claimed to fulfill Christianity, with him at the center.

Interestingly, some parts of how Hitler led were also influenced by other religious models, though not in spirit. One powerful comparison is with the Prophet Muhammad, not in terms of message or values, but in structure. Like Muhammad, Hitler rose during a time of chaos. Like Muhammad, he brought together a broken group of people under a new belief system. And like Muhammad, he built a movement that aimed to change every part of society, not just politics but people's entire way of life.

Hitler spent time studying how the Prophet Muhammad rose to power, and he admired how Muhammad brought together military, spiritual, and political leadership in one. In private conversations, Hitler admitted he was impressed by how Islam helped build a strong warrior culture. He saw Muhammad as someone who didn't just preach with words but also led through action, even on the battlefield. What stood out to Hitler most was how Islam seemed to blend faith with obedience. People followed religious teachings and political authority as one and the same. That kind of unity fascinated him.

But Hitler wasn't interested in the heart of Muhammad's message. Muhammad had spoken of justice, mercy, and humility before God. Hitler didn't care for any of that. He didn't preach peace or prayer. He gave orders. He didn't kneel in devotion. He demanded loyalty. So, when you look closely, the comparison says more about what Hitler wanted to become than any real similarity to Muhammad.

What Hitler tried to copy wasn't the spirit or teachings of Muhammad. It was the blueprint. He saw how one man's story could reshape a whole civilization. He saw how myth could become law, how a message, real or made up, could move millions. That's the part he latched onto. He wasn't trying to be a true prophet or religious figure. He wanted to be the creator of a new kind of belief system, one that wasn't about God but about race, blood, and an imagined destiny.

As World War II dragged on, Hitler's image of himself as a kind of savior only grew stronger. His speeches became darker, more dramatic. He talked about betrayal, sacrifice, and a final, holy struggle. He compared his journey to religious stories, like Jesus in the Garden of Gethsemane, surrounded by enemies, staying true to his mission. When German cities were bombed, he described it like the people were being crucified. When the army suffered, he said their blood was like seeds for a future German rebirth. Even as everything around him was collapsing, he clung to this grand, tragic vision.

In the last days of Nazi Germany, Hitler hid away in the Führerbunker, his underground shelter, while the world above fell apart. And in that dark place, the comparison with Christ reached its final, twisted moment. He was surrounded by destruction, his allies were gone, and his dream was dying. But he didn't show regret. He didn't ask for forgiveness. Instead, he doubled down on his beliefs. He blamed the German people for not living up to his vision. And then, instead of surrendering, he chose to die. His suicide wasn't just a way out. It was part of the story he had built for himself. He wanted it to be a ritual, a final sacrifice. He saw his death as a way to seal his ideology in blood.

But unlike the story of Jesus, there would be no resurrection. No third day. No rising from the grave. Only ruins.

As Berlin burned, all the symbols of Hitler's false religion fell with it. The swastikas were torn down. The banners went up in flames. The same crowds that once cheered him as their savior now stood in shock, surrounded by rubble. And what about Christ, the real Christ? He didn't return with fireworks or loud proclamations. He came back quietly, in the background, unchanged by all the lies that had tried to replace him.

The truth was, Jesus never needed parades, armies, or racial purity to prove his power. His strength was in humility. His power came from love. His victory came through sacrifice. And these were things Hitler never understood and never could beat.

In Christianity, the death of Jesus isn't the end. It's the beginning of hope. His suffering leads to redemption. The crucifixion is followed by resurrection. From pain comes healing. But in Hitler's world, suffering didn't bring peace. It called for revenge. Where the Gospel offers forgiveness and spiritual growth, Hitler's ideology had no room for grace. Inside the Führerbunker, there were no prayers for renewal. No hope. No light. Just a twisted version of religion, cold, cruel, and used to justify hatred and death.

Still, even with all his efforts to copy, twist, and control religious symbols, the deeper truth behind the story of Jesus kept shining through. Hitler could take the words. He could imitate the tone. He could even dress himself up in messianic language. But he could never capture the heart of it: the love, the mercy, the hope. That truth was something he could never fully erase, no matter how hard he tried.

Even among Hitler's most loyal followers, there was a quiet sense of discomfort. Not everyone in the Nazi leadership felt at ease with the spiritual emptiness that Hitler tried to offer in place of Christianity. Some, like Alfred Rosenberg, Martin Bormann, and Heinrich Himmler, openly wanted to get rid of Christian beliefs altogether. They didn't just reject Christianity. They wanted to take Germany back to an older, pagan worldview that worshipped nature, the land, the sun, and the idea of a pure Germanic race. They wanted a belief system rooted in myths about bloodlines and ancient soil.

Others, like Joseph Goebbels, weren't as bold. He shifted between keeping a surface-level connection to Christianity and supporting the new racial ideas. He didn't want to upset the millions of ordinary Germans who still considered themselves Christians, even if only in name. But behind the scenes, a quiet plan was unfolding, one that aimed to slowly erase Christianity from public life. The idea wasn't just to push Jesus out of the spotlight. It was to wipe him from memory altogether.

As the war dragged on, this plan started to feel more urgent. Hitler dreamed of a "Thousand-Year Reich," but he knew that military power wasn't enough. If he really wanted his vision to last, he had to take over people's inner world too: their beliefs, their morals, even their sense of right and wrong. Germany had been shaped by Christianity for centuries, and Hitler knew it couldn't be undone overnight. But he also knew that if you slowly change culture, especially through institutions like schools and youth groups, you can reshape how people think and feel over time.

That was the true goal of Nazi religious policy. They weren't trying to destroy Christianity in a loud or open way. Instead, they wanted to make it fade out quietly, starve it of meaning, push it to the sidelines, and make it so irrelevant that it would eventually disappear on its own. The swastika wouldn't replace the cross through violence alone. It would happen gradually, as a new generation grew up learning a different story.

And so, Nazi youth programs were about much more than marching or military drills. They were designed to change hearts and minds. The Hitler Youth and the League of German Girls weren't just in training camps; they were in spiritual re-education centers. These young people weren't taught the teachings of Jesus or the values of love, humility, and service. Instead, they were fed ideas about racial pride, blind obedience, physical strength, and loyalty to the "Volk," the German people as a racial group. Religious classes were replaced by lessons in Germanic myths, race science, and the story of Hitler's life.

The goal wasn't just to teach. It was to transform. To take out traditional beliefs and replace them with something new: a belief system that didn't kneel before a crucified savior but stood tall before a living leader dressed in uniform and fire.

But there was a problem the Nazis couldn't fully overcome. Even with all their efforts, they couldn't fully erase Jesus from the hearts of the people. He was too deeply rooted in

German culture and personal life. Even among those who supported Nazi ideas, some part of Christianity still remained. Mothers still whispered quiet prayers before bed. Grandparents still held onto their crosses. Soldiers still carried Bibles with them to the front lines.

And as the war went on, as cities were bombed, as young men died on the frozen battlefields of Russia, and as hunger and fear became part of daily life, people started to question everything. The promises of a glorious future were turning into ashes. Hitler, once seen as the one who would bring resurrection, now seemed to only bring death and ruin.

This inner conflict, the gap between what people were taught and what they were actually living, grew louder in the final years of the war. As homes burned and hope faded, people began to remember the old teachings. Not the ones about blood and race, but the words they had once heard in churches and from parents and grandparents: "Love one another." "Forgive your enemies." "Do not be afraid." These quiet words started to rise again, not shouted from podiums, but whispered in moments of pain and silence. And in those quiet moments, the illusion of Hitler as a savior began to fall apart.

Still, even when everything was collapsing, Hitler didn't let go of his belief in himself. Just before he died, he dictated his final political statement. There was no apology, no sign of regret, no admission that he had been wrong. Instead, he repeated the same message, blaming the Jews, blaming the world, insisting that his vision had been misunderstood. He died not as a man humbled by defeat but as someone who still believed he was right. Like other false messiahs in history, he thought his death would somehow give power to his cause.

But there was no shrine built for him, no sacred tomb, no holy book carrying his words to future generations. The resurrection he imagined never came.

Instead, there was silence, and ruins, and the slow, quiet return of something older and deeper than Hitler's false religion. Something that had survived bombs, lies, and betrayal. A message that had always been stronger. Not because it shouted louder, but because it spoke to the soul: love, mercy, humility, and hope. The very things Hitler had tried to erase were the only things left standing.

After World War II, Germany, and much of Europe, was left in a kind of spiritual ruin. The physical destruction was obvious, but what many people struggled with even more was the deep moral collapse that had happened. Millions had been killed in Hitler's racial war, and now people were left to face the painful truth: their nation had followed a path of cruelty and hate. For many Germans, this realization didn't lead to a spiritual awakening. It led to silence, confusion, and emotional numbness.

The churches, which had either gone along with Hitler or stayed quiet out of fear, had lost much of their moral authority. People no longer looked to them for answers. Theologians, those who study religion, had to face the uncomfortable reality that their faith had failed to stand up when it mattered most. New ways of thinking about ethics and morality had to be developed. In this broken world, the figure of Christ didn't return as a symbol of victory. Instead, he came back as a troubling question: how could a country so shaped by Christian teachings, especially the Sermon on the Mount (a message about love, peace, and humility) have turned into a place where genocide was possible?

Part of the answer lies in how Hitler and his followers used spiritual language and religious symbols to serve their own political goals. They didn't try to wipe out Christianity right away. Instead, they hollowed it out, emptied it of its true meaning, and repurposed it to fit their agenda. They took sacred Christian symbols and turned them into tools for the Nazi state. They reshaped biblical heroes to fit their ideas about race and power. They swapped out Christianity's promise of love and redemption for a dangerous promise of racial superiority. In doing so, they didn't just attack religion. They drained one of the world's deepest moral traditions and replaced it with a brutal ideology built on bloodshed, control, and propaganda.

But there's an unexpected twist in history. Despite all of Hitler's efforts to reinvent Jesus as a kind of racial warrior and turn Christianity into a tool for nationalism, it was Christ's original message that outlasted the Nazi era. After the war, as the world tried to make sense of what had happened, through court trials, public confessions, and national reckonings, it was the core teachings of the Gospel that helped rebuild moral understanding. Words like forgiveness, justice, reconciliation, and human dignity, so central to Christ's message, became the foundation for new ethical systems and even helped shape international law.

Take the Nuremberg Trials, for example. On the surface, they were legal proceedings. But underneath, they were driven by something deeper: the belief that every human life matters, that people have a conscience, and that there are moral truths that go beyond any one country or race.

When you look closely, the difference between Jesus and Hitler isn't just a matter of history. It's a matter of values at the deepest level. Jesus spoke of a kingdom that wasn't tied to any one nation or political system. He preached humility, kindness, and love. He healed the sick, fed the hungry, and mourned the dead. Hitler, on the other hand, spread illness, caused famine, and oversaw mass death. Jesus forgave those who hurt him. Hitler turned on anyone who disappointed him. One carried a cross out of love; the other built gallows out of hate. Jesus said, "I am the way, the truth, and the life." Hitler claimed to be the final word in history, but he only brought death.

By looking at how Hitler twisted and tried to replace the image of Christ, we begin to see just how deeply he understood the power of spiritual symbols. He knew people are drawn to meaning. He knew myths can shape how people live and act. And he knew that the real battle wasn't just about land or power. It was about the human soul. Hitler wasn't just trying to take over Europe. He was trying to write himself into eternity. But in the end, eternity rejected him.

Christ remained, not as a conqueror, but as a witness to the truth.

Even though the Nazis tried to reshape Jesus into someone who fit their racist beliefs, it never really worked. There was always a huge gap between who Jesus truly was and what the Nazi regime stood for. In every Gospel story, Jesus is on the side of the poor, the rejected, and the hurting. He tells us to love our enemies and warns that those who live by violence will die by it. These weren't just nice suggestions; they were at the very heart of Christianity. Hitler couldn't delete these teachings. He could only ignore them or twist them into something unrecognizable. In the Nazi version of Christianity, Jesus wasn't the friend of the outsider anymore. He wasn't forgiving sinners or healing the broken. Instead, he was reimagined as a nationalist fighter. The Prince of Peace had been turned into a symbol of racial judgment.

This mismatch created real anxiety within the Nazi leadership. Deep down, they knew that true Christian belief was dangerous to their system. Even as they tried to control or manipulate religion, they saw that real Christian values stood in the way of their goals. People like Pastor Martin Niemöller and the members of the Confessing Church, who stuck to the original teachings of Christ, were watched closely, harassed, imprisoned, and some were even killed. The Sermon on the Mount, with its message of mercy and peace, was seen as more threatening than any propaganda from the Allies. Even whispered in private, the words of Jesus had a power that Nazi brutality couldn't destroy.

And that fear was justified. Many Christians, both clergy and everyday people, did resist, even if only in small ways. Some sheltered Jews in secret. Others refused to join the Nazi Party or stayed silent instead of repeating Nazi slogans. Some held onto their Bibles as an act of quiet defiance, refusing to trade the cross of Christ for the Nazi swastika. These acts, even when small, were powerful. They created a hidden current of resistance in a society overwhelmed by tyranny. In these moments, Christ was still present, not as the fake Aryan version imagined by Nazi theologians, but as the suffering servant standing alongside the condemned.

But Hitler didn't stop at twisting Christian teachings. He also understood that religion lives in rituals, in symbols, in places and traditions. Churches, holidays, music, and even the way people honored the deadm, were all deeply rooted in German culture. If Nazism was going to replace Christianity, it needed to offer people something that felt just as spiritually powerful. And so, the regime set out to build a whole new kind of belief system, one that looked and felt like a religion but served only the Nazi cause.

We saw this new "faith" play out in the massive Nazi rallies. The Nuremberg Rallies weren't just about politics. They were full of carefully planned rituals: marches, torchlight parades, music, flags, and huge crowds moving in unison. It felt more like a religious ceremony than a political event. In these moments, individuals disappeared into the crowd. The nation was celebrated as sacred. And at the center of it all stood Hitler, not just as a leader but almost as a god-like figure. His image was everywhere. His voice echoed like a preacher's. People didn't just follow him. They worshipped him. It wasn't just politics; it was emotional, spiritual manipulation, a kind of false communion.

These rituals reached into everyday life. Births, marriages, funerals, things that were once marked with Christian customs, were now given a Nazi twist. Mothers were honored for giving birth to Aryan children. Couples were married under Nazi banners. When soldiers died, they weren't mourned with prayers of resurrection or peace. Their deaths were turned into patriotic sacrifices, celebrated as fuel for the Nazi dream. The Christian cross at gravesites was often replaced with Nazi symbols, like the iron cross or ancient German runes. The idea of an afterlife was no longer about union with God. It became about living on in the collective memory of the Aryan race.

Even the calendar was reworked. Christian holidays lost their spiritual meaning. Christmas, for example, wasn't about the birth of Jesus anymore. It was turned into a winter celebration of Germanic traditions. Easter, which once celebrated the resurrection and hope, was either ignored or turned into a vague tribute to nature's rebirth and Aryan strength. The Nazi version of time wasn't focused on morality, redemption, or progress. It was seasonal, racial, and circular. In that world, there was no room for Christ.

The Nazi regime's obsession with rewriting the past went so far that they even tampered with the Bible. They didn't just ignore parts they didn't like. They actively rewrote it. New versions were printed with entire passages removed, especially anything that felt "too Jewish" or "too soft." Jesus' background, his words, even the meaning of his death, were twisted to fit racist ideas. In these bizarre rewritings of the New Testament, Jesus wasn't a teacher of love and forgiveness anymore. He was turned into a violent warrior, supposedly fighting for the Aryan race. This wasn't Christianity anymore. It was something completely different, something false and dangerous. But to the Nazis, changing the Bible was essential because they understood just how powerful sacred stories and symbols really are. If they wanted to take over hearts and minds, they had to fill that sacred space with their own message.

And in that space, Hitler began to take the place of Christ. His picture hung where crosses once did. His speeches took the place of sermons. His voice on the radio was listened to with silence and awe. People treated him not just like a leader but like a holy figure. Children were taught to pray to him. Mothers hung his photo in their living rooms. Entire families would stop and stand when he spoke. Hitler was no longer just the head of the country. He had become the center of a new kind of religion. But unlike true messiahs, he didn't offer hope or healing. He demanded loyalty, sacrifice, and fear. He gave nothing back.

What made Hitler's version of faith so spiritually dangerous was that he understood something very real: people aren't just looking for food, shelter, or jobs. Deep down, we all want to feel part of something greater. We long for meaning. We search for stories that help us understand life, especially when things are hard. For centuries, Christianity gave people that kind of story: a story where pain leads to healing, where loss leads to hope, and where even death can lead to life. Hitler offered a twisted copy of that story. But in his version, suffering wasn't something to heal. It was something to inflict. Forgiveness was replaced with vengeance. Love was replaced with loyalty. Instead of lifting up the weak, he crushed them. Instead of grace, he offered punishment. Instead of eternal life, he offered endless struggle.

Still, Hitler believed he had a special destiny. He saw himself as the one chosen by history to lead Germany to its "true" identity. But there was a major difference between him and Christ. Christ came to heal what was broken. Hitler tried to destroy what didn't fit his vision. Christ carried the weight of human sin. Hitler blamed others for it. Christ offered mercy. Hitler offered revenge.

This complete reversal of spiritual meaning left a deep scar, not just on Germany but on the world. The Holocaust, the war, and the ruined cities weren't just political disasters. They wounded something deeper: our shared sense of what's right and good. Hitler didn't just bring destruction. He polluted the language we use to talk about goodness and faith. Trying to take Christ's place wasn't just wrong. It was a spiritual crime.

After the war, many theologians, writers, and scholars tried to understand how such evil could grow in a country that had once been shaped by Christian ideas. This was the land of the Reformation, the home of Bach and Luther and Bonhoeffer. How could it fall so far? Part of the answer lies in Hitler's gift for twisting belief. He didn't get rid of religion. He used it. He borrowed its rituals, its symbols, and its emotional power, then turned them into tools for spreading hate. He saw something that many politicians didn't. If you control people's imagination, what they believe in, what they hold sacred, you can control everything else.

That's why we must remember Hitler not just as a cruel dictator or a ruthless killer, but as a false prophet. He used religious words to spread violence. He stood in holy places not to honor them but to take them over. And like all false prophets, he left behind a legacy not of peace or greatness, but of ashes and grief.

And through all of this, the story of Jesus Christ remained the opposite of Hitler's in every way. While Hitler wanted power, Jesus gave it up. While Hitler demanded to be worshipped, Jesus knelt down and washed his followers' feet. Hitler demanded the blood of others. Jesus gave his own. Hitler died cursing the world. Jesus died blessing it.

This isn't just a religious contrast. It's a moral dividing line. It's the kind of truth that decides the fate of entire societies. That's one of the biggest lessons of the 20th century: when we let others twist our symbols, hijack our sacred stories, or turn our rituals into tools of control, we don't just open the door to dictatorship. We welcome it in.

Hitler tried to reshape Jesus into his own image. But history didn't accept it. The Christ of the Gospels survived the Nazi era. His message outlasted the marching boots. His love outlived the death camps. And in every act of quiet resistance, in every family who hid a neighbor, in every whispered truth, Christ was still there. Not loudly, not triumphantly, but faithfully, defiantly, eternally.

Even after Hitler's death, scholars, theologians, and ordinary people kept wrestling with the hole he left behind. How could one man come so close to changing the way an entire nation thought about morality, faith, and meaning? What does that say about the world we live in? Hitler wasn't a man of traditional faith. He didn't pray. He didn't seek connection with God. But he had a chilling ability to play with the deep longings that religion touches, the need to feel loved, to feel chosen, to be part of a greater story.

This manipulation didn't just stay inside churches. It spread across German life. Words that used to belong to faith, like "salvation," "sacrifice," "mission," or "eternity," were now being used to describe Nazi goals. Even the sacred idea of being a "chosen people," central to both Jewish and Christian beliefs, was twisted into a claim that the Aryan race was special. Religion became politics. The spiritual became strategic. By the time the 1930s ended, many Germans couldn't tell the difference between real worship and political devotion, between God and the Führer.

Still, the Nazis couldn't completely replace faith. There were cracks in their plan, moments when the truth pushed through. One of the most powerful examples didn't come from the Church, but from inside the Nazi military itself. In 1944, a group of German officers tried to kill Hitler and stop the war. It was known as the July 20th plot. Many of the men involved, like Claus von Stauffenberg, were motivated by their Christian beliefs. Stauffenberg, a devout Catholic, said his conscience and faith told him he had to act. To him, Hitler wasn't just a failed leader. He was a spiritual fraud.

That moment showed something powerful: the figure of Christ still stood as a silent judge. Even in a time of darkness, he remained the measure of what was right and just. Not everyone who resisted Hitler was Christian, and not all Christians resisted. But when people did resist in the name of faith, they were almost always looking back to a very different kind of king: one who didn't ride into battle on a war horse, but on a donkey. One who wore a crown of thorns instead of gold. One who told his followers to love their enemies, even when those enemies meant them harm.

One of the strangest and most revealing things about Hitler's attack on faith is that it actually showed just how powerful Christ still was, even in rejection. The fact that Hitler worked so hard to replace Jesus shows he knew just how deeply Christ's message was rooted in people's hearts. In trying to mimic him, he didn't just reject Christ. He revealed his own envy. And by preaching a twisted "gospel" of racial pride and national rebirth, Hitler unintentionally confirmed just how powerful the real Gospel still was: the Gospel that speaks of grace, not race... of human dignity, not domination.

That's why, even now, the strongest moral arguments against Hitler often come from a spiritual or religious place.

People don't just say he was a brutal dictator or a dangerous leader. They say what he did was a violation of something sacred. Building gas chambers in the land of cathedrals wasn't just murder; it was a desecration. Using God's name to justify genocide wasn't just a lie; it was blasphemy.

And sadly, the Church didn't always stand up against it. Many church leaders stayed silent. Some even supported Hitler, thinking he could bring order or protect them from communism. Some believed he would defend "traditional values." It took many years after the war for churches to fully admit their failure. But eventually, they did. Across Europe, churches began to reflect, apologize, and reform. They looked back to the core of Christ's teachings: humility, love, justice, and recommitted themselves to living those values. In doing that, they made it clear: Hitler may have come close to taking over the spiritual heart of a nation, but he didn't succeed. He couldn't erase its soul.

Still, the damage ran deep. After the war, Germany went through what you might call a kind of spiritual memory loss. The horrors done in Hitler's name made people not just reject Nazism, but also lose trust in anything collective, including religion. Many began to see faith itself as dangerous. The cross, once a symbol of hope and love, felt tainted by its association with the swastika. Christianity, in many places, struggled to win back the trust of the people.

Theology had to change. The horrors of Auschwitz and the Holocaust demanded answers that traditional teachings hadn't prepared people for. Thinkers like Emil Fackenheim asked whether faith could even survive after such darkness. Some people turned away from religion altogether, choosing humanism or silence instead.

Yet even in all that silence, the memory of Christ quietly remained, not as a political figure but as a moral guide. In a century filled with mass death and total control, Christ's words still carried a strange and stubborn beauty. "Whatever you did for the least of these, you did for me." Those words, spoken by a man executed by an empire, still held power after the crematoriums. They reminded the world that human dignity isn't based on race or social status. It's something sacred, built into every person. No dictator, no ideology, no false prophet can take that away.

That's the real reason Hitler couldn't destroy Christianity: because Christianity was never about chasing power. It was about giving it up. Its foundation wasn't an idea; it was a person. And that person, so completely different from Hitler in every possible way, still speaks to the heart of the world. Not with shouting, but with quiet strength. Not with force, but with love.

Hitler could ban prayer. He could burn churches. He could even rewrite the Bible. But he couldn't silence the Gospel. He could build grand buildings and fill them with images of himself, but he couldn't keep Christ out of the ruins. After the war, as cities lay in ashes and people were left with nothing, it wasn't powerful institutions that began the healing. It was small, faithful communities. Quiet churches. Individuals who still believed in grace and chose to rebuild, not with flags and armies, but with kindness and truth.

That rebuilding wasn't easy. They had to teach people again what humility meant. What forgiveness meant. What mercy looked like, even when it didn't seem fair. They had to remind a broken people that our worth isn't based on bloodlines or status, but on love. That real greatness isn't found in dominating others; it's found in serving them. That the true Messiah doesn't demand others die for him. He offers his own life instead.

And when you see it that way, the difference between Hitler and Christ becomes painfully, blindingly clear. One fought for a throne built on the bodies of the dead. The other was nailed to a cross between criminals. One launched a war to rule the world. The other offered peace to save it. One thought he was chosen by fate. The other chose to carry the weight of the world. One pulled his nation into darkness. The other rose from the grave to bring light.

Hitler's dream of a "thousand-year Reich" lasted only twelve years: twelve years filled with blood and ash. But Christ's message kept going. It survived the bombed churches, the refugee camps, the war trials. It lived on in survivors' quiet prayers and in the courage of people who chose love over hate. And even now, long after Hitler's body turned to dust, the man he tried to replace still stands: not in power, but in compassion. Not in fantasy, but in truth. Not in domination, but in mercy.

That's the final failure of Hitler's spiritual mission. He didn't just fail to take over the world; he failed to win the soul. He offered fear. Christ offered hope. Hitler built death camps. Christ opened graves. One stained the century. The other still helps to heal it.

As the world moved deeper into the second half of the 20th century, the spiritual wreckage Hitler left behind became something people had to study, face, and learn from. In Germany especially, there was a long and painful reckoning. People had to ask themselves: How did this happen? How did a nation once full of churches and Christian history end up cheering for violence and cruelty? How did sermons echo Nazi slogans? How did people let go of kindness and choose brutality?

The answer, many realized, wasn't that Christianity had vanished. It was that it had been twisted. Its symbols were stolen. Its message was poisoned. Its voice was silenced by fear.

But from that deep self-reflection came something powerful: a kind of spiritual rebirth. Churches across Germany and beyond began to rethink everything. They went back to the roots of their faith, but this time they looked at it from the perspective of the people Christ stood with: the poor, the persecuted, the hurting. Movements like post-Holocaust theology, liberation theology, and radical discipleship grew stronger. Not because people rejected Christianity, but because they wanted to take it back from those who had misused it.

In seminaries, future pastors were taught a hard truth: staying silent in the face of evil is itself a kind of evil. They were reminded that Jesus doesn't stand with the powerful; he stands with the oppressed. Not in palaces, but on dusty roads. Not in comfort, but in compassion. In facing Hitler's legacy, the Church had to face itself. And in doing so, it slowly began to recover not just its voice, but its soul.

After Hitler's collapse, a deep spiritual hunger was left behind. People had lost their trust in governments, leaders, and in big institutions altogether. In Germany especially, many turned away from traditional religion and looked instead to philosophy, literature, and art to make sense of the emptiness. Slowly, though, something deeper started to return. Some people began to rediscover faith, not the loud, nationalistic kind that had been wrapped around Hitler's image, but a quieter, more personal kind. Jesus began to reappear in people's hearts and homes, not as a symbol of power or empire, but as someone close, someone real. The cross, once used to assert dominance, began to mean something different again. It became a symbol of standing beside the suffering, a reminder that even in the darkest times, love could endure pain without giving up, and truth could be buried without ever dying.

In a strange and powerful way, Hitler's effort to replace Christ actually led people back to Christ's real message. The silence that followed the bombings gave people room to think. The horrors of the concentration camps shattered shallow ideas about faith and forced people to ask hard questions. The fake promises and symbols of the Nazis had fallen apart, and people were ready, through grief and soul-searching, to rediscover what was real. They had once cheered for a political "savior." Now, through pain, they had learned to tell the difference between a man who demands worship and a God who stoops down to wash feet.

Hitler tried to present himself as a kind of savior. He twisted light into darkness. He built a kingdom, but it was a kingdom made of graves. And in the end, for all the marches and medals, all the parades and prayers said in his name, he couldn't last. Because kingdoms built on fear, lies, and cruelty always fall when the truth returns, and truth always does.

Jesus didn't have to "defeat" Hitler. He didn't need to. Hitler destroyed himself by trying to take Christ's place. His empire burned. His beliefs were discredited. His name became a symbol of shame. But Jesus, the man from Nazareth, crucified two thousand years ago, his name still brings life, healing, and forgiveness. The contrast between them couldn't be clearer. And in that contrast is the greatest lesson of all: history does not honor the loudest or the most feared. It honors the most faithful. Not the one who shouted orders, but the one who healed the broken.

So in the long sweep of history, it wasn't the Reich that survived. It was the Gospel. Not the false redeemer wearing a crown of steel, but the true redeemer wearing a crown of thorns. Not the one who promised victory through violence, but the one who brought resurrection through love.

This wasn't just a battle of ideas or egos. It was a deep, spiritual clash between two completely opposite visions of what it means to be human. Hitler's world was about control, bloodlines, and conquest. Christ's world was about humility, belonging, and sacrificial love. These two ways of life simply couldn't exist side by side. They collided on every level: political, moral, and spiritual. And yet, even under the crushing weight of the Nazi machine, where nearly everything was controlled, the quiet teachings of Jesus still survived. Not through speeches or power, but through the hearts of ordinary people.

All across Nazi Germany, there were small, brave acts of resistance. Most of them were unseen, many of them deeply rooted in quiet faith. Parents who refused to report their neighbors. Doctors who protected disabled children. Prisoners who prayed in secret, or whispered Psalms in the cold dark of the camps. These weren't big, dramatic protests. Often, they weren't even seen as religious acts. But they came from something deeper: a sense that no law or leader can erase the image of God in a human being. That the light of Christ still flickers, even in the shadow of the gallows.

That's how Christ's message lived on during the Nazi years. Not through institutions, but through people. Through real lives. Through suffering. Through quiet acts of courage and love that defied the cruel logic of the regime. To love your neighbor was, in a way, a form of rebellion. To believe that every person mattered was to reject the heart of Hitler's ideology. Saying "God created all people" was enough to be seen as dangerous, and yet people still believed it.

These quiet acts didn't need crowds or applause. They happened in kitchens, in hiding places, in jail cells. They were invisible to the world, but not to God. And that invisibility itself was a kind of victory, because totalitarianism, more than anything, fears the soul that refuses to bow. And in those terrible years, many souls didn't bow.

After the war, as people spoke about what they had lived through, many talked about Christ. Not as a political symbol, but as someone who had been with them in the worst moments. Some said they saw his face in the eyes of the dying. Others said they felt him in the silence of the camps. For these survivors, Jesus wasn't just a figure in a story. He had walked with them through the valley of death. And the cross, once used as a sign of power, was reclaimed as a sign of love that suffers with the broken.

Out of this reflection came a powerful awakening in Christian thought. People didn't want to protect religion's reputation anymore; they wanted to purify it. For too long, the Church had sided with power and privilege. Now, many believers began to see something much clearer: Jesus could never belong to a government, a race, or a social class. He belonged to the poor, the jailed, the forgotten. His kingdom wasn't "not of this world" because it was irrelevant, but because it stood in judgment of every system that used God's name while ignoring God's heart.

In this new way of thinking, Jesus' story became a way to rethink all of history. The Holocaust wasn't just a moral crisis. It raised deep questions about God and suffering. Where was God in Auschwitz? What does it mean to follow a crucified Savior in a world that perfected crucifixion with science and bureaucracy? Theologians like Jürgen Moltmann began to talk about the "crucified God," not as a distant idea, but as a real companion in suffering. Not a warrior or even just a prophet, but the God who suffers with his people.

This return to a suffering Christ wasn't just an intellectual shift. It was a spiritual necessity. In a world where "redemption" had been used to justify mass killing, the only answer was a Savior who gave his life, not took it. This wasn't weakness. It was the strongest kind of strength. It was a quiet but unshakable answer to every tyrant who ever said that cruelty was justified by the cause. Christ's death on the cross, once seen as a shameful defeat, now became a symbol of pure and incorruptible moral clarity.

So in the end, Hitler didn't just fail to replace Jesus. He ended up proving just how powerful Jesus really is. The more Hitler tried to erase Christ, the clearer the difference became. People could now see what kind of world you get when love is replaced by race, when truth is replaced by lies, when grace is replaced by force. The contrast wasn't just uncomfortable; it was devastating.

In the years that followed, many survivors and those raised in Nazi Germany returned. Not necessarily to churches, but to the person of Jesus. They opened the Gospels again, not as part of tradition, but to meet someone real. They saw him not as a symbol of Western culture, but as a Middle Eastern man who stood up to empire. Not a cheerleader for power, but someone who challenged it. And they remembered that to follow him means to carry a cross, not in pride, but in quiet, faithful love.

This rediscovery has shaped much of the moral progress in the modern world. From liberation theology in Latin America to the civil rights movement in the U.S., from interfaith peace efforts to warnings against toxic nationalism, Christ's spirit has continued to challenge everything Hitler stood for. In every movement that lifts the poor, welcomes outsiders, fights injustice without hate, Christ is present. Not always because people name him, but because his love is alive.

And that love, the one Hitler tried to replace, could never be destroyed. Because it was never built on slogans or pageantry. It was built on love. A love that crosses barriers, forgives enemies, lifts the lowly. A love that walks into the dark and comes out not with revenge, but with resurrection.

So this whole story, Hitler's attempt to erase Christ, isn't just something for history books. It's a timeless warning. It reminds us that no one, no leader, no nation, no ideology, has the right to twist the truth for their own gain. It reminds us that any system trying to own the human soul is not just wrong; it's idolatry. And it reminds us that false messiahs will always appear, but they always fall. Not always because they're overthrown, but because they rot from within.

But Christ doesn't fall. He may be rejected or misunderstood, but he stays. He doesn't conquer with weapons; he enters with presence. He doesn't rule with fear; he leads with faith. And that's why, long after the ashes are cleared, long after the graves are counted, and long after the lies are exposed, the name of Jesus Christ still holds power. Not the power to rule nations, but the power to heal hearts. And that, in the end, is the only power that lasts.

CHAPTER 18

BLOODLINES OF CONQUEST – THE INFLUENCE OF JULIUS CAESAR, ALEXANDER THE GREAT, AND GENGHIS KHAN ON ADOLF HITLER

Adolf Hitler didn't see himself as just another man shaped by history; he believed he was history's final product, the one who brought it all to a head. In his eyes, the truly great men of the past weren't the thinkers or businessmen. They were warriors, visionaries, and leaders with unshakable will, people who didn't just change the world but left their mark on time itself. From the moment he started his political journey to the very end of the Third Reich, Hitler saw himself as walking in the footsteps of three of history's most powerful conquerors: Julius Caesar, Alexander the Great, and Genghis Khan.

To Hitler, these men were more than just successful generals. They were builders of empires, forces of nature, and symbols of what it meant to seize destiny with bare hands. They took broken nations and turned them into mighty empires. They didn't ask for permission; they made their own rules and demanded loyalty. Hitler respected their brutal strength, but what truly captivated him was their bold vision and lasting legacy. He didn't just want to copy them. He wanted to become one of them. His goal wasn't just to rise to power. It was to create a myth around himself, just like they had.

Of the three, Julius Caesar had the biggest influence on young Hitler. What fascinated him was how Caesar wasn't just a military hero. He was a revolutionary hiding in plain sight. He used tradition as a cover while completely reshaping the Roman Republic. Caesar knew how to win over the people, gain military fame, and charm the masses. He took a crumbling political system and replaced it with something new, something powerful. Even his death didn't destroy his legacy; it made him a legend. Hitler saw Caesar's assassination as a lesson in betrayal and fear, how the powerful few often strike when they feel their grip slipping.

Hitler looked at the weak leaders of the Weimar Republic and saw them as modern-day Brutus figures, clinging to a broken system, too scared to lead, too proud to change. So when he tried to overthrow the government in 1923 during the Beer Hall Putsch, he imagined himself as a bold revolutionary like Caesar crossing the Rubicon. The coup failed, but Hitler turned the trial into a stage, and prison into a pause, not an end. Like Caesar writing about his wars in

Commentarii de Bello Gallico, Hitler used his time behind bars to write *Mein Kampf*. Not just a memoir, but a message to the world. It was his personal Bible, his warning, and his dream all in one. Just like Caesar, Hitler cast himself as a man of the people, misunderstood by elites, carrying the burden of leadership while pretending to serve the state.

Caesar's mix of military power and political strategy gave Hitler a model to follow. He admired Caesar's ability to wait, plan, and strike when the moment was right. He also paid close attention to how Caesar used spectacle: massive parades, impressive buildings, and a public image that felt almost divine. Hitler copied this style. The grand rallies in Nuremberg (the bold Nazi symbols, the dramatic speeches), all of it was meant to show not just authority, but a kind of larger-than-life presence. Hitler understood, like Caesar did, that people needed to see power to believe in it.

But Caesar also served as a warning. Hitler believed Caesar's downfall came from trusting people too much, from thinking loyalty could be earned through kindness. Hitler swore he wouldn't make the same mistake. Instead of building his empire on friendships, he built it on fear. When he felt threatened by his own followers, he didn't wait; he acted. The Night of the Long Knives, where Hitler ordered the killing of potential rivals, was his way of making sure no one would betray him like Caesar was betrayed on the Ides of March. Hitler was determined to survive his own revolution.

While Caesar gave Hitler a political model, Alexander the Great offered something else: an image of youthful power, cultural dominance, and almost godlike admiration. Hitler was fascinated by Alexander's fast and sweeping conquests. To him, Alexander wasn't just a military genius. He was a unifier of worlds, a man who brought order to chaos and shaped entire civilizations. He became a legend in his own lifetime, worshipped by many. His face was on coins. His stories were passed down like holy texts. His sudden death only made him more mysterious and revered.

Hitler deeply craved that kind of immortality. He didn't just want to be followed; he wanted to be loved, even worshipped. He created youth groups inspired by Alexander's elite fighters, the Companions (young men loyal to their leader and trained in his beliefs). Hitler saw himself as a new kind of Alexander, a Germanic one, destined to move east, defeat the so-called "lesser races," and create a new empire. This idea formed the heart of *Lebensraum*, the belief that Germany had to expand eastward to survive and grow. To Hitler, the East wasn't just land. It was fate.

Hitler was also fascinated by how Alexander the Great didn't just conquer people; he changed who they were. Alexander didn't stop at winning battles. He spread Greek culture wherever he went. He renamed cities, passed new laws, and combined armies made up of different ethnic groups. It wasn't just about ruling. It was about reshaping identity.

Hitler wanted to do something similar, though in a very different way. He saw himself as someone who could "fix" what it meant to be German. In his mind, that meant purifying the German race, getting rid of anything that didn't fit his narrow idea of racial unity. He wanted to wipe out old regional divisions and bring everyone under one, unified, racial will. Just like Alexander had surrounded himself with loyal followers and spiritual advisors who fed his ego, Hitler did the same. He kept people around him who constantly praised him, encouraged his fantasies, and made him believe he was destined to remake the world. He didn't just want to win land. He wanted to reshape history itself.

But this is where Hitler and Alexander truly parted ways. Alexander could adapt. He took in the customs of the places he conquered. He respected the traditions of the Persian

Empire. He even married local noblewomen and encouraged his officers to do the same. He built his empire by mixing and blending cultures.

Hitler couldn't do that. His idea of racial purity didn't allow for compromise. He wasn't interested in learning from others or finding balance. His goal wasn't to bring people together. It was to wipe certain people out. So while Alexander left behind cities and cultures that carried his name and influence, Hitler left behind destruction. Bones and ashes. Nothing more.

Still, even in his final moments, when everything around him was collapsing, Hitler held tightly to the dream of becoming like Alexander. He believed the world would mourn him. That his early rise and dramatic fall would give him a legendary status. That, like Alexander, he wouldn't just be remembered as a person, but as a force of history.

Then there was Genghis Khan: a darker, more brutal figure, and another one of Hitler's idols. In Genghis Khan, Hitler saw pure, unstoppable conquest. No emotions. No diplomacy. Just total domination. Khan had crushed cities across Asia, built a massive empire, and did it with terrifying speed and violence. Hitler was drawn to that kind of power.

Not just because it was big, but because it was cold and efficient.

In private talks, Hitler often praised Genghis Khan for being willing to wipe out entire populations to gain control. To Hitler, this wasn't evil. It was clarity. He believed Khan had proven that strength was the only truth. That in the end, people don't remember the pain or the bloodshed. They remember who won. They build monuments and draw maps, and the morals get left behind.

This way of thinking gave Hitler the excuse he needed for genocide. In his mind, killing millions wasn't about hatred. It was about building an empire. The Holocaust wasn't just about antisemitism. It was part of his bigger plan to "clean up" Europe and create a pure, racially united empire. Just like Genghis Khan had destroyed cities and replaced cultures with his own, Hitler believed Europe needed to be wiped clean. He saw Slavs as slaves, Jews as people to be eliminated, and Aryans as the future rulers of the world.

Hitler also admired how Genghis Khan used fear as a weapon. The Nazis followed that idea closely. Their Blitzkrieg attacks were designed to shock and terrify, not just to win. The SS, like the Mongol executioners, were more than soldiers. They were symbols of fear and control. Mass killings, public humiliation, deportations…. none of it was random. It was part of the plan. Like Khan, Hitler believed fear would keep people loyal. But he didn't just copy it. He turned it into a full system.

And yet, just like with Caesar and Alexander, there were things Hitler didn't understand. For all his violence, Genghis Khan built something lasting. He created ways for people to communicate across his empire. He rewarded talent. He allowed different religions to exist. He established laws that remained long after he died.

Hitler did the opposite. He destroyed systems. He made himself the center of everything. He silenced anyone who disagreed. He replaced competence with blind obedience. His empire wasn't built to last. It was built to serve him until it burned down.

But even as everything fell apart, Hitler still believed he belonged among the greats. As Soviet troops surrounded Berlin and his generals begged him to retreat, he refused. He believed he was finishing a story worthy of myth. Like Caesar, he wouldn't run from his fate. Like Alexander, he saw his death as the final act of a heroic life. Like Genghis Khan, he thought he'd be remembered as a world-changing conqueror.

He spoke as if history would one day prove him right. That the emotions would fade, and people would understand. That statues would rise, books would be written, and his name would live on beside the men he had worshipped all his life.

But that's not what happened.

Where Caesar's image is proudly displayed in marble, Hitler's face is hidden away, stained by shame. Where Alexander's name lives on in cities across the world, Hitler's is erased from maps and buildings. Where Genghis Khan is remembered for trade, law, and cultural impact, Hitler is remembered only for death. His armies brought no order. His beliefs sparked no rebirth. His war built no empire. It only destroyed.

Still, Hitler's obsession with becoming legendary, his hunger to be eternal, tells us something deeply important about evil. Evil doesn't always look like hate. Sometimes, it looks like ambition. Sometimes, it hides inside dreams of greatness.

Hitler didn't picture himself as a monster. In his mind, he was Caesar with tanks, Alexander with airplanes, Genghis Khan with modern logistics. But his failure wasn't just a matter of morality. It went deeper. It was spiritual. He tried to carve his name into the memory of humankind, but in the end, all he left behind was ash.

To really understand how much Hitler looked up to Caesar, Alexander, and Genghis Khan is to understand the full scale of his dream. He didn't just want to rule. He wanted to be remembered forever.

For him, power wasn't the end goal. It was a way into legend. And that desire didn't come from military meetings or political plans. It came from childhood fantasies, old books about heroic conquests, and a belief that he had a place in history's highest ranks.

The men he idolized weren't just inspirations. They were the standard he used to measure himself.

In Julius Caesar, he saw a master of politics who also had personal charm. Someone who could bend the Senate, win over the people, and turn military wins into political control. Hitler admired how Caesar didn't just fight. He could speak and persuade. And Hitler believed that speaking was his own greatest strength.

Caesar had the Roman Forum. Hitler had beer halls and radios. Both built their power on the idea that the elites were corrupt and disconnected from the people. Both used their popularity as a weapon, to tear down systems that once held everything together.

Hitler didn't just admire Caesar's rise. He studied his fall. He knew that the very nobility Caesar had once served were the ones who turned against him in the end. For Hitler, that wasn't just betrayal. It felt like a warning. A pattern. In his eyes, any leader who dared to challenge a broken system would always be at risk of being struck down by it.

But instead of taking the fall of Caesar as a cautionary tale, Hitler treated it like a puzzle that needed solving. The answer, he believed, wasn't to avoid Caesar's ambition. It was to finish what Caesar started. Where Caesar had been killed by his peers, Hitler would make sure that no such betrayal could ever happen to him. He would not just become a dictator. He would build a system so tightly controlled, so racially "pure," so ideologically united that no Brutus would ever rise again.

This desire to protect himself from Caesar's fate also pushed Hitler to wrap himself in the imagery of sacred kingship. He didn't want to be just another politician. He wanted to be seen as a chosen one, almost divine. When he entered Vienna in 1938, the entire scene was staged like a religious ceremony. The streets were decorated in red, the crowds filled every corner, and his car moved slowly, like it was carrying something holy instead of a man. In those moments, Hitler wasn't just Germany's Chancellor anymore. He saw himself as a modern-day emperor, the true heir of Rome, dressed not in a robe but in the colors of empire.

If Caesar gave Hitler the model for political transformation, it was Alexander the Great who gave him the idea of destiny. Alexander was more than just a general. He was a legend. A boy who conquered nations before turning thirty. A warrior who cried when there were no more lands left to conquer. A man who died young, leaving behind an empire built on the ruins of kings. Hitler saw something magical in him, something fast, brilliant, and unstoppable. He was dazzled by Alexander's mix of genius and fate.

What fascinated Hitler the most were Alexander's eastern campaigns. Just like Alexander had pushed beyond the edges of the known world, Hitler dreamed of pushing eastward too. To him, places like Poland, Ukraine, and Russia weren't just military targets. They were his version of Persia and the Indus Valley. He spoke about the East using racial language, but in his imagination, it was something grander. He saw wide-open land, waiting to be turned into farmland for German settlers, with shining cities built on top of crushed

Slavic resistance. It was his vision of a thousand-year empire, his own version of ancient conquest.

But Hitler didn't just want to repeat Alexander's actions. He wanted to steal his aura, that sense of being guided by something higher. Like Alexander, who was always said to be surrounded by signs and omens, Hitler surrounded himself with astrologers and mystics. They constantly told him he was destined for greatness. Even his time in prison, even his political failures, were turned into parts of the myth, proof that he was chosen, that every step of his journey had meaning. He encouraged people to believe it too. His rise from failed artist to leader of a nation became, in the minds of his followers, a kind of miracle.

Then came Genghis Khan, the third figure in Hitler's imagination. If Caesar had taught strategy and Alexander had inspired vision, Genghis Khan gave him something raw: permission to be merciless. Hitler didn't just admire Khan's victories. He admired the way he won. Fast, brutal, and with no apologies. To Hitler, Genghis Khan proved that leadership wasn't about kindness or complexity. It was about getting results. It was about building civilization on top of corpses, as long as the foundation was strong.

Hitler often spoke about the Mongol conquests with awe. He was impressed by how quickly Khan had taken over vast parts of the world. He admired how focused and straightforward it all was. No moral debates, no compromises, just power, applied coldly and clearly. In Hitler's eyes, that was strength.

This way of thinking shaped how Hitler saw the East. He didn't view the Slavic people as a population to govern. He saw them as something to remove. His invasion of the Soviet Union wasn't just about winning land. It was about reshaping existence. His plan was to clear entire regions, starve millions, and replace them with German settlers. Just like Genghis Khan had wiped out cities and repopulated the land with his own people, Hitler wanted to erase and rebuild.

Even his quiet respect for Stalin, though he hated Stalin's ideology, reflected this admiration for ruthless control. He envied Stalin's ability to purge rivals, silence opposition, and still hold on to power. In those moments, Hitler wasn't just thinking about war. He was thinking about rule through fear, about controlling not just land but reality itself, just like Genghis Khan had done, with myth and terror working side by side.

As his own empire started falling apart, Hitler still couldn't let go of the dream of joining these historic giants. In his final months, when maps no longer matched the truth, he kept speaking as if fate was still on his side. He saw betrayal all around him, just like Caesar had. He believed that the German people, like Alexander's tired soldiers in India, had lost the will to keep going. He didn't just feel abandoned. He felt reflected. Their weakness, to him, was proof of his fading myth.

In those final days, locked in his bunker, Hitler turned more and more to the past. He read about Caesar's last battles. He spoke of Alexander. He mentioned Napoleon and Frederick the Great. But there was no fire left in him. Only ashes. The bold vision he once shouted from podiums had become a quiet echo. And even as Soviet shells fell on Berlin, he still clung to one last belief: that someday, history would see him not as a monster but as a misunderstood hero. A man who had tried to change the world and been punished for dreaming too big.

He told himself that his downfall would awaken future generations. That, like Caesar, his death would spark reflection. That, like Alexander, his youth and vision would one day be honored. That, like Genghis Khan, he would be hated now and worshipped later. He imagined future historians uncovering the "real" him, lifting away the lies of war and showing the truth of his genius. He imagined books written about him with awe, statues built, followers who would carry his torch.

But the world had other plans.

Unlike Caesar, Hitler's death brought no mourning crowds. Unlike Alexander, he left behind no empire, no successor, no cities named after him. Unlike Genghis Khan, he didn't spark a new world. His ideas died with him. His cities were bombed to rubble. His loyalists either vanished or died in disgrace. The monuments he built became ruins. The books he wrote became court evidence. The symbols he once made sacred became illegal.

And yet, his obsession with these ancient conquerors still matters. Not because it elevates him, but because it reveals something about how dictators build myths. Hitler didn't rise on smart policies or strong institutions. He rose on story. He cast himself as the hero of a grand epic. He made himself the chosen one, the heir to kings, the bringer of destiny. And millions followed him, not because he was right, but because his story was powerful.

That's why the real lesson here isn't just historical; it's moral.

Conquest might bring glory for a time, but it also brings pain that no statue can erase. Caesar, Alexander, and Genghis Khan left behind both greatness and deep suffering. Hitler wanted their glory, but not their complexity. He wanted their power, but not their responsibility. He copied their worst traits and turned them into guiding principles. He twisted their ambition into fanaticism, their victories into racial violence. In trying to honor them, he ended up distorting them.

In the end, Hitler didn't join their legacy. He became a warning against it.

They built. He destroyed. They expanded civilization's reach; he shrank its moral compass. They helped shape history. He almost broke it.

And maybe the greatest irony of all is this: none of those men saw themselves as gods. Caesar feared being killed. Alexander wept when his dreams ran out. Genghis Khan made laws to bring order after his wars. They were flawed and brutal, but they were still human.

Hitler didn't want to be human. He wanted to be something more, a voice of fate, a symbol of destiny, the final chapter in history.

But history didn't give him that ending.

It refused him the crown.

For Hitler, legacy wasn't just some vague idea. It was something you could build, carve, and walk through. It lived in towering buildings, massive statues, and carefully staged public spectacles. He believed that the memory of a leader could be shaped not just by victories or history books, but by leaving a physical mark on the world. In this, he tried to follow the example of men like Caesar, Alexander the Great, and Genghis Khan, not just through conquest, but through symbols that lasted. The crumbling ruins of Rome, the silent tombs in Mongolia, and the scattered remains of ancient cities all told stories, not just of war, but of something lasting. Hitler wanted that kind of permanence. Through the sweeping visions of Albert Speer, his personal architect, he set out to create a Reich that would stand forever. Its capital, Germania, would be built to rival the greatness of Rome, Babylon, and Persepolis.

But Germania wasn't just going to be a government center. It was meant to be a stage: Hitler's grand statement to history. He imagined enormous domes that would make St. Peter's look small, broad avenues wider than those in Paris, and arches more glorious than anything Caesar ever dreamed of. These weren't buildings meant for daily life. They were built to shock, to overwhelm, monuments carved in stone to announce a new order, a racial destiny. Like the pyramids of Egypt or Greece's Parthenon, Germania's buildings were designed to whisper through time: "This was greatness." And in the middle of it all, Hitler would stand, not just alongside history's conquerors, but above them.

The spirit of ancient Rome was everywhere in Hitler's plans. He deeply admired how Caesar and Augustus used buildings and statues not only to beautify their empire but to shape the way people thought. Roman art wasn't just for art's sake. It was propaganda set in stone. Hitler believed the same. He thought he could mold the minds of future generations just by shaping the space they lived in. He imagined people, decades or even centuries after his death, walking under Germania's massive dome, feeling in their bones that something powerful had once happened there, even if they didn't know the full story. He didn't just want a footnote in a textbook. He wanted his name etched into granite.

Behind all this was a kind of obsession with the legacies of the men he admired. Alexander the Great built cities, like Alexandria, that kept thriving long after his empire fell. Genghis Khan's empire left behind not just conquests but systems and trade routes that lived on. Caesar wasn't just remembered. He became a symbol of Roman politics, of ambition, of power. Hitler, fully aware that he wouldn't live forever, wanted the same kind of immortality. He didn't just want to be a general or a head of state. He wanted to become a force of history, someone too big to forget. And to get there, he needed to leave behind something too massive to ignore.

But Hitler knew buildings alone weren't enough. A legacy needs a story. He wanted his life to be remembered as a tale of destiny, of struggle, betrayal, sacrifice, and martyrdom. And that story, he believed, could be told not just through architecture but through personal relics and rituals. He carefully saved his uniforms, writings, cars, treating them almost like sacred objects. These weren't just things. They were props in the myth he was trying to build. Just like Alexander's armor or Caesar's laurel wreath, he imagined that one day his belongings would be revered by future generations. That they'd be displayed in museums, admired as pieces of a glorious past. That this "glory" had been built on genocide didn't seem to bother him. Like Genghis Khan, he saw history not as a question of morality, but of magnitude.

But in the end, the whole plan collapsed. None of Germania's massive buildings were ever finished. The only major structure that got built, the Olympic Stadium, ended up becoming a painful reminder of a regime the world wanted to forget. The dream of marble monuments turned to rubble. Hitler had imagined Berlin as the crown jewel of his empire. Instead, it became a symbol of downfall.

And the story he wanted to be remembered by? That didn't survive either. He hoped people would remember him like Caesar, betrayed; like Alexander, taken too soon; like Genghis, misunderstood but ultimately victorious. But that's not what happened. Instead, his name became a symbol of cruelty. His face was something to hide, not admire. His legacy? Not one of awe, but of horror. He tried to rewrite history, to place himself among the greats. But history had its own response: a resounding no.

The truth is, the men Hitler admired didn't just win battles. They changed the world. Caesar crossed the Rubicon to remake Rome, not destroy it. His reforms helped lay the foundation for the Roman Empire. Alexander spread Hellenistic culture everywhere he went. His conquests sparked centuries of cultural exchange. Even Genghis Khan, for all his brutality, built a system that connected East and West and reshaped global trade. Their legacies weren't just about power. They were about transformation. Hitler's legacy? It was only destruction. He didn't create new systems. He didn't inspire cultural change. He left behind nothing but broken cities and broken lives.

What Hitler never seemed to understand was that legacy isn't something you can force. You don't get remembered for simply being loud or brutal. Real legacy lasts because it speaks to something bigger than the person. The men he idolized shaped history by pushing it forward and toward new ideas, new connections, new futures. Hitler, on the other hand, only looked backward. He wasn't trying to build a better world. He was trying to purify it, to shrink it down. While history's giants tried to expand and elevate civilization, even through conquest, Hitler's vision was narrow, fearful, and destructive.

And maybe the greatest irony of all is this: in trying so hard to outdo the men he envied, Hitler revealed how little he truly understood them. He wanted to be Caesar but had no republic to reform. He wanted to be Alexander but had no culture to spread. He wanted to be Genghis but lacked the drive to build something lasting. His ambition wasn't noble; it was misdirected. His obsession with greatness wasn't based on wisdom but on jealousy. He thought power alone would make him unforgettable. But true greatness doesn't come from fear or force. It comes from meaning. And that's what Hitler could never create.

Even at the end, as his world crumbled around him, he kept bringing up those old heroes. He talked about Caesar's last days. He compared his wars to the Mongols'. He tried to paint his downfall as tragic, like Alexander's early death. But it all rang hollow. His armies were falling back. His people were starving. His cities were being bombed into dust. And all those promises of destiny, rebirth, and eternal glory had vanished into the chaos he himself had unleashed.

In the end, all that was left was the man: angry, delusional, and alone. In his final words, dictated in the dark bunker beneath Berlin, he blamed everyone but himself, the Jews, the generals, the world, even the German people. But never himself. Like so many tyrants before him, he couldn't face the truth: that history's respect can't be seized. It has to be earned. And he hadn't earned it.

After the war, as Europe buried its dead and rebuilt its cities, the world looked back at Hitler's shattered dreams and saw no glory, no empire, no lasting vision. What they saw was a warning: a warning that the hunger to be remembered, if not guided by wisdom, can turn into something deadly; that history, while shaped by strong leaders, turns against those who treat it like a weapon; that the line between the conqueror and the tyrant is drawn not by how many battles you win, but by what you leave behind afterward.

And that's the final difference: Caesar, Alexander, and Genghis Khan are remembered for what they gave the world, new ideas, new systems, new paths forward. Hitler is remembered only for what he destroyed. No great cities. No meaningful philosophy. No legacy that survived the daylight. Just graves, ruins, and pain that still lingers.

Even so, Hitler's obsession with those ancient giants holds up a mirror to all of us. It reminds us of how easy it is to confuse showy power with real greatness, to mistake cruelty for strength, to chase immortality by tearing things down instead of building something that matters. And it shows us that no matter how much someone tries to control the story, the truth has a way of standing on its own, especially in an age where memories are recorded, survivors still speak, and the past can't be buried under marble.

When you hear the name Caesar, you think of calendars and empires. His name still marks our months. July, for Julius. Alexander the Great still inspires books, paintings, and movies. Genghis Khan is studied for how he organized a massive empire across continents. But Hitler? His name brings silence. His image is banned in many places or met with disgust. The difference isn't just in what these men did, but in what they came to represent.

And that, maybe, is the most important lesson. Looking back at history isn't about copying it; it's about learning from it. Hitler didn't fail because he lacked cleverness, or charisma, or power. He failed because he misunderstood what makes a legacy last. The leaders he looked up to didn't just take over lands. They left behind something meaningful, something that kept going. Hitler didn't. All he offered was destruction. And destruction, no matter how loud, doesn't last forever.

If building a legacy was his obsession, then the memory he left behind became his punishment. He pictured himself among the legends, standing proudly next to Caesar, Alexander, and Genghis. But the memory of him turned into something else entirely. Not a monument. A scar. While the ancient rulers are remembered, sometimes even celebrated, for what they added to the world, Hitler became a warning.

He wasn't a founder of nations. He wasn't a visionary. He was the architect of genocide. A destroyer. His story didn't become legend or tragedy. It became a study in darkness, something to remember so it never happens again.

And his failure wasn't just about losing a war. It was deeper than that; it was moral, even spiritual. The empires built by Caesar, Alexander, and Genghis lived on long after they died. The Roman Empire kept growing. The Hellenistic world Alexander started lasted for centuries. The Mongol Empire broke into smaller kingdoms that still shaped trade and law across Asia and beyond. But Hitler's empire? It couldn't survive him. The Nazi regime was too poisoned by hate, too wrapped up in Hitler's personal myth, too rigid to last. When he fell, it all came crashing down with him. Not just politically, but in terms of human decency. The world didn't carry his legacy forward. It rejected it.

And that's the real contrast. Caesar might have seized power, but what followed was a working system. Alexander's short life still sparked cultural growth and exchange. Genghis Khan ruled with fear, but he also created trade networks and legal systems that improved life in many regions. Brutal as they were, these leaders left space for something new to grow. Hitler didn't. His vision was rotten from the start. His empire wasn't meant to grow; it was built to crush. There were no cultural exchanges, no meaningful progress, no moments of evolution. Only extermination and control.

And while the ancient conquerors were later reinterpreted, sometimes softened by the lens of time, Hitler's legacy only became more severe. He left no gray area. No one can look back and say, "Maybe he meant well." The truth is too clear. The destruction was too great. The evil too deliberate. The story he wanted to become myth only made his reality more disturbing. He never made it into the ranks of great leaders. Instead, he became a reminder of just how badly things can go when myth is used to justify cruelty.

His failure to rise to the level of his idols also revealed something about the way he thought about power. While Caesar, Alexander, and Genghis all showed flexibility, adapting to new challenges, Hitler refused to bend. He couldn't shift course or rethink his plans. When things didn't go as expected, he didn't change; he just pushed harder. He put ideology before strategy. He clung to his vision of destiny, even as everything around him fell apart. That's where he broke from the historical greats. They knew how to play the long game. He raced toward disaster.

Even in the last days, hiding in his bunker under Berlin, Hitler still saw himself in the same grand mirror. He spoke of Caesar's betrayal, of Alexander's sudden death, of Genghis Khan being misunderstood. He believed that, eventually, the world would see his greatness. That once the war was over, people would understand. But history doesn't reward those who bury the truth in myths. It uncovers them. And what it found in Hitler wasn't brilliance. It was destruction for destruction's sake.

After 1945, the world had to face the consequences of Hitler's failed dream. It had to rebuild cities and borders, yes, but it also had to rebuild the very idea of greatness. People had to rethink what makes a leader worth remembering, and what kind of empire is truly meaningful. And in that new understanding, Hitler became a lesson in reverse. He wasn't a model of greatness. He was a warning of what happens when ambition runs wild without wisdom. His name became a red flag, a signal to watch out for any leader who promises destiny, purity, and total loyalty.

In classrooms, military academies, courts, and churches, his story became the example of how power can corrupt everything. Even truth itself. That's what made him more dangerous than just another dictator. He understood that people believe what they see and hear, and he knew how to control that. But what he didn't understand was that once people see through the lie, it all falls apart. He built everything around his own version of reality. And when that illusion cracked, there was nothing left to hold it up.

The men Hitler admired had something he never had: humility within their ambition. Caesar respected Roman traditions even as he changed them. Alexander learned from philosophers. Genghis Khan took on the laws and customs of the lands he conquered. They reached beyond themselves. Hitler, on the other hand, only listened to his own voice. He silenced anyone who disagreed, not just to stay in control, but to block out anything that might challenge his beliefs. He didn't just hide in a bunker at the end. He lived in one, mentally. A place where no new ideas could enter. He stopped learning.

The sad truth is, if he had really understood the leaders he idolized, he might've known their greatness wasn't just about power. It was about engaging with the world's complexity. Caesar didn't kill every senator who opposed him. Alexander didn't destroy every city. Genghis Khan, even at his worst, built alliances. But Hitler? His obsession with purity made any compromise impossible. In his world, everything was either good or evil, worthy or worthless. That black-and-white thinking doomed him, not just militarily, but in how history would remember him.

And yet, people still talk about him, not because he became what Caesar or Alexander were, but because he tried to, and failed in the most horrifying way. His name stays in the public mind, not as a hero, but as a thief. Someone who tried to steal the stories of great men to justify his nightmare. That's why it's so important to remember him. He shows us how easy it is to twist the language of glory into something dangerous; that even a speech, a statue, or a slogan can be used to cover up something monstrous; that ambition, when not guided by goodness, turns into ashes.

So when we look back at Caesar, Alexander, or Genghis Khan, we also have to look at Hitler, not as someone who followed in their footsteps, but as their opposite. He's what happens when admiration turns into obsession, when myth becomes blind belief, when history is rewritten to serve one man's ego. That's why Hitler doesn't belong in the same group as those ancient conquerors. He's not their heir. He's their shadow.

After the war, in the years that followed, Hitler didn't just fade into history. He became a mirror. Writers, artists, and thinkers kept returning to his image, not to celebrate him, but to uncover the truth behind it. Caesar lives in marble statues. Alexander appears in ancient mosaics. But Hitler? He believed that, eventually, the world would see his greatness…. that once the war was over, people would understand. Now, it unsettles. He doesn't linger as a legend, but as a warning etched into every democracy that rose after him.

And that's the strange twist. Hitler did gain a kind of immortality, but not the kind he wanted. His name survives, yes, but it brings shame, not pride. His life is studied not as a tale of glory, but as a warning of what can happen when power is mixed with hatred. The very tools he used (speeches, ceremonies, myths) have become suspect because of him. Today, when a leader demands total obedience or speaks of racial purity, the comparisons to Hitler are immediate. He's no longer a model. He's a caution sign.

There's one last irony: in trying so hard to model himself after the ancient conquerors, Hitler ensured that people would always compare him to them, but not in the way he hoped. Every time a historian puts Hitler next to Caesar, the gap becomes clearer. Every philosopher who compares him to Alexander sees the failure. Every strategist who examines him next to Genghis Khan finds stubbornness where there should've been vision. His name stays tied to theirs, but only to show just how far off course he really was.

So in the end, Hitler didn't ride through history in triumph. He left behind no great civilization, no classic text, no lasting empire. Just rubble. Just silence. Just a memory that gets colder with time. Where others built, he destroyed. Where others lasted, he vanished. And where others remained human (flawed, complex, and real), Hitler became something less. Not a man to be admired, but a cautionary tale the world must never forget.

CHAPTER 19

THE DANGERS OF FASCISM, COMMUNISM, AND THEIR LINK TO POPULISM IN THE UNITED STATES:

The United States of America was built on big, bold promises and ideas like freedom, equality, and the right of each person to have a voice. From the very beginning, these values were written into the Constitution, which laid out a government built not on kings or dictators but on the will of the people. It's a country where laws matter, where leadership is chosen by vote, and where individuals are supposed to have the freedom to speak, believe, and live as they choose.

But as we move deeper into the 21st century, it's clear that these ideals are being tested. The world is changing fast, and not all of that change is for the better. America isn't just facing threats from faraway places. It is also facing something more complicated, something harder to see coming: dangerous ideas. These are ideas that sound appealing at first glance, especially when people feel frustrated, divided, or left behind. But underneath, they carry the seeds of something deeply harmful.

Two of the biggest threats are fascism and communism. These aren't just dusty old ideologies from history books. Even though they first rose to power in the 20th century, they haven't gone away. They've evolved. They've reshaped themselves to fit today's world, quietly finding support among groups that feel disillusioned or angry. And yes, that includes people right here in the United States.

Both fascism and communism are very different in how they started and what they claim to believe in. One talks about extreme nationalism and the glory of the state; the other about workers rising up and sharing everything equally. But here's what they have in common, and what makes them dangerous: they both tend to lead to authoritarianism. That means power gets concentrated in the hands of one person or one group. Freedom fades. Dissent gets silenced. Everything starts to revolve around control.

What's especially troubling is how quickly these ideas can grow when people are looking for answers. When someone stands up and says, *"I have the solution to all your problems,"* it can be tempting to believe them, especially if you're feeling unheard or fed up with the system. That's where populism often comes in. Populist leaders claim to speak for "the common people" against "the elites." And while that can sound empowering, it can also open the door for manipulation. When fear replaces reason and anger is used to rally people, it becomes easier for leaders to grab more power and harder for everyday people to push back.

That's why it's so important right now to talk about these ideologies honestly. To understand where they came from, what they really mean, and how they can sneak back into public life under new names or slogans. If Americans want to keep the spirit of democracy alive, these aren't things we can afford to ignore. We need to remember the past to make sure we don't repeat it.

The Historical Context of Fascism and Communism:

Fascism didn't start in a vacuum. It grew out of a time when people were desperate. After World War I, countries like Italy and Germany were in serious trouble. Economies had collapsed. Families were struggling. National pride had taken a huge hit. People felt lost, unsure of the future, and deeply angry. Into that chaos stepped strongmen (men like Benito Mussolini and Adolf Hitler), who promised to bring order, restore national greatness, and give people someone to blame.

In Italy, Mussolini rose to power in 1922. He formed the Fascist Party and presented himself as a bold, energetic leader who would "make Italy strong again." Just over a decade later, Hitler followed a similar path in Germany, becoming chancellor in 1933 and quickly transforming the country into a totalitarian state under the Nazi Party.

At its core, fascism is built on extreme nationalism. It glorifies the nation above all else, not just in terms of pride but in a way that leaves no room for diversity, disagreement, or individuality. The state is seen as a living force, something sacred, and everything (your rights, your opinions, even your private life) is expected to serve it.

In fascist regimes, liberal democracy is rejected. That means no room for free elections, open debate, or checks and balances. Instead, power becomes concentrated in one leader or one ruling group. The media gets taken over, opposing voices are crushed, and fear is used to keep people in line. The goal is to create a unified society, but "unity" in this case usually means making everyone conform and punishing anyone who doesn't.

This kind of unity is often based on narrow definitions of identity, like race, ethnicity, or national origin. Fascist leaders are quick to point fingers at certain groups, blaming them for the country's problems. These scapegoats are used to rally support and justify harsh actions. Under Mussolini, political opponents were silenced, and civil liberties were dismantled. Under Hitler, it went much further. The Nazi regime didn't just repress dissent; it orchestrated a massive campaign of terror that led to the genocide of six million Jews, as well as millions of others, including Roma people, people with disabilities, LGBTQ+ individuals, and political dissidents.

Fascism tries to control people and also pushes the idea of militarism. That means the power of the nation is shown through military strength. Fascist governments often celebrate war as something noble and necessary. They prepare for it, encourage it, and sometimes even provoke it on purpose. One of the clearest examples is Germany's invasion of Poland in 1939, which marked the start of World War II. It wasn't just a political move but the result of an ideology that believed in conquest and domination as a way of proving national greatness.

And here's something really important to understand: fascism isn't limited to one side of the political spectrum. Even though it's often linked with the far right, the key feature of fascism is its authoritarianism, its desire to control, dominate, and silence. That can come from the left, the right, or anywhere in between. Any movement that tries to centralize power, suppress opposition, and turn people against one another based on identity or belief can slide into fascism if we're not paying attention.

Communism: The Dangers of Totalitarianism and Economic Control

On paper, communism might sound like a good idea to some. It's built around the dream of a fair society, one where everyone is equal, where no one is poor while others are rich, and where people share resources instead of competing for them. The idea comes from thinkers like Karl Marx and Friedrich Engels, who believed that capitalism, the system where individuals own property and businesses, leads to deep inequality. They argued that the rich would keep getting richer while the poor would always be stuck working for low wages just to survive.

In a communist system, there's no private property. That means factories, farms, and resources, basically everything needed to produce goods, are owned by *everyone* together. But since it's hard for millions of people to manage those things directly, the state steps in and says, "We'll take care of it on behalf of the people." The idea is that the government will make fair decisions, make sure everyone gets what they need, and prevent anyone from getting too much power or wealth.

But that's the theory. In real life, things have looked very different.

Let's start with Russia. In 1917, the **Bolshevik Revolution** overthrew the old monarchy and brought in a communist government led by **Vladimir Lenin**. Soon after, **Joseph Stalin** took over and built the Soviet Union into a massive communist state. But instead of creating freedom and fairness, Stalin's rule became one of the most brutal periods in modern history. He forced farmers to give up their land and work in giant government-run collectives. This forced collectivization led to widespread famine, where millions of people starved to death. On top of that, Stalin carried out purges, where anyone who disagreed with him, or even looked suspicious, could be imprisoned, exiled, or executed. Fear ruled every corner of society.

Something similar happened in China, where **Mao Zedong**, leader of the Chinese Communist Party, tried to reshape the country using radical policies. One of these was the **Great Leap Forward**, which aimed to rapidly industrialize China and boost food production. But it backfired horribly. The plan was unrealistic, poorly managed, and ended up causing one of the deadliest famines in world history. Later, Mao launched the Cultural Revolution, a campaign to wipe out old traditions and ideas, which led to chaos, violence, and the deaths and persecution of millions more. Families were torn apart. People were punished for thinking differently. And education, culture, and stability were all damaged in the name of revolutionary purity.

In all these cases, the idea of equality was used to justify total control. Communist regimes claimed that harsh measures were necessary to build a better future, a classless society where everyone would eventually be free and equal. But in practice, what happened was the opposite: power ended up in the hands of a small group of leaders who controlled everything: the economy, the media, and people's lives.

The truth is, under communism, the state doesn't fade away like Marx imagined. It grows bigger. It becomes a giant bureaucracy that watches everything and allows no opposition. There are **no** checks and balances like in democracies. If you speak out, you risk being punished. If you want to start a business or own land, you can't. The government owns it all, and it decides what you get.

Economically, these systems have not delivered the promised prosperity or equality. When the government tries to control the entire economy, it often leads to inefficiency, waste, and stagnation. There's little room for creativity or innovation because there's no competition, no rewards for new ideas, and no personal motivation to go above and beyond. We've seen this time and again in the Soviet Union, in Cuba, and in North Korea. People struggle to meet their basic needs, and at the same time, their freedom to speak, think, or live how they want is severely limited.

The Link Between Fascism and Communism: Authoritarianism and Totalitarianism

At first glance, fascism and communism seem like total opposites. Fascism is about extreme nationalism and power for the state; communism is about eliminating class and sharing wealth. One praises tradition and national pride; the other pushes for revolution and equality. But when you look more closely at how both systems actually play out, they have some very dangerous things in common.

Both fascist and communist regimes create strong, centralized governments that try to control almost everything, the economy, politics, the media, and even private life. In both cases, freedom takes a back seat to the "greater good" as defined by those in charge. Whether it's about building a perfect nation or a classless society, leaders in these systems believe that their vision is so important it's okay to use force, fear, and censorship to achieve it.

Both ideologies are built around some kind of utopian dream. Fascists talk about restoring national greatness. Communists talk about creating equality and fairness for all. But in both cases, that dream becomes an excuse to silence anyone who disagrees. People who question the system are labeled enemies, traitors, or threats. Propaganda is used to shape public opinion. Surveillance becomes normal. And violence becomes "necessary."

In the end, both systems undermine democracy. They replace open discussion and fair elections with fear, control, and one-party rule. And while their ideas might look different on paper, their real-world results often look very much the same: oppression, suffering, and a loss of basic human rights.

The Rise of Populism: A Gateway to Fascism and Communism

Now, there's one more piece of this puzzle that we need to talk about: something that can act as a gateway to either fascism or communism.

It's called populism.

So what is it?

In simple terms, it's a political approach that says society is divided into two groups: the "good, ordinary people" and the "corrupt, out-of-touch elites." Populist leaders often present themselves as outsiders, people who don't follow traditional political rules. They say they're here to shake things up, fight for the little guy, and take on the powerful.

This kind of message is especially powerful during hard times. When people are facing economic struggles, social unrest, or political scandals, populism offers a simple story, and an easy target for blame. It gives people hope that someone finally hears them. And sometimes, it really does point out problems that need fixing.

But here's the danger: populism can be used to manipulate. Once a populist leader has the crowd behind them, they might start using fear, anger, and division to stay in power. They might oversimplify complex problems, blame minority groups or critics, and claim that they alone can fix everything. And that kind of thinking makes it easier for extreme ideologies like fascism or communism to sneak in, disguised as "solutions."

Populism by itself isn't always bad. But when it's mixed with authoritarian goals, it becomes a powerful tool for shutting down democracy. That's why it's so important for people to stay informed, think critically, and protect the systems that allow for open dialogue, freedom, and accountability.

Populism as a Gateway to Fascism:

Populism usually starts with good intentions. A leader steps up and says they're here to fight for "ordinary people," those who feel ignored, left behind, or betrayed by politicians, big corporations, or global institutions. Populist leaders often talk about "the people" versus "the elites," painting a picture of a country where a corrupt few at the top have taken advantage of everyone else. This message can sound refreshing, even empowering, especially during times when people feel like their voices aren't being heard.

But here's where things can take a dark turn. These populist leaders sometimes use strong nationalist language. They talk a lot about pride in one's country and often bring up the idea that the nation used to be great but that greatness has been lost. They might blame this loss on outsiders: immigrants, foreign influences, or global organizations. This creates a narrative that says: "We were once powerful and proud, but we were weakened by others. Now it's time to take back what's ours."

When this kind of populism gains a lot of support and the leader comes into power, they can begin to make changes that slowly erode democracy. At first, it might seem like they're just cutting through red tape or standing up to biased media. But soon, they start attacking the free press, calling it untrustworthy or even an enemy of the people. They might try to weaken the courts so they can't be challenged. They may shut down or limit the voices of opposition parties. All of this is often done in the name of "protecting the nation" or "getting things done."

And because these leaders are popular and know how to speak to people's emotions, many citizens might support these actions without realizing what's really happening: democracy is being dismantled, step by step. Sometimes, intimidation or violence is used to keep control, and the people who speak out get silenced or punished.

This is how fascism can begin, not with tanks in the streets right away, but with slow and calculated steps that remove freedoms, concentrate power, and turn a populist movement into a dictatorship. And often, it's all done under the banner of helping the people.

Populism as a Gateway to Communism:

Populism doesn't always come from the right. It can also rise from the left, especially when it focuses on economic issues. In this form, populist leaders speak out about the growing gap between the rich and the poor. They point to large corporations, wealthy elites, and broken systems that make it harder for working people to get ahead. Their message is often about fairness, justice, and giving power back to the people, not the billionaires.

Leaders with this message may promise things like wealth redistribution, nationalizing industries (which means turning private companies into government-run businesses), and breaking up big monopolies. They may also promise free healthcare, education, housing, or other social services that are funded by higher taxes on the wealthy or by the state taking control of key parts of the economy.

At first, this message can sound deeply compassionate. And in many ways, it is rooted in real problems that need real solutions. But if this kind of populism becomes extreme, it can also lead to the collapse of capitalism altogether. In its place, a communist system may rise, one where the state owns almost everything, from factories to farms to the media.

What's important to understand is that, just like in the fascist version, the leaders of these left-wing populist movements often begin to gather more and more control. They claim that they need this control to fix inequality and build a better future. But over time, that control can grow into something more dangerous.

In a communist regime, decisions are often made from the top down by a single ruling party. Dissent, people speaking out or disagreeing, is not welcomed. Freedom of choice in the economy and in political life starts to vanish. Citizens may no longer be able to start businesses, express different opinions, or vote for change. What started as a movement for fairness can end up becoming a totalitarian system where the state controls nearly every part of daily life.

So even though the promises may seem noble, the reality (if things go too far) can be just as repressive and dangerous as fascism. Different ideology, the same loss of freedom.

The Threats to American Democracy:

The United States has always been proud of its democratic values; freedom of speech, the right to vote, and a system where leaders are accountable to the people. These principles have helped the country grow and thrive for generations. But today, America is facing a new kind of challenge, one that doesn't come from the outside but from within.

We're living in a time of deep political division. People are frustrated. Many feel that the government isn't working for them, that corporations have too much power, and that their voices don't matter anymore. Social media often makes these feelings worse, spreading anger, fear, and misinformation at lightning speed. This kind of environment creates the perfect storm for extreme ideas. Ideas that once seemed impossible in America to take hold.

Fascism and communism may seem like relics of the 20th century, but the beliefs behind them haven't disappeared. The language may be softer now. The methods may be more subtle. But the core ideas, like concentrating power, suppressing dissent, and replacing democracy with control, are still alive and can be dressed up to sound appealing.

Populist leaders on both the right and the left know how to use people's frustrations to their advantage. They stir up emotions. They divide people into "us" and "them." They offer simple answers to complex problems. And they sometimes use the language of freedom and justice to hide their true goals.

This is why Americans need to talk about these issues openly and seriously. If we don't understand the history and the warning signs, we risk walking down dangerous paths without realizing it until it's too late.

Preserving Freedom and Democracy:

Protecting democracy in the United States isn't just the job of politicians or judges. It's something every citizen has a role in. To keep our freedoms safe, we first need to understand how they can be lost. That means learning from history and recognizing how fragile democratic systems can be when people stop paying attention.

It's not enough to say, "It could never happen here." Many people in other countries thought the same thing until it *did* happen there.

We have to stay committed to the principles that make democracy work. One of those is the Constitution, which lays out the rules and rights that protect all of us. Another is the idea of checks and balances, where no one person or group is allowed to have too much power. These systems were designed to prevent tyranny. But they only work if people care enough to defend them.

That means being informed. It means asking questions. It means voting, getting involved in our communities, and standing up when we see things that aren't right. It also means listening to each other, even when we disagree, because democracy isn't about everyone thinking the same way; it's about making space for different voices to be heard.

The battle to preserve freedom is never really over. It's something we have to fight for every generation. And the best way to protect our future is to stay alert, stay educated, and stay engaged.

Because when the people know what's at stake, they're much less likely to give it away.

Conclusion: The Need for Vigilance and Action

The threats posed by fascism and communism are not just something we read about in old history books. These aren't distant or outdated dangers. They are real, current risks that still exist in our world today. And in some ways, they're growing stronger. That's why it's so important to talk about them seriously, especially as populism is rising again, not just in the United States but all around the world.

Populism often starts with a simple message: "We, the people, have been betrayed by those in power." It taps into real frustration. But when that frustration is used to fuel extreme ideas (either from the far-right or far-left), it can open the door to something much worse. And once that door is open, it's very hard to close.

The only way we can protect our democracy and our freedom is by staying alert, learning from the past, and being willing to speak up. That means having honest conversations about what these ideologies really are, how they gain power, and what we can do to stop them. Education, awareness, and a strong belief in democratic values are our best tools for protecting the future. If we want the United States to remain a place where freedom and opportunity are possible for everyone, we have to stay involved, pay attention, and never take democracy for granted.

This expanded version of the discussion you've just read goes deeper into the history of fascism and communism. It explains how populism can sometimes lead the way to authoritarian rule and why it's more important than ever to talk about these dangers clearly and openly. Understanding them is the first step toward stopping them.

***

After World War II, it seemed like the world had finally buried Hitlerism. The ideology behind Nazism. Its symbols were banned. Its leaders were executed, imprisoned, or cast out. And the crimes it produced (genocide, war, totalitarianism) were exposed so clearly that most people believed such an evil worldview could never return.

But here's the uncomfortable truth: the soil where Hitlerism once grew was never completely cleared. It stayed beneath the surface, waiting. And now, in the 21st century, it's starting to come back. But in a different, more hidden form.

When we talk about the return of Hitlerism today, we're not saying people are marching down streets waving swastikas (though some do). We're talking about something more subtle, more disguised. It shows up as a mood, a style of thinking, a certain way of seeing the world. It spreads as memes, coded language, jokes that carry dark meanings, and vague online talk that hides violent intent under layers of irony.

What makes Hitlerism different from regular fascism is that it isn't just about politics or power. It's a deeper kind of belief system, a way of understanding the world that mixes myth, fear, and a longing for purity and order. It says, *"Some people are better than others. The world is divided between the chosen and the corrupt. Violence isn't just allowed. It's sacred if it serves the right cause."*

This isn't just history repeating but history *mutating*. And we've started to see the signs everywhere.

In countries across Europe, far-right parties that used to be considered extreme have gained popularity. In the United

States, white nationalist movements have gone from the margins to the mainstream. Leaders in places like Hungary, Brazil, India, and Russia have used nationalist and ethnocentric language to build power, often blaming immigrants, minorities, or liberal values for their countries' problems.

The reasons this is happening feel very familiar if you know history. Economic gaps between rich and poor keep growing. Traditional industries are disappearing. People feel their identities are under threat. Fast immigration and cultural change make some groups feel like they're losing their place. And online platforms feed this fear, giving people simple villains to blame and conspiracies to believe in.

And that's the kind of chaos in which Hitlerism thrives. It doesn't need a capital city. It doesn't need tanks or marches. It lives in anger that has no direction, in power that has no rules, in communities that have no shared truth. It spreads in quiet places: online forums, private chats, and websites that look harmless but carry dangerous messages. It doesn't shout. It whispers.

One clear example of this modern Hitlerism is the rise of the so-called "great replacement" theory. It's the belief that white people in the West are being "replaced" by immigrants, on purpose, by some kind of hidden plan. That idea, often connected to antisemitic conspiracy theories, echoes Hitler's own beliefs about Jews being behind the supposed decline of civilization. Just like in the 1930s, today's version finds ways to make hatred sound like logic and violence sound like justice.

These new movements even create their own twisted heroes. People who carry out mass shootings, like the Christchurch gunman in New Zealand or the Buffalo shooter in the U.S., have written manifestos filled with Nazi ideas. They don't see themselves as criminals. They see themselves as fighters, as chosen ones, carrying out a mission. That's what makes it so dangerous. These ideas don't just live in books. They live in actions.

Even more frightening is how flexible and modern this new Hitlerism has become. It avoids using the old language that people would quickly recognize. It rebrands itself with terms like "anti-globalist," "anti-woke," or "cultural warrior." It hides behind sarcasm and dark humor. It uses jokes as shields. And when it's called out, it denies itself: *"Oh, we were just kidding."*

But sometimes, people *aren't* kidding. Sometimes, the joke ends with bullets. The internet has made it easier than ever to spread these ideas quickly and quietly. They don't need a central leader anymore. They don't need a party or a flag. They just need attention at the right moment.

New technology makes this worse. Artificial intelligence can now create fake videos, fake speeches, and even deepfake versions of Hitler himself. Entire campaigns of hate can be built using AI, looking and sounding like real people or real news. In the wrong hands, this could make old fascist ideas feel new, shiny, and believable again.

But this isn't just a digital or political problem but also a spiritual one. Many people today feel lost as if the world doesn't make sense anymore. Everything changes too fast. There's so much information but not enough meaning. People are searching for something to believe in. And Hitlerism offers a dark kind of certainty. It says: *"You belong. You are pure. You are chosen. And everything wrong in your life is someone else's fault."*

That's what gives it power. Not just the lies but the longing it answers. It doesn't offer facts. It offers *identity*. And in a world where many feel rootless, lonely, or confused, identity is a powerful thing to promise.

So what can we do?

We have to look closely not just at history but at the present. We have to spot these ideas as they reappear in new clothing. We have to understand that fascism today doesn't always look like it did in the past. But it *feels* the same in the way it divides, blames, and controls.

Resisting it means more than just remembering the past. It means recognizing its patterns *now*. It means teaching our children how to tell the difference between free speech and dangerous propaganda. It means standing up for inclusion and truth, even when it's hard. And most importantly, it means reminding ourselves that people matter more than symbols, more than slogans, more than power.

Because Hitlerism didn't vanish, it went quiet. It went digital. And it's waiting for the next crisis to rise again.

That's why the final warning is this: Hitlerism might not return the same way, but it *can* return. It won't start with parades or tanks. It will start with ideas. With stories. With blame. With memes.

And if we don't pay attention…..

If we brush it off as just noise…It can grow until it's too late.

The future belongs to those who recognize the danger early and choose not to look away.

REFERENCES

Arendt, H. (1951). The origins of totalitarianism. Harcourt.

Bullock, A. (1991). Hitler: A study in tyranny. Harper Perennial. (Original work published 1952)

Burleigh, M. (2001). The Third Reich: A new history. Hill and Wang.

Evans, R. J. (2003). The coming of the Third Reich. Penguin Press.

Evans, R. J. (2005). The Third Reich in power. Penguin Press.

Evans, R. J. (2009). The Third Reich at war. Penguin Press.

Fest, J. C. (1974). Hitler (R. & C. Winston, Trans.). Harcourt.

Hitler, A. (1998). Mein Kampf (R. Manheim, Trans.). Houghton Mifflin. (Original work published 1925)

Kershaw, I. (1998). Hitler: 1889–1936 Hubris. W. W. Norton & Company.

Kershaw, I. (2000). Hitler: 1936–1945 Nemesis. W. W. Norton & Company.

Longerich, P. (2010). Holocaust: The Nazi persecution and murder of the Jews (S. Pleasance, Trans.). Oxford University Press.

Mosse, G. L. (1981). The crisis of German ideology: Intellectual origins of the Third Reich. Schocken Books.

Rees, L. (2017). The Holocaust: A new history. Public Affairs.

Shirer, W. L. (1960). The rise and fall of the Third Reich: A history of Nazi Germany. Simon & Schuster.

Snyder, T. (2015). Black earth: The Holocaust as history and warning. Tim Duggan Books.

Toland, J. (1992). Adolf Hitler: The definitive biography. Anchor Books.

Waite, R. G. L. (1977). The psychopathic god: Adolf Hitler. Basic Books.

Weber, E. (1964). Varieties of fascism: Doctrines of revolution in the twentieth century. D. Van Nostrand Company.

Welch, D. (2001). Propaganda and the German cinema: 1933–1945. I.B. Tauris.

Zitelmann, R. (1999). Hitler: The policies of seduction. St. Martin's Press.

www.ingramcontent.com/pod-product-compliance
Lightning Source LLC
Chambersburg PA
CBHW051130300726
48978CB00011B/224